ALCHEMY OF GLASS

ALCHEMY OF GLASS

BARBARA BARNETT

Published 2020 by Pyr®

Cover illustration Shutterstock
Cover design by Jennifer Do
Cover design © Start Science Fiction

Inquiries should be addressed to
Start Science Fiction
221 River Street, 9th Floor
Hoboken, New Jersey 07030
PHONE: 212-431-5455
www.pyr.com

10 9 8 7 6 5 4 3 2 1

ISBN 978-1-64506-013-0 (paperback)
ISBN 978-1-64506-014-7 (ebook)

Printed in the United States of America

In love and gratitude to my muse, my best friend,
my most constructive critic: Phillip Barnett

CHICAGO, 1893

CHAPTER 1

G aelan Erceldoune strolled along the water's edge, zigzagging his way through the detritus washed up on the gravel-strewn shore. Stopping, he gazed at the horizon, only now becoming discernable against the black water.

A lone figure, frock coat billowing in the stiff breeze, stood at the distant point of a decaying wooden pier, staring into the dusky lavender of the pre-dawn sky as daylight advanced in slow ascent. Curiosity propelled Gaelan, first one step and then another, slowly down the dock, wondering what so intrigued the man to drive him to that far, perilous vantage, and before the relative safety of the morning light.

The wood bobbed unevenly, precariously, just above the murky brown water, which burst through the rotting boards; the footing was slippery. Midway, Gaelan glanced south over the inlet, glimpsing the remote peninsula where the main exhibition buildings stood, their bright white facades gleaming in the orange-pink radiance of the rising sun, which had now broken the water's surface. The lights of the White City, which all night bathed the Lake Michigan shoreline in an eerie glow, had faded in the dawning light to barely discernable, receding in the far distance like a dying Roman candle.

The boards creaked beneath Gaelan's boots with every step as he approached the distant edge, and he hoped the noise would not startle the stranger into losing his balance. "It is a beautiful sight out here, is it not?" Gaelan said almost to himself.

The stranger wheeled about, arms flailing like a madman, catching

Gaelan off-guard. The small lamp, which had guided Gaelan's steps in the dark, clattered onto the dock before tumbling off the edge and into the lake. But for his ancient walking stick, he would have soon followed suit as he struggled to keep his balance on slick wood.

The stranger's wide-eyed glare burned hot and hard. "People are fools! Complete idiots!" He stopped without another word, wrapping his arms tight about his chest as if to still them.

Gaelan planted his feet at a wide stance, remaining completely still, his wary gaze fixed on the strange man. Perhaps a nonthreatening gesture might serve to calm the fire.

"Forgive me, sir, my intrusion. I shall leave you be." Gaelan turned to make his way quickly as possible toward the safety of the gravel beach.

"Wait a moment. Do not go just yet." The fury had gone from his voice, replaced by a quiet plea.

Gaelan turned tentatively toward the troubled man, who seemed to regret his outburst. "Perhaps you might accompany me to safer, more stable ground, sir, so we might—"

"Do forgive me. Last night I had a spectacular, failed argument with yet another potential financier, and I've been out here all the night ruminating upon it. But I cannot come to any other conclusion. The whole lot of them—fools with no vision whatsoever. No imagination. You need not fear me, nor fear for me. I'm no lunatic. I've no homicidal inclination, nor designs on killing myself, however upset I may be. I thought I'd secured the funding necessary for my most recent invention, and then . . ." He snapped his index finger to his thumb. "Phhht. Nothing. And you would think after my grand achievement at the exposition I might have managed—"

Gaelan breathed out, feeling at last on firmer ground. So, he was an inventor. The exposition was surely the venue for it; the Columbian Exposition was replete with inventors, great and insignificant, the genuine geniuses and the charlatans, side by side. So, which sort was this fellow?

"So, you do understand my annoyance at . . .?" The man shrugged his shoulders. "But never mind all that. It is over."

Crouching, the stranger reached down, scooping up a handful of cloudy water with a gloved hand. It trickled between his fingers, leaving behind an oily, silty residue. "Do you know? Years of harsh winter snows, winds that blow in a gale off the water—neither have rid the place of the Great Fire. And how long has it been? Twenty years, is it? And still, the ash remains. You can still smell it in the filthy water pooling along the edges of Lake Michigan. That distinctive signature. It lives on in the very fiber of a city reborn."

"Whether the remnant of fire or soot from the smokestack, it is a fact of our times, I suppose. It blackens every place where there is industry, from New York to London—anywhere progress moves us forward, it leaves behind its gray, greasy tarnish."

"You are correct, of course," the man continued. "Yet, from these ashes rose up the great White City of the Columbian Exposition. The very future of the world before our eyes. You see, it was inevitable. From out of the fire comes progress. Destruction gives birth to a renewed sense of invention, as it must.

"Case in point," he continued. "As a young man, I had cholera. Terrible business; I nearly died of it. Nine months bedridden in my father's house. Yet, I do not regret it. For out of the fire of my fever—cholera—I was reborn from the ashes to become an engineer. Never would it have occurred had I not become ill."

Gaelan shook his head. "To speak true, I do not understand the connection."

"I was destined for the priesthood, despite my own wishes, but the illness made my father see beyond his own—" The man gingerly removed his dirty, sodden glove, flinging it away, following its flight until it landed in the water with a loud plop. He shrugged. "I suppose I must now buy a new pair of gloves, but I cannot stand it, you know, the filth. I am not sure why I expose myself to . . ."

He trailed off and swept his gaze over the horizon and down into the lake before returning his attention to Gaelan. "But the answer is here. Right before our very eyes. The power of the water, the sun, which already warms us, and is not even yet fully risen from its sleep. Even the wind that defeats whatever warmth the sun may deliver. Whosoever harnesses these elements shall rule the universe."

Gaelan nodded. This was not news to him. "Indeed." The elements of an alchemist's trade: earth, sun, wind, fire. Gaelan knew them well. Since he'd been a young boy apprenticing at his father's side, studying his methods, wondering at his incomprehensible book of healing.

Gaelan walked him back to shore and seated himself on a rotting crate before looking out toward the dawn sky. Venus appeared above the water, a distant orange dot, barely visible before the sun completely obliterated it from view. He blinked and the planet disappeared into the fast-brightening horizon. "Perhaps you are looking at it backwards, sir," he said after a moment. "Sometimes destruction is simply that. Destruction. Not a birthplace for the new and improved, but a grave-yard for what might have been."

"Indeed?" The man alighted upon another rickety crate for a brief second before springing up, backing several paces away. Again, he shrugged his shoulders. "Is there nowhere clean where we might sit, sir?"

Gaelan glanced about. No. This was no Regent's Park. Far, far from it. "Yes. Destruction inevitably follows too-rapid progress. Taking hold and sprinting like Mercury, barreling ahead with no concept of the consequences that otherwise may have been foreseen. The invention of new technologies without the concomitant understanding. There is an inherent danger—"

"That is not the point at all! You have completely misunderstood my meaning. Witness the White City to our south, risen like a great alabaster Phoenix. Yes, the flame possesses unimaginable power. Destructive power to be sure. We have managed, somehow, to harness it, but not yet wrought from it all we may. Yes, destruction is inevitable perhaps, yet, considering what might be . . . the possibilities!"

Gaelan sighed. There was truth there, but he had seen too much over the centuries to trust in unbounded experimentation. Invention for invention's sake. "Yes," he finally agreed. "The electric lights of Mr. Edison. Have you seen them?"

"Bah. Edison." The man strode away, his hands clenched into tight fists. Perhaps better to change the subject. Yet, who could not but admire Edison's achievement, on full display at the exposition?

"As for myself," Gaelan said, "I have come out this morning to walk along this vast freshwater sea at dawn to experience the unbridled power of nature's exquisite beauty. Behold the sunrise, the way it paints the sky in such colors as cannot possibly be described by a mere human." The spray of cumulus clouds just above the lake painted the sunrise in hues of green, blue, purple, red, and orange, such as Gaelan had rarely seen.

"I suppose *you* attribute it to God."

"No. I do not," Gaelan said more brusquely than was polite. "Forgive me, but I have no use for God, at least not as defined by any church. No, sir. God has done me little good."

"At least we might agree on that point. And you are right; quite a spectacular display of nature's power." The stranger hesitated a moment, as if about to venture upon a delicate subject. "Are you perchance aware of a dynamic field, one that radiates from nature itself, in fact, which covers the entirety of very earth upon which we stand, perhaps the universe entire?"

An odd concept, but Gaelan had, at times, reflected upon it, particularly when in the arms of nature's intricate splendor, as he was on this particular morning. Witnessing the raw power of the sun as it lifted above the horizon, setting it ablaze.

Already the temperature had risen by many degrees since he'd first set out, miles down the shore, as sunlight crept further and further across the expanse of water, transforming it from indigo to cobalt to sapphire, like those strange gas-filled tubes he'd seen on exhibit the day before, which captured atoms of gases, igniting them into brilliant colored light. And those globes of trapped phosphorescent chemical compounds with which he would illuminate the dark workspaces of his laboratory so long ago.

The stranger's demeanor softened. "Have you managed to get close, sir, to the Westinghouse exhibit?"

"Yes. The very first day. Incredible, quite. Of course, the remark-able electrical coils. And the Geissler tubes. The conductance of pure elemental gases caught in a glass vessel, and lighted without wires. How extraordinary. I was only just thinking about it. Have you visited yet?"

"Where are my manners? Forgive me, here we have been talking nearly half an hour, sharing this magnificent morning—and debating the future. Still we've not exchanged even the most basic pleasantries! I, sir, am Nicola Tesla. And I am pleased to make your acquaintance. And to know you have appreciated my contribution to the exposition."

Tesla? Why had he not recognized the brilliant inventor?

"I . . . Of course. I must apologize," Gaelan stammered, embar-rassed.

"It is of little matter. It would appear Thomas Edison has quite stolen the show, as it were, from all of us."

"I am Gaelan Erceldoune, chemist, apothecary, and of late, glass-maker." Gaelan extended his hand; Tesla did not take it.

"Are you, too, an inventor, Mr. Erceldoune?"

"No. Not really, and certainly not of your exalted class . . . or Edi-son's. Speaking of which . . . I do believe, sir your coil shall change the world, no matter what Mr. Edison has already brought to electrical invention. Yours can only—"

"Glass, you say?"

"Why, yes. I have always been drawn in by its unique properties, its malleability when liquefied, its ability to incorporate, and seamlessly, elements that either beautify or add to its utility. Glass can give birth to the humblest, yet incredibly durable, vessel or to the most fragile, priceless work of art."

"Have you ever experimented with spectra, as from prisms of dif-fering sorts?"

"Not experimented. Studied, perhaps, as an amateur might. I am quite amazed by the ability of a simple, clear glass triangle or pyramid to bend and deconstruct a simple beam of light, proving it to be any-thing but colorless—or simple. I believe my curiosity about the unique properties of glass has led me here . . . to glassmaking. I am especially keen on the sort embedded with metal oxides—favrile glass it is called."

"I am less in awe of its aesthetic beauty, Mr. Erceldoune, than I am of the beauty of the unfathomable potential of its power. Spectral light—waves of it—in harmony at a unique, perfect frequency. That is power—and at the heart of something with which I have only begun to experiment. What I referred to earlier. It is why I found myself this morning standing out there upon a lonely dock that might at any moment give way. There is something about the spot that drew me to it. Something in an instrument of my own invention directed me there. You would not understand, I do not think, the physics or engineering of it."

"Perhaps not. But I do comprehend that sort of unrelenting magnetic pull an idea might exert. Irresistible and insistent."

"Yes. Exactly that! Tell me, Mr. Gaelan Erceldoune—" Tesla hesitated for a moment as if unsure whether to continue down this conversational path. He held up a finger. "What would you say . . . ? What if I were to suggest to you . . . ? What if we might be able to concentrate beams of light into perfect harmony such that it would create a means to communicate not only from one point to another, say from here to the exposition grounds, but between points in the galaxy, perhaps through time? That space and time might form a convergence of sorts and allow us to—"

If that is why Tesla had been arguing with his financier, it was little wonder he'd been frustrated. The idea was far from reality—and playing with real fire, should it possess even a grain of true possibility. No sane backer would finance such a venture. Perhaps Tesla only meant it as a jest. Yet, knowing what little he did of the inventor . . .

"It is an idea perhaps more at home in Mr. H.G. Wells's fiction than in a laboratory." Gaelan regretted saying it as soon as it passed his lips. He knew better, he had experienced far too much in his life that seemed impossible. The idea that one might bend time to one's will. Intriguing . . .

"Tell me, Mr. Erceldoune. Is there a singular place you have visited or perhaps lived where you felt that sort of overpowering energy, dynamic beyond simple comprehension of the mind? Felt it down to your toes and the fiber of your being? Where nothing seemed beyond the realm of possibility? A spot ripe for such a temporal weak spot, as it were, where one might if only one had the means . . ."

Gaelan considered his father's book, long since missing. A massive tome, its leather cover engraved with a hawthorn tree and mighty ouroboroses. The source of all healing for all time past and yet to come, the key to Gaelan's immortality—and Simon Bell's. But how could he explain it to Tesla, who would, no doubt, think him mad. And it was not an answer to the question. A book is not a place. *Ah, yes. There is one place, cast so far into the far reaches of memory, he'd barely thought of it in decades.*

"There is, but I am afraid little remains but a small church, a few building stones, if that. An herbarium, likely by now gone to weed. In its day, a truly incredible place of tucked-away brilliance. A monastery."

"A house of God?" Tesla laughed unpleasantly. "I am surprised, considering your professed disdain for Him—"

"But I cannot deny the presence there of exactly what you describe. What I experienced when—" Gaelan dared not go further in explanation.

"Perhaps. It is undeniable that each being on this planet—in the universe, each particle, each speck of dirt, granule of glass—we are all interconnected as the stars in the firmament, bound together by an indescribable force. Is this force, then, God? That is a matter of opinion. But it has nothing to do with the institution that defines the indefinable, yes?"

"Exactly so."

Tesla seemed to withdraw into himself a moment, considering something.

"So, this place, you say, no longer exists. Are you certain? Perhaps you've not the eyes to see it. What if you possessed the ability to bend the light, like a prism, at least metaphorically, and see beyond what is visible in the ordinary light? I am certain it sounds preposterous to you, and undoubtedly, you think me quite deranged, as did my finan-ciers."

Gaelan could not disagree more, for he had experienced things more fantastical than even Tesla might imagine. "One century's madman is today's genius," Gaelan offered. "What you suggest would seem to exist solely in the realm of magic and myth. Yet, what is magic, but science—technological innovation—that we have not yet the ability—the eyes—to comprehend? Even twenty years ago, your bril-liant alternating current, your coil, would have been thought a luna-tic's ravings. Three hundred years ago, you might have been burnt alive for witchcraft. Yet, here we are."

An image conjured in the far reaches of Gaelan's memory—the day when as a young lad he'd been forced to witness his own dear papa's execution on the pyre for the capital offense of magical healing. For curing King James VI and his court from a scourge that nearly devoured all of Britain. Not by magic but by science. Not by sorcery but by knowledge, understanding far beyond his time.

Gaelan shook his head, gazing back toward the horizon. The sun was now full up; he'd meant to be back at the fair long ago. The cacophony of gulls filled the air as they dove for prey among the white-caps. The waves sloshed over the rickety dock and the gravel of the narrow beach, pulling the pungent aroma of fish and algae a bit too close by.

"What is this place called, if I might ask, and where is . . . or rather . . . was . . . it located? The site to which you referred—the ruin?" Tesla asked as he scuttled away from the encroaching water.

Gaelan followed. "It was called in its day the House of the Holy Trinity, at a place called Soutra in the Scottish Borders, near Fala." A house of science and study, art, and history. Of medicines far beyond any known capability of the time. And for him, a sanctuary, a rescue from certain death.

CHICAGO NORTH SHORE, PRESENT DAY

CHAPTER 2

Denial. Anger. Bargaining. Depression. Acceptance. Gaelan Erceldoune was dead, and Dr. Anne Shaw just needed to get on with it.

A full two weeks since he'd disappeared down the falls at Glomach in northwest Scotland, mouthing to her over the deafening crash of water, "Trust me." How many times had she passed through the Kübler-Ross stages of grief in those two weeks? Five? Ten? At least. And each time she circled back to denial only to begin the whole bloody process again.

Anne had known Gaelan less than a week, hardly worth the mention. How had he managed to engrave himself into the depths of her soul? She would dismiss the relationship as nothing more than infatuation on the rebound. And then she would recall those few short days and nights. The exhilarating collaboration as they deconstructed his astonishing, ancient healing book with its alluring illuminations, the shared elation of discovering its brilliant magic—no, its hidden and highly improbable science—and, together, watching it work.

Then there was the sweet hesitance of his lovemaking the morning after he'd revealed his deepest secret. Yet how could a man for all appearances her own age be nearly half a millennium old? His shy smile while he tried to explain how it had been nearly two centuries since he'd last been with a woman. And that woman? Eleanor

Bell, her great, great, great . . . grandmother. The way he'd touched Anne—courtly, reverently. His sleepy, stoned gaze in the aftermath of sex . . .

Why did it feel significant pieces of her heart had been ripped from beneath her ribs after this briefest of encounters? Why could she not get on with it when Gaelan Erceldoune should register only as a minor blip on Anne's romantic radar?

She knew the answer to that question. So much better to be swallowed by the agony of grief than deal with a truly failed relationship. Dr. Paul Gilles, who'd sold his soul to pursue riches untold. Never bloody mind the consequences. How could she ever have agreed to marry that venal wanker?

So much safer to lose herself in tormented fury than confront the ramifications of her own research on the immortal jellyfish. *Turritopsis nutricula*, a fascinating biological anomaly, its chromosomal end caps—telomeres—the stuff of wonder and imagination. What-ifs and unbridled quests without constraint. The exalted possibility of curing incurable diseases without considering consequences of the technology borne of it. The price to be paid should it be exploited.

The gentle ebb and flow of Lake Michigan waves washed the rocks at the base of the narrow ravines, thirty meters beneath the long granite outcrop upon which Simon Bell's Highland Park mansion stood. Anne closed her eyes, concentrating to set her breathing to the cadence.

How could she have done telomere research her whole professional career and never reflect—really consider the practical application of *T. nutricula*'s telomeres taken to some nth degree? Human immortality.

She'd been naive not to understand the fortune to be had by someone with zero ethics and a penchant for playing God. Dr. Paul Gilles.

But what, then, to make of one Mr. Gaelan Erceldoune, whose genetic mutation rendered him as immortal as her jellyfish? Infinite tissue regeneration. An embodiment of immortality's promise, but traumatized. Crushed. Tortured. Broken. And decidedly not the product of twenty-first-century genetic manipulation but a biological rarity, centuries old.

She peered out over the vastness of Lake Michigan and out toward the horizon, trying to rid Gaelan from her mind. A futile exercise, damn him.

The wind switched direction, sweeping in off the lake, hard and chilly, transforming the water from mirror calm into a roiling white-capped surf, bathing her face in a cold, freshening mist as the waves thrashed the bluff below.

The fresh green scent of late spring wafted in the breeze, up from deep within the forested ravines and mingled with the flowery perfume of the garden. Not even such lavish aromatherapy managed to lighten her mood.

Anne withdrew Simon's letter from her trouser pocket, the rough fountain pen ink, the flowery cursive, remnants of an earlier era. Simon's era. And Gaelan's. The letter had arrived for her at Mum's by courier back home in the UK a week ago—seven days after she'd last seen Simon alive.

My dearest niece,

If you are reading this, you will know I am dead, and that Gaelan was successful in creating the antidote for this two-cen-turies-long curse of a life I have too long lived. At last, I am free from my beloved Sophie, whose ghostly apparition has plagued me now for almost two centuries. I can now join her in eternity, where we both belong, her grave no longer unquiet and both of us at peace.

As my sole heir, I have left to you my entire fortune, my house, and all future royalties from my numerous books. This information is with my London solicitor, and all you need do is to see him at your convenience. Amongst my effects you will find a series of diaries kept by my sister, Eleanor, who passed on in

1902, and me. I hope you might read them and through them know both of us—and Gaelan too, I think.

As for the house, you may, of course, keep it, or sell as you wish. Its sale and my estate entire will grant you and your family a life of little want.

With great affection,
Your great (many times removed) uncle Simon Bell

What good Anne might accomplish with such wealth at her disposal, begin to make amends for whatever small part she might have played in the wrongdoing perpetrated by her former employer, Transdiff Genomics.

For the moment, Anne was far too jet-lagged and exhausted to focus on much of anything useful. Too little sleep; too little food. Too much coffee. French-pressed and caffeine-rich. Maybe that explained her mood.

That, and the phone call from Paul Gilles. *Fuck him, the bloody wanker!* Until that unwelcome call, every ringtone, every chirp of a notification alert, rang up the faint hope that Gaelan was alive—and on his way to her side.

Dr. Paul Gilles. Who else in her life had the unique ability to destroy everything with a single ring of her mobile? A kick to the gut in the guise of Paul's fawning, feckless transatlantic plea to reconcile. Excuse upon excuse. So many excuses and nothing to remotely explain why he was screwing that tart of a postdoc in *her* bed. *Her* bed! What a bloody, damn fool she'd been!

"You must believe me, my darling. An error of judgment, and that is all." Paul had whined. "It's why I texted you that day."

"Which day? What text?"

"You know, when it all went to hell, and your friend the immortal bloke went off the grid and abandoned Transdiff—and us."

"I got no text message from you. Had I done, I would have erased it, ignored it, and thrown the bloody phone into the Thames."

"You seriously didn't get it? I used one of your favorite ... It was my sole desire, my dearest Anne, to resurrect our moribund relationship. It can't be over. Whatever you need from me, I'll do it and more. I want a fresh start. Bring *us* back from the dead. Like Sherlock. You know ... 'The Empty House.' I can't believe you didn't get the reference."

Paul? That was Paul. *Not* Gaelan?

That had been the moment.

Two fucking, soul-sucking, agonizing weeks she'd placed her hopes upon what was almost certainly a clue. A secret, texted message. Two weeks she'd waited to hear again from him. Where to meet up à la Sherlock and Watson after Reichenbach Falls. "The Empty House."

Two weeks she'd put herself through hell believing that Gaelan Erceldoune was alive and well and would ring her up at any moment. But there would be no Sherlockian "ta-da" comeback on the horizon. No "Empty House" reunion after Gaelan's Reichenbach "fall" at Glomach.

What an absolute fool she'd been. Again. What lingered now were the too-familiar stings of betrayal and humiliation. Anne had allowed girlish romanticism to get the better of her. Again.

She was done. Finished. Better to be rid Gaelan Erceldoune. A tortured and broken man, irresistible in the odd Regency novel, but not so much in real life. She was lucky to be done with him.

Someday, she might even believe it.

And now here she was in a real empty house, abandoned but for the ashes of her benefactor, her ancestor, Simon Bell, his remains sitting in a ceramic urn atop the library mantel. As for the house, Anne had little use for a grand Gothic mansion in a foreign country. She couldn't just pick up and relocate to Chicago permanently, could she?

She turned away from the lake, taking in the lavish gardens, the graceful archways, and mullioned windows of Simon's house. Her house. Impossibly, hers. She could do worse than this magnificent refuge from the muddle of her life.

Glittery pinpoints of refracted light danced against the white pavement of the garden path. The tiny stones of her gem-encrusted labyrinth pendant, a gift from Gaelan the morning he disappeared. The morning she'd tracked him down in Thurso, Scotland, beneath a hawthorn tree. *The* hawthorn tree, its destination somehow encoded into that remarkable book. The ouroboros book, he'd called it.

The book had vanished, he'd explained. Replaced, he thought, by the pendant. Something about Celtic deities. The goddess of healing. The fae. Fairies? *Bollocks.* Or was it?

No more improbable than Gaelan's own existence, was it? A man five centuries old, yet never looking older than thirty-five. And his mutilated left hand . . . his *formerly* mutilated left hand. How to explain that one? She'd seen it. Held it in her hand. Kissed the smooth stump, where, by his explanation, three fingers had been severed more than a century before. And that morning at Thurso? Whole. Nothing she knew of science could explain that one. Why not the fairies, then?

But now, it was all quite beside the point. She should bloody rip the pendant from her neck, chuck it into the lake, and feed it to the gulls.

Better idea. The *useful* graveyard for the detritus of love spurned. eBay.

A large blue heron glided just above her head, distracting her back toward the lake as he alighted, ballet-like. Noisily skimming the water surface on the hunt, he disappeared into the whitecaps. She closed her eyes, inhaling the strange potpourri of fish and algae. Flowers and freshening breeze. Trying to banish all thought of the past two weeks from her thoughts.

Turning from the promontory wall, Anne followed the small path meandering through the garden. White turned-iron benches dotted the way, one at each flower bed. No, not each flower bed. Only the rose beds, each plot a distinct color, a different species of *Rosa*. Some wild, some fringed, impossibly unnatural colors. Some in full bloom, others green, barely buds, full of promise.

"Trust me," Gaelan told her at the edge of the chasm. Was that not his promise to return to her? She assumed he'd staged the disappearance down the cataract at Glomach Falls to throw Transdiff—and the media—off his scent. Or had she misread him so completely? Misunderstood his wistful gaze just before he'd gone over the side?

"Trust me" could mean a thousand things. She scarcely knew him, and certainly not well enough to translate the complexities of a centuries-old human.

It was her own bloody fault. Why had she followed him to Scotland, put him in that position? He'd decided to end his life, and she should have simply accepted it. How unfair she had been to back him into a corner when all he wanted was to escape the hell his life would certainly become, exposed as immortal. A genetic anomaly.

By now, too much of the truth was in the wild: tabloids, conspiracy websites, radio chat shows, podcasts. Grains of truth that would lead to nothing but catastrophe if confirmed. There was only one way to guarantee the immortal "Miracle Man" would remain the stuff of urban legend.

His death.

And now, after centuries, he had the means to do it. Who could blame him?

She had to let it go. Let him go.

Acceptance. Again. For now.

Too weary for one more step, Anne stretched out on a low bench and closed her eyes. Good a place as any for a nap. A blur of fragrance. Of rhythm, of melody, of . . .

An old-school telephone ringtone jangled near Anne's ear, distant at first, jarring her from the first threads of sleep. More and more insistent, it dragged her back. *Bloody hell!*

Resigned to never sleeping again, she answered.

"Dr. Anne Shawe?" An American voice. Male. Unfamiliar. *What was* he *selling?*

She cleared the grogginess from her throat. "Yes?"

"My name is Preston Alcott—"

"Who?" That name. Vaguely familiar, but she couldn't place it. Her stomach tightened. What if he was nosing about for information on Gaelan—or Transdiff? She placed her index finger gently upon above the large red "end call" button, poised to punch it at the least provocation.

"I . . . your name was given to me by a colleague of yours at Salk. In La Jolla. I understand you no longer work for them."

No longer? Leading with the venerated Salk Institute for Biological Studies—not exactly the way to win her over these days. At least he'd not mentioned their quietly withdrawn job offer. Courtesy of Transdiff and Anne's whistleblowing activities.

Something disquieting about the bloke's affable baritone. Silky smooth, a BBC presenter with an American accent. *And that name, Preston Alcott.* It prickled at the outer edges of her memory.

Ignoring her reservations for the moment, Anne summoned her most professional "Dr. Shawe" voice. "Oh! Really! Referred you to me?"

"Yes. I need a physician with your unique qualifications. Someone with expertise in your field of genetics. You're a researcher as well as a doctor, right?"

Straight to the point. Okay, he had her attention. "I've a Doctorate in molecular genetics. And, yes, I'm a medical doctor as well."

"Good. What I have in mind is of great personal urgency. First, do you know anything about me? I mean, have you heard of me? Good . . . bad . . . indifferent . . . ? I'm pretty famous over here in the U.S., but across the pond—"

"I'm afraid not, Mr. Alcott. I'm frightfully sorry, but I don't think . . ." She exhaled as she rose from the bench, casting a last lingering gaze over the promontory wall. *Don't go anywhere! I'll be back!* "Look, I'm out in the garden; hang on whilst I go back into the house. Fewer . . . distractions, I think."

Settling into a cushy sitting room sofa, Anne put the phone on speaker and opened her laptop. "There. Sorry. So. What do you have in mind, then?"

"I'm in the financial end of high tech. Venture capital. Lots of little startups in dedicated incubators all over the U.S.: Silicon Valley, of course, Chapel Hill, Seattle, the Boston corridor, Chicago, Pittsburgh. Well, let's just say I'm everywhere."

He had a warm, genuine laugh. *Do not be taken in by it.*

"Anyway, Dr. Shawe . . ." He cleared his throat. "I . . . I could use your help. I . . . it's . . ." A long beat.

Why had his confident boasting suddenly turned hesitant? Hmm . . . "I'm listening."

"It's . . . it's personal, you see . . . I need a doc. But the right . . . most docs . . ." Another pause, this one longer. "You'll be delighted with the compensation, by the way," he added quickly.

"I'm not sure . . ." Anne wasn't really a clinician. Not since just after med school. And she had little interest in taking on a patient. Besides, she lacked any of the paperwork to practice medicine in the States. On the other hand, maybe she could consult. She definitely needed some sort of new project. A job. Anything to divert her from Gaelan Erceldoune. Just enough to see her through . . . No. Not a good idea. Not before she know more about this Preston Alcott fellow. "Look, I'm on holiday right now. For an extended period. I've been through a bit of an ordeal and—" She typed his name in her browser address bar.

"Where?"

"I beg your pardon?"

"I mean, are you here in the U.S.? Or the Caribbean? South of France? Mallorca? Greenland? Where do you Brits . . . holiday, anyway? I can be in the air in an hour and meet you . . . wherever. I'm anxious to . . . I'm used to transactions on the fast track. Mine is a business of minutes. Five minutes late, and another guy swoops in. Of course, this isn't about my business, like I said. It's personal. Very. And I don't want to discuss it over the phone."

A flood of matches scrolled down her ten-inch screen. Page one was all business and biography. The meteoric rise of the thirty-five-year-old multibillionaire Preston Alcott, founder of DigitX services, which drew the increasingly Internet-entangled world ever closer with his holographic meeting service. "HoliNar: like being there, only better."

Ah. That Preston Alcott. Anne had attended two HoliNar-hosted meetings over the past year. Impressive—and it was almost like live.

So. What interest would he have in her? Did he want to step things up further, with some sort of bio-component? Remote medical exams? Virtual genetic testing? Intriguing possibilities there. No. He'd said it was personal, not professional.

"Dr. Shawe, are you still—"

"Sorry. Got distracted. You were saying . . . Actually, can you give me a minute? Sorry."

She clicked "Next," taking her to the second of an infinite number of pages and 2,762,587 hits. She stopped at hit number three.

"Telomerase Research Results in Creation of First Immortal Rat." *That's a new one. How the fuck they manage that?* And how did Alcott figure into it?

Anne had read every morsel of legitimate research on telomeres and telomerase, was a peer reviewer on three major journals in the field. Never had she read one word about *any* lab producing an immortal mammal. Immortal cell lines, yes. Organ-specific, telomerase-enhanced reverse transcriptase—TERT, yes. No mammals. Full stop. Never. Not yet.

She sucked in a breath and opened the article. *Bloody fucking hell.*

Anne scanned down the article. She wasn't impressed. Bad science . . . and the rat? Virtual, not real. There it was, Alcott's name.

Best known for his groundbreaking HoloCall and HoliNar services . . . wading into the ancient quest for immortality . . . cracking the secret to immortality . . . true fountain of youth . . .

"Dr. Shawe??"

"Yeah. Yeah. Another sec. Sorry." Maybe he'd hang up; maybe that would be better. She continued to read . . . more carefully.

Alcott claims he isn't involved with the secretive antisenescence think tank Galahad Society, but sources close to the organization say he has a large financial stake, one that may soon be paying off. The group claims to be on the brink of a huge discovery with its immortal rats. Alcott denies any interest in funding basic research on curing rare genetic diseases, such as the one that claimed his wife last year. She stopped and reread that last bit twice more before returning to the call.

"You still there, Mr. Alcott?"

"Preston. Yup."

"Sorry for the interruptions. I *am* sorry about your wife—"

"You know, then—"

"What I don't know is what I might offer you. I'm no practitioner, if that's what you're hoping to find. Haven't been for years. My research takes—"

"Like I said. Rather not discuss it on the phone, if you don't mind."

"Look, Mr. Alcott, I'm quite in the midst of something right now . . . Might I ring you back in say an hour? This number?"

"Yes. Of course. My cell."

Holiday. This was . . . is . . . supposed to be . . . a holiday. Not a happy, carefree, lay-on-the-beach-have-an-affair-with-a-stranger holiday, but still . . . Chicago had men, right? And beaches. She did not want to contemplate work. Not yet. And who the hell can't talk about a personal medical issue by phone?

Anne scrolled up to the source of the immortal rodent story. *NewsFax Daily.* The tabloid? "All the News—Unfiltered, Real Stories, Beyond the Facts." A license to destroy careers and lives in the name of someone's version of the truth. On the other hand, whatever the source, the fact Preston Alcott was at the heart of the story was unnerving at best.

She opened a second article and froze as her own words stared back at her.

Science fiction describes cyber-beings—brilliant machines with human tendencies. The simple fact is all beings—from the tiniest microbe to the T. nutricula jellyfish at the center of my work to the highly honed machine of a superstar athlete or Nobel laureate—are also machines, imperfect, but of the most elegant biology. Like the androids of Star Wars or any other of your favourite science fiction classics, human lifespan dictated by the failings of structure. The question is, can the fundamental structure of living beings be restored, rejuvenated, rebuilt at the cellular or even molecular level so that the superstructure—the body—never actually dies? Senescence becomes a choice?

Buried three paragraphs down from the quote, a mention of the Galahad Society and more speculation that Alcott was involved, at least financially.

A minor part of a lecture she'd given six years earlier on the ethical issues of applying her research in a practical setting. Indeed, it was beneficial to explore the use of telomerases to forestall cell death in diseases. Already it was becoming reality. But the temptation to take it to its ultimate degree . . . ? And she wasn't talking about immortal rodents.

NORTHWEST COAST OF SCOTLAND, PRESENT DAY

CHAPTER 3

The seacoast, at last. Cape Wrath, Scotland. Gaelan Erceldoune had lost count of the days since he'd parted ways with Anne and lowered himself down Glomach Falls. The cobalt glass of the small vial glinted in the sunlight as he gave the poison a slight shake before gently replacing the bottle in his coat pocket, relieved it made the journey intact.

Now that he finally possessed the means, it was time to end his life. A poison. An antidote to five hundred years of living. *Sola dosis facit venenum*—the dose makes the poison, said Paracelsus. In this case, the poison *was* the dose.

A foolish move to give Anne that spare vial, but she'd cornered him. Trapped. Conflicted. The plea in her gaze had nearly undone him. *Nearly*. Part of him wanted to go back, fall into her gaze, her arms. But he couldn't do it. To either of them.

Besides, she'd bloody well known the plan. He'd made it plain enough back in Chicago. She'd understood, at least she'd said so. But she had to muck it up and follow him to Scotland. So, he'd given her one of the two vials and lied. "Trust me," he'd said, when she should do anything but that. How could she have known he'd made a second dose—just in case? *Always have a backup plan.*

He'd been moving for days now, ignoring the injuries tearing at him from within. The struggle against searing agony and gnawing lethargy beckoned at the crest of every new hill. But he pushed on. No choice.

But for a missed foothold on the descent at Glomach, he might have made it through the falls cleanly, as he'd done so many times as a lad. Each contusion and broken bone, cracked rib, and ugly gash provided an exquisitely painful reminder of just how vulnerable he was for an immortal fellow. Left untended, the injuries would mend in a matter of days. Gaelan had no plans to be alive even that long.

The tether holding him aloft just this side of conscious thought and forward movement had nearly disintegrated. Encroaching apathy and a mosaic landscape of blurred images now waged war against his bloody-minded determination to reach this, his final resting place. Leaning his back against a large, algae-covered boulder at the mouth of a sea cave, Gaelan slid to the ground, exhausted and broken.

Cape Wrath, a poetic location to end his life. Here he would put the vial to his lips and drink, savoring it like a one hundred-year-old whisky. Allow the tides to do the rest. After more than nearly five centuries, it would soon be over, his body forever lost to the sea.

The bracing surf pummeled Gaelan, cleansing him of grime and sweat, blood and regret; the tang of bitter salt lingered in his mouth. Anne Shawe had played in the shadows of his mind the entire way. Now she hovered just beyond the shore, haunting him, taunting him, a siren calling as she bobbed in and out of view, disappearing into the waves only to appear closer a moment later. He blinked and the image disintegrated, cascading into the white foam, a looming mirage conjured of guilt and fear. Remorse. She would despise him into eternity, but there was nothing to be done about that.

Soon enough, Anne would move past the brief moment that had flared between them in Chicago. And his promise, made in a moment of weakness, mouthed at the ledge of the abyss. "Trust me."

To do what? Trust he would choose life, and they would live happily ever after? Until she'd grown old and he did not? Until she died, frail and elderly and he lived on, eternally a young man? For Gaelan "ever after" was forever. And ever. And never a happy ending.

Gaelan had loved three women in all his long years: Caitrin Kinston, Lady Eleanor Bell Braithwaite . . . and Anne Shawe. He'd been drawn to Anne in some indescribable way. Visceral. Incandescent. Transcendent. But she would move on; he would die. Full stop.

A cormorant landed on a nearby rock, eyeing a flock of puffins bobbing just off shore. Another day, a different time, Gaelan might simply sit in peace for hours, transfixed by the stark, unearthly seascape, its surreal rock formations, stone creatures forged by millennia of North Atlantic storms and the calm evolution of slow erosion.

Doubt lingered in the periphery of his thoughts as centuries passed him by in a flash. Centuries of being witness to discoveries small and significant. The constant but slow motion of civilization's thrust and parry—darkness into light into darkness. Enlightenment that too often wasn't. Genius ignored, dismissed, discarded until it was too late to acknowledge the achievement.

Gaelan had touched greatness, played in the shadow of genius: Newton and Tesla, Wells and Conan Doyle, Louis Tiffany. Benjamin Bell. Giants. *Sláinte* to them, one and all. Yes, he regretted not being privy to the next chapter, but he was done, and ready for the end.

Anne hovered in the near distance, just beyond the whitecaps. He tried to ignore the mirage, but it refused to vanish in the faded northern light of early spring.

The vision dissolved just as he reached out toward it, as it mutated into an army of grotesques swallowing everything in its path. Setting the sea ablaze. Gaelan closed his eyes, but the image remained, burned into his retinas.

A blink, and it all disappeared, leaving in its wake only the whirlwind of sea and foam. No monsters. No Anne.

He breathed in the cold, sour salt air, hoping the spray would numb his injuries, aches, and pains. All it managed was to make him wet and cold. His sodden jeans clung heavy to his thighs and his suede jacket, blackened by freezing salt water, hung about his shoulders like an anvil.

He really needed a smoke, if only for a bit of warmth. But everything in his pockets was drowned and useless. Even his vintage Zippo.

A voice buzzed at his ear. Familiar and unwelcome as a mosquito.

"For fuck's sake, Erceldoune, take the damn poison already."

That voice; he knew it like his own. Simon Bell. "I thought you were dead, Simon."

"I could say the same to you. Clearly, *you're* still quite alive. Whereas I—"

If the entire thing wasn't so completely pathetic, Gaelan would laugh at the absurdity of conversing with a . . . ghost . . . auditory hallucination? Just the same . . . "It worked, then?"

"It did! And what are *you* waiting for, hmm?"

Gaelan patted his jacket pocket. "The vial. It's right here."

"Yet, you've procrastinated, and nearly a week. And, by the way, you're a bloody arse for disappearing on *my* dear niece, the delectable—and brilliant, if I might say—Dr. Anne Shawe."

"Go the fuck away."

"That what all this hesitation is all about, then? Not sure you want to shuffle off this mortal coil just yet?"

No, quite sure. I have suffered more slings and arrows than any mortal man may endure. I am done.

The sea was on the move, and the high tide would come in soon, infiltrating the cave, higher and higher. A slithering snake consuming everything in its path. And Gaelan was ready for it. He would drink the poison and wait for the blessed blanket of death. No more hallucinations, no macabre visions to invade his days and nights. No more fucking PTSD. No Handley. No Braithwaite. No Tremayne. *No Simon Bell.*

But, for the moment, Simon floated in and out of view, bothersome as ever.

"Why did you send Anne to me? Tell her my coordinates? You had no right!"

"Thought you deserved a chance after all you'd been through—"

"Bollocks. What are you doing here, anyway? Haunting me? Aren't you busy reconciling with your dear departed Sophie? It's all you've whined about for decades."

"Having, I suppose, is not so pleasant a thing as wanting, in the end."

"Quoth the philosopher Spock. Go away, Simon. Leave me be."

Again, it was quiet, but for the flock of puffins, which had now relocated to the shore, scavenging the sand and gravel, tiny, feathered clowns with painted beaks, hunting dinner an earnest mission to complete quickly, before the tide roared back and hid the booty.

Gaelan took a final look around and, hands shaking, carefully tipped the vial to his lips. He closed his eyes and waited. The taste was not unpleasant—like cheap orange vodka—as it stung down his throat. He tried to identify each ingredient he'd mixed into the deadly elixir, its taste, the sensation on his tongue, in his throat, as it slithered into his bloodstream.

It would not be long now. He hauled himself into the sea cave and collapsed at the base of a massive boulder, awaiting a long-overdue death to claim him, as Simon Bell's ghost lingered in the shadows.

Blinding flashes of light exploded in the dark periphery of Gaelan's vision, a strobing rhythmic pulse in sync with a dull humming roar. Something was forcing him down, further and further. An anchor, sucking the air from his lungs like a vacuum, and in its wake, an overpowering crushing in his chest. He struggled to breathe against the screaming agony, a dagger piercing his lungs.

Then it was over, swiftly as it had begun, leaving Gaelan gasping for air and plastered to a jagged, rocky surface. No sound. No light. Complete and utter nothingness.

Suddenly, he was floating, drifting, aimless in the void on a bed of gauze and feathers. Would there not soon appear the famous white light to guide him directly toward heaven's gate?

Or was his fate, instead, a place in the pits of hell? For now, he was falling. One level to the next until . . . what? The eighth circle of Dante's inferno, reserved for those who'd dabbled with nature's laws— where alchemists and sorcerers were condemned for all eternity?

Fire ignited the air, filling the chasm with dazzling, blinding light. From the depths of the blaze materialized the lone figure of his father, unbending, unrelenting, the flames licking at his boots, his clothing, lapping like waves, surrounding him. Yet, there Papa stood, still, and staring into Gaelan's eyes, as he had that terrible morning nearly half a millennium ago, speaking words impossible to hear as they evaporated into the chaos of burning embers.

Gaelan could do nothing but watch in horror as, so very slowly, Papa's clothing burned away, melting into his flesh, his bones, turning them to ash.

The fire sparked and spitted, engulfing the entire courtyard, reaching the high parapet, where, all-powerful, James VI, king of Scotland, smiled, pleased with the fiery execution. The inferno crept closer, scorching Gaelan's face, as it had that morning in 1598.

Then he heard it, thunderous and deafening, a surging wall of water, coming at him from all sides. The cacophony of the tides thrust deep into the narrow cave, only to be sucked out again. Further out to sea this time, as high tide retreated. And he was still alive.

The poison vial, still clutched tight in his fist, was empty. Why was he not dead? *How* could he not be dead?

Gaelan's heart pounded in his ears as the steady drip-drip of water echoed off the sea cave walls, dragging him back to full awareness as the remnants of the tide drizzled steadily from chalk white stalactites inches above his head. How had he gotten all the way up there?

Did some innate survival instinct force him ever upwards to escape the inundation? Up the boulder and just above the tide line? Or had the force of the tides pulled him out to sea only to deposit him here, atop this boulder as they heaved their way to and fro?

A furious storm battered the rocks outside, slamming a new swell through the cave's mouth, which surged up the boulder just below Gaelan's precarious perch. Lightning turned the night into day and beasts of the sea loomed on the cave walls in silhouette.

At least Simon had shut the fuck up.

Above the whip of wind and foam as the sea rushed in and out about him and the eerie whistle and screech of the gale sweeping through the cave, a sweet voice lilted in modal chant high and pure. He knew the ballad. The tragic tale of the Great Silkie, the man-seal creature who dwelled not far off from this bit of seacoast—at Sule Skerry.

The storm slowly receded along with the sea. Bioluminescent algae deposited by the retreating waves shimmered in bloodred puddles surrounding Gaelan's boulder. He eased himself down from the slick rock and let go, landing in a shallow pool. Soaked through and shivering, he tried rubbing the cobwebs from his brain, the searing pain from his forehead, where he must've bashed it during the storm.

Think, Erceldoune! Why had the poison not worked? How could he still be alive?

He had been precise in its preparations. Every detail. Exactly following the instructions in the ouroboros book.

"*Pondere per singula*—one dose. *Celeri morte*—a swift death. *Certa mors*—certain death." Euthanasia in a bottle. He'd made no mistake—not with the poison. Yet, here he was. And lacking a Plan B.

In the distance, the notes of a familiar ringtone. Gaelan searched through the darkness for the familiar glow of his phone. How could it not be waterlogged and dead by now?

The ringing stopped.

If only he could concentrate, wrangle his brain into some semblance of clarity. Five centuries of looking over his shoulder had trained him; even when he'd been dead drunk or wasted into oblivion, his instincts were always reliable. Now there was only freezing wet fog and weariness. Coherent thought was, at best, an elusive notion, a meteor storm of disconnected thoughts.

The mobile went off again; the white of its bright screen pulsed among the algae. He pounced upon the phone, seizing it, determined.

Dragging himself through miry sand and slimy ropes of the luminous algae, Gaelan now stood at the base of a towering cliff just outside the cave entrance. He hurled the phone with as much strength as he could muster—barely enough to reach the fleeing sea as it swept ever westward. For a moment the phone bobbed on the crest of a wave, and then disappeared.

The effort sapped Gaelan of all strength and he staggered against rocks. The stars had begun to emerge, and he tried to focus on the western sky; always the heavens provided his most reliable guideposts as he navigated the worst of times. Perhaps they would now help him make sense of the mud and muck in his head.

But the expanse of sky was distorted into a confusing, pock-marked blur. Disorganized pinpoints of hazy light, one object indistinguishable from the next. He could not connect them into constellations. The northern sky danced a ballet of color, indistinct. An impressionistic painting of the aurora borealis. Not even the stars made sense this night.

His eyes drifted closed as sleep descended, he hoped for the last time. The vortex of the next high tide would propel his lifeless body, then, into the waiting peace of a deep-sea grave. Awareness faded into the ceaseless rhythm of the tides, transporting him on the wings of time.

CHAPTER 4

Silence. Ominous, like the void in the eye of a hurricane when the sky is clear, but for the creep of a scarlet-tinged black cumulonimbus mustering on the horizon, planning its attack of death and destruction. Strange, almost pastoral. The quiet before a flock of panicked birds flee into the sky ahead of any human understanding that catastrophe is but a moment away.

July 1916, it had been, an hour before dawn. Gaelan had been there too long, on this field of death. The distorted ground was strangely uneven, almost alive with movement, just beneath their feet as they moved, always forward. An eerie sensation as they marched above the invisible graves of the Somme. Soldiers whose names would be ever unknown, their bones crushed with each step into white powder, mixing with the quicklime that lined each grave. Inches beneath their boots, buried in the clay, forging a treacherous path for the still living.

The dawn light glinted off the mud and mingled with blood and flesh and the dull gleam of cannon fodder dotting the entropy of the battlefield, too distant to be heard. And with the dawn had come the renewed bedlam of war. The endless procession of good lads swarming like rodents catapulted over the top of the trench, pushed forward, endlessly forward, only to fall like so many dominoes: green and red, not black and white.

"Keep moving." The commander whispered over and over. "Do not bloody stop." Until the next trench. The acrid scent of gunpowder and mass graves covered with lime burned his eyes, his nostrils. Hell's perfume at the banks of the River Styx.

Gaelan was vaguely aware he was dreaming. A flash of memory a century old.

The silence broke, replaced by the soft tinkling of glass . . . wind chimes? Sprites in his ear. The atonal elegance of the notes lacked cohesion yet vibrated distantly through his head. The high strings of a harp randomly plucked, sustained, note blending into note, enough to rouse him to full wakefulness.

Gaelan groaned, casting off the final remnants of the dream. His joints cracked satisfyingly as he stretched. His arm was better; his ribs no longer throbbed with every slightest motion. He was warm and dry. Comfortable. Evidently, some time had passed since he'd taken the poison—enough for his injuries to heal, but how long? And he was no longer, as far as he could discern, in the sea cave.

Was this death? He didn't *feel* dead, but would he know? Or was this yet another dream? A dream within a dream?

In the blank blackness, the constant *tlink . . . tlink . . . tlink* of the wind chimes began to grate. Definitely *not* the sea cave.

Tentacles of panic slithered along his spine. *Think, man. Assess your situation.*

Fact: you are flat on your back in a cot. No pillow. No sheet. You can move but not see. You are in a twisty little maze . . . An amusing memory from the most ancient of old-school computer games. Good old "Adventure." But this was no game. This was a puzzle decidedly real.

The moist air pressed down on him, heavy like bricks. A familiar mustiness and windowless closeness of the air reminded of prison. Was he being held captive? But where? And why?

Gaelan's imagination, fueled by too-vivid memories of his imprisonment in Bedlam nearly two centuries earlier, manifested before him in a tableau of rusty knives and scalpels, tongs and hand-saws—the disembodied tools of Dr. Francis Handley's torture. Five years of infinite cruelty. Until the day the mad doctor severed Gaelan's fingers one by one—an "experiment" to see if they might grow back. They hadn't. He blinked away the vision.

But this was not Bedlam, not Newgate prison, not any other cell Gaelan had been unlucky enough to inhabit. There had to be a logical explanation.

The simplest explanation, Mr. Occam, is that the poison is taking its bloody time and is having quite the jolly time screwing with my mind. Ensnaring it in some sort of lucid dream. A Sartre-esque hell.

Well, there was no exit discernable, at least not from Gaelan's vantage on the bed. In the pitch black of wherever this was. *L'enfer, c'est les autres.* But no other people around to hold up that eternal mirror to his damned soul. *Fuck Sartre.*

Working theory: this is real, I'm actually awake, and somehow *not where I was before I blacked out. Further, the poison did not work, for reasons yet to be determined. But what went wrong with the poison? And how to fix it, make it right.*

Those damnable wind chimes shattered any small shred of concentration he still possessed. He needed to find them, and crush the fuckers to sand. *No time like the present.* One more stretch and Gaelan sat on the edge of the bed.

Socks. How the devil had socks got on his feet? Thick woolen socks, warm and quite comfortable. But where the devil were his sandals? If only he could see . . . anything.

Gaelan seriously needed a smoke. Patting down his jeans and shirt he remembered this was not his clothing. Yet, there in the shirt pocket, a pack of fags. Not his brand, but . . . ah, well . . . At least they weren't soaked in brine. Damp, but worth a try.

More patting. This time for matches. But the box was a sopping mess of wet cardboard and sticks. He had no working lighter. And where the fuck was his wallet? Desperate, he struck the first match. Nothing, not even a spark.

Six more futile attempts, before he gave up.

Bloody fag probably wouldn't burn anyway.

He pitched the pack and the matches into the black, listening, waiting for them to hit a wall, the floor, anything that might make a sound besides that infernal tinkling. Help him gauge the size and shape of the room. *Might as well have cast them into a black hole.*

He sighed, resigned to simply wait out whatever this all was. Preferably death and not imprisonment. Unless *this* was it—his dying fate, as it were, his personal circle of hell, not even a bloody smoke for company. Trapped in a life devoid of light and color, his only companion the irritating monotony of glass wind chimes.

That would be poetic, would it not? Surrounded into eternity, haunted by glass. His laughter at the irony of it reverberated through space and against rock, absorbed by the tinkling of those fucking wind chimes, which only made them louder and more irritating.

Gaelan reached out into the near darkness, hoping for a clue about his surroundings wondering absently why hadn't thought of that earlier. A table sat just to the right of the cot. He slid his hand up its rough-hewn wooden leg through a maze of cobwebs and dust, finally reaching the edges of a flat surface.

A wide, tall candle, half-consumed sat at the edge. Grimy and dusty, but hopefully useable.

Et voila! A *dry* box of matches! *Progress. Now to find those bloody fags!*

On his knees, Gaelan groped blindly though a carpet of dust along the cold stone floor in the direction he'd flung the cigarettes, until . . . *Yes! There you are!*

Sitting cross-legged on the floor, Gaelan hungrily sucked smoke into his lungs, eyes closed, savoring the cloak of fumes as the nicotine worked to settle the jangle of his nerves. The cigarettes were truly awful, but you couldn't be choosy with a life raft.

Now, to that candle! He retraced his movements back to the cot.

"Let there be light," he shouted into the emptiness of the room, finally igniting the wick. Tiny sparks flew in all directions as the candle crackled and sputtered, burning off years of dirt and dust as it bathed the room in a dull haze of amber light. Indistinct shadows lurked about its curved walls and dark floor.

But for the cot, the table, and the candle in its holder, the room was quite Spartan. An unopened case of bottled water sat on the floor beside his feet, and the clothing he'd been wearing were neatly folded at the end of the cot. When had he changed clothes? Bought fags— and water?

How had he managed to ramble about Scotland, purchase provisions and find shelter, completely unaware? He had no memory of it.

Gaelan chugged a full liter of the water, the cool moisture restoring his flagging energy as it slid down his parched throat. He finished another, only then realizing just how thirsty he was. How many days since he'd had food or drink?

Perhaps if he'd the sense to acquire a case of water, he'd been lucid enough to buy food as well, but, alas, no sign of so much as a wrapper or tin. He lit another cigarette and put it out before the first drag. *Best not go through them all in one sitting.*

The candle flickered on the table. The stick was quite old. *Midsixteenth century?* A long time since he'd encountered one of its like. The signature aroma of tallow. Ever the dealer in antiquities, even now. Not that it mattered much anymore. Long as the flame held out.

An arched opening provided the only exit from the room. *Time to explore.*

Coiled and wary, still uncertain he was alone, and not someone's prisoner, Gaelan held the candle aloft and crept through the corridor, conscious of every footfall thudding softly on the dirt floor, echoing against the hard rock of the walls. He seemed to be a tunnel system of some sort.

There were many such networks among the caves at the Scottish seacoast. Perhaps he'd stumbled into one of them? The items left there by some other wayfarer another time. That would make some sense. *More* sense, anyway.

Gaelan wound his way through labyrinthine series of corridors, which linked numerous additional chambers, eroded and smoothed by time into glossy black. And then he saw the sconces. Gargantuan metal hands, every few feet, each bearing a candle much like the one he held. Each stuttered to life as Gaelan held his flame to the dusty, dormant wicks.

He'd seen sconces of this sort before when he'd been a young lad. Not uncommon, he supposed, during the sixteenth century. Perhaps he'd happened upon an ancient privateer's hideout, abandoned centuries earlier. It didn't explain the clothing, water, or the fags, but . . .

Gaelan turned, peering down the serpentine passageway. He'd lit at least twenty candles along the way. The flames reflected off the walls, painting eerie shadows along the rough-hewn glossiness.

He turned down a new corridor corner and froze in his tracks. Memory, not of the past few days but of centuries earlier, flooded back in a torrent. Sagging against the wall, stunned and confused, he realized exactly where he was. Out of context and completely impossible. A place he had not visited in nearly two centuries. Had not resided for more than four.

LONDON, 1826

CHAPTER 5

*T*ap . . . tap . . . tap.

Gaelan Erceldoune awoke, gasping for air in the sweltering heat of his workroom, the last vestiges of a nightmare shattering into faded amber, merging into the dull candlelight and dying embers. It was the same nightmare he'd had nearly every night since moving to Smithfield one week past, always awakening to the pungent, sickly odor of burning flesh. Never would he rid himself of that morning in 1598—the execution of his father.

The mantel clock read two o'clock, four hours since he'd last looked. When had he fallen asleep?

Tap . . . tap . . . tap.

A dull, muffled rapping through the apothecary alleyway door, out of rhythm with the clock. Who would visit in the dead of night?

Rats. Had to be . . . or worse. No, nothing fouler than vile rats, lying in wait to burrow through the alleyway door, scratching, tapping at the wood until they'd broken through. Breeding everywhere pestilence and death. This section of London was rife with prey and the rats were sharp enough to know it.

Two centuries since the Plague of 1625 had taken more than forty thousand, and Gaelan still shuddered at the lingering memory of Shoreditch that summer. The rodents brandishing death in dagger teeth, murdering everyone in their skittering path. They were to blame for destroying his life. Rats.

They would not, this night, at least, slink in past his solid oak door. Not if he didn't open it. And there was little reason to do so. Not at this hour. Peppermint oil would do to keep them at bay. Until the morrow.

His walking stick would do well this night to chase them away, should the need arise. If, that is, he managed to locate it amongst the crates ported from Hay Hill, too few of which he'd emptied.

Gaelan yawned and stretched, setting aside the heavy leather volume he'd been perusing. The tapping had stopped. Perhaps he wouldn't hear it from upstairs in the flat, where he might manage a few hours more rest.

A quick glance up toward the staircase. What would be the point? A full night's sleep had eluded him since he'd opened shop in Smithfield. Why should this night be different?

Gaelan yawned again, picturing the hundreds of items he'd yet to place upon the shelves he'd so meticulously cleaned and repainted: soaps and elixirs, herb teas and potions—for remedy *or* pleasure. If he could not sleep, at least he might put the time to clever use.

He pried open a small crate, removing several bundles of dried herbs and flowers, garlic bulbs, and colorful dried peppers. He would hang them first, draping the window, welcoming, friendly. Then set the bottles and jars of brightly colored elixirs, names no one—save him—could pronounce, and jars of fragrant teas to line the shelves behind the long counter.

With the blinds open, the bowed glass panes would catch the morning sun, reflect off the bottles and paint the plain walls with refracted streaks of colored light. Would that he'd have someone with whom—beyond the odd customer—to share such simple pleasures.

Late at night, alone, Gaelan often lamented his long-standing vow to take no wife. The loneliness had begun to exact too dear a price. Distance always had been a necessary part of survival, relationships the inevitable casualty.

Hay Hill had served its purpose well these past ten years. Not one of the elegant ladies entering Erceldoune's Hay Hill Apothecary, for all their flirtatious glances, would elicit more than a polite smile and slight bow before a return to the business at hand. A very sharply drawn line, and one he never dared cross. Gaelan knew his station in the world of Hay Hill.

Smithfield was a welcome change. A busy London market teeming with activity—and disease. And poverty.

Few *gentleman* physicians would dirty their gloves in this filthy, vermin-infested place by stepping so much as a toe beyond the King Henry VIII Gate at St. Bartholomew's Hospital. As for the so-called surgeons *practicing* in these impoverished parts of London, they were too often little more than butchers in filthy shop-fronts preying upon the illiterate and desperate. Like rats, they bred with patent cures and so-called miracle tonics.

Here, Gaelan's practiced skill with knife and pestle, his vast experience as apothecary and surgeon, would do some good. And even better, the transience of Smithfield's populace provided an anonymity that would certainly serve him well for many years to come.

Gaelan opened the next crate, this one crammed to the top with handwritten manuscripts. To all appearances, a stack of ancient, yellowed papers; to Gaelan a rich legacy of knowledge and lore. Wisdom and practical medicine.

The acid aroma of old ink and vellum swaddled him in the perfume of memory: his father hunched over his desk at home in Edinburgh, writing for hours into the night his meticulous medical notes; the wondrous stories of his ancestor Lord Thomas Learmont de Ercildoune and his strange, ancient book of healing said to be given him by the queen of Elfenland herself. Gaelan had only ever known the massive, illuminated manuscript as the ouroboros book for the tail-consuming snakes that decorated nearly every page. He kept it hidden up in the flat on a high shelf and out of his sight. And with exceptionally good cause.

Gaelan removed a large, heavy journal from the top of the crate, admiring its deeply burnished leather cover, engraved with the family coat of arms. In the center, a single red rose with the Learmont motto, "I hope."

Tap . . . tap . . . tap.

This time more insistent. Too loud for a rat. A feral dog?

Plenty enough of them roaming round Smithfield, skinny and for-aging for market-day leavings, sniffing about for a warm hearth.

Tap . . . tap . . . tap.

Now, an erratic scratching rhythm. Perhaps it was not a living thing at all, only a branch brushing up against the door on a windy night.

Gaelan hoisted the journal, hurling it at the door in utter frustra-tion. "Go away, and let me to work!"

The tapping paused—again. He waited. Nothing. *Good.*

Whatever it was, he'd scared it off to bother someone else. Sighing, Gaelan fetched the journal from the floor, relieved to find it undam-aged.

Yes, Smithfield would be a refreshing change, if not as financially lucrative as Hay Hill. Gaelan possessed a fortune adequate for a com-fortable life. The flat above the shop was spacious enough—and the laboratory, after a few sore-needed renovations, would provide him a welcome sanctuary. The tall arched windows were perfect for his tele-scope.

He opened the journal. "*De curatione dysenteriae et alia practica nota querellis,*" his father had inked in a large, elaborate hand. "On the practical treatment of dysentery and other known ailments," by Lord Thomas Erceldoune, physician to the court of James VI, king of Scot-land.

A historical record, compiled by his father from those who'd pre-ceded him, adding his own observations and those of contemporaries from all parts of Europe. Three centuries on, it remained a valuable guide for which many a practitioner would pay a fair penny. Espe-cially for some of its strange formulas and procedures more resembling alchemy than modern treatments.

Most compendia of this sort were long ago cast into so-called purifying fires, destroyed as sorcery along with the practitioners, his father and grandfather amongst them. The thick vellum pages had, over time, softened and yellowed with age and use. But of all the works in Gaelan's library, none was so useful a treatise. A rare treasure, even unpublished.

Gaelan turned to the final page of the journal, reading the fluid Latin of his father's hand.

All courtiers fallen ill by this vehement sickness have recovered; fevers subsided. His Majesty, King James, is once again in good health, the danger at last passed. Thanks be to God on high, the Book of the Healers, and the goodly brethren at Dernwode House nearby Eildon for their healing medicines and wise counsel.

The final entry was unfinished, spilled ink blackening half the page. He remembered that terrible night; he had been sitting on a low stool at his father's side when the king's guard burst through the door, swords drawn, demanding his father appear at court. And life was never the same.

Gaelan had his own reasons for thanksgiving to the black-hooded brethren of Dernwode House. There, he was nurtured, tutored in languages, science, medicine, alchemy, literature. Mathematics. It had been home and sanctuary for years after Papa's execution.

The flash of a fleeting memory forced a smile as his gaze caught a glimpse of a dried sunflower on his workbench, its unique patterning of the Golden Spiral. The Dernwode brethren had delighted in demonstrating to Gaelan for the first time the unique mathematical pattern unifying all of nature. For days hence, he saw it everywhere, in everything, as his tutors pointed out more examples of the pattern, writ small, writ enormous as the entire universe.

Centuries hence, Gaelan could not fail to peer into the night sky through his telescope, or appreciate a tree or pine cone in the forest without recalling with fondness Dernwode, and pondering the Fibonacci mathematical sequence: 1, 1, 2, 3, 5, 8, 13, 21 . . .

Tap, tap, tap. Tap, tap, tap.
Damnation!

But something had changed. A strangled moan? Not feral, but quite human. Desperate, anguished, but muffled—and very weak.

Oh, dear God and I have delayed and delayed all these minutes . . . "I am coming!" He sprang to the door, nearly tripping over the open crate. What had he been thinking to dawdle so with someone in urgent need—and at his own threshold?

Gaelan cracked the shop door a sliver and peered up and down the dark alleyway. Only the moonlight filtering dimly through the mist, casting its gloomy halos about the gas lamps. A cat the size of a small dog in hot pursuit of three rats fled through a tenement archway and out of sight. He must have been mistaken . . .

Then he saw it. Still and in a heap beneath a large cloak at the foot of his doorstep. He opened wide the door and it fell across the threshold, a small mound of ivory velvet and lace petticoats, muddied and wet—and edged in the familiar red-black of fresh blood.

CHAPTER 6

"Hush now; only a moment, lass, and I'll have you safe inside." Her moans and whimpers, pleas for him to stop, could not forestall Gaelan's task, he could do nothing for her standing in the doorway.

He crouched to where she lay. "Gently, gently now. Can you lift your arms about my neck, so I might . . . ?" She complied, but with effort; she was trembling. No so unexpected. "Good lass. Now . . ."

The distance was not great to the examining room, where he lowered the girl to a small cot fitted with white muslin. Blankets, bandages, and cloths were stacked neatly beside it, along with his implements, clean and ready in their black leather case.

Her eyes were closed as she continued to whimper, words barely audible and weaker than in the doorway. "No . . . no . . . please . . . ?"

"Lass, can you say what befell you? Did you fall? Were you attacked?" She flinched.

In Smithfield it might be anything from an ill-placed cart to a swaggering, pissed-up market man brandishing a butcher's knife and an unrelenting want for a disobliging whore. The streets swarmed with all manner of villain, and a young girl—especially a prostitute—would be easy prey.

The body snatchers were the most terrifying of the lot. Smithfield buzzed with rumors of folk gone missing only to turn up dead, corpses stripped clean of their internals. Or never to be found at all.

No one much cared about the fate of vagrants, lunatics left to fend for themselves on the streets of London, prostitutes. Yet, this one was too smartly dressed for a Smithfield whore, too well, indeed, to *be* of this place at all. How could he have been so heedless of her knocking? What was he thinking? Rats, indeed.

The whimpered pleas stopped; she'd gone completely quiet now, but for her rapid, shallow breaths. Still alive, though barely, no thanks to his delay. *Damnation*! He would be run out of Smithfield, a lady—a gentlewoman, no less—dying under his care the first week he'd arrived. Who would trust him then?

The velvet was soaked through and sticky with blood and tissue from hem to waist. He pulled the cloak away to reveal her skirts—and a clue to the problem. But he needed the particulars, not so much the "why" as the "how."

The blood alone failed to explain whether someone ended her pregnancy surgically or gave her an herbal preparation of some sort.

Loss of blood might explain the pallor; the pink spittle at the corners of her mouth, still dribbling down her chin, suggested poison, taken not too long ago. An abortive to lose the child. But which one? The difference between life and death. Or life with nevermore the possibility of bearing children.

He sighed, observing her as she stirred. Too young a woman for such a wretched plight. But what brought her to Smithfield? To him?

Gaelan looped his finger about her small wrist, waiting with close-eyed concentration for a pulse to thrum through his fingers. Nothing. He pressed more firmly. There. There it was, but just barely so. Erratic, weak. Her eyes fluttered open as she stirred, her gaze blank and unaware.

"Miss, I must learn what happened. What you *took*—"

"Oh!" She tensed, gazing frantically about the room, as if surprised to find herself not alone. She stopped, turning to Gaelan. "Forgive me, but where . . . am I? What is—?"

"You are at an apothecary. In Smithfield Market. Do you recall—?"

"Yes. Yes, I—" Her lips drew tight and she closed her eyes. "Female pills, she called them." Her voice trailed off into a puff of air. Again, she grew still.

Cover-shame. Of course. Savin juniper? Savin was efficient, yes, but it was easy to misunderstand the dose, turn it to a fatal poison. Too few practitioners treating women in her condition understood the fine line between too much and not enough.

He had to be quick—*if* that was her only problem. If *unadulterated* savin juniper was the entire story. Nothing further attempted to end the pregnancy. Too much he did not yet know, could not know, until she was full awake—and properly examined.

Still, he was not clueless of what to do. The needed ingredients were up two stories in the laboratory. "I shall return in a trice," he whispered, knowing it was unlikely she heard him.

Gaelan bounded the stairs quickly as he might, racing to her side once satisfied he'd prepared the dosage properly, praying there was yet time to save her.

The lady's eyes remained closed as he sat beside her. If possible, she'd grown paler by degrees in the brief time he'd been upstairs.

"My lady—"

Nothing.

He took her hand. It was ablaze with fever. "Miss, please—" he said more keenly.

Her eyes fluttered before opening a mere slit. She was shivering again. "Sorry. I seemed to have drifted—"

"No, that is a good thing. You must sleep. But first . . ." Holding a small beaker to her lips, he entreated her to sip the bubbling elixir. "I know it has a taste most foul, but I've no honey to sweeten it. I am sorry. It will make you better—and help you to sleep whilst your body recovers from this . . . this bungled . . ."

He managed to refrain from spitting out what he really wanted to say. The butchery by unskilled, unpracticed hands preying upon vulnerable girls in their most fragile state of mind and body was something he could not stomach.

She nodded weakly and sipped, drinking it all. There was naught to do now but wait it out and hope for the best. An hour or two, and he would know whether it took—and if she would survive the night.

Herbs and oxides, an ancient formulation, learned long ago at his father's knee, would counteract the savin. A delicate balance, and he could only guess at the exact dose required. Gaelan sucked in a breath and noted the time.

An hour passed; the candle flame sputtered and faded to gray smoke, and its pleasant tallow aroma infused the room, mingling with the sick-sweet odor of blood and tissue. Gaelan's eyelids drooped heavy, drifting shut as the battle to keep watch over his charge faded.

A sudden pounding on the door roused Gaelan from the first whispers of sleep.

What manner of devilment is this to disturb me yet again this night?

The girl was awake, staring at him through terrified eyes. She grasped for his arm, her gaze a plea. "I beg of you, kind sir, tell not a soul of my presence. *No one.* Please, I—"

More words than she'd uttered since her arrival.

A quick nod as he fumbled with the buttons of his frock coat, endeavoring to cover the blood, which had stained his shirt and trousers shoulder to knee. "Who comes to call at this hour?" Gaelan shouted as he approached the shop's front door.

Dawn had already begun to brighten the sky, rendering the morning fog in halos of light. Gaelan glared at the visitor through window glass, suspecting he was quite aware of the too-early hour.

"Open the door, apothecary! I implore you! It is of the utmost urgency!" Caped in a rich greatcoat and top hat, assuredly *not* a man of Smithfield, the man continued to pound the glass, his voice raspy and harsh as he repeated his demand several times more in rapid succession.

Had this visit anything to do with the young lady in the examining room? A husband worried for his wife? The bairn's father? Her father? No, he appeared much too young for that. A brother, perhaps? No matter.

Gaelan sucked in a breath and opened the door; he did not mask his ire at the intrusion. "Have you an idea, sir, of the time? It is just barely dawn; I do not open for some hours to come."

"You have a woman here."

"I beg your pardon?"

"A young lady. She is ill, perhaps in the direst straits."

The guilt-ridden lover it is. Whoever this fellow may be, Gaelan had little inclination to be dragged into the midst of what appeared to be a family matter. Yet, the girl's haunted expression, even as she'd tottered at the edge of consciousness, compelled him to comply with her request to be still about it.

"I assure you, sir, there is no lady about. Indeed, I have, this day, seen to several requiring my care, men *and* women. None remain under my roof, particularly at this hour. Now, if you please . . ."

The man ignored Gaelan's polite but insistent sweep of an arm toward the door. Instead, he pushed his way to the center of the shop and paced the floor some moments until suddenly stopping before a long counter. He pounded his fist on the glass, then wheeled on Gaelan, just inches away. "If you do not mind, sir, I shall have a look myself. She is wont to hide, this one; perhaps she has snuck in, tucked herself away beneath a staircase or . . ." The stranger directed his gaze toward a curtain behind the counter. ". . . in your examining room?"

Who the blazes is this . . . gentleman come bursting in at such an hour? "You speak of this woman, *my good sir*, as if she is but a stray cat, not a lady. And, yes, I *do* quite mind. I do not like your tone, nor your insinuations, and I would ask you to take your leave. Immediately, for I have indulged you quite long enough. Who are *you* to barge in here at this hour—and with a demand to inspect my shop, hmm?"

Gaelan had already decided. The baby's father, most definitely, who had either been opposed to or arranged the abortion. In either case . . . "I am not easily intimidated, sir, even by one of *your* station. I tell you, no other person is about these premises."

Gaelan needed no trouble, and not so soon after in the move from Hay Hill. He retreated behind the counter, fuming as he tried to tamp down his anger.. He'd seen this sort too many times before, all puffed up and arrogant. Thinking they'd the right to do whatever to whomever they desire.

"I will ask you courteously once more to leave these premises, but my patience is wearing thin, sir."

The man's shoulders slumped, and the intensity of his gaze evaporated into resignation, but he made no move to leave. Instead, he removed his hat, placing it on the counter as his fingers drummed the glass.

"Please forgive me, sir. I realize I must appear to you quite the lunatic. I assure you, I am not. You see, I have been seeking her . . . any word of her whereabouts . . . all the night."

Gaelan stood his ground, unwilling to let down his guard just yet as the stranger commenced to pace again. However, the man's state was now obvious. The unkempt hair, cravat undone; he was unshaven, his boots caked with mud. Lines of sweat streaked from brow to jaw through the grime on his face. A man distraught, indeed.

He came to rest once again at the counter, examining Gaelan with an accusing gaze, as if he could see through to the bloodied shirt hidden beneath his coat. He nodded slightly, seeming to consider his next words carefully before speaking them aloud.

"I believe . . . I have some reason to believe . . . you may have in your keeping the cousin of a good friend. He has asked me on behalf of her family to fetch her. I am a physician, you see, and they desire for me to . . . see to her . . . to her . . . illness. My *only* motive is to be of assistance to the young lady in question. *Discrete* assistance, if you catch the drift . . ." The man arched an eyebrow. "I am certain you can understand."

Gaelan struggled to answer. Why should he believe this . . . stranger, calling himself a physician? A friend of the girl? She was emphatic, was she not, that *no person* know her whereabouts? "You are sore mistaken, sir. I understand your worry, but I repeat." Gaelan shrugged his shoulders. "I am quite alone here. Therefore, unless there is something else of an urgent—and relevant nature—with which I might assist you at this hour . . ." Gaelan gestured toward the door.

The man sighed and removed his coat. "As long as I am here, yes. There is another matter. May I?" he asked as he draped it across the counter beside his hat.

Gaelan crossed his arms across his chest. *If this will rid me of the intruder* . . . "Go on, then—"

"Perhaps there is. Something else. You are, sir, Mr. Gaelan Erceldoune, the apothecary lately of Hay Hill?"

"Yes, that is me." He snapped, refusing to keep the annoyance from his tone.

The physician held up a conciliatory hand. "Hear me out, sir, if you would. To speak true, Mr. Erceldoune, the family is much grieved about the daughter—"

"You, sir, have the distinct advantage of knowing my name, yet—"

The physician combed nervous fingers through his short dark hair. "Forgive me my lack of manners, for I have been running about London this entire night, hoping for . . . My name is Dr. Simon Bell."

Gaelan well knew the name. "You said there was another matter—"

The man held up a finger. "Please, if I might first—"

Gaelan said nothing, drawing his arms tighter about his middle before nodding.

"She . . . they are quite concerned for her . . . for her . . . well-being. Her cousin has confided that she fled to Smithfield in a condition, shall we say . . ."

Gaelan could guess the rest.

Bell turned away for a moment, tapping his foot as if to consider his position. "If you should happen to see . . . if she *should* come your way, I beg you, please to help her in whatever way you might, but do not send her back to her family. I wish her no . . . Her family are set on shipping her to the continent. To France and marry her off to a man twice her age. She would never see these shores again. If she *is* in your keep, I would wish to express to her these sentiments. Should she wish to contact me, have her know I only desire to be a friend to her, and would not . . . She should not return to her own kin. For to do so would cost her never-ending despair. Of this I am most certain."

"Is that not what you aim to do . . . should you find her? Return her to such—"

"No. That is what the family *desires* of me; not what I would *do*, should I discover . . . should I find her safe and *before* she is discovered by her kin."

"And what are you to this . . . woman . . . girl, truly . . . beyond good friend of her cousin? Lover? Not good enough for her? Or she not you?" Gaelan was aware he treaded a fine line here but would explode if he stayed silent even a moment longer. Yet, he needed to mind his tongue, not arouse suspicion. Besides, he was certain Bell noticed he was covering . . . something.

"Not at all, sir. I am but friend to the family. Their occasional physician. The young lady is to me nothing beyond acquaintance. I would see to her well-being, help in any way I might. And if you should . . . if she should come across your path—"

"Very well then. I shall heed your warning with regard to the girl. Should she come my way. And now, I bid you a good morrow."

Finally, Bell seemed ready to depart, and Gaelan quickly ushered him to the door, opening it to the dawn chill. Already, he had been too long gone from the girl.

His hand on the knob, Bell stopped. "Another moment of your time, and I then I shall leave you be."

Whatever else might he want of him so early? "Well, then?"

"I wish not to leave your company on such difficult . . . This is not the first time I have heard your name. Your reputation precedes you and I have long desired to make your acquaintance."

What had the physicians of Hay Hill to say of him now he'd gone? Disappeared with nary a word. "Indeed?" Gaelan was curious, but he thought he'd heard the girl stir beyond the curtains.

"From brother physicians. They have only to say you are quite gifted, if not a bit . . . impertinent." The corners of Bell's mouth quirked into a crooked smile. "They laugh at your impudence for the number of times you have altered their instructions, the medicines they prescribe. Privately, they cannot deny the number of times you have—"

Saved them from embarrassment? Forestalled the fatal error that would have killed a patient through sheer stupidity?

"Suffice to say, Mr. Erceldoune, you are missed, despite the widespread perception in Hay Hill that you were chased away for forgetting your station—and dabbling in business for which you are ill qualified."

"And you sir? What do *you* say?"

"I, sir, do not know you, and have no reason to either trust or distrust you. I do know I have seen it with my own eyes—the recklessness, the folly of my brother physicians. And evidence that your methods, however unorthodox, are effective—at least more so than theirs. I have for the past week, in fact, been seeking to locate you for counsel on a medical matter."

At another time, perhaps, but any moment, the lass might . . . He forced himself from turning toward the quiet rustling behind him, hoping Bell had not also heard it. "Perhaps you might return in a few hours when you . . . and I . . . are in a better state to discuss—"

"Of course. I shall return. Say, eleven o'clock?"

Finally, he was gone. Gaelan closed the door, locking it, waiting as Bell mounted a carriage and disappeared into the morning mist. He blew out a long breath, relieved, yet disquieted about what had transpired. He had even forgotten to ask the girl's name. What devilment had he gotten himself into?

Gaelan drew back the curtain. "My lady, he's—" She was gone!

CHICAGO NORTH SHORE, PRESENT DAY

CHAPTER 7

"**B**eyond Methuselah: The Immortality Option." Anne held her breath as she read the title of the article, staring at the screen until her eyes burned and she saw nothing else on the Google search page but a blur of light and letters. Dreading what she might discover beneath the headline, not in a tabloid or conspiracy rag but a respected pop-science magazine. Finally, her fingers shaking, she clicked. Three times she read the piece in horror.

Two hours now since Anne had promised to ring back Preston Alcott. Any moment, he would take the initiative on his own. And therefore, God created the "ignore call" button.

The Galahad Society once again seemed to be at the heart of the story.

Our goal, claimed its CEO John Brady in paragraph one, *is to benefit all of us, eradicate disease through identifying a truly immortal strain of cells, human cells. People will live longer—disease-free and with a quality of life unknown to humankind here and worldwide.*

Dozens followed Anne's work on telomeres with keen interest, less to do with the *T. nutricula* jellyfish than its practical application extending human life—infinitely. A fairly benign pursuit, and so far into the future as to be a futile quest in any of their lifetimes. The subject of amusement over drinks at conferences, and little more. Most of her colleagues had their "fans," who regularly emailed with theories most often wild and occasionally quite logical, but simply beyond the realm of known science. And would be. For years to come.

She studied the article a final time and sat back in her chair, nauseous. The Galahad Society seemed a particularly aggressive new strain of immortality junkie. Their scheme? Use their collective vast wealth and connections to procure, the youngest, healthiest, strongest, most attractive athletes—volunteers, all, the CEO claimed—to donate "gallons of their perfect" blood to the "greater good" so members might inject themselves nightly before bed. The one goal? Forestall the inevitability of aging—forever.

Her revulsion turned to anger and then panic. Had her own work, however indirectly, fueled this mad drive to achieve immortality? More unnerving than anything conjured from the mind of Bram Stoker or Anne Rice. No fantasy. This was reality.

Move over Nosferatu; step aside Count Dracula. No black and purple cloak needed, no fang teeth to dig into the neck of an unsuspecting victim. These were twenty-first-century vampires—not drinking blood but mainlining it, complete with IV tubes and infusion pumps.

No photos in the article, fortunately, but the description was monstrous enough to see it clearly without the visual aids: wards filled with young men, their blood transfused to . . . whom? Employers? Masters? Patrons? A macabre experiment aimed at living forever.

The Galahad Society. In a weird way, the name fit. Be the first to claim the Holy Grail of immortality, as the Arthurian knight had done, but only in the realm of legend.

What was Alcott's involvement in all this? His name appeared nowhere in the text of the article. She hit the "find," button which brought her to the tiny font of a photo caption. A group shot. Eight men, glasses raised, smiling into the camera. "Billionaire tech guru and venture capitalist Preston Alcott drinks to his latest project, called Galahad, at an exclusive club in Los Angeles." This list of people in the photo included Dr. Anthony Cantwell. A name Anne knew well. And, according to the caption, Galahad's chief technical officer.

The grandfather clock chimed four. The day had bled half away. When had that happened? And Alcott hadn't called. Maybe he'd moved on to the next geneticist on his list.

Elizabeth Bathory. The name popped, unbidden, into her head. A BBC documentary on the so-called Blood Countess. Hungarian royalty, unlimited funds, accountable only to herself. She'd murdered more than six hundred virgins and used their blood as bath oil in— what was it—the sixteenth century? And all in the vain pursuit to preserve her youth. Anne had seen the program only the week before. Little had changed in this danse macabre with immortality, but for the costumes and the music. And the technology.

Oh, screw it all. She really did need a break.

The spicy sweetness of clove and cinnamon, ginger and cardamom greeted Anne as she stepped into Simon's large, airy kitchen. She breathed it in, let it settle about her like a cozy blanket. The gnawing ache behind her eyes that had commenced with Preston Alcott's phone call began a slow retreat.

Simon's housekeeper sat at the table, working a crossword puzzle.

"Dr. Shawe. I thought you might like some tea. I took the liberty of—"

"Thank you. Perfect."

Mrs. O'Malley had doted on her since the morning she'd arrived. Fresh biscuits, homemade soups, pressed clothing, and scented towels. Already, Anne felt quite spoiled. Simon's housekeeper had been kind but held Anne at a—slightly intimidating—formal distance.

"It was Dr. Bell's favorite. A custom blend. Do you take milk and sugar?"

"I do."

Anne plucked three brown cane cubes from a bone china bowl and stirred them into the steaming mug along with the proffered milk.

"Anything else you need?"

"Please, Mrs. O'Malley. Do join me for a moment."

"Very well. I am here to make your stay comfortable and as enjoyable as these things might be. Is there anything amiss?"

"No, of course not. You have been more than kind."

Mrs. O'Malley took the seat opposite Anne.

"How long were you in Dr. Bell's employ?" Anne asked, sipping from her mug.

"Seven years, and a more gracious man you'd never find, but odd, if you don't my saying. A real odd bodkin, some might say. I asked no questions; kept my tongue. Perhaps if I had been more . . . if I . . ."

Mrs. O'Malley had no clue, then. "With suicides . . . Well, it is difficult to know what . . ." What could she say?

"Well, he'd not be dead, would he, had I been minding? And such a young man. I came in just as I always do—I'd been to visit some friends in the city, you see—found him sitting at the dining table. Two glasses and an empty bottle of whisky. I thought he'd gotten drunk, but then—"

Anne pictured Gaelan and Simon that last morning after she'd left for the airport. A final drink together. Two hundred years they'd known each other. How bizarre it must've felt for them both, knowing by the next day they would both be dead.

"Dr. Bell's funeral, was it at least well attended?"

"Just me, I'm afraid. Private affair. And Dr. Bell's solicitor. You'd have thought that strange friend of his would have been there, for all the help Dr. Bell's been to him over the years."

Ah, Gaelan. "Do you mean Gaelan Erceldoune?"

"Something like that, yes. Erceldoune. British chap. Bookseller, I think. Anyway, the solicitor came in from London and it was all very quick, and according to Dr. Bell's wishes. Two days after I found him, it was all over. Done. I might've expected *you'd* come sooner, being his heir and all. Been at the funeral at least. Not my business, is it dear? Well, the ashes are on the living room mantelpiece—"

"I had affairs to attend in the UK. Besides, we were not close."

And no, it was absolutely not her business.

The housekeeper stood sharply. "The *ashes*," she continued, ignoring Anne, "are to be scattered at a particular location near Gattonside, according to the solicitor's instruction."

Mrs. O'Malley fetched a small note from a tin near the coffee maker. "These, I believe, are the GPS coordinates. The solicitor thought it a strange request since there had been no Bell estate on those lands for more than one hundred years—gone the way of many such estates of the upper classes . . ." Another glare. "As I am certain you are aware. Apparently, the lands were sold off long ago, but for a very small parcel, razed to the ground near the turn of the last century. Nothing there but a field, he'd said. A few gravestones. Bell relatives, I'd suppose."

"Perhaps there was some other draw to the place. The setting of a Holmes novel? I'm certain he had his reasons."

"He was an odd one, that's for sure. Well, if there's nothing else . . ."

Anne glanced at her watch. Three hours. Alcott had given up. *Thank God for small favors.*

"Very well, Mrs. O'Malley. I'm just going out back for a bit of stroll in the garden. I thought I saw a path down to the beach, actually."

"Big storm coming. It'll be pouring buckets quite soon. I was just going to give you a flashlight in case the lights go out. They often do in an intense storm, especially out here by the shore. The winds whip through the bluffs something fierce. You don't want to be caught out down the rocks in a storm. The path's not maintained and quite slippery when wet. I'd leave it for a nicer day, if you don't mind my saying so."

"Thanks for the warning." Maybe she would go out there anyway, let the spring rain flood over her, purge her pain, soothe the remains of her headache. Shoeless and coatless. Stand out there until someone rescued her like the heroine in a Jane Austen novel. "And for all your help these past days," she added, stepping through the garden doors.

Except such romantic salvation did not exist. Not now. Not ever.

The temperature had soared since she'd been out earlier, joined by sauna-level humidity and beads of sweat quickly sprouted on her forehead and above her upper lip in the saturated air.

Where's a good onshore breeze when you really need it?

Charcoal-purple clouds bulged low and foreboding in the western sky, a study in contrast with the cloudless deep blue sky over Lake

Michigan to the east. The sun diffused through the leading edge of the clouds to stipple the lake with crested points of silvered sapphire.

A heron harassed two white and gray gulls riding the tip of a whitecapped wave, an amusing diversion. She could stay here all day, a whole lifetime, a life to which she could easily grow accustomed. Far from her phone. Far from worry about Gaelan. Far from thoughts of Preston Alcott. A respite house. A sanctuary.

And why not, now she'd become an heiress? Screw everything else. She could afford it. And it was more than tempting.

The low growl of thunder echoed to the west, far into the distance as the sky had, in the span of only a few minutes, darkened above her head. The rumbling grew more insistent, each crescendo rolling into the next as the storm drew closer and the air thickened further with the rich, moist scent of impending rain.

Lightning crisscrossed the sky from cloud to cloud as she gauged the distance from where she stood at the edge of the cliff to the house. *Plenty of time to make it back.*

What was that formula she'd learned at school? One second per mile between lightning and thunder.

She counted aloud. "Seven . . . eight . . . crash." Eight miles, give or take; the storm's leading edge would be closer. Yet, she resisted the urge to flee before the last possible minute.

Bring it on!

Catharsis, that's what she needed. Desired, hoped for. Always the hopeful one, wasn't she? "Hopeful romantic," they teased back at school. Scoffed. Derided. Her, and her chronic naiveté.

Huge raindrops began to splash, leisurely, like the plinking of violin strings, ricocheting off the brick ledge and the wrought-iron benches. The gulls and heron had already fled the oncoming storm, and ice pellets, which stung like cut-glass shards, spat from the sky. Slowly at first, building to a barrage that drowned the quiet while coating the garden in crystal.

Lightning shrieked across the sky in a continuous barrage as the rain pelted, cold and stinging. Beethoven's Sixth—the *Pastoral*—in real time. Drenched and shivering, Anne bolted across the garden, flying through the French doors just as her mobile rang.

Had to be *Alcott.*

Rallying the presumptive combative tone she usually reserved for telemarketers and phone scammers, Anne touched the green button. She was ready for him.

"Yes?" No name, no niceties.

"Dr. Shawe?" *Not Alcott.* Yet, the voice was familiar. "It's Andrew Samuelson. From Evanston Lakeshore Hospital in the U.S.?"

Andrew Samuelson, who'd hoped to engage her in his unthethical little scheme to study Gaelan's DNA. *What the fuck does he want?*

Anne understood the temptation. What would it take, after all? Pilfer a bit of surgical waste from a man whose biological regenerative abilities defied imagination? What's the harm? And what self-respecting scientist wouldn't be intrigued? Never mind the slew of ethical violations involved, given Gaelan's adamant refusal to consent to any genetic analysis of any sort.

On the other hand, she suspected Samuelson's boundaries were highly flexible, easy to stretch for a good reason—or price.

"Dr. Samuelson. As I recall, the last time we spoke—"

"Yes, and I took what you said to heart. I never touched Mr. Erceldoune's DNA. Never tested it, never crossed my mind after—"

"Really." Yeah. After she'd threatened to report him to the medical ethics board.

"Look, we have a bit of a situation. It doesn't involve you directly, but you might get a call about it. An inquiry about . . ." He hesitated. "I wanted to—"

"Oh, dear! Well, I hope it's another not-immortal immortal happening into your trauma center." She put him on speaker as she ran up the stairs to the bathroom, dripping water everywhere.

"If only. It's what's walked *out* that's the problem."

Hmm. Zombies? She hadn't spoken to Samuelson in weeks. And only one case would concern her—Gaelan. The Miracle Man, whose critical injuries miraculously commenced to heal in full view of a roomful of doctors. She waited for Samuelson to continue, which he did not. Her turn. "*Dear me! Walked out?" Yeah. Zombies.*

Where the hell was her bathrobe?

"So, there were several samples of our Miracle Man's tissue scheduled for biowaste destruction. At least one is missing. Possibly up to three."

"Got to them before you had the chance, hmm?" She was in no mood to be kind. "It's been, what, two weeks and only now you've figured it out? And what's it got to do with me, in any case?"

She flung her wet clothes in the tub and draped her huge chenille robe about shoulders before reclining in the ancient brocade chaise lounge at the end of the hallway.

"That's not fair—"

"Which part?"

"You know which part, Dr. Shawe."

"Yeah. I do. And I'm being entirely fair, by the way. Last I recall, you very much wanted to steal those samples for yourself and have me run the DNA once I got to Salk with their high-tech machinery. Never mind all of that is illegal without consent. Which, to my knowledge, *he* never granted."

"Look. I told you. I didn't—"

"Maybe someone else had the same idea. Besides, don't you think it's rather a moot point, Dr. Samuelson? Our 'Miracle Man,' as you call him, is dead." Anne still had not forgiven Samuelson. The medical ethics board paperwork was still on her computer—unfinished, but . . .

"Look, Dr. Shawe, I confess to a momentary lapse . . . the idea of having a chance . . . And don't tell me you weren't curious and . . . Wait! How do you know?"

"Know *what*?"

"That he's dead."

Oh, for fuck's sake. She wasn't supposed to know him—or care. *Double fuck.*

"Erm . . . It was all over the British press two weeks ago. Suicide. Gone over a waterfall in Scotland. Crushed at the base. Nothing left.

Dead. Mystery over. *Finis.* And after the entire Transdiff fiasco, I'm
the ultimate bête noire to the Salk Institute. I'm finished." *Not badly
handled, that.*

"Do you really believe it?"

"What? That I'm professionally done for?"

"That he's *dead.*"

No caustic rejoinder for that question. She had no bloody idea, but
there wasn't a moment of hesitation in her reply. "Yes. And, by the way,
we're no small part of what drove him quite literally over that edge."

"So?"

So? What a fucking arse. She sighed, hoping he'd heard her exas-
peration loud and clear. "What *exactly* do you want of me, Dr. Samuelson?"

"Andrew. Just giving you a friendly heads-up, that's all. You might
get a phone call—questions. They're talking to anyone with access
or an interest in the case. Right now, it's only the hospital biohazard
people. Tomorrow it could be the county, the state, CDC. And I'm
just sayin'. It wasn't me. If they ask, that is."

Anne sucked in a breath. "It's a nonstory. Nothing dire about a
missing tissue sample. And, as far as I know, no biohazard risk. Our
so-called and very nonmiracle man fell off a cliff, didn't die of plague.
What? Are you worried I might suggest you're behind the missing
sample?"

"You and I are not the only ones who know the truth about that
guy. His off-the-charts genetics? Despite what's been played up in the
media. The official line about anomalous errors in the machinery,
human error, all that? 'Conspiracy of errors,' they called it. Officially,
anyway."

"*But—*"

"You know the 'but.' There's not one EMT, not one nurse, not one
tech or doc who'd been in contact with him believes that story. Plenty
who were there know it's all BS. All I know is, a lot of bonuses and
raises being given out to those folks. Like it's Christmas. And it's not.
Christmas, I mean. To keep it quiet."

"Maybe the samples went missing because someone was careless. Full stop. Recorded the wrong number . . . Didn't write something down . . . maybe they were destroyed and never recorded. A million reasons. It happens."

"Yeah. It happens, but not often—at least not here, it doesn't. And our biowaste recycler is the best in the business. No. I think someone stole them. I think the big, convenient suspect is your former company."

"Transdiff Genomics? In the UK? They'd have to have fabulously long arms to manage that one." He wasn't entirely wrong—if Transdiff were still in business. Which they were not. "Would it not take quite an elaborate conspiracy to carry it off? And from long distance? Not to mention, they no longer exist in any meaningful way."

"Usually our recyclers take it all out of our hands. Routine pickup. But we'd—"

And there it is. She heard it in his voice. "You'd set aside Miracle Man's tissue." For future use. Lovely. "And someone made off with it. I'm *shocked*! Simply shocked! Stealing from the thieves! What *is* medicine coming to these days? And you still haven't answered the question—what has *any* of that to do with me?"

"Like I said, you were on the team."

"For a day at best. At any rate, you've come to the wrong player, Dr. Samuelson. And I've no intention of getting involved."

"You are anyway, so just the heads-up for now. Look, I'm trying to be collegial. Just in case they call. No need to jump down my back. Hey, they might not even call. Since you're . . . where . . .? London?"

Loud, baroque chimes filled the air, reverberating through the two-story foyer. Anne jumped at the unexpected clamor. The doorbell. *Fuck!* She pulled the robe closer about her.

"*Yes.* London," she answered with no hesitation. "I have to run. Someone's at the door." She clicked off and padded barefoot to the door, carrying a dry set of clothing. "Coming! I . . . Can you wait a moment?" she called through the door as she traded the bathrobe for jeans and a T-shirt.

She opened the door, immediately regretting it.

The man leaning against the carved lintel looked exactly like his photograph. Wild salt and pepper hair curled down to his collar, framing a tanned angular face and narrow eyes, the color of smoke. Though he was taller than she imagined.

"Dr. Anne Shawe?" He extended a large hand. "When you didn't return my call, I figured it was easier if I just drop by than play telephone tag until one of us gave up or gave in. I had a pretty good hunch you weren't going to let me get two words out before you hung up anyway, so—"

"I'm . . . um—" How the hell did Preston Alcott find her in the United States, much less in an out-of-the-way suburb north of Chicago?

"I hope you'll forgive the chutzpa of employing a little technological abracadabra. Gotta love what you can do with GPS!"

Of course. She had used her cellphone. Not exceedingly difficult, she'd imagine, for a communications technology genius to triangulate her location. *Fucking hell*. Was there *no* privacy at all, anymore?

"I actually don't. Love it. How dare you violate my privacy? In the UK there are laws—"

"I dare because I have to. It's how I've gotten ahead, and what I gotta do now. So, forgive the intrusion, but I *really* have to talk to you, and didn't know any better way to make that happen. And quickly. To be honest, if I'd pinpointed you in Europe, I'm not sure I'd have gone to the trouble, at least not today, but since you were only a short skip by corporate jet—"

His drawl reminded her of Texas cowboys and her dad's obsession with American Western television programs. She despised every bloody syllable of it emerging between Preston Alcott's lips, no matter however much cultivated affability exuded from every pore. "I'm sorry to have wasted your time. I've no interest any project, from you or anyone else right now."

"You really should be more mindful of what you read on the Web. A hellhole of made up stories, alternative facts. Fake news, haven't you heard? I know you went straight to the shrine of Google and looked me up. Learned all sorts of vile bits about me. Very few of them are accurate. Or true."

"You trolling my Internet usage as well?"

"No. Common sense. I know *I* would, if the roles were reversed. Which is why I chose not to wait for you to hang up on me, buy a new phone, change your number, and disappear back into the UK. So. May I come in?"

SCOTLAND, PRESENT DAY

CHAPTER 8

Dernwode House. A place not in existence for centuries. Yet, inexplicably, there he was. But how?

And how had it taken so long to realize it? The sconces should have given it away immediately had they not been completely out of context.

But the stairway. *That* stairway. The entrance to the monastery cellarium, its network of caves.

Gaelan remembered the morning he'd carved into the bottom stair his family's sigil—the single red rose of House Learmont. And now, more than four hundred years later, there it was, exactly where he'd engraved it.

Two hypotheses vied for dominance in Gaelan's mind. Either he'd traveled the distance from the coast to the Scottish Borders completely unaware—or he was in the throes of full-on delusion. Neither one a welcome proposition.

Three hundred miles through rough terrain from the northwest coast to Eildon. This particular place, so hidden within the jaw of two hills, had been near impossible to find *before* it was flattened centuries ago. He'd never have managed it, much less with no recollection? Had he walked? Driven? Hitchhiked? On foot it would have been days and days of travel. Dazed and injured? Much longer. More than improbable.

He was less fond of the more likely scenario. Hallucinations and flashbacks were nothing new to Gaelan. The torture at Bedlam. His father's execution. Visions of Mama. Eleanor. Caitrin and wee Iain? The healing goddess Airmid. She'd come to him too, time to time.

Gaelan's mind had always provided a fertile landscape for such horrors and delights to conjure from his unconscious at will. To terrify or soothe. Yet, his mind had never before ventured here, to this place, neither in dream nor vision.

Yet, why would it not, other than it hadn't? And why *not* now, at long last, a dream of safety he'd not felt for hundreds of years? Why *not* this place? And who knew what havoc the poison had wrought?

Ah, the poison... Was this his death, and this his singular heaven?

For the moment, Gaelan was satisfied to avoid the question and go along for the ride—wherever it took him. Not that he had much choice. And that meant, for now, up the staircase and out of the stale air of the cellarium.

The narrow, steep stairs spiraled up toward ground level, and Gaelan stayed close to the retaining wall, a small lantern his meager guide up the pitted and cracked stones.

The hospice Dernwode House had been notorious in its day. A place of mystery, its black-hooded brethren but phantoms, the remnant few of a once-grand monastery at Soutra, most of whom had been executed long before Gaelan was born. Yet, a small band survived, said the legend, haunting the Borders in perpetuity. Gaelan believed it a tale perpetrated by the brethren themselves as means to an end—keep the secret and continue their practices of medicine and scholarship. Work and study.

Yet, Dernwode, even in its veil of secrecy, became welcome sanctuary for those in need of its generosity, and the skill of the monks, whose medical skills were far more advanced than any known in Britain. Skills gladly offered, but only on the promise of absolute discretion beyond the hospice walls, well sequestered within the arms of the Eildon Hills.

For Gaelan, Dernwode House had been sanctuary and more.

A third of the way up the stairs, Gaelan was breathless, drenched in sweat. The trek up to the surface was more arduous than he recalled; his injuries must have been worse than he'd imagined. He needed to rest.

Sitting on a mud-caked stair, he raked filthy fingers through his equally filthy hair and closed his eyes, elbows on his knees. The voice of his tutor Brother Hugh echoed softly through the dark, reminding Gaelan of the first time he'd been down these stairs as a lad of twelve and only just arrived. Turn of a new century, 1600.

"We are a house of healing, a house of learning and work. A hospice to those who have need of us, who will find our door, no matter how hidden we are—or whom we shall find, as we did you, my lad.

"Your dear papa and grandfather we considered great friends and allies and could never forsake. We worried for your safety after the execution, lad, and grieved the loss of them, both bright lights in the darkness of ignorance, which flourishes yet upon these shores."

Two years it had been after King James burnt his father alive on the pyre. In the midst of winter the Dernwode brethren had found Gaelan half-frozen and barely breathing, nearly dead of starvation, only a short distance from the monastery gates.

Two years living beneath the oppressive thumb of his mother's father in the cruel emptiness that followed the horror of that morning, which still preyed upon him four centuries on. He had little choice but to carefully pack all that remained of his father's work and flee.

Gaelan sighed and the memory disintegrated, as a large spider crept silently into the periphery of his vision, ambling its way along the wall. Another joined it, and another after that. Soon, they covered the entire wall, weaving away at a complex web. Gaelan blinked, and they'd vanished.

Oh, for fuck's sake.

He looked up, noticing now, not so high above, the orange-black of early dawn. Or was it twilight? With no watch, Gaelan had no idea.

Time to push on.

The stairs were ever-more eroded and cracked the higher he

climbed, many of them separated by gaping crevasses. He paused before a particularly wide gap, wiping away the sweat dripping into his eyes. Twenty-one more steps to the top.

The land whereupon Dernwode House stood had once been part of his own family's estates. Centuries earlier, long before even his grandfather was born, House Learmont forged an eternal bond with the black-hooded monks of Soutra. Lord Thomas Learmont de Ercildoune, poet, philosopher, prophet, friend to the fairy folk, keeper of the great book of healing.

Thomas had shared the book with the monks—Augustinian Canons—of Soutra. Airmid herself had insisted upon it after releasing him from his seven years' captivity in the thirteenth century, or so said the legend.

"They will understand how to interpret these cures," she'd explained to Thomas, who explained it to his sons and their sons after until the story was passed on to Gaelan, not by his father but by his tutor Brother Hugh. On these very stone steps.

"The Quhawme Brethren shall for you and your heirs ever be friend and ally. No matter what comes to pass. We are all that remain of the Black Canons, who long ago dwelled here, but we dare never admit it. To any. This be Dernwode House now, and we but mere lay folk here, who do endeavor to continue their goodly works."

Gaelan departed Dernwode—all that remained of the Soutra legacy—after three years, not to return for more than two hundred after that. By then, the monks and their legacy were long gone, the hospice consumed by tall grasses and dense woods. There'd been little remaining of its grounds, its buildings and gardens.

The amber glow of the lantern reflected against the retaining wall, drawing Gaelan's eye to something just above his head, just barely visible beneath centuries of grime. He moved closer, boosting himself up to the next stair to take a closer look.

It required nearly half the case of water bottles Gaelan had found to clear away the centuries of mossy filth. By the time he finished, he was drenched with sweat; he gripped the wall for support as a wave of dizziness fell upon him and leaned his head against the cool, rough stones for a moment's respite.

Holding the lantern close, he saw it clearly. An inscription carved deep into the wall and clearly the work of an experienced artisan—of a time very long past.

"'Twas there above a beam o' light danced owre them mair bonnie than starshine. Wi' green scarves on, but ane that rade foremost, and that ane was a good deal larger than the lave wi' bonnie lang hair, bun' about wi' a strap whilk glinted like stars. They rade on braw wee white naigs, wi' unco lang swooping tails, an' manes hung wi' whustles that the win' played on. This an' their tongue when they sang was like the soun' of a faraway psalm."

Gaelan knew this story well; had heard it over and over as a boy—this telling of the Rhymer's abduction away to Elfenland. To Elfenhame. The fae, their queen, and her court on parade. Visible, but only in the blink of an eye, a shadow in the periphery, but no more than that—and only then to those who knew *how* to see them.

The inscription glowed in the amber light, penetrating through the centuries, the letters dancing, as if they themselves *were* the fae, arrived from another plane.

Gaelan's ancestor was called by many names in legend. Lord Thomas Learmont. True Thomas. Thomas the Rhymer, borne away by the fae queen Airmid and kept as her consort for seven years. Abducted quite near this very place they rode through on the hallowe'en.

The Scots inscription nudged at the far reaches of Gaelan's mind and lapped at the slipping bonds of Gaelan's wakefulness. Before him, in the peculiar light of the stairway, marched the fae, dressed not in green velvets but in rags of faded color, not on white steeds with braided manes and decorated tails but on foot, slow and weary. Their song not a psalm but a plea for help. They stared at him from within the vision, gazes dark, desperate.

Gaelan blinked and they vanished. Desolate, alone, frustrated that the poison had not, evidently, worked—or worked so strangely as to drive him insane—he'd had enough. Powerless to do anything about it, he wept.

Tears cascaded down his face unabated, his hands, his now-filthy shirt, his jeans, bathing him of everything that had transpired in these past several days. Or had it been weeks by now? The last century. The past five. Of regret and revenge. He wept until his eyes were dry and the tears dried to caked streaks as sleep claimed him.

A single ray of sunlight split the dark space of the stairway. Enough to wake him. Gaelan stood, stepping into its unexpected warmth. His mood had not improved.

"Enough!" he shouted up through the stairway until it reverberated all around him, disembodied voices. Until he was hoarse, and his throat was as dry as burnt paper. "Enough!" Until no sound had the energy to emerge from between his parched lips.

He pounded on the stairway wall until his fists bled. Ignoring the pain, and the itch of blood trailing down his forearms, Gaelan again leaned his head against the cool stone, exhausted, spent of all reserves.

A block of cracked masonry disintegrated in his hands when, finally, he pushed away, and a large granite block popped out of its place in the wall. No matter how hard he tried to force it back into position, it would not budge an inch.

Now what?

Gaelan edged the heavy block from the wall, resting it carefully on a step, and dusted off his hands. What the hell had lodged itself behind the block? He squinted into the opening, the dim lantern light no more help than the scant rays of sun filtering through from above.

A petrified rodent? Vines? A jug of five-hundred-year-old rum?

Now that *would be worth the effort!*

Groping far into the breach, Gaelan located the offending object. A sheaf of papers bound up in a leather cover, secured with braided cords and a heavy strap, brittle with age. But not even decades, centuries, of grime and dust, moss and mildew could completely mask the richness of the tooled leather.

He'd been an antiquities dealer too long to risk opening something ancient and fragile in the dark, difficult stairway. Curiosity tugged at him, recharging his flagged energy, and he trudged up the remaining stairs, mindful of the increasingly fractured stone, finally reaching the top.

The midmorning sun cut like a laser, too bright after however much time he'd spent below ground. The cool cleanliness of a spring morning replaced the oppressive, dark chill of the cellarium. The fresh air swathed him, and the forest perfume wafted down from the hills, swaddling him against the dark spirits that had just before threatened to suffocate him.

Holding it up to the light, Gaelan examined the cover. The leather tooling was crude, certainly not professional. A primitive sketch. Random lines. Rubbing away more of the grime revealed no useful clues about the document's age or contents. It was old, yet not so much as Gaelan imagined a document hidden within the subterranean wall of a medieval structure might be.

The handwriting was neat. Quill.

First of May 1930

It is no figment of my imagination, and despite what my critics write about me and my penchant for the fairies and their world, I must here finally assert they are all wrong. I am at last vindicated! There is no mistake, and I am proven no fantasist.
I have seen them with mine own eyes, and have acquired hereabouts—or from your perspective, dear reader, thereabouts—validation of all I have for so long believed true, though perhaps not exactly as I'd imagined. Sadly so, I am sorry to report, for

their condition—their world, just a hair's breadth beyond our own—is far from what is fancied. However, after writing for so many years, indeed, most of this decade, of others' personal encounters, I am happy at last to give in these pages my very own accounting.

You may think I do not know the Cottingly fairies are but a hoax. A bloody good one, but a hoax nevertheless. Yet, despite my knowledge of it, you may further wonder why I did not expose it, and, indeed, did embrace the very idea of it. Most assuredly, it was neither pride nor vanity—an old man refusing to say out-right he has been fooled, and so soundly at that. For the fairies do exist, real as you and I, and I did not wish to harm my own case by dispelling the Cottingly prank.

And so, this journal I leave for whomsoever may discover it, wanderer or plunderer. Consider it the ravings of a madman or the insight of one who has seen beyond normal seeing, perceived beyond the everyday of life and into the world of the fairies. I am a journalist of some reputation still, and I only ask you consider that as well.

This was madness. It could not be. Conan Doyle's writings? *Bloody hell. Conan Doyle?*

He closed the cover. How was it possible?

A red fox bounded across the field and into the shadow of the hills in hot pursuit of a hare. Gaelan's stomach growled in protest. How long had it been since he'd eaten?

Conan Doyle had lived not far from this place, and it was not uncommon to read, even in the American press, of a newly discovered unpublished manuscript turning up in a nearby attic or cellar. Was this yet another? A story? An unfinished novel? Would Holmes pop up on the next page or the one after that? Gaelan continued reading.

My hope for some time has been to track down the history of an elusive, perhaps magical, book of healing attributed to a par-

ticular sect of the fairy folk and given over to our world through Thomas of Erceldoune, a man of legend and ballad, to be sure, but also of historical significance. That I have been unsuccessful is of little matter, for what I discovered was of far greater import. Hard to fathom it has now been more than a quarter century since first I set out on this hunt for what you might suggest is the great white whale of my existence. But at long last, I am successful, knowing that although I am not long for this world— perhaps a year, perhaps less—I have my proof of the existence of fairies in my own hands.

Conan Doyle died only two months after the date of the entry. July 1930, years after they had last been in contact. As Conan Doyle more and more concerned himself with the supernatural world of ghosts and fairies, Gaelan placed himself at an increasingly safe distance from the author's often too-probing inquiries.

He quite understood Conan Doyle's obsession, his dogged pursuit of facts to support his understanding of the fairies, despite the risks to his reputation. Conan Doyle obviously witnessed something. And had written it down for posterity. But why stash the papers here and not at his home in Sussex?

More likely, and far more tragically, these papers represented the mad ravings of an elderly, dying man. His last testament to a theory for which he could never acquire even the merest threads of evidence.

Never mind the unlikelihood of Gaelan, of all people, discovering it here, and now. The idea that all this was his grand delusion weighed heavily. If ever he awoke from it, would he still be in the sea cave? Had the poison destroyed his sanity and left his body alive? A cruel fate, if true.

The probability of discovering a journal—or whatever it was— documenting events triggered by his own conversation with Conan Doyle more than a century ago—insane. And mention of Gaelan's healing book to boot! What other rational explanation could there be? A madness brought on by the poison he'd consumed. Yet, he was curious enough to learn where this delusion led.

You undoubtedly think me insane, or this entire diary a fiction fabricated for the benefit of my loyal readers, perhaps to be published in The Strand *as an addendum to* The Coming of the Fairies. *But where that was anecdote, this is a first-hand chronicle, worthy of a journalist of my standing. I ask only, dear reader, that you keep about you an open mind—open to the holding possibility that what I suggest is true and no fairy tale, as it were.*

As Gaelan set the folio on the ground, a piece of glass fell from within the sheaf of papers. Curved as if blown and not cut from a plate. Smooth as weathered quartz. Opalescent.

Turning it in his hand, he held it up into the sunlight with an artist's eye. The piece was in perfect condition, no cracks. No weathering or erosion.

Then it hit him. And he froze, stunned, as if struck by lightning. *That* piece. Crafted by his own hands, missing for more than a century. Impossibility upon impossibility. None of it made any sense at all, but how could he not believe his own eyes? Not trust his own memory of it? The feel of the glass, its smoothness, the weight of it in his hand? What next? A white hare bounding by, asking about the time?

Clasping the piece to his chest, running his thumb along the curve of it, Gaelan closed his eyes, picturing . . . *her.* His beloved. His wife.

LONDON, 1826

CHAPTER 9

The girl could not have ventured far, not in her condition. What had she overheard of the conversation with Simon Bell through the thin curtain? Enough to scare her off, no doubt.

The constant threat of discovery. The terror of inevitable catastrophe, a noose about the neck. The endless fear of it gnawing away from within, a crushing stranglehold about the middle, refusing to loosen its grip. The ticktock of Gaelan's life. Two hundred years of it. That same terror, writ plain in the girl's countenance as she'd pleaded with him.

Her velvet cloak lay in a heap on the floor beside the cot where he'd left it, the blood dried to brown. Yet the lustrous ivory velvet incongruously shimmered in the candlelight like fire opal.

There was nowhere for her to run but up the dark, steep stairway to his flat. She'd never have made it even halfway. Holding his breath, Gaelan quietly turned the handle on the mahogany door.

She barely stirred as she sat on the rough floorboards, back against the banister, sobbing into her gown. He waited in the doorway; he dared not frighten her and risk her scuttling up the stairs. Finally, she looked up, meeting his gaze. In the gleam of the candle, her eyes glittered dark and terrified, liquid blue-black indigo, split by the reflection of the flame.

With a nod, she granted leave for him to approach. Fresh blood pooled beneath her skirts. Her arms were crossed tight about her middle as she shivered, saying nothing. A cornered animal observing warily, expecting attack.

Gaelan crouched low beside her, maintaining a cautious distance between them. "He is gone, Miss. You've nothing more to fear."

Gaelan did not believe it, even had Bell spoken true. "He is called Simon Bell. Do you know him?"

Her eyes fluttered closed, but she said nothing. There would be time enough for discussion, but later.

Confident she would not struggle, he set down the candle and collected her in his arms. She was asleep by the time he resettled her into the cot, swaddling her with blankets to still her shivering.

He dragged himself to the washbowl and poured out the remaining fresh water from a large glass ewer, reminding himself to collect a new supply from the sand filter apparatus he'd fixed to the rooftop cistern. He managed to scrub the blood and grime from his hands and face, but not the fatigue of yet another sleepless night.

Gaelan sighed, lamenting the day he'd let go his last apprentice before securing a new boy. But an opportunity had arisen for the lad, and Gaelan could hardly deny him a better position than what he could promise in the squalor and stink of Smithfield Market.

The Apothecary's Hall had sent him four candidates in short order, and not a one worth the tidy sums their fathers promised for their training and keep. Two were clumsy fools, one a dour complainer, and the fourth could not read a word of Latin. Useless. If a capable young man would not come soon into his employ, he would have little choice but to suffer whatever doltish lout next came through the door.

Gaelan ground the heels of his hands into his eyes, in a futile effort to force away the throbbing in his head. He dragged a low stool to the cot and sat close by the young lady's side.

Her long hair was drenched and matted; perspiration trickled from her forehead, running in rivulets down her pale face, wending their way into the hollow of her neck. This was her body fighting off the poison from within, purging it from each pore. At least she was no longer shaking. Optimistic signs, yet too soon to know the outcome for certain.

He touched the back of his hand to her damp brow. Cool. Her

hands were no longer afire. With luck, by morning's light, the worst would be past. From the corner beckoned his deep-cushioned wing chair. Perhaps he might find an hour or two of rest in its arms before opening the shop, and without leaving the girl's side.

"Please sir, I am too hot. I do not want all these . . ."

He was halfway to sleep when she woke. "What—?" he mumbled sleepily.

She thrashed about, struggling with the bedcovers.

"Ah," Gaelan yawned. "You are awake. That is an excellent sign," he said, endeavoring to keep the fatigue from his voice. "And I am happy to remove *one* coverlet, and only that for now. I pray the other you would keep close about you just a while longer." Her eyes were no longer glazed; she seemed alert enough. And he had many, many questions—and the need to better examine her.

"Now. Might you tell me your name, miss, and what has brought you this night to *my* apothecary? Indeed, to Smithfield!"

The young lady spoke haltingly. "I would beg your forbearance, a short while more—"

"I do not wish to grieve you, but I must call you . . . something—"

"Call me . . . call me . . . Cate, if you must, but please do not oblige me to give my true name, nor the circumstances that have brought me here. I implore you, Mr.—"

"Erceldoune. Gaelan Erceldoune. I am the newly installed apothecary here in Smithfield. In any case, I am glad to see you awake and much improved since first you arrived on my doorstep."

"Am I? I think *not*."

An odd reply. "Forgive me . . . Cate . . . but are you not in a peculiar area of London for a young lady of your station?"

Her only response was a rueful laugh, hard-edged, with a brittle bite, which provoked a coughing spasm.

Gaelan held a small cup of water to her lips when it stilled. "Here, sip this."

She pushed away his arm. "My station! Indeed!" She spat out the words, breathless, and the coughing recommenced.

"Please do allow me to help you sit up; it *will* help. And drink. All of it. And slowly. Your body endeavors to exorcize the poison—the savin juniper given you by—" She would never say who it was gave it to her. London crawled with incompetent "doctors" whose specialization was in expunging unwanted pregnancies—at an exorbitant cost, and in much more than pounds sterling.

"What is this?"

"It is but ginger water. Drink!" Ginger, honey, and vinegar. All credit to Hippocrates and his brilliant oxymel. Gaelan had only just tinkered with the formula. Refined it a bit. Finally, she sipped.

"Good. Yes. Slowly now."

"Thank you, sir. You have already been too kind, and your care and medicines have much improved me. I am now quite ready to take my leave." She pushed off the blankets and stood. Far too quickly. Gaelan was already up and at her side before she lost her footing completely.

"Please do not . . . allow me to assist—" He eased her to sit on the cot before she swooned. "There, now. Slowly, my lady." He did not remove his hand from her back.

Tears collected at the corners of her eyes. "What time is it, pray?"

"It is not long past dawn—"

"Have you gotten no rest at all this night, tending to my . . . ? I am—"

Gaelan shrugged. "Do not trouble yourself about my well-being." He attempted his warmest smile, trying his best to make it genuine. "It is my vocation to thus help whomsoever needs medical attention, no matter the hour."

"Please. Do not stay on my account. I am certain you have much else to do. More important than tending to my . . . problem."

"I cannot yet leave your side; you are not quite out of danger. And I've yet to . . ." He had to examine her more thoroughly. But he needed her complete trust for the task. And he needed better lighting than the single candle could afford.

"I shall be but a moment, Cate. Here, lie back. One blanket. I promise."

After placing a light covering on her, Gaelan moved about the room, sifting spoonsful of a gray phosphorescent powder into several glass globes, taking a flame to each. By the time he returned to her side, she was asleep. Extinguishing the candle, he was satisfied with the blue-green glow provided by lamps. Adequate to continue the unpacking, but not so bright as to disturb her slumber.

A quarter hour later, she was awake again, and sitting up. It had been a vain hope that she might sleep a bit. He dropped the book in his hand and was immediately by her, attentive but frustrated. He pinched the bridge of his nose, steadying his nerves. "It would do better . . . Cate . . . if you would at least *attempt* to sleep."

"I am not sleepy, not at all. And it is too difficult to talk, lying prone, whilst you work at the far side of the room. And I seem rather suddenly disposed to be gregarious. Perhaps it is the fault of the potion you gave to me."

It was not the medicine but her fear, and hardly unexpected. Twice already, he'd watched her flail against some unseen enemy from within her fitful sleep. He understood better than most the monsters looming in the shadows of a peaceful dream, waiting for the moment to shatter it, to terrorize, to . . .

He could only imagine what horrors ravaged Cate's sleep. Arguing with her would do little good; he could not *force* her to rest and drugging her might well do more harm than good.

"Might I read to you? It may serve to settle you, although I confess, the books in my library are hardly suited to young ladies. Boring texts, they are. Botany and chemistry. Anatomy." He laughed. Wasn't that, after all, the point? "I dare say, they would put most *men* to sleep in a trice. Soon, you shall be asleep."

"I confess I do quite enjoy your voice. There is music in it; I would love to hear you read, no matter the . . . content. And if it will serve to still my nerves, all the better."

She'd lent him a notion. Perhaps he had no need of a book at all. He closed his eyes and thought upon earlier, better times. Peaceful times.

"There was a lad," he began, "long ago, time out of mind, who dwelled in a magical, secret place, hidden in the shadow of three peaks." It had been so very long ago. The tale of his own youth, the happy times before James VI betrayed his father, murdered him, and destroyed his family. He would skip past those wretched years to his rescue by the monks of Dernwode House. But the lass had again fallen asleep. His own battle against sleep was lost, and Gaelan drifted on the memories of childhood, hoping, at least for a few hours, the demons of his past would be kept at bay. That he would dream of his time at Dernwode, and not once again be visited by the flames of his father's execution. But it was not to be.

"Are you all right, Mr. Erceldoune? You were shouting as you slept. And now you weep . . ."

"What . . . ?" Gaelan leapt from his chair, startled.

Cate stared at him from the cot, concern plain in her countenance.

He rubbed away the grit from his eyes, trying to cast off the last vestiges of a nightmare. How long . . . ?

He glanced at the mantel clock. Three hours had passed? Too long. He must not delay the examination a moment longer. Make certain no vestige of the birth remained within her.

Damnation. Soon enough, the savin would be the least of her worries. But to gain her cooperation for so an intimate examination . . .

"Miss . . . Cate . . . you seem to be in far better a state than when first you arrived, and I must, if you would allow it, examine you more thoroughly. Internally, if you understand—

"I do—"

"Good. Your clothing must go, else it will get in the way of . . . You might do with one of my nightshirts in . . . exchange. At least for purposes of . . . Besides which, your skirts are fouled beyond washing, and I fear . . ."

She nodded.

"Excuse me, then; I'll be but a trice."

By the time he returned to her side, Cate's skirts were in a heap on the floor; she'd wrapped herself in a goose down quilt. Happily, there seemed no obvious signs of bleeding beyond the expected drainage.

"I must be certain all has been expelled from the womb; nothing can there remain of it, else . . ." Too often, the abortion was incomplete; tissue remained, leading to far deadlier problems than caused by savin juniper.

Conversely, the deed was a total butchery, and the poor unfortunate girl was rendered entirely unable to bear children. He'd seen it too often and could tell her none of it.

She nodded, pulling the quilt closer. She was trembling again, but it was no chill caused it.

"I shall be swift as possible, and painless as I can manage, but I need to—" Gaelan gestured to the area below her waist.

Again, she nodded. "I do understand." She lay back on the cot. "Must I remove the coverlet, or—"

"There is no need. In fact—" Gaelan placed another of the blankets about her legs before immersing his hands in a glass basin, which he had filled with a pale green liquid.

"What is it you are doing? It smells of citrus. Lemons?"

"It is a practice I learnt long ago. Strange, is it not? *Lime* and a salt powder dissolved in water. My father insisted that washing this way before performing such an examination . . . as this . . . I mean to say, any internal examination—no matter what for, is better for the patient. Fewer fevers, many fewer deaths . . . Do forgive my bluntness. I do not know why it works, not exactly so, but I have found it to be true in my years of practice."

Conversation seemed to distract her well enough while Gaelan prodded about the birthing canal and cavity above. If the examination caused her distress, she did not show it. "If I might be so bold to enquire . . . who it was dosed you the—?" He was nearly done.

"The cover-shame? Such an appropriate name for it, is it not?

An old woman—a midwife, she insisted, but I think not. Madame Browning, she is called. She is well known ..." Cate stopped, unwilling to say more. "Two pills and a foul-tasting liquid, and she showed me the door forthwith. I think I remember falling, or nearly so, but then staggered my way about before—"

"Here, in Smithfield she . . . practices?" He'd not heard of a Madame Browning, though he suspected he would likely see too many more of her victims in the months to come.

"I do not believe her address is in Smithfield, but it could not have been too far, do you suppose? I had nowhere to go ... after ... and was of a mind to take a room at an inn nearby. The White Owl?"

"Yes, I know it, but it is good fortune you had not done, for likely as not you would be—"

"The cover-shame. It is poison?"

"Not always. And it is effective, when given in the correct amount ... The dose makes the poison, it is said. Very true. She likely mixed it with something else. Turpentine, perhaps. Opium? I do not know, but very likely, forgive my bluntness, you would be dead had you not fallen over my threshold."

She was fortunate. The birthing canal seemed clear enough, the uterus intact as far as he could tell. He removed his hand, discretely toweling away the blood, which covered him fingertip to elbow. She was not yet out of danger, but he was convinced she would soon be recovered.

"Perhaps it would have been much the better, sir, should I not have done."

He placed his hands in the basin, allowing the green solution to skate down his forearms before drying them with a fresh towel. "Truly you cannot believe that! You've your whole life before you—"

She blushed and turned away her face. "It was my cousin," she blurted.

"Your ... ? Did what? Brought you to Madame—?"

"That did it ... took me ... I did not want to ... He forced ..." She was sobbing again. "I'm sorry; I cannot talk about—"

Gaelan's hands clenched into tight fists. Too often he'd heard this same unforgivable story. A cousin. An uncle. A father. A brother. Hers explained much. She would have little standing to remonstrate against the blackguard.

A change of topic was in order. "I brought you something to wear; it is not much, but I fear I've nothing better to offer. It should suffice for the moment, as you shall not be venturing out for a day or two at least. I have given you a preparation made from ergot to stem the bleeding, but you will yet be weak, and must be watched closely."

She nodded, her lips drawn into a tight line.

"There now. We are done. All appears in good stead. Dress. I shall be in the shop should you need assistance." He bowed slightly, and taking up the bowl of green liquid, went through the curtains, pulling them tight.

By the time he returned, she had dressed in his nightshirt and was sitting on the edge of the cot.

"Good. Now, if you do not mind, I believe the settee in my flat might make for a more comfortable . . . and private . . . sanctuary for your recovery. There, you will also find soap and water to wash. Use it. A bath will need to wait . . . a day or two."

She would not make the steep stairs, even with his help.

"I shall need to carry you; the stairs are out of the question for now. Are you ready?"

Again, she nodded tightly.

"Arms about my neck—like before." He gathered her up, and slowly managed them both up the dark turns of the staircase.

"There. Much the better up here," he said once she'd been settled on the settee and a fire lit on the hearth. "Forgive the chill. It will be warm in a trice."

"You have been more than kind, sir; I should trouble you no longer than need be. Most assuredly, by tonight I shall be away. Already, I am much improved and—"

"Did you not hear what I have spoken only a moment ago?"

"I cannot think to put you out—"
"You must rest, my lady, and we shall take up the matter later."
"Why did you not let me die? Why . . . ?"
She was asleep before she finished the question.

CHICAGO NORTH SHORE, PRESENT DAY

CHAPTER 10

Preston bloody Alcott, standing in her doorway. What the fuck was Anne supposed to do with that? Of all the self-important gall. She slammed the door and waited to hear the slosh of his boots all the way to his Jaguar. She peeked through an adjacent window. He hadn't budged from the lintel.

She couldn't very well leave him standing in the downpour; he'd still be loitering on her doorstep come morning. Trapped.

Fine. As long as he was here, she could confront him about his appalling Galahad Society personally, face to face, and not through the anonymity of email. Directly involved with those postmodern vampires or not, he certainly was bloody aware of their activities.

The door banged against the wall behind her as she opened it with a force she hoped would throw him onto his bum. *No luck with that.* "Fine." She sighed. "You've the time it takes us to have dinner. But not here. In a restaurant. And then I have several questions for you."

"All I'm asking, then fire away. Any questions you want. I know the perfect place. Evanston. Near Northwestern U. Hung out there when I was in grad school there."

"I'll get my coat and be right out."

"May I come in?"

"No." She shut the door again, less violently this time, and locked it behind her.

By the time they got into the red convertible, the sun had again emerged. She wasted no time to begin her interrogation. "Tell me about the Galahad Society. Are you a member?"

"The Frothy Pint is like stepping back into another time. A real institution," he explained. He pushed a button and the car's roof disappeared behind them, the wind effectively extinguishing any possibility of conversation as they whipped through the snake curves and hairpins as the road twisted and turned along the shoreline.

What was she thinking? Dinner? What a bloody bad idea. Each red light, Anne contemplated bolting and catching a taxi home. Then, Alcott stopped the car beneath an enormous neon beer mug. *Too late.*

"And no, you can't take her out for a spin," Alcott admonished the valet with a grin, handing over the keys to an eager young man. He led her through a door and into a darkened restaurant, greeted by the strains of the Moody Blues. "Nights in White Satin." Evidently the "another time" was the 1970s.

"Like I said, the place is sort of a landmark."

"A time machine, more like," Anne said, eying the black walls decorated with garish posters, concert flyers, bumper stickers, autographed photos of George Harrison, Paul McCartney, Freddie Mercury, et al.

A massive island of a salad bar dominated the middle of the crowded restaurant. They slid into a tall wood banquette, graffitied with carved initials, hearts, emojis, generations of youthful symbology. "I'm just going to do the buffet," Anne said as an earnest college student appeared and began to list the day's specials.

Alcott knew exactly what he wanted. "Onion blossom and burger. With fries." He watched as the server left the table, waiting until he blended back into the crowd, before turning back to Anne.

"So, Dr. Shawe. I'm glad you agreed to—"

"I want to ask you about a mutual acquaintance—"

Alcott cringed; she noticed it even in the votive-lit booth. "Ah. Tony Cantwell."

"You do know him, then?"

"Got your name from him, in fact. Of course, you read about . . ." The scent of grease and onion filled the air. He rubbed his hands together dramatically. "Perfect timing. The rings have arrived. Best thing about this place . . . 'cept for the ambience, that is."

"How can you eat those? My LDL is skyrocketing just watching you salivate over them!"

"Bah! *Never* a take a doctor to dinner! Guilty pleasures, Dr. Shawe, when taken in moderation are good for the soul—"

"If not for the heart! What's your connection with the Galahad Society? And Anthony Cantwell?"

The server reappeared, setting a chilled pewter salad plate before her.

"None and none. Tony is an acquaintance. Hardly call him a friend. I financed a small venture of his a few years ago. End of story. Onions are a vegetable, you know. This is practically health food."

Full-on fucking charm offensive of forced affability. She wasn't buying it. "Yeah. I'll keep that in mind as I make my way around the salad bar! And *not* 'end of story.' What about Galahad?"

"Lot of guilty pleasures there, I'm sure. At the buffet. Galahad? Wasn't he some sort of knight? King Arthur and the Round Table, right? Or was that Lancelot?"

"I'm waiting—"

"I honestly don't know that much. An investment. To help out a friend's startup. I'm not actually involved. At all. So, I don't know what I can tell you. Beyond what Google already has."

"Enough!" She brandished the pewter plate and headed for the buffet. He was lying; she knew it. Layered good and thick as pudding with that . . . façade of fake niceness . . . There had to be a way to get out of this . . . colossal mistake.

The salad bar was huge, but nothing appealed; her appetite bled away as the crowded restaurant closed in around her like the walls of a cave. She had to get out of there. Now! To think. To . . . something.

Anne glanced back toward the banquette. Alcott was on his mobile. A short-term fix, but she saw her chance as a boisterous entourage of university students congregated in the restaurant foyer. The perfect camouflage.

Slipping away from the buffet, Anne pushed her way into the pack of kids, leaving a trail of apologies as she maneuvered her way toward the exit, still gripping her salad plate. Setting it down gently on a newspaper box just outside the restaurant door, Anne took a half-second to breathe in the fresh air before dodging around the corner. *Now what?*

To one side, the elevated tracks roared to life as a train flew by, creating a small cyclone of leaves and dust on the ground before her. Instinct screamed to call for a taxi, go straight to the airport, buy a one-way ticket home, and never turn back.

No! She would not allow that puffed up billionaire vampire to intimidate her. No fucking way. She stared at the home screen of her phone as she walked down the block, crossed and continued, wondering if even now Alcott was tracking her, expecting his red Jaguar to wheel about the corner any second. Nothing. Maybe he'd gotten the message. A girl could only hope.

Think, girl! Use that considerable brain of yours and bloody think, damn it!

Wait a moment—something familiar about this street. Alcott had said they were in Evanston. Gaelan lived . . . had lived . . . in Evanston. She stopped and looked up, finding herself directly across Gaelan Erceldoune's bookshop.

Her heart caught in her throat midway between horror and the relief of not being completely lost in a strange city. His shop would make for a dandy escape from Preston Alcott. And she had the keys right there in her bag. On a keyring, alongside Simon's.

Candles small and large, plain and elaborately carved, flowers of every variety—single roses, large bouquets, baskets of them—took up half the sidewalk in front of his door. *Bloody hell.*

She remembered the night they'd first met, staking out his shop, sitting in wait among the flowers—a shrine, not unlike this one. To Miracle Man.

Gaelan had despised it. The attention it symbolized, and with good reason. She'd cleared it all away that night. A gift. A peace offering that managed to break all the way through his formidable fortress of defenses. Now he was dead. Or so far off the grid he may as well be. The tributes had returned; he never would.

For hours now, she'd not given one stray thought to Gaelan Erceldoune. Now here she was. His home. A deep breath and she crossed the crowded street to his front door, stopping before wreaths of English lavender and baskets of wildflowers. And notes. So, so many notes. Stuck in the door jamb, in the window sash, scattered among the flowers, tied to baskets and black balloons.

She plucked a note from the ground, expecting to find within it proposed sainthood for the Miracle Man of Evanston, Illinois. She needed the laugh. Even, perhaps especially, at Gaelan's expense. *Miracle Man, indeed!*

> *May you find the peace and wholeness that has eluded your years here, it began. The rest of the note Anne devoured, rereading it twice more through a haze of tears. From your lectures to epic chess battles late into the night, I learned more Renaissance science history listening to you than from any other prof. Half my doctorate rightfully belongs to you. Rest in peace, Professor E.*
> *—J.F., (newly minted) PhD.*

Could she be mistaken? Were they all like this? Not a shrine but a memorial. Placing the note in her pocket, she collected another, and another, each evoking a similar sentiment. Eulogizing his teaching skill, his way with words, his knowledge—as if he'd lived the times, one said. Oh, if only they knew the truth of it.

These were not tributes to Miracle Man but remembrances of a kind friend, a teacher—so much more than an expert in "antiquarian books and antiquities."

How little she knew him. Not really at all. Jealousy and shame constricted about her like a vise. They'd all understood him in a way she now never could. The way he didn't quite fit, his terrible loneliness. Grief sucked the breath from her, pouring over with an unanticipated fury, burying thoughts of Preston Alcott beneath an avalanche of sorrow.

Whatever brought her to this threshold, she needed to be here tonight. To finally say goodbye. To accept his death. To be among his books. To sleep in the bed they'd shared that beautiful early morning as they both teetered on the edge of the abyss. To ask his forgiveness for the wrong she'd done him that morning in Scotland, goading him into a promise he could never keep. She opened her bag, retrieving the ring of keys left for her at Simon's house, finding the one marked "GE."

"Dr. Shawe!"

Alcott. *Shite!* She hadn't heard his car pull up.

"Look, Doc. I get your point. I'll leave you be. I'm curious as hell about why you've got the keys to the Miracle Man's place. You friends? Lovers? Rhetorical question, you understand. Don't feel compelled to answer, 'cause I'm sure you won't. Why should you? You don't know me; you don't trust me, and I don't really blame you. So, I'll leave you in peace, but ask you to keep an open mind about what you do—and do not—read in the online press. About me, your Miracle Man—or anything else."

"Thank you." She did not turn around until she heard the Jaguar's engine roar down the street. *And good riddance!*

It was early evening, and the shade of the train trestle painted the shop's interior in sepia hues. The shop smelled of old leather and spice tea, the essence of Gaelan Erceldoune. She felt like a cat burglar, slinking about in the semidark, wondering if she dared turn on the lights.

He'd left all of it behind, taking nothing save a sleeping bag and his passport. Everything he owned left to her, certified in a letter from Gaelan's Chicago attorney. *We will be happy to dispose of the estate and settle it in cash after you've taken for yourself any keepsakes from his shop or home. Please advise.* The letter was dated the day they'd left for the

UK on separate flights. The day before Glomach. The day before he'd told her "trust me," and then betrayed her. She understood better now the why, but it still smarted.

What the hell was she doing here, anyway? What did she hope to find? A souvenir of a relationship that lasted less than a week? What did it matter that he was connected to her family through a many-times removed aunt who'd died more than a century ago?

The books were valuable, and meaningful to her. Those, she could embrace—a purely professional interest; no emotions need be involved. An incredible library of medicine's history, of discovery from ages long past. She'd wager most of his collection were originals, one-of-a-kind books, and in perfect condition. Worth a bloody fortune.

Almost involuntarily, she opened the door at the back of the shop, and climbed the steep staircase with an impulsive, urgent need to know him, to understand him, his relationship to her family, every-thing about him. She knew the clues lurked not in his shop, among the books, but upstairs in the sanctum sanctorum of his private resi-dence.

A pungent infusion of marijuana, cigarettes, and whisky ambushed Anne as she stepped through the doorway and into Gaelan's flat. After weeks, the haze of tobacco smoke and weed had long settled from the air and saturated every surface.

The overpowering chaos of aromas matched the entropy of the sitting room. Papers, folders, electronics, empty bottles of Lagavulin strewn about in a heap on the floor just as he'd left it. A fit of frustra-tion, he'd said with no further explanation save a shrug of the shoul-ders. Well, she wasn't about to clean it up now, but at least she could open the windows. As many as possible.

The small pass-through kitchen was as organized as the sitting room was disastrous. A full canister of coffee beans, vacuum sealed, sat near a coffee maker. She could use a cup right now, despite the hour. Fair trade, single-origin Costa Rica estate. Perhaps later.

Resigned to the task of weeding through the accumulation of Gaelan's things, Anne grabbed a wastebasket and dropped to the floor beside a large mound of papers and files. The task appealed to her inner detective.

What might she uncover beneath some random yellowed envelope? What rare find hiding inside a circa 1940s manila folder? *What insights might this mess reveal, Gaelan Erceldoune, about yourself, about my family? Yours?*

Ariadne. Wasn't that his daughter's name? His and Eleanor's. Lady Eleanor Bell Braithwaite Langford, her very own ancestor and the origin point of that strange genetic line in her family tree. All those long-lived women for generation upon generation. All descended from Ariadne, her aunt—many generations removed. What might she discover about them?

Disappointingly, most of the papers seemed to do with his business. Of minimal interest, but for one letter, several pages, and in French. Photographs of a well-preserved but very old book were stapled to the corner. Anne's French wasn't good enough to decipher the letter, but she got the gist. A medieval French medical book of recipes. Yellow highlighter marks and margin notes in English, most likely Gaelan's, covered practically every inch of the letter. "Facsimile" was scrawled in red marker across the photographs. "Decline" had been written with a flourish at the top of the letter.

How could Gaelan have determined with only a small photograph that the book was a copy and not genuine? Yet, could she not distinguish a genetic anomaly by simply glancing at a photographic fingerprint? A chromatograph filter? An expert's eye can see well beyond the obvious. One need only possess the proper eyes to see, trained and in harmony with the subject. He had that extraordinary gift—apparently, something she often lacked, especially with men.

She gathered the remaining papers and piled them as neatly as she could next to Gaelan's laptop on the large carved desk, which stood as a boundary between the kitchen and the sitting room. Curiosity compelled her to open the desk drawers, but they were locked. No visible key anywhere; probably somewhere in the chaos of the sitting room. The laptop was another thing; she was tempted to open it, peek inside like the voyeur she'd now become. No. She would leave it be. Besides, he would have certainly password protected it, and although she was equally certain she could puzzle it out, she would let it lie unmolested.

The thought of remaining a moment longer in the flat grew cold. It was morbid to stay here—his tomb. The tomb of all that remained of Gaelan R. Erceldoune, a genetic enigma wrapped in a mystery. Besides, by now, Alcott was long gone, halfway across the country. Her excuse for staying had evaporated.

As Anne grabbed her bag from the counter, she noticed a small electronic keypad. Beside it, a closed door. She tried it, but it was locked. And she had evidently triggered some sort of alarm; the keypad flashed red and emitted a piercing *beep*. A warning to *keep out*.

CHAPTER 11

Anne stared at the keypad until her eyes stung and vision blurred. Why the bloody hell would Gaelan need a locked room? She rolled her eyes. *For his most valuable books, that's why, you idiot!* Probably had all sorts of dehumidifiers and gadgets in there to preserve the ink and paper. Little mystery there.

But she was too curious not to see for herself. But how to get in? The chances of guessing a numeric code were infinitesimal minus a clue.

She considered the puzzle. Gaelan had tasked her with disposing *all* his possessions, had he not? Bequeathed the bloody lot to her, so the code would likely be found somewhere within the papers his solicitor had sent her. Simple enough. But the papers were back at Simon's house. And she was here. Now.

A challenge. A diversion. Exactly what she needed.

Did she really know Gaelan well enough to figure it out? That was the real game, wasn't it? Unlikely, but worth a shot.

Firstly, the passcode likely would be something only he would understand. Something unexpected, but not impossible to remember. Not random, but obscure enough to seem so.

She brewed a cup of coffee, breathing in the brew's rich citrusy cocoa notes. *What did you love, Gaelan Erceldoune? What amused you? Gave you joy? Is that the secret place where the password lies?* His books. Of course.

She scanned through his several massive bookcases. He'd ordered the volumes by subject: alchemy, astronomy, chemistry, pharmacopeias from at least five eras, none more modern than the nineteenth century. History, Holmes—Conan Doyle—and A.C. Danforth aka Simon Bell. Mathematics.

The code was numeric, but not likely the obvious: address, phone number, birthdate . . . She smiled. She had no idea of that one. And the year . . . ?

Maybe she was wrong, and the code was entirely random and ever changing, which would render the lock impossible to open without the key, and she was completely wasting her time trying to puzzle it out on her own.

One more scan of the shelves before giving it up. Two shelves of mathematics books caught her eye. They were perfectly arranged just inside the lip of the shelf except for . . . a single volume, A very, very old volume, turned on its side, "Liber Abaci" engraved in gold on its spine. This was silly. Useless. What or who the bloody hell was a *Liber Abaci*?

Not Liberace, the pianist, but two words. And among the mathematics, not music, books. Music, mathematics . . . connected, she'd once learned from a maths prof. A bit of a reach, but . . .

She withdrew the volume and opened it to the first page, half expecting the door to mysteriously open as she did. The text was in Latin, which, she reckoned, Gaelan could read with the fluency of primary school English. Was Gaelan playing with her? A farewell gift to her, conjured even in the depths of his despair? Had he found some delight teasing her with a puzzle he never might have imagined she'd find? Of course he hadn't. When would he have found the time? *Down to Earth, girl!* She glanced at the door. *Still closed. Back to reality.*

There was something about the book. She knew it. Perhaps a clue within it for *him*, unwritten—a reminder of the code. Like a string around his finger.

She pushed a button on her phone. "Look up . . ." She glanced at the book's spine to be sure. "Search Liber Abaci on the Web."

"Liberace . . . more than three million citations. Twentieth-century American pianist. Biography . . ."

Fucking useless electronic so-called wizard! "Cancel." Old-school time. She slid her finger around the keyboard, annoyed when the autocorrect insisted she'd meant to type 'Liberace.'"

Finally. "Liber Abaci. Landmark mathematics text by thirteenth-century mathematician and philosopher Leonardo of Pisa, also known as Fibonacci."

Fibonacci. Of course. That name, she recognized. His brilliant numeric sequence that ordered all the natural universe, from the sunflowers that grew out her window back home to the most distant galaxy in the night sky.

That would be perfectly Gaelan, would it not? Obscure medieval mathematical treatises. She glanced over at the keypad. *Hah! Not so hard to figure out, are you, Mr. Erceldoune?*

Now to test the hypothesis. She knew the first few numbers by heart: 1, 1, 2, 3, 5, 8. What was next? A prime, that much she remembered. Thirteen? The sum of the last two numbers produced the next in the sequence. Five plus eight? Thirteen, then twenty-one.

That Gaelan Erceldoune was a polymath, she'd already guessed. She'd seen first-hand his incisive analytical skill at languages and chemistry. Try as she might to follow Gaelan's thought process as he'd deciphered the healing book, she'd always been paces behind him with no real chance at catch-up.

She tried the first several numbers, pausing after each. She'd no idea how many numbers he'd programmed into the lock, much less the combination. It beeped and blinked red after the fifth digit. So . . . five. But which five? And how many tries would she have until a lockout code required resetting the lock? Then she'd be screwed.

One more attempt. All she'd risk. Occam's razor. The simplest answer would be to try the first two adjacent numbers that would make five digits. She did the sums in her head. Eighty-nine plus one hundred forty-four. Eight, nine, one, four, four. Fingers poised over the keys, she held her breath a moment before entering the digits. The LED glowed yellow, then green, and then the purr of electronic tumblers giving way. *Small victories.*

The door opened automatically into a narrow room bathed in a red glow that reminded her of photography class, silver nitrate and spirals of exposed camera film—back before everything went digital.

Anne pushed a button on the wall, and bright white light flooded the room, reflecting off the chrome and stainless steel of a long labora-tory bench lined with chemicals, equipment, and a large, expensive, microscope fixed with a camera. An old-school centrifuge sat beside it. In the corner, a small incubator set to thirty-seven degrees Celsius. Sterile swabs and pipettes, Vacutainers and disposable syringes, all neatly arranged in small storage drawers.

In the kitchen fridge, a covered bin containing stains, reagents, and all the other fixings needed for T-banded karyotyping. Mr. Erceldoune had set up for himself a nicely outfitted but basic DIY genetics lab, not a complex thing to do. With it, he could accomplish little more than a university first-year laboratory exercise: collect a blood sample, spin it down in hypotonic solution, treat with colchicine to freeze the mitotic chromatids in metaphase, put them on a slide, stain with Geimsa, and snap a photo for posterity. Why go to all that bother? *Why, indeed?* Undoubtedly trying to understand something about his genetic makeup. What made him . . . immortal?

Anne began opening drawers and cabinets in search of more clues. *Voila.* A file folder and an old-fashioned green-flecked data notebook. And a stack of human karyotype images, each dated and a year apart. She removed the first image, examining the chromosome banding. Well executed, but primitive. The banding was clear enough, but . . . there were others; he'd used several different techniques. Some she rec-ognized, a few she didn't.

Another folder, more karyograms, more sophisticated scans, but these he never could have accomplished with the equipment here. They'd required radioactive dyes, special scopes, and cameras.

He would have needed help, but from whom? Gaelan didn't seem the type to trust very many people, and besides, how would they explain the results if they demonstrated in living color the genetic anomaly that was Gaelan Erceldoune? He'd never put himself in that position.

Anne held an image beneath a magnifier light. There was some-thing odd, not in the banding but in the structure of the chromosome itself. Yes, the telomeres were elongated. She'd expected as much. Not a complete surprise in someone whose tissue regenerated so quickly.

But there was something else—differences in one image to the next. Artifacts? Mistakes in the preparation of the slides? A bad sample? The mistakes of an amateur—a talented amateur, but . . . She picked up a grease marker from the bench and circled the regions of concern. She'd take a closer look later.

The genetic makeup of a man half a millennium old in her hands. *What a find!* And no wonder he'd kept it hidden behind lock and key. Along with the blood sample he'd left with her, and the notes for the ouroboros book he'd so carefully written out for her use, she could write an important text. A landmark work. Reinvent her career . . . But not yet. Not until she was certain Gaelan Erceldoune really was dead. All was fair game after that.

She rifled through the pages of the notebook, looking for the name of whoever helped Gaelan with his experiments. *Eureka!* A business card. Dr. Dana Spangler, Department of Medical Genetics, Northwestern University. Bingo! Anne would ring her up first thing.

A forty-dollar rideshare later, she was home, back at Simon's, too spent to trudge up the stairs.

PRESENT DAY, SCOTLAND

CHAPTER 12

Gaelan held the glass piece in his hand, staring at it from every angle, running a thumb along the smooth surface. *It cannot be.* It could not be *that* glass piece. Logic dictated the impossibility that a small piece of glass, missing since 1893, lost in Chicago, should turn up now, here. In Scotland. Yes, it was a teardrop quarry. And opalescent. And about the right size for it.

The piece had gone missing halfway through the Columbian Exposition, and Gaelan had searched the grounds for hours, for days, before giving it up as lost forever.

The quarry was warm in his hand despite the spring chill; held up to the sun, the full range of its colors, their depth—the entire spectrum held captive—bursting to escape. Color merged into color, light into light, the glass fluid, yet solid. White into turquoise into cobalt; from a different perspective, blood orange swirled iridescent into red and back to white.

He'd crafted it as something extraordinary, the process taking him days of effort in his workroom to be worthy of *her*, worthy of the stained-glass panel he'd designed as a memorial to her. An image of how he'd known her, not when she lay bleeding on the apothecary floor when they'd first met, but as he beheld her the first time, he witnessed her genuine delight. Made her smile with the gift of a simple glass bauble.

Its very existence, here, now, added much fuel to his gnawing belief that none of this was real. A mad fantasy conjured of a broken mind, random flashes of memory, a conflation of four hundred–some-thing years of experience, with just enough reality to make him doubt his disbelief.

Only two months earlier, he'd retrieved from storage the original favrile glass quarries to recreate the panel, an exact duplicate of the original. Remake the missing opalescent piece to replace the one lost and complete the work. He never finished it.

Gaelan weighed the teardrop in his hand, turned it over, scruti-nizing it. He could be wrong and this was simply what it appeared to be. A peculiar, interesting piece of glass, fragment of a stained-glass window, smoothed over time and the elements.

Likely thousands of them lay scattered about the field, bits and pieces of the elaborate windows that once adorned the Dernwode House buildings. Crafted by the Quhawme Brethren who'd lived there, who taught Gaelan the craft in the first place. He'd studied each quarry each window, transported into the intricacies and workman-ship. Magic, but not. Solid, but not. Fluid, but not liquid.

What an insane, romantic notion that the teardrop should materi-alize thousands of miles away, here, in a place he could not be, reading the ramblings of a man he'd known, dead now nearly a century. What additional evidence did he need of his derangement?

He should hurl the bloody thing against the stones. Watch it refuse to shatter. Prove it all an illusion. The slimmest of doubts stayed his hand.

Instead, Gaelan pocketed the piece of glass and pushed himself up, inhaling the clean Borders air deep into his lungs. Several boulders and large flat stones were scattered among the sparse, dry grass of the large barren field. They fit together well enough to craft a rather rickety bench, yet it was a bit of a physics experiment to locate the exact balance spot where he might sit without toppling the entire thing. Placing the Conan Doyle papers beside him, Gaelan welcomed the bracing chill of the Borders morning.

Why could he not remember getting here? He had no recollection of anything from the moment he drank the poison.

A conundrum. A riddle to be solved if Gaelan had any hope of . . . Hope of what? Going back to Anne? Living a normal life? Returning to the status quo from which he'd only just escaped?

What if, and without knowing how, he'd survived the poison, mind intact, and found his way to Dernwode House? Improbable, yes. But was it impossible?

Gaelan turned back to the Conan Doyle.

I freely admit I have for all these years been obsessed with finding this truth, which has so eluded humanity in all but minstrelsy and legend. And up until now, I have left open the possibility I have been wrong, welcoming all naysayers and sceptics, no matter their opinion of me, including my dear friend Mr. Harry Houdini. Ah, Houdini, I so deeply regret that our friendship has been a tragic casualty of this disagreement.

I have placed within the pages of this document a small piece of glass, which will, I hope, find its way to you, dear reader, and not erode with time. I do not know how—or why—but I do know this far-from-simple piece of glass is a device to gain entry into their world—the world of the fairies. It is a key, if you will, through a portal of some sort. And it is why I so carefully stashed these items safe within the walls of this ancient structure. It is my proof that the fairy world exists alongside our own.

When I have held this small glass bauble secure in my hand, I am transported, as if by magic, to their realm. To see it, to experience it. To dwell amongst them in their most fantastical environs. A genuine gift. But once the device—for that it is—is set down or placed it in my waistcoat pocket, I no longer am in the Otherworld, but once again find myself in a dank and lonely catacombs.

How very like Conan Doyle to perceive mystery in even the simplest object. But a key, and to the "otherworld"? No wonder Conan Doyle had stashed the papers in a place no one would find them.

Gaelan first met Sir Arthur Conan Doyle on a cold London night in January in 1902, dragged to a dinner party by Simon Bell. Already in a black mood, Gaelan had no patience that night to be quizzed about his surname and its connection to the fairy folk and their otherworldly domain. But Conan Doyle had been insistent.

And yes, Gaelan had been provocative, drawing Conan Doyle into an argument impossible to win by being truthful about his past. All Gaelan could do was deny and evade every assertion.

Conan Doyle, the keen journalist, was hot on the trail of proof. The existence of fairies. Conan Doyle believed Gaelan knew more than he admitted. And based upon only his unusual surname.

Conan Doyle pursued Gaelan through polite correspondence for years afterward andGaelan refused to be pulled into the endeavor. He knew too much, and Conan Doyle was too clever not to perceive even the slimmest shred of connection—a risk Gaelan was unwilling to take if it meant exposure.

The light began to dim as the sun slipped behind a cloud. High above, a single red kite swooped and dived, seeking its prey, its magnificent wingspan stretched across the sapphire sky mighty as a fighter jet, silent, majestic. Free.

It glided lower and lower, spotting dinner, a white-gray hare loping in great strides across the field until it disappeared into a stand of trees. The kite, denied, soared higher once again, altering its flight path as it scissored its long tail, until it, too vanished into the hills.

Their world is far, far flung from what I expected; they are not a wee, wee folk, nor green, nor winged like a butterfly, but quite human in their way. And quite tragic, from what little I've overheard them discuss amongst themselves. I can see them, hear them, have so far been unable to interact with them directly, which grieves me.

Before the end of my journey, I would so like to meet the Rhymer. Lord Thomas Learmont of Ercildoune. After all, these are his ancestral lands, and quite nearby in Earlston sits his tower. Legend tells us the fairy queen endowed him with life immortal. And local lore professes the Rhymer yet dwells beneath the three hills of Eildon, not far from where I have placed this document.

It has long been said beneath the hills of Eildon exists a world between worlds, a portal through time and space. Since time out of mind when the great Scottish hero Michael Scot split one mountain into the three peaks of Eildon, some eight centuries past. And it is this small object—this glass bauble—that connects the worlds. This miraculous discovery of mine would astound even my dear friend Mr. H.G. Wells.

Gaelan closed the folio with a sigh. Intellectually, Conan Doyle's writings could be read only as the folly of an elderly man with dementia.

The sun had slipped behind the middle peak, encircling it with a halo. Michael Scot. A true genius, unrecognized in his time and for a long time after. A man of philosophy, science, languages from Latin to Greek, Hebrew to Arabic. Mathematics.

The Fibonacci numeric sequence.

The Dernwode House brethren had trained Gaelan's mind well to visualize the pattern that centuries later continued to fascinate him. Gaelan possessed an edition of Fibonacci's most famous work on the subject, which the mathematician had dedicated to Scot.

Gaelan stared up through a nearby stand of trees, looking for Fibonacci in the organization of the branches. Order from the wild chaos of nature. Complex biological structures to the simple elegance of the periodic table to intricacy of quantum physics. To the elegant harmony of Gaelan's glass panels, which themselves adhered to the Fibonacci principle. *Phi.* The golden ratio: $a + b$ is to a as a is to b.

Were the designs in the ouroboros book arranged according to Fibonacci as well? Would it have simplified the task of understanding it, long ago? He'd never considered the idea. *Fool.*

Yet, for all his brilliance, Scot had been dismissed, derided, even cast by Dante into the flames of hell in his *Divine Comedy*. Darkness won as it had too often. Was Gaelan now guilty of the same error by dismissing Conan Doyle?

Gaelan stared at the crest of the middle hill. If he squinted, he could see the ancient hawthorn, its branches barren, incongruous in the green of springtime. "As long as the thorn tree stands, Erceldoune shall keep its lands." Gaelan remembered the saying, passed down some three hundred years from the time of Lord Thomas from father to son and, finally, to Gaelan's father.

Conan Doyle had sought out the Rhymer; Gaelan never considered it a credible enough possibility to try. That was the difference between them; Conan Doyle had always wanted to believe—did believe—too easily, willing to destroy his reputation and relationships in the process. Fairies, ghosts, phantasms of a world beyond our own, beyond the laws of science and provability.

Gaelan was a well-trained skeptic. To him, true wonder lay in the realm of this world—both what we knew of it and the discovery of what we did not yet. Magic, his father told him, as did his tutors at Dernwode House, was but science we'd yet to understand. Logos and mythos and the interstitial space between them that was exploration. Different perspectives of the same thing, seen with different eyes, differing experiences. In different times.

Gaelan stood, taking in the whole of the field, allowing his mind's eye and memory to locate his bearings in this barren place. He was standing in the middle of what had once been Dernwode courtyard. Possibly. To his left would be the grand marble fountain, guarded by chubby alabaster cherubim, their wings tipped in gold.

A bright white pebble caught his eye and he stooped to pick it up. It bore some resemblance to the teardrop, but smaller, rougher. The alabaster fragment of an angel's broken wing? He shook his head and hurled the stone as far as he could. *Even alabaster cherubs die, and medieval monasteries, and everyone but you! Fuck you all!*

He concentrated, and before him spread out familiar paths and buildings that hadn't existed for centuries. Towers and turrets, the filigree of stone and bronze of arched windows; the pungent stink of the piggery. The fragrant aroma of yeasty bread as he would pass by the bakery. The heavy oaken doors deeply engraved that led into the main church with its carved, painted naves and vivid stained glass that lined every exterior arch window.

The stark, spare, nearly windowless dormitory buildings. When he'd been a lad, he'd count the footsteps from the fountain to the tower, first in English, then Gaelic, then Greek, and then Latin. Later, as Brother Gregor taught him, in Aramaic, Arabic, and Hebrew. Six hundred ten. Two hundred thirty-three to the bakery, and three hundred seventy-seven more to the fountain.

Gaelan had last been to Dernwode in 1826. He'd been shocked even then at the deterioration of monastery, by that time an abandoned ruin with little left but for a stray boulder of significance—perhaps two. Gaelan suspected that many homes in nearby villages had been built with those very ancient stones.

The afternoon sun had now dropped behind the hills, back-lighting them with a rusty glow. Better make his way back to his rabbit hole before it vanished into the dark earth and he was stuck outside for the night with no shelter.

The lantern was where Gaelan left it, on the top stair. Yet he was not quite ready for the catacombs. He would wait for the stars. Would they, too, seem off-kilter and surreal?

Gaelan gazed up into the twilight sky. Vega—Alpha Lyrae—dropped into the heavens from nowhere, just above his head, the brightest star, so near and vivid, with no light pollution to dim its light. A mere twenty-five light years away. Someday . . . a short commuter flight.

There was so much we did not yet understand of the universe. Would it be so far a stretch to believe Conan Doyle's fairy world? Perhaps not.

Removing the glass piece from his pocket, holding it up to the lantern light, he half-wondered whether he'd be magically transported to Conan Doyle's "otherworld" as he descended the long, dark stairway.

LONDON, 1826

CHAPTER 13

With Cate comfortable and asleep in the flat, Gaelan descended the stairs into his shop to wash up and prepare for the day.

"You Erceldoune?"

What in the . . . ? A stranger sat atop the counter, top hat, gloves, and walking stick beside him.

"Who the devil might *you* be? And more to the point, how have you managed to get in here?" Gaelan was in no mood for another disruption.

The intruder stood, dusting off his trousers, his left hand perched on the countertop, his right on his hip, smiling. "I, Mr. Apothecary, am Lyle Tremayne. You may know my name already. And it has come the time for us to have a conversation."

"I am Erceldoune," he said finally, with no effort to mask his impatience. "But I have not yet opened for business this morn. Please return . . ." He glanced at his pocket watch. "In two hours' time." He paused, reconsidering. "Unless this be an urgent—*medical*—matter."

Gaelan had heard the name, whispered by the good people of Smithfield in hushed tremble, gazes terrified and downcast. By their accounts, Lyle Tremayne owned Smithfield, holding a sharp blade poised on the necks of the merchants, demanding tidy sums from all . . . or suffer the cost.

The Man O' War Public House, his fortress, an entourage of cutthroats, wielding daggers and clubs—and unafraid to use them—his court. Rumors carried even far as Hay Hill of certain business pursuits at the Man O' War, which undoubtedly this day brought him to the apothecary.

Gaelan had no time for this blackguard, not today. Send him on his way with a smile and a bottle of his best shaving tonic. And nothing more.

Tremayne's fancy velvet suit of clothes and studiously manicured fingernails did little to conceal the danger in his hooded gaze, the menace of his ruddy, weathered face, crisscrossed by jagged scars, forehead to chin. Gaelan never had taken well to tyranny, and Tremayne was little more than the pettiest of tyrants, preying on the vulnerable good people of Smithfield. Yet, it would not do well to provoke him needlessly, make an enemy of him for no good reason.

Tremayne settled himself into Gaelan's favorite chair. This was not to be a simple social call.

"I could do with a whisky, if you've a good old one—"

Gaelan followed Tremayne's gaze to a half-empty shelf—and a full, cut-crystal decanter.

"Of course." Gaelan poured two tumblers and sat opposite him. On his guard.

Tremayne swigged down the amber liquid in one swallow, slapping the empty glass hard against a small inlaid table. "You've right good taste, apothecary. Now. Mr. . . . Erceldoune. Down to the matter at hand, if we may. My visit is more purposeful than a cordial drink between men of business."

Tension slithered down Gaelan's spine like spider. Not a spider. A snake. "I am listening."

"Mr. Erceldoune, I have been asked by a father—a gentleman of some means—who is at this very moment beside himself, quite desperate to learn the whereabouts of his daughter, a young lady he believes may have wandered, perhaps unawares, into this . . . my . . . *our* little part of London. She has not been heard from since early last evening. He is gravely concerned for her well-being.

And perhaps, if she has fallen ill . . . or . . . she would have done well to seek out your goodly services and medications for aid and comfort."

Tremayne's baritone whisper was a mere notch above malevolent, an implied threat underscoring each word. Did he already suspect the girl had come to the apothecary, or was he speculating? Had Bell observed more than he'd let on, and then gone straightaway to Tremayne and secured his assistance? Baiting the hook? Or was he fishing blindly?

Tremayne's gaze darted from the half-bare shelves to the unopened crates that lined the walls as he nervously tapped his finger on the tumbler's edge. Was this but the first stop of many in search of the girl, or did he really know something?

"To speak true, Mr. Tremayne, no young woman has visited the shop in past day, at least."

Tremayne's eyes narrowed, judging. He raised an eyebrow. "You seem to me a fair bit weary, sir, for so early an hour. Not much sleep, eh? The noises of Smithfield more feral than those of Hay Hill?"

"Hay Hill?"

Tremayne leaned in close enough for Gaelan to smell the threat on his breath. "It is my business, Mr. Erceldoune to well know the residents of my . . . domain."

Gaelan pushed back his chair and retreated behind the counter, refusing to allow Tremayne to provoke him. "If you do not mind, I've a business to open shortly and much to do." Gaelan gestured toward the array of partially unpacked crates lining the shop walls. "And I've yet to settle completely into the apothecary. As you can see."

"You've not slept, even I can see that. Sure you've not been tending to our lovely young lady, hmm? Or maybe it be the ghost of William Wallace steals the sleep from ya?" Again, Tremayne gestured, broadly this time, his hand sweeping in a wide arc like an actor onstage. He laughed, and the sound reverberated through the shop like thunder echoing through the Highlands.

"William—?"

"Executed right here at the very corner where your shop now stands. Him and his traitorous band. Drawn and quartered, he was. It's said he haunts the market, most especially this place. Driven out more than one apothecary from these premises. Never you worry— it's but a tale. A good old ghost story for a chilly Hallows Eve, eh?" Tremayne's raucous laugh shifted into a phlegmy cough.

"I have a tonic that might soothe the hacking, sir—" Gaelan placed a bottle of honey elixir on the table, an offering.

Ignoring the gesture, Tremayne cleared his throat into a lace-trimmed handkerchief. "And haven't I heard you're needing an apprentice? No need to look further, Mr. Erceldoune. I've just the lad and shall send him 'round by afternoon. You will find him an able assistant, I am certain."

"No, sir . . . I thank you for the kindly offer, but I mean to have *well-qualified* apprentice in my employ. My standards are quite difficult, and I have interviewed several already. I shall have one in my employ by week's end."

Gaelan could quite imagine the apprentice Tremayne might send to him, more like to spy on his every move, his every prescription, every ailing soul to cross his threshold. Collecting gossip, exacting his price. That Gaelan could not countenance.

"Very well. There is one other matter . . . perhaps two . . . I wish to discuss, and being as I am here already—"

"Out with it then, Mr. Tremayne, for I've no time to dawdle. The sun is full up, and I am not yet ready for the trade." There was fresh water to fetch, and he desperately needed a cup of good, strong black tea.

"There are thieves and highwaymen who perpetrate their ill deeds in this wild place—"

"Indeed." Gaelan imagined that most, if not all, were in Tremayne's employ—if the rumors and warnings he had heard since he'd come to this place rang true.

"I only wish to be at your service, sir. As I am to most of the district. Offering my protection from such evildoers—"

Ah, there it was . . . extortion for the simple benefit of not being

robbed and burnt out. What exaction would be required? It little
mattered, for Gaelan refused to become the next bit of prey for this
rogue.

"I've a proposition for you, Mr. Tremayne—"

"A proposition?" A broad smile split Tremayne's countenance, his
dark mustache spreading the breadth of it above a set of well-repaired
teeth, one molar gleaming gold.

"Indeed, sir . . . The men . . . and ladies, perchance under your
employment, no doubt, from time to time require attending to their
. . . medical needs. And I, sir, would be most honored to provide . . ."
Gaelan's stomach clenched at the very notion of honoring Tremayne at
all. "Honored to be at your service in that regard. At no charge to you,
of course, but for the medicines alone."

Tremayne laughed and the rheumy cough returned. "Perhaps I
will quaff down a bit of that tonic after all."

Gaelan handed him the bottle. "It is yours. Keep it. No charge."

"Include the medicines as well, and you've a bargain. I will guarantee the safety of not only you but all in your household and, whilst
in your shop, all those to whom you minister. And I've no propensity
to tell the authorities of any . . . services you might render beyond the
purview of a simple . . . apothecary. You are, of course, no physician,
and here in London—"

"Much obliged," Gaelan replied quickly. "Then it is settled?"

Tremayne rose, placing the honey elixir in his coat pocket.
"Indeed, it is, sir. Pleasure to finally make your acquaintance and to
do business with you. You will of course let me know forthwith should
you come across the young lady of whom we spoke?"

"There was a second matter of which you wished to speak, sir?"

"Ah, yes. Of course."

Tremayne had not forgotten—he was merely gauging Gaelan. A
test?

Tremayne cleared his phlegmy throat. "As you are, I understand,
a surgeon as well as an apothecary, I personally invite you to visit me
of an evening soon at the Man O' War. You will find it, I trust, quite

the experience. Quite more entertaining than the White Owl, your usual—"

He shuddered to imagine what entertainment might be found there. "The Owl, I think, more suits me. But I do appreciate the kind invitation."

"I've a hefty interest in the place, and many a surgeon finds there a lucrative trade . . . going both ways. It is, shall we say, a meat market like any other of Smithfield, but dealing in a more particular sort of animal flesh."

Yes, Gaelan added only to himself, and when demand outstrips availability, London body snatchings surge and resurrection men grow rich and fat.

"I have, sir, no need. Rest assured. I am no anatomist."

"No, of course not. Not what I meant at all, Mr. Erceldoune." He drummed his nails on the table. "But should you . . . come across a fresh . . . erm . . . Your predecessor and I had a very lucrative business going. Quite lucrative for us both . . . and for the progress, shall we say, of medicine, eh? For example, a young child, near death, perhaps dead already, family with no means to repay you for what all you have done by your goodly works . . . Let us say, you've only to call on me, and you shall be more than compensated for your travails. And you will be doing more than your . . . part . . . to supply our teaching hospitals . . . with the, shall we say, 'parts' for their continual needs."

Gaelan had long ago visited Man O'War Public House—long before Lyle Tremayne was born. Even then, it boasted a special "room" lined with corpses stripped bare of anything valuable, any means to identify them. Waiting, fresh for the picking. Some dead of illness, but many others who'd met less natural, and far untimelier, deaths. Gaelan understood the need; he'd studied his fair share of cadavers in his time. Yet, this hideous practice, condoned by the silence of most who might stop it—that he could not countenance. Men of medicine eager to pay much and ask few questions.

"I think not, Mr. Tremayne. We have our bargain, and I pray it is enough."

Tremayne finally stood to leave, nodding his assent.

Gaelan breathed, moving swiftly to the door, holding it to usher his guest into the damp morning air.

"I shall say no more about it, Mr. Erceldoune. The invitation remains. I bid you, then, a good morrow, sir."

The door locked, and Tremayne disappeared into another shop. The unexpected encounter with Tremayne, the lack of sleep as well— all of it sapped Gaelan of all strength. Collapsing into his chair, he shut tight his burning eyes, waiting until the pulse now throbbing behind them slowed and the room stopped spinning when he dared open them.

As for Tremayne's ghost tale of William Wallace, indeed a strange coincidence the execution had occurred in the exact location of the apothecary. The stories were famous, of course, of the great knight and his exploits, told over and over until he could recite them from memory when he'd been but a lad and play them out in the palace courtyard. And his own ancestor Lord Thomas Learmont a confederate of the Scottish hero.

Gaelan never much believed in ghosts and hauntings. If old William did happen to be about, not likely it would be to harass him, but to stand guard against Tremayne and his ilk—more terrifying than any specter of a heroic Scottish knight.

As his thoughts faded, Gaelan gave in to his growing drowsiness. A few slim moments of sleep, and no more, he promised himself, knowing, despite his unusual physiology, like any man, he would soon collapse from the lack of it.

CHAPTER 14

Simon Bell arrived at precisely eleven o'clock in the morning, looking less frantic than he had only hours earlier. "Do have a seat. The kettle is on, and I hope I might interest you in a cup. My special blend."

"Of course."

"Forgive my appearance and that of the shop. As you know, I have only just relocated to Smithfield, and business has been perhaps brisker than I would have thought. You were saying when you visited earlier you wished to consult on a medical matter. I am both surprised and admittedly a bit flattered. And I assure you, I am quite prepared to provide for all you might require—"

"You have somewhat of a reputation, I must say, for saving the necks of my brother physicians, who are at once slightly in awe of your uncanny abilities and at the same time resentful that you are . . . forgive me, I mean no disrespect, Mr. Erceldoune . . . merely an *apothecary*."

Gaelan had to credit Bell for the admission, couched as it was in the usual slight. At least Bell appeared to be less the dandified gent than many of his colleagues.

"Bell," Gaelan said after a moment, ignoring the affront. "The name means something to me. Might you be a relation of the famed Scottish surgeon Benjamin Bell of Edinburgh?"

"My grandfather, sir. He is, naturally, long since departed from this earth."

"Of course. He was a singular talent, was he not?" Gaelan would need to take care and not reveal anything of the brief time he'd apprenticed to the legendary surgeon. "I have studied his writings so thoroughly, I feel I know his techniques as if I'd learned at his elbow. It would be my great honor to serve the grandson of such a giant."

"Indeed! It is said, sir, you have experience with diseases few physicians have met in Britain. Might I enquire how that might be? Certainly not from the study of my grandfather's writings. Have you traveled the world? The army, perchance? Or a ship's surgeon?"

"No." Gaelan was not keen to reveal he'd spent a year at sea. Surgeon on a privateer a century and a half ago. If Bell had any experience at all with *modern* seafaring, Gaelan would be ill prepared to discuss the subject.

He'd not been to sea since that difficult voyage. Slashed by a cutlass breaking up a row, Gaelan's wounds would surely have been a mortal blow for a normal man, and several shipmates had witnessed the extent of it. He'd hid away in his quarters for days afterwards, waiting for the wounds to heal, and then he denied the entire business as a drunken tale.

"I confess, I read quite a bit. Practice technique when I'm able. Cats, usually. The occasional rat . . ."

"You've no taste for dissecting human corpses, then?"

"I've little opportunity to do so, nor the funds to pay the resurrection men. No, I have done quite well with cats and rats to understand physiology. Humans are not so very different."

"The resurrection men would disagree with you on this point—"

Gaelan laughed. "Right you are! And there are ideas more important than one might discover in a corpse. I endeavor to make my horizons as far-reaching as possible. Indeed, there are times when a modern cure proves less effective than something ancient and long forgotten. Dismissed and derided, even outlawed as magic in less enlightened times."

"Very few such resources remain anywhere on these shores, I understand."

"Not all are vanished, destroyed, and I have found it useful time to time to reconsider these old ways, but with modern eyes. What baffled us in ages past, viewed through the prism of modern understanding and the gift of hindsight . . . Ah, Dr. Bell, we have before us the rich and too-often untapped vein of history to plunge."

Bell slapped his hand on the table between them, a smile ear to ear. "Quite right you are. And it is exactly something my grandfather would suggest. I do hope you will forgive me my behavior last night . . . or should I say . . . earlier this morn. The family were frantic with worry, and I must admit when the young lady's brother prattled on about his sister last night, her rumored whereabouts in Smithfield of all places, I had to wonder if she came to you seeking help."

"They have located her, then?"

"No. Not as far as I know."

"Why would the brother not seek for her on his own? And why the presumption about me?"

"As I said, you've a reputation as a gifted practitioner, and especially kind to those in the greatest of need. Perhaps you'd been recommended by a friend of hers. I admit it was more wishfulness than anything. That the young lady found herself at *your* door rather than . . . As for the brother, he is a preening fop, more interested in his social status than the well-being of his own sister. I doubt she would have come home with him, in any event, which is why I'd set out on my own, you see. And in her situation, she is better off to cut the tie entirely, find help elsewhere. Therefore, Mr. Erceldoune, I must ask again . . ."

Gaelan needed to tread carefully. Admit to nothing. "And I repeat to you. I have treated not one young lady in the past day. Nor do I have knowledge—"

"Please, Mr. Erceldoune, I have no wish to antagonize you. As I said, she is better off on her own than—"

Gaelan could not contain vehemence of his anger, which crept up on him unawares. He stood, hands balled into tight fists, and stalked to the far end of the shop. "You would wish her alone and friendless *here?* In Smithfield? I assure you it is safe enough by day if you've a notion how to handle yourself, but it is a place of ruffians and cutthroats at night, after the markets close shop. There lurks about the district a band of body snatchers who would not hesitate to kidnap a young woman, slit her throat and turn her over to the anatomists and surgeons for study. Or, if she is more the fortunate sort, might find herself in a bordello." A young, genteel lady would be easy prey. "Be that what you'd want for her, Dr. Bell?" Gaelan turned back, hoping his glare fixed a saber-sharp point on Bell. "For a young lady you call a *friend*?"

He had to stop, lest he give away even the smallest clue about the girl being under his roof. He turned to stare out into the market until he might continue on calmer footing. "Forgive me my outburst, Dr. Bell," he said before returning to sit opposite his visitor. "It has been a taxing sort of day already."

Now, Bell stood and paced the length of the long room. "Of course it is not what I would want for her . . . for anyone. I would hope . . ." He stopped, coming to rest again at his chair. He took up his cup and sat. "What does it matter what you or I might hope?" Bell blew out an exasperated breath before continuing. "Perhaps . . . *Perhaps* she will find sanctuary with some kindly family. That is what I pray. She is a free spirit, that one; she knows her own mind. But a girl on her own? She is barely nineteen years, and despite a fierce independent streak, she is naive as any young lady of her station."

"Then let that be an end to the matter, and hope she finds refuge, eh? As for the other thing you wished to discuss? Despite whatever reputation others may accredit me, would you not be better off to seek the services of an apothecary in a more convenient part of town?"

"The local apothecary is adequate, but somewhat a fool with his strange concoctions at steep prices—and, I might add, to dubious effect."

"There *are* those who discredit the trade . . ." Too many, and they lent to all apothecaries the stink of fraud.

Bell sipped the tea. "This is quite a wonderful brew!"

"Orange peel, cinnamon, ginger, cardamom, clove—and cayenne, which I infuse with bergamot and black leaves." Gaelan waited for Bell to come to the point of his call.

"Mr. Erceldoune. I have in these past several days been confronted by a rather perplexing illness I have never before seen in my many years of practice."

"Indeed. Please go on." Gaelan's curiosity was piqued by the whiff of a thorny medical riddle.

"Chills—tremors head to toe. Poor wretch's teeth were chattering so, I thought he might bite right through his tongue."

"There are, sir, a great many illnesses that commence thus. A high fever no doubt followed suit—and a weakness more than any fatigue the patient has known? You would know all this, surely. And this patient, I would assume, is no pauper living in filth and ten to a room, but a man of some means?" Undoubtedly, Bell saw few patients suffering the ailments Gaelan treated daily in the years he had practiced his trade in rat-infested slums, teeming with people crowded into impossible living conditions. He had at his disposal no magic potions—only the benefit of several centuries treating the worst disease had to offer, a keen eye, and a gift for making connections others too often refused to see. "Indeed, your patient must suffer from other, more peculiar, symptoms—else why search beyond your own experience and insight?"

"This is no ordinary influenza or at least nothing of its like I have seen. The rapidity of the onset . . . I tell you. He is in extremis, and only over the course of hours, his condition has deteriorated from a state of good health to near death."

"Have you a complete reckoning of the illness's course over the past day?"

"His wife says it commenced with a mild headache. No more than that. Breathing difficulty followed within two hours, she says, and then chills, fever, shortly thereafter. By the time I came round to examine him, his chest rattled with every breath. And as I said, all in the course of mere hours."

Gaelan roved about the shop, his gaze darting from Bell to the open crate of books and back again, evaluating the order of symptoms, discarding possible diagnoses one after the next as either highly unlikely or so obvious Bell would have already considered it himself. "To speak true, Dr. Bell—"

Bell shrugged. "You see, I am at a loss. I even fear bleeding him in his present state. The practice does little good in any case, and I am afraid I might make his condition worse for the tampering with him. I can scarce manage a sip of elderberry tea down his throat. He coughs it up and cannot catch his breath. Oh yes, the delirium. His wife says it is the drink, but I cannot say for certain."

Few physicians would be so circumspect as to balk at bloodletting. Gaelan was impressed. "You made no mention of digestive—"

"None I've observed."

"Sweating. Not simply the expulsion of fever, as might be expected, but so extreme—"

"Yes! Yes, so profuse his bedclothes were sodden. I have not considered it as a symptom so much as an effect of the fever—"

Gaelan dismissed a niggling in the periphery of his mind. A most improbable idea. Yet, it fit this particular set of symptoms. He thrust the notion aside, but it buzzed about his head, in his ear like a troublesome gnat.

No, not improbable. Impossible.

"The disease, Dr. Bell, sounds like nothing I've encountered personally; however, I've a notion about the symptoms you describe. I would ask that you return later today, after I've had the opportunity to think upon it."

"Well, then, what is it? Time is of the essence. By afternoon, it may indeed be too late."

Yes, Bell was right. Perhaps it already was. "I quite understand, and your patient may be beyond helping at this late . . . You must forgive my reluctance, but if it is what I think . . ." He could not further travel this path with Bell. Not until he was certain.

"If you've a notion, I insist you say it!"

"Still. If I am wrong, we will have wasted . . . You see, what I am thinking . . . it is quite obscure and . . ." Gaelan needed more clues to summarily dismiss this prickling feeling, move on to a more conventional diagnosis. "Let me ask you this. You've not mentioned a rash—"

"Dear Lord. I nearly forgot. He developed a rash soon after the sweating began. I'd forgotten to mention. Forgive me, but I have been up all this night."

"Indeed. And the husband is the only one thus far to—"

"Yes. It has not spread. It seems not necessarily contagious."

Gaelan nodded. "The wife, children, servants—any of them? No matter how mild the symptoms? Complaint of a mild headache? The rash? Especially that."

"Not any of which I'm aware. The symptoms are an odd mix, are they not? Of course, I am worried for his wife. Their three children have been sent off to the country."

One in a family falls ill, then the rest. Little to do but listen, observe, and measure against one's own base of knowledge of ailments and treatments, medicines and procedures. Leaches and bleeding, laudanum, the standard fare, and pray the patient made it through the night. Few practitioners possessed the imagination to do more. "Dr. Bell, please. If you allow me to spend some few hours at least thinking upon it, say, until two this afternoon. Perhaps, by then—"

" . . . my patient will be gone. Is there nothing—?"

"I am no magician, sir. And it is not in my nature to offer elixirs of false hope. I can, however, send you off with a tonic. Something of my own invention. It will mitigate the worst effects of the sweating, if nothing else. It will assure that the loss of fluids from the body will not rob his physiology of essential elements. Give me but a moment and I shall prepare a bottle for you."

"Essential elements? Whatever do you mean?"

Gaelan had no desire to elaborate, only to have the idea discarded as fakery and fraud. "Only know, sir, it works. That it will prevent him from growing yet weaker than he is already. A simple combination of certain salt compounds, a bit of vinegar and molasses to make it more palatable, all dissolved in fresh water."

Gaelan removed a large amber bottle from a cabinet behind the counter, filling it with water and powders from several small bottles. When he turned around Bell was scrutinizing Gaelan's inlaid chess table. "This should help, at least. Until mid-afternoon, then?"

"This is quite a remarkable board. Ebony?"

"Agate and onyx. It is quite old." Gaelan was inexplicably drawn to the young physician. Was it the resemblance to Benjamin? That, and the fact Bell did not appear to sneer, *a priori*, at the apothecary's craft. "Do you play?"

"What? Not . . . I really must be going—"

"No, not *now*, of course. There are far more urgent matters at hand, for us both, I daresay. I do like a good game; I seem to think best with my mind occupied by chess. Oftentimes, in my experience, the answer to the most perplexing question presents itself in the guise of a clever move. My own, or an opponent's."

"I do play, and quite well."

"Perhaps once this crisis of yours has passed—"

"Indeed, I would like that quite a lot."

"Go then, and I shall think upon the illness and pray stumble upon . . . something. For this affliction seems a feral thing, and should it spread . . ."

"Until two o'clock, then." Bell gathered up his belongings and tonic and took his leave with a slight bow.

Gaelan's first priority was to mix more of the salts tonic, especially with no other treatment at hand. He did not completely understand the mechanism whereby it worked, but work it did, and far better than water alone. A discovery he'd fallen upon quite by accident some years earlier.

A chance draught from his freshwater barrel after a hard ride on a blazing hot July day revived Gaelan much more swiftly than expected. The water possessed a strange taste, and he noticed only later the spilled tin of potassium chloride salts beside the barrel. Perhaps some of it had gotten into the water, explaining the odd taste. But what of its reviving properties?

Curious, Gaelan searched through the ouroboros book. True wizardry in the skilled hands of his father. But he was not his father. Would he somehow manage to find the secret of the salt water somewhere within its strange illuminations?

An obscure reference to several chemical compounds—salts— and their relationship to physiology, tucked away beneath the tentacles of an octopus that blazed in metallic hues of orange and red, taking up an entire corner of a page on treating fevers. He'd stared at the page for hours, until, with a flash of clarity, he understood.

Symbols hidden within its tentacles pointed the way to the bottom of the image, a deep, almost black-blue sea bed, which spewed forth sprays possessed of a phosphorescent glow amidst easily identifiable alchemical elemental symbols for sodium, potassium, and magnesium. Enough to guide Gaelan's hand in creating his remarkably effective reviving tonic.

To use the ouroboros book was always to play with wildfire. As Gaelan knew too well. Yes, he would consult it to help make sense of one of his own discoveries, but only that. Yet, to follow even one of its healing recipes equipped with only his limited knowledge and experience would always risk consequences far beyond the realm of anyone's control.

The symptoms of Bell's patient were unique in his experience but fit too well an ancient pattern he could not quite dismiss. But would he once again need to dive within the treacherous waters of the ouroboros book to quench the fires of this deadly illness? Or was Bell overreacting? That was the question.

CHICAGO, PRESENT DAY

CHAPTER 15

The sharp edges of a migraine, fringed in a frustrating rainbow of auras, invaded Anne's already fitful sleep, waking her to a groggy blur that would soon enough blossom into a full-blown throbbing if she didn't get to her meds ASAP. Digging her thumbs hard into her forehead, she hoped to delay it at least until she found her bag, which was hopefully up in the bedroom, twenty-five long, head-lacerating steps up.

She stretched, nearly tumbling from Simon's drawing room sofa. Dragging herself to an upright position, she realized she'd never removed her shoes. Or turned off the reading lamp before conking out sometime late last night.

Pinching the bridge of her nose, Anne failed to will away the tightening vise circling her head. Gaelan's karyotype images were scattered everywhere: the floor, the coffee table, the sofa. Her bag was hiding out beneath an empty folder. She dove for it, if a bit too quickly, retrieving the small pharmacy bottle. Choking back the two small pills dry, she switched off the lamp, closed her eyes, and waited for the medical magic to kick in.

The disconcerting creaks and pops of an old house settling were hardly restful, and she needed to fall back asleep. Knew it was not to be, despite the drugs.

Perhaps a stroll in the pre-dawn air—a quiet sit-down among flowerbeds. Allow the quiet murmur of Lake Michigan's lapping waves to loosen the tension.

The garden air was thick with dew, the grass damp and cooling. In the distance, the splash of water licked the rocks far below her. As her eyes adjusted, Anne found her way to the edge of the promontory and leaned against the wall.

Soon the sun would creep over the horizon. Eyes closed, she drew breath from the sounds of dawn, the sensation of a cool breeze on her face as it wisped through the garden and down the ravine. The agitated cackling of a large seabird struggling with a catch perhaps a bit too lively for its ability.

What creatures dwelled in such a freshwater sea as this? Did Americans have their own monsters of the loch? A Great Lakes Morag? A North American Nessie? A freshwater Silkie?

Now *there* was a tragic tale to fit her mood. A seduction gone all wrong. Lesson: never fall for a supernatural being. And Anne would include in that group immortal apothecaries.

But Gaelan wasn't supernatural. Hyper-natural, perhaps, but he was quite human, enhanced in a way science hadn't quite figured out. Yet.

Was that what Gaelan was working on behind that locked door? Trying to understand the genetic mutation that had altered his telomeres such that they never degraded, rendering him essentially immortal?

Gold streaks slithered across the mirror-smooth surface of the water as the first rays of sun bled over the divide between sky and the vastness of Lake Michigan. An unfolding magical display of light as it reflected off the low morning clouds and refracted into every hue, painting them orange, red, purple, magenta, and colors she could not even begin to identify.

By the time the sky lightened to cornflower blue and the clouds began to burn off, her migraine had faded to a dull memory. She returned to the house much improved, greeted by the strong, nutty aroma of fresh coffee, and Mrs. O'Malley.

"Good morning, Dr. Shawe. I didn't expect you to be such an early riser. I hope you slept well."

"Late night. Bit of a headache earlier—"

"Going to be a scorcher today, dear. Upwards of ninety, they say. I'll make sure the air conditioning is set. Oh. There's a package for you. It was sitting on the front step. A bit early for FedEx, but perhaps it came late last night. I left it on the foyer table."

"Thank you."

"I've got good old-fashioned Irish oats in the cupboard, if you fancy."

She was famished. "That would be amazing. Brown sugar?"

"Of course. Twenty minutes?"

Perfect. Enough time for a quick shower.

The cool marble of the shower stall contrasted with the hot water, coursing hard as needles on her neck, her back. She was content to stand in the stream, eyes closed, relishing the loosening of knots from her shoulders, from . . . everywhere. She breathed out, imagining all her cares washing down the drain at her feet.

She'd had such high hopes that this trip back to the States to sort Simon's affairs would be a respite from the past months: blowing the whistle on Transdiff's despicable actions; coming to the realization that Paul Gilles, her now *ex*-fiancé, was the most venal of men; losing a coveted research post at Salk.

Add to all that the real stunner about Gaelan Erceldoune. His genetics. The book. Her book . . . *his* book, not that it mattered anymore. The impossible ancient tome of healing and its complete understanding of modern pharmacology. Of genetics. Of medicine. Their familial tie—and the elemental bond between them she'd perceived tying them together heart and soul and mind.

That bloody book. She sighed, shivering as the water grew lukewarm, then cold.

Fairies, indeed! Yeah, life needed a good rethink.

Wrapping herself in an enormous, thick towel, Anne stepped onto a small rug, refreshed and clearer. Yesterday's clothing would do her no good. Cigarette smoke from Gaelan's flat clung to them with a vengeance. Wrinkling her nose, she tossed them in a laundry bin and selected a fresh set.

The sweet, rich aroma of caramelized bananas and hot porridge greeted her as she descended the grand staircase. Perfection.

"My dear Mrs. O'Malley! That smells amazing!"

"I had some overripe bananas; I hope you don't mind."

"Not a bit. I'm starved! Erm . . . I've a question. You are planning to leave the service of this household, yes? And soon?"

"Yes . . . as I explained."

"Of course. Is there a chance you might delay it, at least for a bit? I have no skills about the house. I can't cook, and I cannot begin to imagine keeping tidy even a small flat, let alone an enormous house like this one . . . I understand if you—"

Mrs. O'Malley joined Anne at the table, wiping her hands on her apron. "At the same salary? I don't mean to be pushy, but Dr. Bell paid me quite well, you know."

"I would gladly match your salary, if you would give me, say, a month? Six weeks tops. By then, I should be on my way back home to the UK."

Mrs. O'Malley nodded. "Six weeks it is. But I think—"

"Fabulous. And by the way, I know for all these years you have come back and forth each day to work. Simon . . . Dr. Bell was quite jealous of his privacy, I am certain. I am much less so and would appreciate the company of having you stay here. Lord knows there are enough bedrooms to house three families at least, so—"

"Very well. You have a bargain. To be honest, I've always loved this house. And my apartment is a lonely place since my Henry died last year."

Anne extended her hand. "I'm so sorry. I didn't know. He was . . ."

" . . . my dog. A beautiful red border collie. Fifteen years old."

"Ah . . . well, then. Let neither one of us be alone for now."

"You'd best eat it before it gets cold, you know."

One taste of the porridge, the sweet crunch of the burnt bananas, and Anne realized exactly how starved she was.

"Oh, Dr. Shawe, don't forget about the package." Mrs. O'Malley placed the package on the table between them before leaving the room.

No return address. Likely more papers from Bell's solicitor.

Inside, a large sheaf of papers banded together in brass clips. And a note.

Dear Dr. Shawe,

I don't blame you for running away last night. I suppose I would have too. My reputation certainly precedes me, but not all things reported on the "Interwebs," as I'm sure you're aware, are true. Whatever you may think of me, despite the grains of truth, my aims are and always have been to find a way to help my young daughter live out a normal, full life. I lost my wife to a rare genetic disorder five years ago. GPC—guanipravis congenita. I'm pretty sure you've heard of it. My wife was forty-six. My eight-year-old daughter—her name is Erin—suffers from the same disease, diagnosed after my wife's death.

I ask only that you read her attached medical records, and the academic papers I've also included. I have, literally, unlimited funds, and I would gladly spend every penny of them to find a cure and spare my daughter from this terrible disease. If others benefit, great, but not really my concern. All I ask is that you keep an open mind; forgive my aggressive behavior. I promise I was not stalking you. You have a reputation as a compassionate person and brilliant researcher in the field of telomeres. That's all I needed to know. You have my number, so it's your move. I await your call.

—P.A.

Yeah. A serious rethink!

Guanipravis congenita. GPC. A horror for its victims; sometimes the symptoms didn't present until early midlife—after there were children, and a new generation left to inherit it. Anne took a deep breath and sank into the soft cushions of Simon's sofa, Erin Alcott's three-inch-thick medical file open on her lap.

Mother of patient developed pulmonary fibrosis at age forty-three. Patient exhibited no other characteristic signs at the time. Within one year, new symptoms presented, increasing in severity and at a rapid pace, including bone marrow failure, suppression of red and white blood cells and platelets, and death. Progress of disease from first diagnosis to death—three years. No mutations at any of the signature genes for the disease were identified in multiple genomic assays. However, chromosomal studies revealed extreme telomeric shortening in a high percentage of the samples examined.

Patient's father did not recall other potential GPC sufferers in her family, although he did report that the maternal grandmother had a history of breathing problems and skin anomalies. Death in the grandmother occurred at an early age (mid-30s).

Damn. Anne would have to be heartless—and violating her medical oaths—to dismiss a priori a distressed father's pleas. She didn't need to read any more to know for certain that Erin Alcott had inherited her mother's condition.

There was no treatment, full stop. Not enough was yet known about the disease origins to do much about it but treat the symptoms, and if you believed in God, pray.

What else might she add that other, more prominent, physicians hadn't already tried? There were jacket notes from the National Institutes of Health Rare Disease Center, so they'd gone the best route, the best clinicians, the best research available. She'd spent a career studying jellyfish, not doing clinical trials and experimental protocols for telomere deficiency diseases.

Setting aside the folders, Anne glanced at her watch. Gaelan's friend at Northwestern should be in her lab by now. The brief time she'd known him, she imagined Gaelan reclusive, studiously avoiding anything beyond the simple pleasantries of business. She had a hard time thinking of Gaelan having any social relationships.

Stopping at the fridge on the way out to the garden, Anne grabbed a water bottle. At the back of the shelf, sat the Styrofoam box with the blood sample Gaelan had given her that last night in Simon's drawing room before . . .

A universe of his molecular secrets sealed in a Vacutainer—Gaelan's parting gift. That and the labyrinth necklace. The blood sample, particularly the double helix of Gaelan's immortal DNA, was much more valuable, and for her, far more interesting.

Infinite tissue regeneration. Perhaps Gaelan's remarkably stable telomeres could unlock the elusive cure for Erin Alcott's disease—if. So many "ifs."

A cloudless day greeted Anne as she walked the garden; the lake had once again transformed, now a shimmering turquoise against a deep blue horizon. No sign of an oncoming storm—a perfect day to sit outside. An aromatherapy intensive at its most natural, no diffusers needed.

She punched in the number for Gaelan's friend, Dr. Dana Spangler. A female voice answered.

"Dr. Spangler, please."

"You've got her." A young voice. *Oh, great!* Anne meant to Google her first. "Only got a couple minutes. Finals week. Gotta babysit a roomful of undergrads in ten. Lab final."

"My name is Dr. Anne Shawe—"

"Why do I know that name?"

Anne hoped it wasn't her connection to Transdiff.

"I've got it. Telomere research! Dr. Anne Shawe. Cambridge. I think we met at a conference a few years ago. Calais?"

Calais. Yes. She'd given a paper. She was ashamed to admit she'd no recognition of a Dr. Dana Spangler. "Yes. I was there. Three years ago?"

"Yeah. I was still an indentured slave . . . I mean . . . grad student. I have now vaulted all the way to postdoc. Not much of an upgrade in salary, but more prestige, I suppose. I still spend eighteen hours a day in the lab."

Anne remembered those days all too well. "Listen, Dr. Spangler. Can we meet sometime over the next few days? I don't want to keep you now, but I believe we have a common acquaintance. Mr. Gaelan Erceldoune?"

"Gaelan. You've heard, right?"

Heard what, precisely?

"Really sad. We all loved him. Hard to believe he's dead. His shop was the best place in Evanston to get a cup of tea or . . . whatever. Brilliant mind—in everything. The real deal, you know. Look, I'm late now. Can you stop by tomorrow, say twelve-thirty? I should have the afternoon free. Find me at Califax. Evanston campus, not downtown."

"Right. See you then." *Where the bloody hell was Califax? No matter; the gods of GPS would guide her.*

Two bright orange birds with black wings fought over a worm, squawking angrily until it tore apart, and they each flew off, disappearing to their own corners of the garden, each victorious. Pure instinct, no rumination required. If only life for mere humans were that basic.

The rest of the day was free to have a go at Simon's papers. Why had he not left it all to his solicitors to take care of? His literary agents and managers? Why her? Because she knew his secret? What difference would that make now he was dead?

The mobile's ringtone interrupted her ruminations.

The caller didn't wait for a greeting. "Dr. Anne Shawe?"

An unfamiliar voice. "Yes?"

"My name is John Fry. I am with the Evanston Lakeshore BIT."

"BI . . . what? I don't—"

"Biohazard Investigation Team. We have a question or two we'd like to ask regarding several missing tissue samples."

Ah. Andrew Samuelson's warning.

"Missing samples? I—"

"You did a consult last month on a trauma patient . . . a John Doe brought into the ER. Big deal case with some more-than-usual weirdness. Weirdest of all in some quarters, a few of the leftovers from his surgery disappeared from the biohazard disposal cabinet."

"That was weeks ago. And you're just now getting round to it?"

"Oh, we've been investigating since then, just got around to you. We know you weren't directly involved in handling them, but we've had nothing but dead ends. So, can't hurt to check if you might know something, right?"

Surgical waste was a big deal only when infectious. Maybe when a crime was involved. Or . . . perhaps when the case was strange enough to . . . "I'm sorry, I don't know anything about missing biohazardous anything. I returned to the UK very shortly after the consult. I've been back home ever . . ." She'd better be totally honest. These days, it was easy enough to check. "I've only just returned to the States for a brief stay."

"Why is that?"

"Beg your pardon?"

"Why you returned."

"I don't see as that's really any of your business, to be perfectly honest. I have no clue about missing tissue or any other surgical waste. And I'm really terribly busy. You'd be better off to check with people at your own facility."

She clicked off, annoyed at the intrusion. It wasn't her fault they couldn't bloody keep up with proper records keeping! If that's what it was. If it was not . . . yet more reason to stay as far away as possible.

Preston Alcott and his daughter nudged at the edges of Anne's thoughts. She couldn't shake them off. Was he one of those poor, gullible souls who bought into every miracle cure offered up by online frauds with empty promises and phony science? A grasper at futile straws?

Didn't much matter that he was a bioengineer, a hugely successful businessman. He possessed all the traits of an easy mark for medical sharks. How many fool's errands had he already chased down, for his daughter, his wife before that?

A decision made. She would agree to examine Alcott's daughter. Once. And, if at all possible, help her. But it was the most unlikely of "ifs."

Apprehension shimmied up her spine as she touched his number on her phone. Three rings. She should hang up. Now.

"Dr. Shawe, I'm so glad you called. You don't know how grateful I am. I was sure I'd never hear from you—"

"GPC is a death sentence." She'd not meant to be quite so blunt. "But I will see her. Understand, I can't promise a thing. Everything her doctors have done has been exactly as I would have—"

"I'll bring her to you," Alcott insisted gratefully. "I can be there by tomorrow afternoon. A corporate jet has its benefits. And I do understand this is a 'Hail Mary,' and, believe me, I also get your skepticism about the disease, me—"

"I have no office, no examining room. I've no privileges at any hospital. No work visa—"

"Done. Taken care of. As soon as we're off the phone. Major alumni donors can sometimes work, at least, nonmedical magic."

"*If* all that can be worked out, I'd rather speak with her physicians first—before I see her. So it could be days . . . there's no rush to get on a plane just yet—"

"There *are* no other physicians. I've fired every last one of them. They haven't done a damn thing but waste my money on nonsense. Fuckin' snake oil. I'm sure I can get you everything you need. State-of-the-art equipment, credentials, the works. I have plenty of connections at Northwestern. My alma mater, right? That good enough for you?"

Anne sighed. Alcott sounded . . . different. The brashness was gone, replaced by a desperation she well understood. An earnestness borne of hope. A flimsy, likely fruitless, hope. A father of a sick child with no future. She tried to ignore her unease that there was more at play here than a little girl and a genetic disease. And the fear this would all spin out of her control.

SCOTTISH BORDERS, PRESENT DAY

CHAPTER 16

Shadows crept the catacomb walls as Gaelan made his way through the narrow corridor. The last vestiges of lantern light faded and extinguished. And that damnable tinkling again. *Where the fuck was it coming from?* Burrowing into his head, it had become a discordant concerto, disorienting and setting the darkness to relentlessly spin around and through him.

With one hand, he held close to the greasy, slick walls to keep his balance; in his other, the useless lantern and the glass teardrop. In the far distance, the glow of the sconces he'd lit earlier; he would make it that far.

Just fucking keep moving. Find the damn wind chimes and smash them to bits. The broader question of "what next?" could wait.

Gaelan followed the sound further and further into the cave network, finally reaching a chamber distant from the stairway. The strident grating grew more deafening the nearer he drew to the chamber, the sound transforming by the second: a wail, a shriek, the roar of a million panes of glass crashing in upon themselves over and over and over again.

The flame of a candle he'd snatched from the wall wavered and danced from the vibration, finally snuffing out as he entered the room. Stumbling in the complete darkness, confused and drowning in the chaos of the wind chimes, Gaelan collapsed to the ground, grateful as the noise evaporated along with all thought.

A female voice echoed through his sleep, deep from within a nightmare. Fragments of hideous monsters dissolved before him, camouflaged in a relentless gray fog. Their eyes stared vivid, dark and hollow. Blank. But human—and alive. The vision faded and the voice grew urgent as it threaded through Gaelan's semiconsciousness, adding to his confusion in the nexus between sleep and wakefulness.

"Come! Quick, before the Burkie-boys find us. You're not one of them, are you? Nah, don't look the part." A young woman, long hair pulled back in a braid and dressed in a gray metallic tunic, materialized, looming above him where he lay on the ground, hands on her hips. Her gunmetal tunic rippled as she impatiently tapped her foot.

Gaelan sat up, his head still spinning. "Who the bloody hell are . . .?"

She either was not listening or chose not to answer as she extended him a hand. He did not recall falling. The chamber, yes. The infernal chiming . . .

But this place was not . . . And the discordant clanking . . . gone. Dreams within dreams within dreams, swallowing him alive like a vortex.

"We have to be quick! Let's go!"

Gaelan dusted a powdery substance from his jacket and trousers as he stood unsteadily. The chamber had vanished, and he sensed he was somehow outdoors, yet all seemed strangely nebulous, like a black-and-white movie, dulled and streaked by age. A gloomy landscape suspended in the cool, dense air. Even the girl blended in, colorless but for the pink of her hands, the olive cast of her cheeks.

The glass piece, still clutched in Gaelan's hand, glittered, sputtering as if wakening to life, emitting a dim, almost ghostly, glow in the amorphous achromicity of their surroundings. Just what the fuck was this—act two, scene one?

"I was dreaming," he said finally, not really expecting a satisfactory answer. "How did I get—?"

"No time! We need to get inside. Now."

Gaelan followed her through the fog until they reached the

middle of a cul-de-sac. He was ankle-deep in a soft gray-white powder, which resembled more than anything else pulverized sand. It spun up miniature eddies with each step, his footfalls silent, absorbed by the substance. It burned his eyes and nostrils, the acrid sting familiar as its odor. Gaelan turned to ask the woman about it. But she'd vanished.

In the distance, the shadows of towering buildings loomed dark against a clay sky, blending into it, their rooftops disappearing into the fog. Crouching, Gaelan scooped up a handful of the powder, observing as it drifted through his fingers and floated to the ground, fine, like cornstarch, like the diatomaceous sand of a Caribbean beach.

To his right, a low range of hills spread against the near horizon, gray, of course, like the finish of a silver automobile dulled by time and neglect. A rhythmic pulse cut through the silence nearby, like the gentle lapping of tide against a breakwater, but erratic, randomly fading entirely until it returned, resuming its cadence.

Shadows scurried past in the periphery of Gaelan's vision, wraiths, dark and huddled. Silent—like everything else here—keeping their distance, watching, listening. The monsters of his dream, returned.

A whisper near his ear and Gaelan jumped, startled. The girl had come back.

"Do not trouble yourself with trivialities—it will only make your brain hurt. Now if you're finished exposing us both out here, please, follow me!" She reached for his hand.

A strange quality to it, corporeal, like the empty space where the fingers of his left hand had been severed by Handley's knife. Phantoms to fill in the emptiness. Soft, but too soft. Not quite gelatinous, not liquid, not solid.

His hand slipped from hers as they ran. And ran. Gaelan could barely keep apace as she called back toward him to hurry, her voice a garbled blur as she accelerated, until she seemed almost in flight, too far ahead, until she disappeared from view.

"We can rest here for a moment. I don't think anyone's—" She was waiting for him to catch up.

"That skyline . . . something about it—"

"Skyline?"

"Yeah. Back there, I saw it in the distance . . . perpendicular to those hills." Gaelan swept his arm in the general direction.

"Hills? Ah . . . the hills. Our fortress walls. Cool, huh? The magic of light and imaging. Hard times for people . . . like us. Gotta use what we can to protect ourselves on our little island, you know—"

Gaelan struggled to understand. "Like *you*? What are you talking about?" Mirrors within mirrors within mirrors.

He searched his memory back to Chicago, to the poison he'd created. Had it contained a hallucinogen? He did not recall one among the ingredients he'd added. Yet, it was possible in the mixing . . . a chemical reaction . . . If so, this was one fucking train wreck of a trip.

The girl had disappeared again. Perhaps he only couldn't see her for the powdery mist. Gaelan called out. "Hello? Where am I?" *Heaven, hell, purgatory? Or some sort of existential nothingness?* Or something entirely "other"?

Just ahead, the sound of water again, closer now; he turned toward it, curious.

"Not that way. In here."

Ah, there she is. They now stood inches from the base of a gray hill. The young woman craned her neck in all directions before placing her right hand flat on the surface. Silently, the hill slid open and a light from within beckoned them to enter.

"Never mind all that nonsense. Through here and be quick. If you're the one, we'll find out right away. If not . . ."

"The one . . . *What*?"

"Come on. You're nearly—"

Gaelan stood his ground, refusing to follow. He had too many questions to follow this woman—anyone—blindly. Hallucination or not. "No. If not . . . what, exactly? Who do you think I am? I'm not going in anywhere until I—"

He was just so bloody tired. He could not manage another step; every bit of his strength bled away into the amorphous gray. He sat in the dust as large, dry flakes fell all about him, like lake effect snow, but not cold. Or wet. It gathered in his hair, on his shoulders. Perhaps he should simply stay put, wait for the dust or ash or dirt, or whatever the hell it was, to bury him alive. Gaelan's eyes slipped shut as he gave into the silence.

Gaelan woke lying on his back; no longer outdoors, no longer covered in a strange powdery sand. The wind chimes had recommenced, no longer a dissonant noise, but pleasing, a plaintive harmony.

He blinked, gaze drifting up toward the ceiling as his eyes adjusted to the semidark. This place he knew.

The Quhawme Brethren of Dernwode House had constructed for their monastery a room of great arched lead glass windows reaching through the forest canopy and high above the grounds. From the ceiling they'd suspended a series of prisms—a pattern designed to maximize the effect of the small amount of natural daylight in their hidden location. The seòmar-criostalan—the room of crystals.

Every afternoon the sun would pour through the windows, painting the walls in refracted hues. Every color of the spectrum, reflecting off the glass and onto every surface. A lavish feast of color and light, a demonstration of nature's power. The brethren insisted it was God; the young Gaelan knew such a splendid God would never take from him his entire family. He'd not changed his opinion, not even hundreds of years later.

Gaelan spent many hours waiting in the middle of the room, speculating upon the exact moment when the sun was at the proper trajectory, week by week, season upon season. How to make sense of the ever-changing facade of color—paintings not painted with anything but light and glass.

Then the moment would come, and the glass would transform the room as if by magic. Majestic magic borne of physics, by mathematics, by the ingenuity of the monks, so far ahead of their time in so many ways.

"Already we are hidden in the hills, Master Gaelan," Brother Hugh explained so long ago, "and direct sunlight is a rare privilege. One day, we may be forced to hide yet further from the sight of those who do not understand our ways, who seek to destroy us. Perhaps survival will require retreating below ground, where creating such an approximation of daylight will be yet more crucial."

And so they had. Transplanted the seòmar-criostalan to the cellarium.

"It will never be adequate to grow our herbs and food—except those that do not require light," Brother Hugh said. "But a garden is a garden, and they are difficult to squelch, and especially one as hidden as ours. Ours will grow long past the time we are all gone from this Earth." Had that, too, survived the long centuries somewhere among the brush and rocks of the ruins?

Or was this another hallucination? Dream? Or the simple haze of memory from a distant time past? Gaelan stood, steadying himself with a hand upon the wall. Reaching up, he plucked a small prism from the ceiling, running his hand along its jagged edge, slicing his index finger, cherishing the pain.

The skin peeled away, and he observed as the blood flowed freely from the wound, pooling in the cup of his hand. Real enough, but perhaps more unsettling than if all this were an elaborate nightmare. He did not wait for the gash it to repair itself, as he knew it would. A piece torn from his shirt would do for a bandage.

The black walls suited the prisms, rendered the refracted color more intense as they arced off the glossy basalt. The orange and yellow at the base of each refraction—miniature rainbows—bathed the chamber in soft light. Where was its source?

The teardrop! As the prisms glittered, drawing light, life, from each other, the opalescent glass piece, which now sat on the floor beside Gaelan's foot, glowed, radiating up and around itself, caught by the prisms.

An idea burrowed through the chaos of Gaelan's mind. He raised the drop, directing it toward the central prism; the light intensified, illuminating the entire room, bathing it in a damn good simulation of daylight.

"The glass object is a key to a portal," Conan Doyle wrote in his journal. If Gaelan had, indeed, traversed this so-called portal, it had been into quite a desolate place, as distant from Conan Doyle's magical mystery world of fairies and their domain as heaven was from hell.

To my sceptical friend, Conan Doyle long ago inscribed to Gaelan in a first edition Holmes. *Someday you shall know me to have spoken true; mark here my words. I know a secret far greater than your own, my friend.*

He'd signed it, *For strange effects and extraordinary combinations we must go to life itself, which is always far more daring than any effort of the imagination.*

Was that what Gaelan had experienced? The strangeness of a world beyond their own? Conan Doyle's world of fairies?

What utter nonsense! Whatever Conan Doyle had seen, it had been only of his own making, his own peculiar imagination. Perhaps senility had reduced him to a shadow of his former self, holed up in a deluded world of fairies hidden beneath a godforsaken Borders valley. Gaelan's own experience best explained as *folie à deux* as he was sucked into the delusion.

Gaelan shuffled through Conan Doyle's journal to the end.

I understand how difficult it must be for you, my dear reader, to embrace a truth I have known all my adult life. I know now that I am not a doddering old fool believing in fairy stories and crowing about some fanciful Otherworld for all to deride me. No. I know it is true.

Indeed, as I have seen, and you shall, if you but look beyond the expected. The likely. The probable, and into the Otherworld I have now known. I have proof at last that there exists amongst us an entire world in parallel to our own. It is

*there for our reaching. Call them fairies or by some other name
if you must, but they exist.*

*I have written the following words before, but only in dis-
tance of faint possibility. I see them now as more prescient than I
might have imagined when first I set pen to paper, and perhaps
they will be useful now to restate: 'We see objects within the
limits which make up our colour spectrum, with infinite vibrations, unused by us, on either side of them. If we could conceive
a race of beings which were constructed in material which threw
out shorter or longer vibrations, they would be invisible unless
we could tune ourselves up or tone them down. It is exactly that
power of tuning up and adapting itself to other vibrations which
constitutes a clairvoyant, and there is nothing scientifically
impossible, so far as I can see, in some people seeing that which is
invisible to others.'*

*The answer lies in these very ancient catacombs, in its pecu-
liar prism chamber, in the patterns that govern all things in the
universe—theirs and ours. It is mathematics; it is cosmology; it
is biology and chemistry. All are governed by it, and through
this universal truth it is possible to experience the seemingly
impossible. The utterly unknowable to those not adept at this
sort of perception. Not exactly as I envisioned in my seminal
work on the fairies, but not far as you might find them not useful
in your pursuit.*

Gaelan had always been able to perceive beyond the ordinary.
He'd learned the skill at an early age, and hundreds of years later, it
had rescued him more than once. Perhaps it would again. Beyond his
own, he'd saved lives countless more times. As he had a century ago.
In London.

LONDON, 1826

CHAPTER 17

*S*udor *anglicus*—the English sweating sickness—had vanished from Britain's shores some thirty years before Gaelan was born. It murdered indiscriminately: the rich, the impoverished, slinking away as mysteriously as it began, as if by some magic incantation, never to return to these lands. Yet Gaelan could not wrest from his mind the similarities between Simon's patient and those described in his grandfather's notes on the illness, uncrated and placed on the shelf only a day earlier.

Perhaps it was nothing more than mere coincidence, a theory conjured from too-convenient clues. For were the notes not now fresh in Gaelan's memory, would he make the connection at all?

The morning was proving mercifully quieter than Gaelan had anticipated as he considered Bell's patient. He stepped into the dusty boisterousness of the street, having forgotten for the moment he was no longer in the tranquility of Hay Hill. That he would not be breathing in lavender and chrysanthemum wafting over from the park, easing his mind to birdsong.

Instead, his senses were bombarded by the stink of offal and dung, blood mingled with sawdust. The discordant symphony of cackling chickens, grunting pigs, and agitated cows and sheep herded tight into their pens blurred the mumbled "Good morrows" to mime.

Bell would be right to think him mad even to suggest *sudor anglicus*. There was too much else, known and unknown, that could be the cause. And it was but one patient. Yes, an overreaction fueled by

Gaelan's too-lively imagination and his grandfather's papers. *Cholera?* No. There had been no intestinal distress. Or an influenza.

What if it was Bell overreacting to a simple fever—a cold. After all, what did Gaelan know of the man's skills, beside the familial connection to Benjamin? Most likely the salt tonic would prove satisfactory, and Bell would return shortly with good news about his patient's recovery. Or not return at all. Yet . . . those symptoms continued to gnaw at his curiosity.

The door swung open and in rushed a harried woman, startling Gaelan from his ruminations. Slim as a reed she was, but even after only a few days, he knew this one was a force of nature unto herself, and no one to be trifled with. He'd witnessed her resolute gaze and unbending stance as she dealt with the other market purveyors. She was tough as any man in Smithfield.

"Good morrow, Mrs. Faust, in what might I interest you this fine day?"

"Good morrow to you, Mr. Erceldoune. Have you any rose water today? I've used my last dregs, and as you know, I find a bit dabbed in front of the ear masks the ripe odors of the market stalls—"

"Indeed, I've several varieties, brewed myself. A moment, if you please."

Gaelan returned from his workroom with a small cobalt blue bottle decorated in white enamel. "This is Damask water. Quite pleasant. From Damask roses. The oils are especially potent in this brew and should serve the purpose well, I think." He had sold barrels of it to the ladies of Hay Hill. An endorsement unlikely to impress Mrs. Faust.

"It looks quite dear, and I've only—"

"Never mind all that; I'll not accept from you a farthing. I've a greater need just now. If you would, Mrs. Faust, put aside for me a nice fat hen from your stall, and deliver it to Mrs. Mills for cooking into a stew. I would consider it an honor to give this to you in a more than fair trade."

It had not gone well for the lady. Her husband shot dead by a highwayman, she had become both proprietress and mother to their small children—a difficult life, and she could ill afford the cost of such an extravagance. Hens she had in abundance.

"Thank you, Mr. Erceldoune. Good day to you, sir. And God bless you."

Gaelan bowed slightly and ushered her from the shop, hanging the "closed" sign in the window. He needed peace and solitude to think. Should any have need of his services, he would hear the door quite well from the workroom.

First to check on Cate. Mrs. Mills's stew would make a hearty dinner for her, rich and thickened with beef bone marrow. She was improving quickly, but she was not yet out of danger. A small downturn could plunge her into the direst straits, and with little warning.

She was asleep on the settee when Gaelan entered the flat. She'd eaten the luncheon he'd left for her, drunk the elderberry tea and salt tonic as well. All very good signs. Quietly, he gathered what he required and returned to the shop, settling into his chair, his grandfather's notes on the illness at his side.

The idea had implanted itself too strong to simply ignore, and his fear of its return refused to be shaken loose. Had Gaelan ever *seen* the disease? Of course he had not. His understanding came solely from reading the meticulous and comprehensive accounts of his grandfather from 1528 and 1551—the last known occurrences in Britain. And Grandpapa's correspondence with other practitioners. But had reading them, and within the past day, biased his assessment of the current situation?

Should Gaelan even suggest to Bell they might well be confronting the sweating sickness, he would rightly dismiss anything Gaelan might offer by way of treatment as ridiculous, illegitimate. Perhaps fraudulent! He would be laughed from the Apothecary's Hall for suggesting anything so absurd. Remove from him the Licentiate of the Society of Apothecaries, which granted him his small modicum of legitimacy in the practice of medicine. Place him squarely amongst the street mountebanks with their piss-infused elixirs and cure-all tonics. It would ruin him forever. Yet . . . would he be remiss to discount the idea entirely?

The symptoms and their progress matched Bell's patient. Yet, mightn't they also match the influenza—La Grippe—albeit not any manifestation Gaelan had seen? Was it not, however, a much more likely diagnosis?

And what of the two men Gaelan had treated the day he'd moved to Smithfield? Their symptoms were similar to those of Bell's patient, and he had not considered at all that it might be the sweating sickness. Perhaps Gaelan should not have been so quick to send them on their way with only a jug of the invigorating tonic, an elderberry fever elixir, and promise to visit before the week passed. What if . . . ? He would visit their home as soon as he finished here.

He removed a blank paper from a stationery box and his pen, carefully opening the ink bottle before dipping in the nib to write down his own observations—and Bell's. How well did they match with the account of his grandfather? Gaelan needed to create his own picture of the present illness, its nature.

Devastating as it had been in England, the sweating sickness never reached the Scottish court at Edinburgh. Word spread, his grandfather explained in the journal, that a magical incantation had vanquished the disease. Or it had been divine judgment for the heresies of the English Crown, and the English Crown alone. Superstition before knowledge, he'd said, was the way of the world. No magic but his grandfather's skill alone slayed what he'd called the demon disease, halting it at the border.

Gaelan opened the journal, taking care with its ancient condition. The brittle pages were fragile with age, and the writing, though fine, had faded. A challenge to decipher.

1528, 14th June

There be little way to block this dragon of a disease at the border, and I fear its spread from England across the River Tweed and on to Edinburgh. Yet I feel it is within my powers as a man of science and medicine to fight its onslaught, protecting our sovereign nation and the young king, His Majesty, King of Scots, Seumas V Stiùbhairt. For the king has been in his short life through much all ready. No, I shall not, as the king's physician, allow this fever, which already has devoured much of the English court, even unto King Henry's household, to descend upon Scotland.

The sickness is painful, to the head most especially, and sharp like a knife's blade thrust behind the ear and lancing through to the other side. The pestilent fever sets the flesh ablaze, pouring forth sweat as if to douse it, but to no avail, until blistering the skin in the tenderest of places. But most worrisome be the fetid, corrupt, putrid, and loathsome vapors taking hold close by the heart and the lungs until such time as breathing constricts, which magnifies and increases and restricts of itself further until death take the sufferer.

There be a cure for this in Airmid's great book of healing, gratitude be given unto her and her fae kin, the Tuatha de Danann. For only in this book lay the recipe for the protective medication, which will prevent the disease from flaring unto these shores. I do not rightly know from whence comes their great knowledge, far beyond the ken of this humble man. Or any mortal walks this earth. If this be magic or this be medicine, I cannot tell ye. But only that it doth work to cure the sweate.

Airmid's book. "The ouroboros book," and too far beyond Gaelen's comprehension to wield it as skillfully as his forebears, as he'd learned during the Plague of 1625, when he'd used it to cure himself, only to leave him burdened with this accursed immortality.

Since he'd discovered he did not age, and healed with the rapidity impossible in a mortal man, Gaelan rarely opened the manuscript, except to savor the exquisite illuminations, painted in jeweled inks, nearly alive and of beauty beyond description. He hoped the diagnosis

for Bell's patient would require only consultation with Grandpapa's
notes and nothing more.

*Each symptom, one by one, must be by itself treated if the sick-
ness is not discovered in the first hours. It is the only way. The
sweating, the malign shivering. The breathing—that be the
worst of it. And should each sign be attended and hastily so, the
patient shall mayhap recover. Oftentimes the symptoms present
simultaneous as one, and quick of onset and of swift progress.
Even thus, we must discern them each unto itself as be possible.*

*Yet, it be in the preventative preparation wherein lies the
key to taming this dragon of a disease, which spreads as wildfire,
knowing no distinction neither of station nor standing, afflicting
the nobility as it does the poorest wretch in London town. It is a
tricky thing the preventative potion, for to convince a soul with
no sign of illness to allow the insertion of the medicine through
an incision in the skin is unlikely, nay near impossible. But done
it shall be, and by royal decree if required.*

Gaelan continued reading, forming his own opinions of it, of
Bell's patient, his own. By the time he looked up again, the light had
dimmed, and hours had passed. The day had been as quiet as he'd
hoped, and perhaps this all had been for naught.

His grandfather's account was far from definitive. Yes, the similarities were irrefutable; still, Gaelan doubted it. After all, the sweating
sickness was quite contagious, and but for the two possible cases he'd
seen earlier—and Bell's single patient—where was the expected spread
of it? Would it not already have sickened many more? And the likeli-
hood for it to appear again after centuries . . . ? As for Bell, he'd yet to
return. Perhaps with good reason.

Gaelan stretched, and went out into the day, taking a step into the
busy market.

"Mind your feet, there!"

Gaelan jumped out of the way as two large men ran at a near trot, carrying between them the carcass of what been an enormous hog, nearly knocking him off his feet. No. No sign of illness. The market was as bustling as ever.

"Mr. Erceldoune! I am so sorry. I am hours past when—"

Bell. Finally. "It is of little matter, sir, if your patient is—"

"Recovered! I daresay, remarkable! He was dying; I would swear upon it. But for that tonic you prepared for me. Salts, you say?"

"Please do come in, Dr. Bell." Gaelan ushered him from the street. "Sit awhile. I assure you, the tonic was not intended to cure anything, simply to . . . I am afraid I cannot take credit for simply restoring your patient's bodily harmony, as it were. I confess, I've some success with it, but the mechanism of why it works is quite beyond me. *When* it does, which I am afraid to say is not as often as it fails."

"You are too humble, my dear sir, not to credit yourself—"

"Perhaps my success comes from my reticence in bloodletting. I do not believe in it, nor do I believe it works, and may in fact make matters much worse, despite the common and so-called wisdom of many physicians—"

"Here, here, sir. Do not insult—"

"No, I do not mean you, nor the truly wise amongst physicians, and yet . . ." It was useless to explain. Bell would take any blunt comment as an affront to them all. "I do know, Dr. Bell," Gaelan continued, returning to safer territory, "the tonic revives one who has lost a great of deal of fluid—sweating, diarrhea, vomiting—perhaps, with your patient it was a simple fever, in the end. In any event, I am glad to hear he is much improved—and that you thought enough to report it to me." Gaelan bowed slightly. "And I am deeply grateful. Once again, I apologize for any perceived—"

Bell bowed slightly. "Accepted. And you must be preparing to close for the day. I shall not keep you. As for that chess match, I would quite enjoy the prospect of winning against you. And playing upon that quite magnificent chess table of yours.

"I must say, I would not mind the diversion of a good game, if you've the time now. I've been unpacking crates all week long, and the prospect of a match tempts me—perhaps over a glass of *very* old whisky?"

Even after only a week, Gaelan missed the intellectual challenge of a good game. The goodly folk of Smithfield were much concerned with assuring their families had enough to eat and providing for the most meager needs of their children and wives. Little time for the pleasurable pursuit of a game when survival was forever in doubt.

"I've the time, if you've the whisky—and a set to match that table!"

Gaelan smiled. "That I have. A moment, if you will, and I shall set the board."

A frisson of guilt as Gaelan thought of Cate upstairs, but he'd set a fresh kettle and cakes by her as she slept, so she could take tea when she arose. She'd no need to know Simon Bell was about.

Gaelan brought over a decanter of the spirits from behind the counter with two tumblers. "I've only just uncrated the pieces. They're quite delicate—old. A family heirloom."

One by one, Gaelan withdrew and unwrapped the pieces, setting each in its place.

Simon drummed his fingers on the table, his gaze roving the spare shelves and Spartan appearance of the shop, which contrasted unfavorably, Gaelan knew, with shops in more fashionable parts of London.

"I need no pretense of refinement, Dr. Bell. You see, the people here neither desire nor can afford the sorts of lotions and perfumes the residents of Hay Hill may consider essential. To them a dab of rose water is to stem the stench of a meat market—a practicality here, I am afraid."

"Why *here*?"

Gaelan shook his head. "Why what?"

"Why would you move . . . here, of all places? It is quite the subject of gossip amongst physicians in London. It is said you vanished with nary a word!"

How to explain? Time came for Gaelan to move his shop to a new venue, lest inquiring eyes begin to notice that after ten years, he'd not aged a day. His patrons' faces lined with age and their bellies fattened with realities of too much living, Gaelan was ever frozen at a fit age of eight and thirty. Not young, but never to grow a day older. Never a gray hair would infiltrate the dark auburn of his fine, long hair, no salt and pepper in his beard when he would be too lazy to have a shave. Someone would notice, if they had not already.

"Did you not pay your rent? Slip it away to . . . shall we say . . . more humble quarters? Perhaps it was a lady made you flee." Bell's grin was as broad as it was smug. "Or," Bell whispered, leaning in conspiratorially, "have you fallen in with the resurrection men, who've their headquarters no so far from this very spot, hmm? 'Tis said quite a lucrative trade may be made by a surgeon with a steady hand and a taste for riches."

"Black or red?" Ignoring the interrogation, Gaelan held out his fists toward Bell, who tapped the left hand. "Red it is, then."

"So it shall remain a mystery."

"I suppose it shall. No, I have my reasons, and, I can tell you, naught to do with the goings on at the Man O'War!" Gaelan thought of an answer befitting the cheek of Bell's suggestions. "No, sir, my move has perhaps more to do with the fact that despite the proximity of St. Bartholomew's to this place, few of your colleagues would dirty their gloves beyond its gates, and certainly not in the service of those for whom payment is too dear."

It was as good an explanation as any. Better for the grain of truth to it. Gaelan was curious about Bell's reaction. Would he take it as provocation?

Simon's head bowed. Touché. Perhaps the inquisition would be at an end.

"These chessmen are rather unique. Quite old, you say? Are they bone? I confess I've never seen their like."

"Indeed. Carved walrus tusk . . . I am told. They have been in my family many generations into antiquity."

The board was new; the pieces belonged to his great-grandfather.

Bell hoisted the queen in all her contemplative solemnity, examining her before setting down the piece, laughing. "They are quite comical, do you not think, with their bulging eyes and rotund forms? And the bishop, biting his shield in terror whilst hiding behind it—"

"I do not believe they were intended as comical. But I concede the point. Your move?"

Bell made his first move. Pawn to queen's four. After three more moves, Gaelan could guess Bell's next five, all predictable. Clearly, the physician was not as good a player as he believed himself to be.

Gaelan seldom repeated his own openings, preferring to confound his opponent. Of course, he had two hundred years' experience playing the game, not all with pieces and a board. A strategy of surprise. Ever a contingency plan at the ready.

"Tell me more of your patient, Dr. Bell. Was his revival sudden or over some hours?"

Gaelan moved his queen across the board with great relish. Not so many years ago, Her Highness could move but one square. "Check."

Simon surveyed the board before castling, protecting the king. "Ha! No, it was only after he drank the contents your tonic. What was in it, really? Or is it an apothecary's secret?"

"As I said earlier. Salts: magnesium, sodium, potassium. It's an old formula, learned long ago, and as I told you, I've no idea why or how it works, other than to infuse him with liquid—and salts."

"Still, I would not mind knowing how to prepare it myself."

"Then you would have no reason to consult me—and pay me the exorbitant sums you shall."

"So it shall remain a secret. How much do I owe you for—?"

"This game is payment quite enough. Perhaps you might supply the whisky next time." Gaelan sighed and took Bell's queen. "Checkmate, I believe. Would you mind jotting down your patient's full range of symptoms, onset times, the path and time of his recovery?" He eyed the board, careful to keep his index finger poised atop the knight until Bell felled his king in resignation.

"To what possible end?"

"Curiosity, I suppose. An odd illness crosses my path . . ." He made no mention of the sweating sickness. The point was, at this juncture, irrelevant. Gaelan carefully replaced the pieces on the board. "Another go?"

"I should be off. I shall be meeting several colleagues; supper at the club. Would you care to . . . ?" Bell stopped midthought; his face reddened, as he looked away, his gaze roving everywhere but toward his host.

"Would I care to . . . what?" Gaelan tensed, keenly aware Bell could never finish that sentence without causing great offense.

Bell stammered. "I don't . . . It is not that . . . You see, the club requires . . ."

"I *do* . . . see . . . quite well. I've not the time in any event!"

Bell stood, stopping at a tall built-in bookshelf. He ran his finger along the spines, wide-eyed, removing a large volume from its place, turning to face Gaelan. "May I?"

Gaelan nodded, deciding to let go the slight.

"Is this a first edition Culpeper?"

"Aye, it is at that. Dated 1659, if memory serves." Anticipating the inevitable question, he added, "Found in a dustbin, if you would believe it!" It was a lie, of course; Gaelan acquired it from Nicholas Culpeper himself. "His life might have been . . ." Mine—Gaelan nearly said it aloud, thinking about his friend and colleague, shunned and humiliated as a witch, much as befell Gaelan's own father. "He died at too early an age, before his work had been recognized and accepted." It satisfied that Bell was so admiring of the work of a once-discredited . . . apothecary.

Gaelan recalled when Nicholas had gone off to war, the Battle of Newberry, to prove himself, and he never returned the same. "Consumption."

Bell looked up from the page. "Consumption?"

"Yes. Erm . . . Nicholas Culpeper. He died from it, you know. A terrible loss to the trade—to medicine." Gaelan struggled to not betray the wistfulness in his voice. "He was a gifted apothecary, Dr. Bell. Now, as you have your supper awaiting you at your club, so have I, upstairs in my flat. Then if you will excuse me, sir—" Gaelan bowed from the neck.

"Of course—"

Both men leapt, startled at the frantic pounding at the door. It rattled the blinds and threatened to loose the wood from its hinges.

Gaelan opened it a crack, and a tall man pushed through, nearly toppling the apothecary from his feet. The man was panting as if he'd been pursued for miles on foot. His gaze was wild, terrified, darting from Bell to Gaelan and back.

"Which of you be the apothecary . . . Erceldoune?" he croaked between breaths.

"I am Erceldoune." Gaelan observed the coiled demeanor, the way he seemed poised to pounce like a rabid dog. He bid Bell to leave, and quickly, but the physician did not move an inch from his place, transfixed.

"Mr. Erceldoune, you must come with me quick as can be."

"What is the problem, Mr.—"

The man suddenly lunged toward Bell, grabbing hold of him about the neck. "Who be *this* man, if man he be? Satan! Satan, I tell ye!" He collapsed in a heap at Bell's feet.

CHAPTER 18

A moment later the man was again awake; he scuttled to the corner, his wild glare akin to a frightened wolf. By now, Bell had retreated to the other side of the shop, his fearful gaze never leaving the madman.

"Get 'im . . . away from . . . me! He be . . . be a demon! A . . . demon, I say!" The man quaked violently, teeth chattering between each word.

Gaelan gestured Bell toward the door with a hasty sweep of his arm. "Perhaps it may be better if you make yourself scarce."

"Of course." Bell eyed the door for a brief moment, before nodding his head toward a curtained area. "Would it be alright if I remain to . . . observe?"

Gaelan shrugged. "Suit yourself." *Hmm.* Perhaps the display on hand was more fascinating to Bell than dining with his brother gentleman physicians.

Gaelan crouched to the floor, the same level as the wild man, but at a distance, reluctant to approach too close. The man had settled some since Bell disappeared into the examining room, but just a wee bit. "If you please, sir. I cannot be of help if you—"

"What is this place? Why am I here? Who are *you*?" Confusion, now, and the shaking had worsened considerably, despite the blanket he'd managed to throw over the man.

Gaelan ventured closer, now sitting cross-legged on the floor close by the man, nonthreatening as he could manage. He spoke softly, gentle as to a wee child. "I am Mr. Erceldoune, the apothecary. You came to me only just moments ago, sir, for my help. Do you not remember? You asked I follow you . . . somewhere. To your home, perhaps? Has illness taken your family? Your wife, perhaps? A child?" He eased a calming hand on the stranger's bare arm. Ablaze, just as Gaelan suspected. Fever, ravaging chills, delirium.

Bell stood in the entrance to the examining room, watching, a grim expression darkening his features.

"Dr. Bell, is this—?"

He nodded. "Yes. Yes. It is. Do you see? This was my patient . . . although not exactly. I daresay he did not make me out to be a demon. I thought to seek you out immediately, but then, you see, the business with the girl. Do you desire my assist—"

"Better you should stay where you are for the moment." Gaelan turned his attention to the man. "I should like to ask you a few questions. How is your head?"

The man closed his eyes, as if to concentrate, before slowly nodding. "It throbs, sir. Like the devil himself's inside it tryin' to get out. Please, sir, a blanket? Do you not have a blanket? I am terrible cold," he complained.

Gaelan tucked the blanket about the man more securely, but no amount of warm coverings would suffice to stem the fever chills wracking his body. "Do you think you can walk?"

He nodded. "I can try, sir. I cannot promise my legs will hold me—they tremble so. I am terrible cold, you see."

"Alright, then. Let's give it a go, shall we? Perhaps you shall find more comfort in the nice cot I've got ready for you in my examining room." Gaelan helped the man to stand, looping an arm around his back and steadying him against his side as he avoided Bell, urging him out of the way. "Right?"

He waited a moment, until the man nodded again.

"Good. It is but a few paces to the left. Can you tell me your name?"

"Barlow. I be Zacharias Barlow."

"Very well, Mr. Barlow, I am Mr. Erceldoune, and I will do my absolute best to make you comfortable and see you back to your family, and in good health. But I must know a few things, and my friend, Dr. Bell, might be helpful in that regard. Might I bring him to the room as well? He is no demon, I assure you."

Barlow was faring better than when he'd first come in, much calmer, the delirium subsided. But Gaelan remained on his guard lest it return and be directed toward him.

"Yes. Sorry, sir. Didn't mean to . . . Don't know what I meant, to be honest. I know there ain't no demons 'round here! That's for fairy stories." He started to laugh, and it triggered a fit of coughing, nearly sending the two men sprawling to the floor.

Gaelan secured him more closely to his side. "Only another step or two now. Do you need to stop and rest?"

"Nah, I'm all right."

"Nearly there now." Gaelan settled Barlow into a low cot and placed several more blankets about him. "Right. I shall return in a trice."

Gaelan hoped Bell hadn't taken the opportunity to flee; he needed to know how precisely Barlow's symptoms matched those of his recovered patient. But Bell was standing in the shop, his hat, gloves, and stick in his hand.

"Dr. Bell, I wonder if you might look in with me on our Mr. Barlow."

"Now why would I do that?"

Gaelan grimaced. The exertion of practically carrying Barlow into the examining room had been more tiring than he'd have imagined. He brushed his long hair back from his sweat-slick forehead. "You would not agree his delirium was caused by fever?"

"Of course I do. But I daresay he doesn't want *me* about. And you've that wonderful salt elixir to bring him round, eh?"

Bell was looking for a way out. To get to supper—at the club. Of course. "*I* do. I would very much . . . appreciate . . . You need to confirm for me that the symptoms match your patient's. Or do not. Already, Barlow's arms and hands are afire. The shaking too. The order as well as the severity. If you would be so kind, sir. And as I explained earlier about the salt elixir—"

Bell returned his belongings to the counter with a weary sigh. "Very well."

Gaelan pulled the curtain. "Mr. Barlow, this is Dr. Bell—" Barlow had fallen asleep. At least, it would make the examination less difficult.

"There, do you notice, Mr. Erceldoune? The sweating. Pouring from him. The profuseness of it. My patient, exactly."

"He also complained of headache. His breathing . . ." Gaelan pointed to Barlow's chest. "Do you see that even in repose it is labored?" Gaelan removed two pillows from a shelf, covering them with muslin before setting them below Barlow's neck and head. The man barely stirred.

"Yes. It is exactly what I observed, though Mr. Barlow is not, by many a mile, quite so extreme. I was certain my patient was mere hours from death. Quite certain, and yet . . . And yet, he recovered. It is a strange ailment, this one. I've never seen its like, and if this man too—"

Barlow sat straight up, his eyes glazed, darting everywhere. "Please, sir, my wife, my lad Johnny, they're in an awful state. You must help them! There. Do you not see them? Sitting right there, atop the table. There she is. She is awful terrible pale; death's upon her, I fear. *Please!*" Barlow's arms flailed wildly in the direction of a large secretaire.

The delirium had returned; Barlow was growing more agitated with every second.

"Where do you live, Mr. Barlow?"

"In Page Street, sir. But she is right here, not at home. Not anymore. Do you not see her sitting—"

Bell turned to Gaelan. "Go, Mr. Erceldoune, with haste. I shall keep watch over our patient until your return."

"I thank you, Dr. Bell. There is a bottle on the shelf. It is the same elixir I prepared for you earlier. Have him drink it. Small sips, until the bottle is half empty."

Cate! In the urgency of the moment, he'd forgotten her. What if she should need him? What if she were to come down the stairs? Surely then she would come face to face with Bell, which would not do. "I've only to run up to my flat, and I shall be off."

He fled up the stairs to warn Cate that Bell was about, and she'd best stay quiet. When Gaelan returned to the examining room, Bell was sitting beside the patient; he'd removed his frock coat and folded up his shirt sleeves to the elbow. He was speaking in soothing tones to Mr. Barlow.

"Ah, Mr. Erceldoune. There you are. You're off then, to the Barlows?"

A nod.

"Good. Our patient is dreaming of the little people, it seems. In his mind, they are everywhere about your shop." Bell chuckled. "I daresay, sir, you have quite the esteemed guests in residence."

Gaelan echoed Bell's laughter, more anxiousness than amusement. "One never knows where the fairy folk might take up, eh?"

"Mr. Erceldoune!" Barlow tried to sit, resting his weight on his elbows, his voice coming in short gasps. "Mr. Erceldoune. Come closer. I need . . . they say . . . the fairy folk . . . they insist . . . you must . . . a picture . . . a pretty painting all aglitter, they showed to me. Blue and green. Snakes. Many, many snakes, and dragons . . . and . . . dragonflies. For you, she said . . . You must . . ." Barlow sank back into the cot, exhausted, his breath yet more labored, his lips blue and parched.

Gaelan froze.

"You see, Mr. Erceldoune. The fever. Delirium has overwhelmed him; his breath is barely . . . He will not last the night, I should think. I daresay, his family, *if* they yet live . . ."

Gaelan nodded, his lips in a tight line. He gathered several bottles and small pouches into a leather satchel and slung the strap across his chest. "I am off, then."

The image conveyed by Barlow's fevered vision had by now planted itself Gaelan's mind as he headed down through the market toward Barlow's home. It was the dragonflies, not the snakes, that gave him pause. Blue-black and emerald green caught up in tall grasses. An image in the ouroboros book Gaelan knew well. Barlow had not described it in detail, yet it resonated deeply. Did not Grandpapa's notes reference dragons, dragonflies? Like as not, simple happenstance. Yet . . .

The street lamps had not yet been lit but the sun was too far behind the buildings to provide much illumination, shrouding the market in a dreary gloom as Gaelan reached the address Barlow gave him. The house was in a far corner, down a bleak alleyway. The stench cut right through to his gut. Smithfield was ever a hothouse of vile odors, he learned during his first days in residence, but this was different. The decay of death. Not even rose water would do to disguise the stink.

The day had been sweltering hot. No breeze—not that a breeze would ever make its way into this claustrophobic corner of London. He opened the door just a crack, and the smell of putrefied flesh stung his eyes and nose, overpowering his senses. He lit a candle and counted the bodies, already half-overspread with bottle flies and vermin, silhouetted in candlelight—every orifice prime property for propagation.

Three—the wife and two children, gender indeterminate from the doorway. Gaelan pulled the door closed on the tomb gently as he might. How long had they been dead? Surely days, not hours.

As he made his way back to the apothecary, Gaelan could not help but notice quiet. The sun was dying to the west, but on such a warm summer's day, would there not yet be stall keepers hawking sausages by lamp? The lowing of cows, the cacophony of poultry, the backdrop of porcine squealing as stall keepers closed for the day seemed to have faded into a peculiar silence.

Sally Mills paced in the mud outside the White Owl, hands on her hips. Gaelan did not need to see her face to read her concern.

"Mrs. Mills, whatever is the matter?"

"Do you not feel it, Mr. Erceldoune? A foul wind do blow hereabouts. Upon my life there is, thick with the reek of death."

"Are you ailing, Mrs. Mills? Have you fever? Chills? Anything of the sort? Perhaps you ought follow me to the apothecary. I have—"

"Nah. Me, I'm fit and fine. No choice but to be anything but the picture of health! I've much too much to do. Ha! And a full house tonight at the Owl. But sense it, I do."

Never had Gaelan seen Mrs. Mills quite so uneasy, and for no reason. He did not know her well, yet . . . He managed a smile. "Indeed, something may well be about. Not an evil, but an illness. Only just that." Gaelan bowed and took his leave of her, rounding the corner to his shop. He paused a moment, peering in through the double bow windows before entering. Bell was waiting for him, appearing far more bedraggled than he had.

"Dr. Bell! Is all—?"

"Barlow's gone, I am afraid. Died only just moments ago. I hope you don't mind; I sent a boy for the undertaker. His family?"

Gaelan shook his head.

"Have you a clue?"

Indeed, he had, but he could not say it. Not yet. "Possibly, but it is a too far-fetched a notion, and I am not certain. For now, there's naught but treat the symptoms, one by one as they appear. *If* there are others." Barlow's symptoms had come one upon the other, and in such rapid succession. In a discernible order. "It is the best course; do you not agree?" The only course.

"Yes, but—"

In no circumstance could Gaelan suggest even the remotest possibility they might be confronting a disease some two hundred years extinct. And Barlow's dragonflies? The ravings of delirium, yet the image insisted itself into his thoughts. They nipped and fluttered, an echo of a memory. Too long ago, Gaelan learned never to dismiss out of hand anything, no matter how ludicrous on its face.

"I do have an idea," Gaelan said finally, "some notes I jotted down after your last visit, thinking they might be of use for your patient. I must consult something upstairs in my laboratory first, and it will take some time. Perhaps on the morrow I shall have something more . . . substantial . . . than a simple salt elixir to offer. You will return?"

"I've other patients to attend, none of whom are exhibiting . . . Although, I must plead to an acute curiosity with regard to this ailment, and what treatment your musings tonight might produce."

"I bid you a good evening then. Perhaps you will not be too late for your *supper*."

Bell glanced at his watch and sighed. He gathered his hat and coat and left Gaelan alone in the shop with the expired Mr. Barlow.

Dragonflies.

CHICAGO NORTH SHORE, PRESENT DAY

CHAPTER 19

The drive from Simon's home in Highland Park to meet Dr. Spangler at the Northwestern Campus was tricky enough without having to mind the correct side of the road. Narrow, two lanes. The lakeside lane plummeting far down jagged, forested cliffs. The road twisted and wound along the shore, descending to the water's edge until the bluffs now towered above her to the west. Finally, the land flattened out completely.

"Northwestern University Welcomes You," read an enormous purple and white digital display. A beautiful campus, its ivy-covered Gothic buildings reminded her of Cambridge, but far more modern—and transplanted to a beach. She squeezed into a parking space on a side street and wandered toward the middle of campus, looking for Dr. Spangler's building.

Anne had never been to the Califax Center for Molecular Biology, but she'd met several faculty members at conferences and conventions. Perhaps she'd look them up, before she returned to the UK. Although she was not keen to answer questions about Transdiff—or Salk. For that matter, why she was in the States at all.

Dr. Dana Spangler looked young enough with her short-cropped hair and small round specs that she might easily have been mistaken for a first-year. She greeted Anne in the building lobby, extending a warm hand.

"Have you had lunch yet?"

"No. Famished."

"Have you eaten a slice of real Chicago pizza?"

"Can't say I have."

"Well, you're not allowed to leave Chicago without at least trying it, so . . . no time like the present."

"Sounds like a plan."

"So, most of my work is downtown at the Medical Center. I figure we can catch the inter-campus shuttle and be downtown in less than an hour. There shouldn't be that much traffic now. We can talk on the way down. And one of the city's best pizza places is right on the water. Ah, there it is now. Perfect timing."

They climbed into the small purple and white bus. There were no other passengers. Anne cleared her throat.

"I know a few of your Northwestern colleagues. I did . . . do . . . research on telomeres in tissue regeneration. *T. nutricula*. Other invertebrates as well—"

"I've read your work. Required reading." She blushed. "I don't mean that I wouldn't have read it if—"

"No problem at all. So . . . you're . . . were . . . a friend of Gaelan's?"

"Not friends really. Acquaintances. No one really *knew* him, right? One of a kind, though. I think that's what people dug about him."

She remembered all those memorials left on his doorstep. "So, he taught here?"

"Not really. Guest lectures. Adjunct prof a couple quarters, I think. Not in the sciences, though it could've been. Easily. He knew a lot of stuff about a lot of stuff."

"History?"

She nodded. "Literature, mythology . . . Then he'd disappear from campus for a while, then come back. He never explained where he'd been but to say 'traveling.' I think he had bouts of depression, real serious, like. Drugs? Maybe—"

"So how did you know him?"

"The bookstore. Have you ever been in there? It's amazing. Real old-school. No bestsellers, but really rare stuff. Do you know him from back in the UK?"

"Not really. I . . ." How could she explain it? "Family connections, I suppose." At least it possessed a scrap of truthfulness. "So you must be wondering how I came to contact you."

"He told me a while back he'd developed, as he put it, 'an amateur's curiosity' about genetics. I suppose it was triggered by you, huh? Trying to impress you with his knowledge—"

Anne blushed. "No, of course not. I had no idea—"

Dana shrugged. "Didn't think so. He wasn't the type to try to impress anyone about anything, but he did it all the time. So. What can I do for you, Dr. Shawe?"

"Anne, please. I found a folder full of karyograms in Gaelan's flat, and your business card. He'd created a series of—"

"Yeah. He was fascinated by the idea you could actually take photographs of chromosomes, see the banding."

"So, the images. You helped him produce them?"

"Yeah. How else would he get them?"

"He's pretty resourceful. You know he had a lab in his flat?"

Dana's left eyebrow disappeared beneath her bangs. "No idea. Never been up there. He wanted to learn, I suppose so he could do it himself. Undergrad experiment. Expensive equipment, though, to do a simple karyotype."

"So that's all he asked? To show him how, and develop the images?"

"For a while. Then I think he got bored. It's not very exciting as far as cytogenetics goes. I have to say, though, he was particularly interested in the telomeres. Wanted to examine them up close. Knew a lot about it too. More than some of my grad students. Come to think of it, I lent him a couple of special dyes. Said he wanted to try some things himself. Couldn't figure out how, but now the DIY lab makes sense. I would have loved to know what he was trying. Why the obsession? I never heard from him after that. Two months later, he had that awful accident up Sheridan Road in the Ravines."

As if Gaelan would tell her. But Anne had figured it out. Not that it was difficult if you knew Gaelan's real story.

Serial karyotypes with an emphasis on the telomeres. He was looking for clues. What made him . . . him. Infinite tissue regeneration. He'd learn nothing solely by examining the telomeres. He would need to comprehend the underlying mechanism that caused his DNA sequence to perpetually renew itself. And that was beyond even the best karyotype image. "All that horrid publicity. Poor man," Anne said finally.

"Crazy stuff. A lot of people around here thought he was some kind of superhuman mutant or something. A real X-Man."

"Did *you*?"

"Nah. I know too much about tissue regeneration to believe it."

The bus stopped. "We're here. Welcome to the Gold Coast of Chicago. Lunch awaits after a short walk down to the pier."

They followed the shoreline along the breakwater. How much calmer the water seemed down here. It lapped gently, the steady "glub-glub" against the dock.

"Restaurant is down there." Dana pointed to a spot at the far end of the pier.

Anne looked up, shielding her eyes against the sun. "What a fab Ferris wheel. Reminds me of home."

"And I quote, 'The original wheel was created for the Chicago World's Fair.' The Columbian Exhibition of 1893. That exposition? It set the stage for the brave new world of the twentieth century more than almost anything else at its time: from Daniel Burnham's White City of the future to electric lights and the zipper on your handbag. God, I'm sounding like a tour guide. Sorry. Born and bred. Can't help a little bit of Chicago pride."

"I have sheer terror of heights, so I'm not begging for a ride on the wheel!" Anne smiled. "But it is quite cool."

"Obviously, it's not the original. The fair was a few miles down the beach. One of the few structures remaining from it is our Museum of Science and Industry. Never knew about a connection between the museum and the World's Fair. Gaelan's the one who told me about it. Been going there since I was a kid and I dragged Gaelan with me to see it. Knew he'd get a real kick out of it. But when we got there, he had the strangest reaction. Started talking about the World's Fair, how it had been 'right there.'"

Anne fidgeted with her phone. "Well, I'm certain he loved the place. He loved anything to do with science. I know that much, at least."

"That's not what I meant." Dana stopped, turning to face Anne. "No. Like it was deeper than that. The way he talked . . . as if it was some sort of . . . He went on and on about the magic of that moment. That how the people who'd brought their inventions there risked their reputations for all the potential benefit. It was a real visceral reaction. I don't know. Strange. I'd never seen those coal-black eyes light up like that. Like I said, he was some sort of history genius."

"He never taught a course or gave a lecture about it?"

"Never. At least not as far as I know. Like it was something for him only, I guess."

She'd seen his eyes blaze like that—as he deciphered that healing book with but one goal in mind. To create a means to end his life—and Simon's. He'd been so delighted that morning he'd exited the make-shift laboratory in Simon's bathroom, stoppered bottle clutched in his fist. A great success, he'd hoped. She could picture it as if . . .

Anne gasped as something occurred to her, hitting her full force in the stomach. "I need to sit a moment, please."

"Sure."

No. Not one vial. There had been two of them. He'd created a second dose! Of course he had done. How had she not remembered that? Gaelan was meticulous as any scientist, and when the result could never be duplicated—ever—he would have created a backup. He'd given her one vial and kept the other to himself.

The realization hit her with the force of a thousand kilograms of steel pressing in on her chest. Gaelan Erceldoune was *not* off the grid, holed up in hiding, run away to Antarctica or Tahiti. He was *dead*.

Really dead. She whispered his name, realizing she'd said it aloud.

"Yeah, I know. Sorry, I shouldn't have been so . . . I miss him too, I guess."

"I'm sorry, Dana. I think the last few . . . Haven't had much sleep, and it's hit me full on just now. Where's that pizza place? I could use an espresso right about now. And something to eat."

"Their coffee sucks. But the beer's pretty fine. All local craft beers."

"That'll do."

They found a table in the nearly empty restaurant; the quiet of early afternoon while school was still in session, Dana explained.

"Medium cheese, deep dish. Caesar salad for a start," Dana said to the server, glancing at Anne for confirmation.

"I'm fine with whatever you order. Like I said, I'm famished. Besides, I'm the visitor to your city."

"Great. And a chocolate stout for me. You?"

"Pellegrino. Orange if you have it. So, was this a favorite place for Gaelan?"

Dana shrugged. "It's a big drinking place at night. Gaelan never drank—at least not when he was out with me. I think he was more into good weed."

The collection of empty Lagavulin bottles in his flat suggested otherwise.

"He wasn't really a hang-out type anyway. I don't think he was really comfortable in crowds unless it was in front of a lecture hall. And even then . . . He was hard to find, except by email—or in his shop—sort of on his own turf. I think he was, on the whole, a troubled soul." She lifted her glass just as the pizza arrived. "To Gaelan, wherever he may be."

Anne nodded tightly, trying to change the subject before she lost all composure. "Erm . . . The pizza. It's delicious. I've never had anything of its like. Pizza is usually flat, not—"

"Chicago style. The best. But don't tell New Yorkers that." Dana smiled.

"So . . . This place is called Navy Pier?"

"Yeah. Oh, and there's one other connection I forgot to mention. I mean about the World's Fair. So, there's an exhibit down the pier a bit. Stained glass from the Columbian Exposition . . . the World's Fair. It's enormous, takes up the entire lower level beneath the Great Hall, way at the end. It was closed for a couple years, but just reopened six months ago. Apparently, someone, some organization, I suppose, procured almost all the surviving stained glass from the exposition. It's pretty spectacular, but no one knows who funded it. Completely anonymous. So it's just called the rather prosaic Glass Museum of the Columbian Exposition. Mostly Tiffany stuff. Gaelan cajoled me into going with him just after it opened. He had a real thing for glass."

Anne nodded. It sounded like him.

"I'd love to see it. Is it open today?"

"Should be."

The pizza was more food than she was used to eating, especially the past month. She finished her Pellegrino. "I'm ready when you are."

"Shall we?"

The Grand Hall was nearly a mile down the pier, past tall ships, excursion boats and yachts, attractions, and market kiosks and stalls. Finally, they reached the great domed building with its twin Byzantine towers, standing guard over the waters.

"Through here."

Down a dim stairway and through a darkened corridor until they came to a black curtain, which opened just as they stepped on the welcome mat. From the dark into the light.

Stunning was inadequate to describe the hall. The brilliance of glass and light, colors that matched every hue and tone, set into lead, set into stone and wood. The room's only sign suspended from the ceiling, set in stained glass: "It is a kaleidoscope of the world that furnishes a passing panorama of life in every zone—John Eastman, 1893."

It *was* as if they'd stepped through the looking glass and into the barrel of a giant kaleidoscope, every move, every breeze, every step representing an altered perception, a changed perspective.

Tucked away in a corner of the room was a small unfinished display of glass tubes, bent and twisted into strange shapes mounted into large black boxes. Beside it a small sign: "Coming soon: Tesla's Tubes—Magical Neon of the White City."

Where had Gaelan been in 1893? London? Edinburgh? The Highlands? Or had he been here in the States? Anne stopped before an enormous stained-glass panel.

The center of the panel was a three-dimensional labyrinth, bathed in moonlight. At its center, Dionysus and the Minotaur in fierce battle; beyond the fray watched Ariadne, cloaked in silver and gold. The top third of the panel was in shades of indigo, solid but for the moon and a constellation identical to the one Gaelan pointed out to her in the night sky above the lake—Ariadne's Crown—the Corona Borealis. No wonder Gaelan had a fascination with this place. She imagined him spending hours staring at this one panel, the inner complexities and colors of the panel to him a representation of his life, bearing the name of his and Eleanor's daughter, Ariadne.

Her gaze drifted to the artist's signature at the base of the panel. It was tiny, barely legible in the far-right corner. "G.E., 1893."

Anne sucked in a breath, losing her balance and finding it as she lowered herself to the carpeted floor, inches from the panel. Gaelan a glass artist? Admittedly, the notion hadn't crossed her mind, but why not? Why not be in Chicago at the turn of the century? Or was she reading something into the stained glass, placing Gaelan right in the middle of it, when it might well have been not Gaelan Erceldoune but George Edison, or Gregory Eastlake, or any one of a thousand "G.E."s?

"Are you okay?"

Dana Spangler. She'd forgotten she wasn't alone.

"Yeah. Fine. This is amazing. Brilliant. Thank you so much for bringing me here. I never would have . . ."

Anne turned, and there it was, proof. Another panel, and an exact copy of the page from the healing book. The Diana's Tree Gaelan had shown her to demonstrate his theory about how the book worked. And again, the initials "G.E."

She rested her fingers over the inscription, her eyes closed.

"Gaelan."

SCOTLAND, PRESENT DAY

CHAPTER 20

A whisper borne upon a faint breeze wended its way through the prisms as Gaelan sat on the dirt floor of the crystal room. "Gaelan." He was certain he'd heard it.

"Anne," he called out, almost involuntarily, knowing the voice was hers. Impossibly. An overactive imagination at play, part of the grand delusion in which his life was now enmeshed. The strangeness of the visions, his presence in these particular catacombs. Conan Doyle's journal.

Shaken, fingers trembling, he turned to a random page. A distraction.

They dwell in a high castle, which stretches to the heavens, glittering crystal, bounded by turquoise streams and emerald rivers, waterfalls and trees adorned with lacy mosses, intricate as filigree.

Gaelan had observed no castles, no palaces, only a desolate place, permeated by a foreboding air of desperation, of fear. Certainly, there had been no sight of a river, turquoise or otherwise. Everything he'd seen had been desiccated, colorless.

I have always believed the fairy folk to fly like birds or dragon-flies, lithe and graceful as they hover above and move swiftly. Leastways, that is how they have been in my mind depicted,

perhaps fueled by the fairy stories told me in my youth here in
the Borders—a magical land, if ever there was. Indeed, they do
fly, their wings neither flesh nor feather. Nor aeroplane.

Besides their ability to fly, they much resemble humans, yet
perhaps more perfect specimens of our best selves. Unblemished,
perfect skin. All carry with them a lithe youthfulness incon-
gruent with their melancholy. A heavy weariness that might
only be borne after a long life of disappointment and tragedy.
They are waiting, I'd heard them say so very many times, but
for what? For whom? I never learned, only just 'We wait.' An
answer, but to what question?

Gaelan wondered if Conan Doyle had been projecting his own
lifetime of disappointment, despite the success of his career: the death
of his beloved son, the ridicule at his belief in fairy folk, in spiritualism.
His falling out with their mutual friend Houdini because of those
beliefs. Conan Doyle's account ended:

My only regret in this adventure is that although I see them at
play, at tea, at conversation, and can quite clearly hear them,
they do not acknowledge my presence amongst them. They seem
quite real as you or me, yet not quite corporeal in nature. I reach
out and my hand passes through all in their world—as if I am
the ghost and they the haunted.

It quite pains me, for I long to have even one conversation
with their kind, so many years I have longed for it. To learn
more of their world. Perhaps I am not adequately skilled in
wielding this glass bauble—the apparent key to their singular
plane of existence.

I was quite right, however, in the end, to choose this place—
amongst the hills of Eildon—for my search. I have long believed
that if any place on Earth would hover close to the world of the
fairies, it would be here in the Borders. These hills have ever
been a place of enchantment, the stuff of legends and ballads,

the spark of brilliance in poetry, prose, theatre. Arthur, Nimue, Morgana, Merlin, the Lady of the Lake, and the Rhymer.

That is one fellow I should like to meet, for his descendent I count amongst my most treasured friends. It was he, after all, some quarter-century past, who sparked this small quest of mine to finally come face to face with the fair folk and their extraordinary world.

And now alas it is time for me to return to Southampton and home, lest I cause undue worry amongst my dear family once again. I do hope to return, to complete this chronicle and at last to meet them, not simply observe as if from afar. Yet, I cannot help but believe this is the end for me; I shall not return. I leave it to the next sojourner who might find his way here, to this chronicle, and the glass key to a magical world beyond our imaginings. Bon voyage to you, my friend. —ACD

Gaelan rubbed his thumbs into his closed eyes, trying to chase away the ache that had taken hold there, surprised to notice the finger he had earlier nicked still stung quite painfully beneath its makeshift bandage. Unwinding the fabric from around his index finger, he winced as he came to the site of the wound, which stuck to the material. He yanked at it, and blood trickled from the gash. He stared at it for some moments, following the narrow trail of blood with bewildered fascination as it wound down his finger and around his wrist. It had not healed.

Light-headed, Gaelan let his eyes drift closed as he leaned against the cool black of the cave wall, taking hold of the opalescent tear drop as if it would keep him upright.

"Ah, there you are! I wondered where you'd got to! Thought I'd lost you—out there." The same young woman he'd spoken with earlier gestured toward the back of the tiny, bare room in which they now stood. At least they were indoors, and no longer in the gray desert. And it was bright enough to see clearly.

"Stand still and the . . ." Her voice was blotted out by a loud whirring; gray dirt mounded all around him in small piles. "There. That's better. Don't worry about the floor, it's self-cleaning."

Scooping up a handful of the substance, he now realized it wasn't gray after all. In here, it sparkled in every hue. Fine as diatomaceous sand, yes, but it seemed to be a sort of ground glass. Infinitesimally tiny grains, worn down and ground as if by time and the harshest of conditions.

"I'm sure you have so many questions, but not as many as we have. Gaelan Erceldoune, aren't you?"

Gaelan could only nod, confused . . . by everything.

"Good. Be terrible if we got the wrong guy. Almost did, like a hundred years ago."

"But—"

"Patience."

She removed a dirty green velvet cloak, revealing a long flowing tunic of silvery silken fabric. She placed it on the floor, which was now completely bare, no trace of dust or sand but what he clutched in his hand. She touched the wall and it slid open to a new room. The fine grains slipped between his fingers, vanishing as if by magic into the floor beneath him as he followed the girl.

They were in an enormous hall as spacious as the first was claustrophobic. Graceful beams arched up and up until they vanished into a glare of light many hundred feet from where they stood.

"Imposing, isn't it? But it's an illusion, created by a precise placement of mirrors and colored glass."

"What is this place?"

"You will find out. Promise." With her index finger, she drew an invisible "x" over her heart. "But not yet. After."

"After . . . what?"

"You'll see. Sorry I can't be more forthcoming. It's way above my pay grade. Come on; you'll see."

Gaelan had a vague notion this all was a dream, that he was still asleep in the crystal chamber. Or was it the sea cave? Or . . . in his confusion, he couldn't quite recall where . . .

No context to tether him to even the slimmest notion of reality. The opalescent glass piece still glowed within his hand, warm to the touch. An anchor into the past. Was that any more real than anything else surrounding him?

Once again, his head began to throb, which only added to the entropy of his thoughts. He was desperate to ask the girl, "Is this death? Are you my escort?" But the logic of inquiring escaped him. If she answered "no," what then? He'd be in the same place, following behind the same strange girl through a stranger place set into an even stranger dreamscape. One he seemed unlikely to escape. For now.

Gaelan's last reliable memory was when he consumed the poison; everything afterwards was shrouded in a surreal fog. Like LSD, but not quite as colorful. Had the poison caused this aimless drift between memory and imagination braided together in his mind, familiar, yet vastly different than remembered?

A backward glance, and Gaelan realized they'd walked quite a distance from where he thought they'd entered. Yet, it seemed only a few minutes had passed.

"This way."

They veered down a long, narrow path lit by tall glass domes every few feet, bathing the way in a pleasant amber-pink that seemed as foreign as it was familiar. There was something about it, like the ambient light during a near-but-not-quite solar eclipse. Or sodium vapor street lamps that would, of a winter's night, diffuse and scatter the planes and angles of snowflakes into an unearthly pink-amber glow.

Another door slid away, and they stood now on a spit of land at a confluence of rivers, a remarkable contrast between the dusty gray blankness of the "outside" and the lushness of this place.

The air was green, like after a storm, and rich with the perfume of dense vegetation. Above him the pounding of a waterfall cascading down a circuitous cataract so high he could not see the top, its destination far below where they stood, perceivable solely by the thundering pulsation of the pale turquoise river at their feet. A blue more reminiscent of the Caribbean Sea. The second river was emerald green, the color of the Chicago River on St. Patrick's Day when it was dyed to match the celebration. Lacy Spanish moss draped a small stand of cypress, their twisted roots exposed—a landscape befitting a Van Gogh painting.

It was as Conan Doyle described it, but ever so much more. But why was Gaelan able to interact with them when Conan Doyle had not?

"We're nearly there, but we must get to the far bank. This way, Mr. Erceldoune." She extended her hand toward him. An inaudible hum, sort of an electrical sensation, passed from her hand to his as they touched, not unpleasant, but rather odd. They stood at a precipice with no obvious way to cross to the other side.

She turned toward Gaelan, motioning to their left and up a mossy, steep, ridged incline. There was no way scale it—not without proper climbing equipment.

"This way," she mouthed, pointing upward. She clamped her hand over his and with a slight shudder, soft hooks latched over the fingers of his left hand. "Don't worry. I've got you."

From within the metallic mesh of her gown radiated several small devices with tiny rotating blades. They were flying. Not so much flying as hovering alongside the cliff face, a steady upward motion that churned Gaelan's stomach. He was an experienced climber, had hiked Rainier, but this . . . ? Instinct told him to reach for the ropes, but there were none. No footholds, no handholds. They were suspended in air. Was this the flying Conan Doyle described? No wonder it had baffled him.

They reached a high ridge and set down behind the waterfall. Gaelan gazed out over the chasm below, stepping closer to the edge to catch a bit of the cooling spray from the torrent. The water droplets refracted into concentric arcs suspended across the divide, looping in and around each other.

"Please, Mr. Erceldoune, we must go. They are waiting."

Gaelan breathed in the aroma of springtime in the Highlands.

That was real enough. The moist, fertile soil, the luxuriant grass, the first budding of hill flowers. They walked in silence, finally reaching the other side, where another woman met them, older, draped in a lustrous emerald cloak, almost invisible in the verdant dreamscape, but for her outstretched hand. Her long hair was fastened tightly into a snood at the back of her head, lending her a severity both seductive and unnerving. Her ice-blue gaze was both kind and commanding.

"Welcome. Please follow me."

Gaelan's escort nodded slightly and let go of Gaelan's hand, before turning back, sprinting along the walk. Gaelan's gaze followed her until she blended into the scene and disappeared from view. *That voice.* Vaguely familiar . . . another time, another context . . .

"Come. You must have many questions. I know we have many for you, Mr. Erceldoune."

Gaelan stopped, refusing to travel another foot before he received some answers. "Yes. I have several questions." *May as well rattle all of them off, eh?* "What is this place and how am I here? And what is outside . . . the bizarre gray desert I . . ." Gaelan looked up, trying to see beyond the dense forest canopy. He could see nothing but darkness above. No stars, no moon. Only blank blackness.

"Please have patience. It's only a short way longer. Come." They proceeded through a heavy black steel and glass door that seemed to materialize from within the forest. "I will answer all your questions as soon as you are settled and comfortable. Ah, here we are. The tea is steeped and ready for us. Come. Sit. You fancy spice tea, do you not?"

He didn't even consider asking how she knew. What would be the point? He nodded, willing to go along for the moment. What choice did he have?

"I'll be but a moment." The woman retreated into the forest as Gaelan settled into a comfortable chair. He leaned back, and an ottoman came up from beneath his feet like a recliner chair, but not quite; it curled about him closely—memory foam, but not quite. He was tired enough that he could easily be asleep before his host returned. But that voice . . . where had . . . ?

"Ah, I see you've made yourself comfortable. Good." The woman reappeared and set down a tray with two steaming mugs of tea. The aroma of cinnamon and cloves revived him. Orange peel and jasmine penetrated his unease. He breathed it in, savoring the familiar aroma, realizing it was his own blend. If only it had a dash of cayenne . . .

A small sip. A vague awareness that it might be drugged flashed through Gaelan's mind and dissolved into the sweet, spiciness of the tea. Yes. Cayenne. The exact proportion. The woman smiled, seemingly satisfied. Gaelan's eyes slipped shut; fatigue was beginning to overwhelm his curiosity, his desire for answers.

From within the cushions, soft, rubbery tentacles stretched, accompanied by a low whirring as they looped securely about Gaelan's wrists and ankles. They did not hurt, but he couldn't move. Another twisted around his chest, settling itself into place with a loud "click."

He should cry out . . . to someone . . . anyone . . . to set him free. But who would listen?

"Mr. Gaelan Erceldoune." A man's voice behind him, but he was unable to turn around and see his face. "You, sir, are quite the person of interest!"

CHAPTER 21

Gaelan struggled against the restraints; a sort of metallic something, but malleable, even comfortable, but ultimately unforgiving. The man came around the chair, sitting on a low stool at Gaelan's feet. His jet-black hair, pulled into a band at the back of his neck, twined halfway down his back.

Gaelan's momentary calm had evaporated. Perhaps now he would get some answers, but it seemed absurd to continue asking where he was. A slightly different tack was in order. "What is your interest in me? And who are *you*?"

"Our interest is significant. And you can call me LaSalle, as in the street. You know, the Loop? Financial district? Admittedly, a lifetime or two ago. I was a pit boss at the Board of Trade. Anyway, enough about me. I have more than a few questions for you, Mr. Erceldoune."

Gaelan searched his memory for the name and came up empty. "Should I know your name?"

"No. I don't think so. I mean, unless you were you a trader . . . you know, back in the day?"

"No. Why do you know my name?"

"Who doesn't? You are quite famous. A legend-ish."

Gaelan had lost his mind. Had to be it. But how could he know for certain? Wasn't self-awareness of insanity positive proof of sanity? "Catch-22," he said flatly.

"Catch . . . Ah. You suspect that I, this place, your coming here is all in your mind." LaSalle poked lightly at Gaelan's forehead and Gaelan recoiled. "You're wrong."

Said the spider to the fly. Gaelan squinted past his immediate surroundings, his gaze darting in every direction, desperately searching for something familiar. Context. He needed context. He needed focus.

"That poison you consumed," LaSalle continued, "eating away at your mind, even as we sit here sipping tea? That would be a tragedy, wouldn't it? To live out eternity, alive, but crazy as a jaybird—if jaybirds still lived. Which . . . oh, well." He shrugged indifferently. "I assure you this is all the real deal. Even if you aren't ready to accept it. Yet."

The tea. His favorite blend. He breathed in the fragrance of citrus and clove as it drifted up from the delicate china teacup, sweet and spicy. He ran a finger across a small chip in the cup handle.

"The eighth circle," Gaelan whispered sotto voce, his eyes closed as he considered one possible answer to his unanswered questions.

"The what?"

"The Divine Comedy. The Malebloge—the Eighth Circle of hell."

"Okay. Let's go with that for now. Why not? Eventually, you'll need to accept this as reality. Fine. You might say our world reeks of the River Styx—outside the safety of our enclave. You've seen that already. The tenth bolgia—the tenth ditch—within the circle would be most fitting in your case, I suppose. The place where alchemists and sorcerers suffer for eternity. As for your crimes, nothing so harmless as promising to conjure gold from lead. No, sir." LaSalle wagged his finger back and forth. "Not your style. Your alchemy had a much greater impact. Genuine, human consequences. Enormous repercussions that continue to reverberate . . . But I'm getting ahead of myself."

LaSalle was baiting him. But wasn't he right? Unlocking immortality was miles beyond anything alchemy ever managed, despite the effort. But consequences? Simon, of course, that was one unintended consequence . . . What did LaSalle mean . . . repercussions?

Gaelan shuddered. *A vision. That is all this is. A fevered, poison-induced hallucination.* He needed to remember it. Keep it close by. A chant. A mantra.

Dante was a poet, *La Divine Commedia*, a work of fiction. A poem, and nothing more. There was no Malebloge, no circles descending further and further into hell. Right?

Still . . . vile disease. Disfiguring disease. The punishment of the tenth bolgia. And was not madness the most horrific of diseases?

Breaking the mind, but not the body? Disfiguring the spirit with uncertainty and constant fear? Was this justice finally delivered for what he had done to Simon all those years ago in London? Was this man the gatekeeper determining Gaelan's fate? LaSalle's breath fluttered against Gaelan's ear.

"You were an alchemist, were you not?"

"Not as many would define it," Gaelan replied, a bit too defensively. "No more so than were Paracelsus, Isaac Newton. Culpeper. They were men of science, misunderstood, dismissed. But only until the rest of civilization caught up with them."

"And you place yourself amongst those great men?"

"Of course not. They were geniuses—"

"Let us return to Dante's eighth circle. You believe you belong there." Not a question.

"I . . . A moment, please." Gaelan's discomfort return, growing into full-on panic. Perspiration trickled down his face, itched down his spine. LaSalle swayed and quivered before him as if in a funhouse mirror as Gaelan fought against a growing dizziness. "What is this place?" His voice wavered, weak, distant.

"Pay attention! We were discussing your crimes against humanity. Your proper placement in hell. Your father was said to have perverted God's laws with magical healing. Must run in the family, hmm? Maybe you'll be reunited at long last."

Fight it, for fuck's sake, Erceldoune. Focus! Gaelan drew a long breath. "Perversion of natural law is a subjective accusation, a matter of perception. History often vindicates . . . vindicates many who supposedly play God with nature." Gaelan swallowed hard, trying to stem the quiver in his voice. "Otherwise," he breathed, "otherwise, how would medicine . . . science, have advanced from the Dark Ages? But how did you know . . . ?"

LaSalle was talking, but Gaelan had lost the train of it. Random thoughts, indistinct babble filtered through pulsating shadows. If only he could get hold of word, a phrase, concrete and discernable, to tether him to reality.

There. Out the corner of his eye, a fleeting glimpse of something in the far distance. *Fuck! Where did it go?* Colored steel girders, incongruous among the dense forestation. Vaguely familiar, completely out of context, like seeing a bookshop client in an unfamiliar setting.

A flash of an image. Gaelan concentrated, clamping down his eyes, searching for it in his mind's eye. To remember why it seemed . . . Faded pink. Then green, also faded nearly to colorless.

"Mr. Erceldoune! Pay attention!" LaSalle barked again, this time, too near Gaelan's ear.

Startled, Gaelan loosened his grip on his glass piece, forgetting it was still clutched in his fist, catching it before it reached the ground.

"You're bleeding." LaSalle pointed to Gaelan's hand. "You should get that looked at. Might be infected." An ugly laugh in his ear; a chill slithered down Gaelan's spine. "That's impossible, isn't it?"

Gaelan stared at the bandage, soaked with blood. How many hours had it been since he'd gashed it? He couldn't remember.

"I . . ." The light faded, and darkness enfolded him like swaddling.

"Gaelan!" A whisper in his ear, close.

He blinked. LaSalle was gone, and he was back in the prism room, still on the floor. The opalescent glass piece had fallen from his hand and lay just beyond his grasp. The light within it dimmed, the dying embers of a bonfire.

"Gaelan." The lightest touch—a downy feather—stroked across his knee. His eyes fluttered as the sensation wrapped around him accompanied by the scent of lavender soap. *Anne. Again, Anne.* She crouched before him, a subtle shadow in the darkened room, lit only by the glimmer of glass. "Anne. When did you . . . ? How did you find me?"

Her voice was a whisper floating on the breeze, melodic, soft and warm. "A kaleidoscope of the world . . . a passing panorama of life in every zone. Every zone."

"What? What are you talking about? A kaleidoscope of . . . what? What are you doing here? How did you find me? Why didn't . . .?" There was something quite not right about her in the strangeness of the prism light. As if . . . He rubbed his eyes. A dream? But . . .

A delicate breath in his ear, an arousing purr. "Ariadne's labyrinth."

He flailed his arms, trying to catch her up, but there was nothing for him to take hold of. "Where are you?" he howled into the prisms, which merely tinkled in response. They swayed gracefully above Gaelan's head, their music peaceful, sweet.

Four matches it took Gaelan with trembling fingers to relight the candle he'd earlier left on the chamber floor. The strange vision of Anne continued to dance in and about the suspended crystals, searing into his mind as he stared up into the pattern.

The Quhawme Brethren of Dernwode House had taken incredible care to remove them from the monastery and create below ground this seòmar-criostalan.

Refracted light arced between and around the prisms like a spider's web of translucent color. A pattern, Gaelan was certain. A distinct order, not only of the arrangement but also of their size relative each to the next. *No! Not a spider's web.* The combination of light and glass branched like the arms of the Milky Way, ever outward along the ceiling, the walls and the space between.

Gaelan blinked to refocus, see the whole of it as one. The Golden Spiral, its arms growing in constancy with phi—1.618, the golden mean. Or was it only what he wished to see? Needed so desperately to order the chaos of his mind. Brother Hugh had drummed the Fibonacci numbers into his head, never missing an opportunity to point it out. "It is everywhere. In everything, both expected and astonishing," he would explain. An ever-present reminder of the recurring patterns in nature. A unifying principle of all existence: physical, chemical, biological. The harmony, the energy that connects all things.

Gaelan painted an imaginary a box around the entirety of the prisms. The length of the side of a larger square to the next smaller square is in the golden ratio. He hadn't the instruments to measure precisely, but he could easily visualize the boxes as well as the whole.

Fascinating. If he sought them out, would he discover other Fibonacci representations throughout the catacombs? Were the chambers themselves so arranged, not random but following Fibonacci's rule? Or was that too far a leap?

What was it Nicola Tesla had suggested to him the day they'd met during the Columbian Exposition so very long ago? They'd debated much in that one brief conversation on a chilly morning, but on this one point they agreed. The elegance of Fibonacci's work. Tesla had insisted it was the key to true comprehension of the universe, and the fragile field of dynamic energy holding it together.

Interesting, yes. But where did it get him in his present situation? A thousand-piece jigsaw puzzle with the reality hidden within optical illusions, fitting together properly only once you accept what the eye alone cannot perceive. A leap of understanding running counter to the obvious, yet, in the end, making perfect sense when it all clicks together into a wondrous panorama.

Was Gaelan Erceldoune ready to make that leap?

LONDON, 1826

CHAPTER 22

Dragonflies flickered, amorphous images only just out of Gaelan's plain view as the undertakers removed Mr. Barlow's corpse from the examining room. An ill-afforded distraction; he'd nearly allowed . . .

"A moment, please." Gaelan stopped the men just as they opened the alleyway door. "Do not, under any circumstance, deposit Mr. Barlow at the Man O'War. Nor his family, lying deceased at their home, should you be called there. I say this with the most urgency. And it would do you well to pass the word about amongst your brother undertakers."

Gaelan withdrew several sovereigns from his purse and sent them on their way. He did not know what took Barlow—or his family. The ailment was strange enough; it would not do to have Mr. Barlow's corpse hanging about the Man O'War, passing it on to the living.

Indeed, the bed linens would need burning. On the morrow would be soon enough. He was far too weary and would as like set ablaze the entire building.

When Gaelan entered the flat, Cate was sitting in his favorite chair, reading by the soft glow of candlelight. She didn't see him at first, and for a moment, Gaelan looked upon her from the threshold. What a piteous future had this young woman before her. If she'd a mind to relent and return to her family, she'd quickly find herself married off to a man of wealth twice her age with no better prospects than the hand of a ruined lass. Such was her fate. And if not that? What then? The streets? And what of Simon Bell? Would she not be wise to trust him? Perhaps he . . .

Cate looked up, her expression puzzled. "What was the racket below?"

"A man . . . a man fell ill," he stammered, distressed he'd been caught out staring at her. "Sadly, he is no longer amongst the living." Gaelan wished not to burden her with his worries. "I was also visited by a physician who was quite concerned about a missing young lady who might well have found herself in a bad way. I can only assume he meant you. He did not share her name, nor did I ask it. He claimed to be a friend of hers. A certain Dr. *Bell*." He regarded her, curious of her reaction. "Do you know the name?"

She tensed, recoiling deep into the chair. "Simon? Or James."

That second name Gaelan did not recognize, but clearly, she well knew to whom he was referring.

"It was *Simon* Bell. He insists you are friends?"

She seemed to relax, if only a bit. "I know him but slightly. A stout-hearted fellow. He is betrothed to a distant cousin—Sophia Wallingford of Gattonside. I do not wish him to know I am in residence here. Our circle of acquaintances is small enough that before long, my father will know of my presence here, no matter Simon's undoubted promise of discretion." Her eyes widened. "What did he . . . ? What did you . . . say?"

She was on edge, ready to flee at the smallest provocation.

"He merely asked if I had, perchance, treated this particular young woman. Seen her about. I assured him I had not. I told him nothing of your presence here, even with much reason for me to suspect the young woman of whom he spoke was you. I did not so much as ask the girl's name. And the subject was dropped for a more pressing matter."

"Thank you, Mr. Erceldoune, for all you have done these past two days."

"I have done nothing but what any man, any practitioner would do in a like circumstance, I assure you. Now rest; you are not as strong as you might believe yourself to be. It is easy to be fooled into too much exertion, too early."

Their eyes locked, her gaze pleading. "It is too much to ask that I impose on your hospitality any longer. Yet, until I've somewhere—"

"Only a day or two more, until you've regained your strength. And then I might suggest . . ." Exactly what? Sally Mills's busy public house? Cast her out into the streets? "Have you someone you might trust? You might send for? Bell, as you say, seems a good man. Perhaps—"

She shook her head. "No one. I have no one. Even should I trust Simon completely, the chance he might . . . even inadvertently—" Her lip quivered, and tears gathered in the hollow beneath her deep-set eyes.

"Do not trouble yourself now; think upon it and we shall discuss on the morrow."

"I am sorry to impose on your good graces—and your continued discretion. I am most fortunate to have landed on your doorstep, and not . . . another."

Indeed. The plate of food was scarce touched. "You should eat. And drink the elixir I left for you. You must drink it all."

"I've little appetite, but I have finished the drink."

She opened the book she'd been holding on her lap. "I have been quite captivated by this volume from your library. I've never seen anything of its like. The illustrations are glorious. Mysterious as they are unusual. Wherever did you come by—?"

Gaelan pinched the bridge of his nose. He had no time for idle discussion. "Cate, I apologize. Perhaps we might talk later, but I must go up to my laboratory for . . ." He stopped midsentence as he noticed for the first time exactly what had so beguiled her.

Damnation. What was he thinking to have left the ouroboros book in plain sight?

"My lady!" Gaelan wrested the book from her hands, too roughly, placing it behind him on a table, and out of her view. "I adjure you not take up that which is beyond your ken."

The rebuke might well have been better directed toward himself, not Cate. She folded herself further into the deep brocade of the cushions, now fully sobbing. Now he'd frightened her.

"Please, Mr. Erceldoune, I did not know . . . It was atop the table, and I was drawn, sir, to its great beauty. A work of art more than a book. And—"

Gaelan closed his eyes, calming the storm brewing behind them. "Please forgive my outburst. There is no excuse for it. You are a guest in my home—and a patient. I should not have . . ." Every excuse he mustered fell flat to his ear. He shrugged, embarrassed.

He had set that terrible fright in her eyes. "Do not grieve yourself, my lady. It is but a book, though quite rare. It has been in my family for centuries, and I fear for its . . . for its fragility. It might be—"

She sniffled, the tears slowing. "It is no matter. You did say to avail myself of your library." The merest hint of a smile creased the corners of her mouth.

"Indeed, I did." He gathered the book to his chest. "This book, in any case, I've need of it just now. But take care, please do not . . . In future . . . It is not for your eyes or anyone's but mine. But I am sore grieved to have frighted you so. Please, my lady, forgive my outburst. And now, with your indulgence, I shall take my leave."

Without awaiting her reply, Gaelan retrieved several manuscripts from the dining table, and avoiding her gaze, fled up the stairs and into the welcome isolation of his laboratory. The young lady was a distraction he could ill afford just now.

Gaelan seated himself at a large writing table in the corner and arranged the papers about the top of it. No matter how he weighed the symptoms of both men—Bell's patient and Mr. Barlow—his thoughts always returned to the English sweat. No matter how little the sense of it. The least plausible diagnosis; perhaps the simplest to consider and discard quickly. If he could not, Gaelan would have his answer, improbable as it was.

The Sweating Sickness: A Boke or Counseill Against the Disease Commonly Called the Sweate or Sweatyng Sicknesse. John Caius's 1552 work on *sudor anglicus* sat open on Gaelan's desk. Each of Barlow's symptoms matched exactly to Caius's descriptions, their severity and order of presentation. How had it returned from the dead, when it had been gone from these shores these three centuries past?

John Caius wrote there was no cure for it. Why that conclusion, when Grandpapa had managed to prevent the sweat from crossing the border to Scotland some twenty-five years before Caius's text?

And what of Barlow's dragonflies? Were they but the ravings of a man on the brink of death? Then why did they nibble so relentlessly at the edge of Gaelan's thoughts?

He searched through his grandfather's journal for any mention at all of dragonflies. Perhaps . . .

Although I do propose that treating each symptom individually as they appear may prove effective, we must see the dragon as a whole—not scales and wings and tail, not fire, nor fangs, nor jagged teeth. Granted, each may appear simultaneous and malicious, each burning with its own mortal danger, but we must distinguish them one from the other, as much as be possible; fight the fiend with shield and sword. It is only in so doing singularly and as one that we tame the dragon disease into a harmless fluttering dragonfly. On this I've but one source for good counsel, and that is the words of the healing goddess Airmid. "Leabhar ghalair agus a leigheas luibhean Airmid."

Gaelan sighed. Inevitable, was it not? "The book of diseases and medicines—of Airmid," Gaelan translated aloud. The ouroboros book. Grandpapa's journal continued:

And once again, I must rely upon the goodly brethren of Dernwode House and the splendor of their healing gardens, sprung direct, I would aver, from the most secret cloak of Airmid herself, deny it though ever they have done.

Grandpapa lamented the decline of the monastery as the monks, stripped of their stature, continued the work to which they'd long ago committed, but as laymen, and in the shadows. Yet their medicines and their artistry were much hidden from the king and his men.

Deep in the shadows of the hills of Eildon, away from curious eyes, the gardens yet thrived, their rare plantings in combinations found nowhere else on Earth, with healing powers unknown but to a few, and ever at the service of the House of Learmont.

An annotation lettered in red drew Gaelan's gaze to the encircled paragraph:

Should this dragon invader cross the border despite our goodly efforts, and indiscriminate slaughter, burial alone suffice not to quench the disease of its thirst. We must take care to cover over the corpses in their burial pits with quicklime, and then take to it flame so nothing of them remain to tempt the dragon's return.

Twenty more pages of detailed notes and Gaelan was convinced of the possibility that the Barlow family may well have succumbed to an extinct disease. If it was indeed the English sweat, his grandfather's notes pointed a way to slay the dragon before it consumed London. But to proceed would require him break a vow taken two centuries earlier to never again use the ouroboros book for any but the most academic purpose.

Gaelan looked up from his grandfather's notebook, pinching the bridge of his nose. The laboratory was dark but for a single candle flame, barely aflicker. He had lost all track of time.

It would by now be long past midnight. Ideas had begun to take root, yet he had no answer to the question nagging at him since he'd first thought of the English sweat. How had it returned? Without an answer to that question he could not very well argue his case to Bell—or anyone else. And why Barlow and his family? And why Bell's patient? No others fallen ill, at least none come to the apothecary. Was that, then, the counterargument? The most significant clue that it mightn't be the English sweat at all.

Frustrated, and back at the start, Gaelan closed the book and looked up from his writing, rubbing his eyes, which burned with the need for rest. Cate would by now be asleep, and to go down into the flat would be to waken her needlessly. Instead, he lay on a small cot and tried to sleep, knowing he would not.

CHAPTER 23

Dragonflies zigzagged, fairy-like wisps of blue and green, diving about the cattails and reeds as they flitted in and out of Gaelan's view, dropping one by one, dead, into a scarlet pool. A constant refrain, "sudor anglicus," buzzed loud and insistent from within the dream. He shoved away the coverlet and lit a fresh candle. There would be no sleep this night.

Sudor anglicus. What if Barlow and his family were not alone? Had others already succumbed, unbeknownst to Gaelan? Others that may even now be dying or dead in their beds? To ignore the possibility could well cost many lives.

Yet, could it not be just as well a form of the influenza he had yet to encounter? La Grippe. A murderous disease as it cast its shadow, village upon village. Ten days, two weeks, the patient would live; the patient would die.

Barlow died in a matter of hours. His family, likely the same. Death had come to them with the swiftness of dragon's fire, fierce and more powerful than he had ever experienced with La Grippe. One day, two, perhaps. This was no ordinary influenza.

For some moments, Gaelan stared at the unopened ouroboros book, fingers trembling. Little choice now but to confirm his suspicions—or refute them, yet he was hesitant to embark on a thing he might regret. Long ago he'd vowed never again to use its recipes. For lifetimes, he would pay dearly for having done so two hundred years past.

Mightn't the risk be too great? *Sudor anglicus* would sweep through a town, but vanish with the first winds of autumn, leaving death in its wake, taking its due, but randomly. Was that not the way as well of the influenza? In that case, would it not be best to allow the disease its course?

Not best. Easier. For him, alone. And cowardly. For then he could ignore the ouroboros book. Place it back on its shelf—a curiosity to be admired for its artistry, not its alchemy. But it would be wrong, and should this fever indeed be the English sweat, the deaths of too many would haunt him, not only for the span of a normal life but for an eternity of them.

Running his hand across the engraved leather of the cover, Gaelan allowed his fingers to absorb the deep jeweled colors that seemed at one with the leather, pools of liquefied sapphire, ruby, emerald, amber. Diamonds. The large hawthorn tree at its center, branches knotted with ouroboroses, the tree itself entwined in fire of copper and gold, flames licking at its trunk, yet not consumed by them.

As a lad, Gaelan could recite from memory, naming the central image of each page—in order. Hard experience had proved that rote memorization of pretty pictures was a pitiable substitute for understanding of their context—and content. Perhaps this time, with his grandfather's notes to guide his hand and prompt his mind, it would be enough.

A frisson pulsed through his fingers, electric and strange, bid him open the cover and set to work. Hastening past a frightening Karkinos, the luminous Diana with her bow, intertwined snake-trees consumed by fire, improbable gardens and marshes alive with fairies and sprites at play, Gaelan stopped at the page he'd sought. He took in the whole of it—a tranquil pond; every figure, every line and corner of hidden text, the smallest image, pulsed with life. Yes, the image in the dream.

He must get this exactly right. And if he did not? *Sola dosis facit venenum*, said Paracelsus. The dose makes the poison. Too little and no effect at all; too much might well unleash consequences yet unknowable.

He dipped his pen in the ink bottle and took account first of the myriad languages embedded within the scene, bending and twisting into distinct patterns: Scottish Gaelic, Scots, Old English, Latin, Greek, Hebrew letters that he remembered were not Hebrew but another, more mystical, tongue derived from it; Arabic as well. He must be methodical about it. Faultless. The risk was too great for error. Yet this was the easiest task, the simple deciphering. The more challenging tasks would follow—to make sense of it, and then conjure the treatment needed to slay the pestilent dragon.

His index finger poised just above the page, Gaelan hesitated to touch it directly, lest the ancient inks flake away in his hand, marring the exquisite images. Yet, it was too difficult to follow the texts as they traversed branches, entwined within the wings of tiny sprites, and threaded between the tall grasses and cattails.

A fresh goose quill would do quite well to trace along the text. He chose a single line of Latin script, following it as it looped back on itself, shifting every few words from Latin to Gaelic and then back to Latin, the letters forming a large bloom—a rose, perhaps, colored in a deep scarlet, shimmering in the sun. Within the rose sat a sprite, wings tipped in gleaming emerald as endlessly deep as it was fragile—the fluff of an eider's down. And within the wings, symbols.

The margins, decorated in inks of black, gold, silver, copper, framed a scene of dragonflies, pansies, violets, narcissus, and other radiant flowers: blues of several hues, greens and purples, a pond of turquoise teeming with life, even as it lay two-dimensional on the page. A stream, its current swift and powerful, doused a wildfire raging amongst a patch of reeds.

He could happily spend hours lost inside this page alone, untangling every twist and bend of letter; interpreting every dot of color within color within color. The opposite page had been similarly embellished, but rendered in the reds, oranges, and greens of fire-breathing, winged monsters born of the most ancient legends. Behind a hawthorn tree he lurked, a hideous, jeweled dragon, ready to ambush.

The two pages converged; one upon the other, the dragon slowly merged with the dragonflies, bled together like a butterfly emerging from a cocoon. The dragons shed their intense reds, which were transformed to purples, then blues and finally placid green as they metamorphosed to dragonflies. Gaelan remembered these images but had never understood them.

Using his grandfather's notes and his own, rather eroded, skill in the languages, Gaelan meticulously translated the page into a single readable text. Hours later, he was finished, but for comprehending the significance of the dragonflies—if there was any to be had. Perchance the drawings were but artifice—to disguise and distract, draw scrutiny away from the texts with pretty pictures. Not all eyes had the ability to see into a book such as this.

On the other hand . . .

The laboratory door opened behind him; Gaelan jumped, as the unexpected sound split the silence. The metal pen slipped his grasp, and its glass nib shattered on the floor. He looked up, squinting through the bright light pouring in through the window glass. When had the sun come up? Indeed, the morning sun streamed into the laboratory, glinting off the smooth stone edges of the bench tops.

"Good morrow, Mr. Erceldoune. I have been looking all about for you. And here you are!"

Cate stood in the doorway, enmeshed in a sunbeam that surrounded her in a halo of light. He rubbed his eyes, for a moment unsure who—or what—he was seeing. Indeed, his eyes ached with fatigue and from hours of working in the dark, never noticing the candle flame had gone out.

Gaelan was irritated by her presumption to come up to his laboratory uninvited, but there was little point in reproach. He was not pleased by the interruption, yet it was good a time as any to pause in his work. For a moment. Raking trembling fingers through his unbound hair, he endeavored a futile attempt to make himself presentable.

"You should not have mounted those steep stairs in your condition, my lady. You've nearly recovered by now, and your adventure to find me may well have thwarted it all."

He approached, gently taking her elbow, leading her to the sole chair in the room before retreating a respectful distance from her side. There was no sign of fever; indeed, she seemed stronger today. Beneath her shy smile, roses in her cheeks, a good sign. Very. Yet, her condition was still fragile. "You *are* much improved. Nearly—"

She stood up suddenly, hands on her hips, approaching, perhaps too near for comfort. "I am bored, sir, and have been imprisoned in your flat now for days."

"Hardly that, my lady, and you are no prisoner! And if . . . I have kept you here only until such time as—" *What on Earth has brought all this on?* Ah, his earlier outburst.

She sat again, her eyes softened by gathering tears; they glittered, cut emeralds caught in a sunbeam. No, not anger. Fear. Fear he would send her on her way, return her home. He recognized this look well enough.

"Not that I am complaining, Mr. Erceldoune. Much to the contrary. You have been beyond kindly, sir. Beyond . . . Please forgive my—"

"Hush now. I'd have done the same for any—"

"The risk, sir . . . My father—"

"Knows *not* that you are resident here. And shall not, unless you tell him yourself. You are ready to return home in any event, should you desire it. In fact, I see no reason for you to stay, if that be what you wish. Or to find other accommodation. Simon Bell might perhaps—"

"No! I do not trust Simon. I have no one—"

"I cannot keep you here indefinitely, whatever you—"

Steadying herself against the laboratory bench, she took in the breadth of the laboratory. "This room is . . . it is glorious. As beautiful as my father's solarium! What is this place?"

The change of subject was not unwelcome. For the moment. "It . . . it is where I work when not in the shop. Here I prepare the recipes: the elixirs and lotions, poultices, items I employ in my trade. I am new to this part of London, and I hope in a time not too distant, this will be a busy place, as I make myself better known to the physicians hereabouts. Although I daresay, in the brief time I have been here, I've seen nary a one—save Dr. Bell. I do not expect that many of them would attend the ill here, but—"

Cate laughed. "Did you think even one of those dandies might dirty their breeches or boots in Smithfield? I aver not, sir! Very few would come here amongst what is called by many the 'vile zoology' of the place. And they do not, I daresay, refer to the animals sold in the market. Do you think, no matter your reputation elsewhere, any would deign to visit you here? Indeed not!"

She was right, of course. He had said it himself many times over. "It grieves me, but I know it to be true. I've had my doubts about the medical care afforded the people here resident. It is poor, to be sure. But no physicians about at all? And with St. Bartholomew's so nearby, I'd hoped I was mistaken, but feared it. Which is why, in part, I've chosen Smithfield. The folk here are in sore need and I've no lack of skill," Gaelan said with more pride than he'd meant. "Yet it angers me that . . . You would think, if only out of a sense of duty to Hippocrates . . . The suffering alone would—"

"Would not signify amongst a single one of them, sir! At least not amongst the physicians with whom *I* am acquainted."

Gaelan snatched a glass flask from the workbench, clutching its slender neck until he thought it might shatter in his hand, infuriated at the lot of them—Bell included. For where had *he* been, this descendent of the brilliant, compassionate Benjamin Bell? And yet, well-qualified apothecaries were scorned by medical society, when they should be welcomed as equals in practice.

Cate approached the workbench, cautious, yet her intention was clear, her gaze fixed on the flask still clenched in Gaelan's fist, her hand held up to stay his. She was too near, yet he applauded her effort to settle his ire. The girl was quite something. Clever did not begin to describe her.

"Fear not, dear lady. I've not a mind to shatter the vessel. I've need of it in the hours to come. And many more yet to craft."

"What an exquisite and unusual vessel it, Mr. Erceldoune. Its neck is delicate and . . . those arms, so magnificently curved. It resembles a bird to my mind—odd to be sure, but perhaps a shore bird. I fear your grip on it is so fierce . . ."

Gaelan glanced from the flask to his guest. Shrugging, he placed it gently on the countertop and wiped his hands on his waistcoat. "Aye, birdlike indeed. It is, in fact, called a pelican retort. Of quite an ancient design. Medieval . . . if I am not mistaken," he added quickly.

He held it out to Cate, inviting her to examine it. "Some ascribe a spiritual purpose to an implement such as this, but I find it is quite effective in rendering my preparations the purest possible, which has very little to do with the soul, but much to do with healing the body."

"Wherever did you find such a thing?"

"I fashion all my own glassware. Do you fancy glass, then? It is an odd occupation for a lady such as yourself—"

"Not so odd as you might think. When I was a girl, my father would delight me with baubles from his glassworks. He owns . . . I mean to say, up north . . ." She turned away briefly. Clearly, she had said more than intended. "Suffice to say," she continued after a moment, "I've an eye for glass wares, and—"

Gaelan searched her countenance; her cheeks reddened under his scrutiny. "You are Lord Alfred Kinston's daughter." An accusation more than a statement. He regretted the tone of it immediately. He knew the man only incidentally, but his glassworks too well. Of all the people to venture past his threshold in seek of help, he'd not expected . . .

"I . . ." Cate's eyes fluttered and Gaelan was beside her in two steps, catching her before she fell to the wood planks.

"You should not have come up here," he said too sternly, setting her back into the chair. "The climb is too sharp and perhaps I was hasty in thinking your recovery—"

"No, that is not it. Not at all. It is that you . . . Why did you say that? That my father is Lord Kinston?"

Gaelan ignored the question. He poured a tumbler of water from a blue glass carafe. "Drink this—"

She waved him away. "I *must* know how you guessed it. Or have you known all along and have been planning my return, even today? What did he offer you? Or was it *Simon Bell* made the offer?"

"My lady, do not agitate yourself. You've nothing to fear from me. This is but cool water. It will freshen you in a trice. I promise."

She nodded, sipping slowly before handing it back to him.

Gaelan sat on the floor beside the chair. He needed to calm her; it would not do in the midst of this crisis to have her relapse. "I swear it, until you made mention . . . I lived for a time in the north of England and knew of a glassworks there—between Liverpool and Sheffield. Kinston Glassworks, owned by Alfred Easton, Earl of Kinston. There are other glassworks in the north, of course, but . . ." He shook his head and shrugged. "It was but a *guess*."

CHAPTER 24

Gaelan had known Lord Kinston when the earl was but five and twenty—and the most ruthless of masters. The burns, the overwork, the disease from too many hours and too much exposure to poison in the windowless purgatory of the Kinston Glassworks. So, the girl was yet another of Kinston's victims. Gaelan peered at the floorboards, refusing to look up into Cate's gaze.

Finally, she spoke. "I do not know what to say, sir. You now have the power to return me to the one place I cannot go, that I detest with all my heart. My father would indeed pay you *well* for that service. I ask but one thing. That you allow me but a day's head start. I shall be out of your hair, whatever comes to pass."

There was a steely boldness in the tenor of her voice. She was strong; that much was obvious. But force her to withstand her father's certain cruel judgment? He could not do that to her. He could not deny her whatever small amount of protection was in his power to offer. "I would not betray this confidence, nor the trust you've placed in me by confessing it, my lady. Please do not trouble yourself ere you work yourself into an awful state. Be assured I've said nothing about you. Not to Bell. Not to anyone."

Gaelan retrieved a small amber bottle from a shelf, placing three drops into her water glass. Again, she waved him away. "You ought drink this; it will hasten your recovery. For despite how well you might be faring now, a turn for the worse is not out of the question. Not yet, especially as you seem quite insistent upon climbing stairs and moving about when you should be resting!" He could not suppress the small quirk of a smile.

She was beautiful, this young lass, and Gaelan imagined how a smile would brighten her countenance and lighten the heavy burden she wore in the grim line of her mouth and her luminous, sad eyes. He stood to go back to his work, needing desperately to break the sudden intimacy gathering between them. "Please allow me, my lady, to return to the task at hand. I've yet a few hours' work ahead of me before—"

"When I was a child," she began, ignoring him, taking a further step toward him, "my father would bring me trinkets from the glassworks; they were precious to me as the crown jewels."

There it was—the beginnings of a true smile. He took several steps backwards, moving to the other side of a long workbench. "It is, indeed, a miraculous thing—a magical thing, glass is, but I must insist . . ."

He retreated to an area in the far corner, clear but for a large cauldron set atop several large, flat granite tiles. She followed. "Please, my lady, allow me to attend to my work. I must insist—"

"Caitrin. That is my name, and now you know who I am, there is little purpose concealing it from you."

"Caitrin, then. Greek in origin: pure. Quite fitting you. And an improvement over 'Cate.'" Tapping the edge of a tile, Gaelan ignited a blaze beneath the cauldron, drawing out his watch and noting the time.

She frowned, her lower lip trembling. "I am quite the opposite of pure, and that you know only too well, sir."

He should not have made mention of so sensitive a point. "I cannot agree. Yet, perhaps a distraction might be in order to forestall an argument on the subject of purity. And I've just the thing, and it will not at all keep me from my work."

Of all chemistry's creations, none was so magical as glass: amorphous and liquid, jewel hard, yet not solid—no crystals to be seen in its composition. Yet. Sand and soda ash and lime. Iron and whatever else his heart desired, set afire and transformed into something so fragile, so beautiful, and yet so practical.

"You see, I have always fashioned my own glassware. No baubles, not often, only what is required in my trade: flasks, cylinders, tubes. I learned the craft as a boy, and it has stayed with me always. Quite an extraordinary thing to transform simple sand and metals into something durable and at the same time so very fragile. Alchemy at its most elemental—fire, earth, the air needed to fuel the fire. Water to harden it."

"You insist on its practicality, yet you speak of it as a poet might."

Ah, there it was—the full smile he'd hoped to elicit from her, softening every feature. The instant transformation left him breathless. His face grew hot, and not from the fire beneath the cauldron. He turned away from her, retrieving a few needed implements from a low shelf.

"I've a need just now to craft several vessels quite soon should I have need of a particular prescript. And if you promise to keep your distance . . . for your safety of course . . . I would not mind if you would stay and observe. That is, if it might amuse . . . distract you . . . from your troubles."

"It would that, Mr. Erceldoune."

Her eyes sparkled with a light he'd not seen in them. Anticipation. Curiosity. He could not hope to divert her from her thoughts with a simple beaker, nor even a swan flask. He knew exactly what would spark her imagination and demonstrate the true magic of glass.

Gaelan collected a few items from the workbench before returning to the cauldron. "I should like to fashion for you a Rupert's drop. It will serve both to test the readiness of my cauldron . . . and as a bit of an apology for my earlier brusqueness."

He would lose a moment or two, but to see her laugh, even that smile once again . . . Had he but the time, he would play the court magician, revealing the trick with an actor's flair. But he'd too much to do; besides, he'd never been much the showman, unlike too many, less scrupulous, fellow apothecaries, who'd the canny instincts to gather about them all manner of passersby. Pied pipers with horse-piss tonics.

She shrugged, and her hair cascaded about her shoulders—a blaze of sunlight captured on a fine summer's morning. "I do not understand. A Rupert's . . . what?"

"A Rupert's drop. Do you not know what that is? Did your father never let you witness the brilliance of it?"

His tutors at Dernwode House, who'd taught him the trick, would scold him when he'd dare call it magical: "This is not magic. Magic is for fools and heretics"—reminding him that his own father had been executed for wielding *so-called magic*. "This is science. Manipulation of God's Nature, as we are intended to do, and nothing more."

Indeed, they had been right, but as a lad . . . Magic. Science. The two were entwined and inseparable—a matter of perception. One era's magic was another's great scientific achievement. After more than two centuries, he'd seen it proven over and again.

Gaelan glanced at his watch again and returned to the cauldron, pouring the contents of several small jars into the pot. Caitrin followed to stand at his side.

"Not so close by." He ushered her to a large crate—a safe distance. "Please, my lady, do remain seated whilst I work."

"What are you doing, sir? What do you stir into that pot?"

"Potash and copper oxide, a small amount of a silver compound as well, together I blend them under the immense heat of—"

She began again to rise from her place, her countenance ablaze with curiosity. He held out a forestalling hand. "Please do keep your seat, and not draw too near. The heat will singe your hair." Gaelan stirred the brass cauldron with a metal rod, tapping his foot to the stone tile a second time.

"Where is the furnace to heat your mixture?"

"It is hidden in the stones, where it might safely do its bidding without setting my shop and half the market afire! An invention of mine, and quite sufficient, I assure you, for my purposes."

He withdrew the rod, and with it, a syrupy ball of molten glass, which resembled blue-green molasses. "Now watch, my lady, and you shall see!"

The small ball dangled from the tip of the rod, transforming into a large blue teardrop as Gaelan manipulated the metal implement over a second vessel filled with cold water. Lower and lower it dropped, thinning at the very top into a glistening thread no wider than a spider's silk, before it snapped, sinking into the water.

"A moment." Gaelan held up a hand, admonishing Caitrin not to rise from her place. Plunging his hand into the water, he withdrew the drop and knelt on the floor before her. "I am no magician, I fear; I've no flair for theatrics, yet there is little else as magical as this piece. From liquid to solid it has journeyed in the span of mere seconds. Yet that is not the best of it."

He opened his hand, revealing the turquoise teardrop, iridescent and gleaming.

She gasped, her hand to her heart. "It is exquisite."

"It is hard as diamond. I might take a mallet to it, and it would not break, yet—"

"Oh, do show me. Please!" she asked. Her eyes sparkled in delight and curiosity. She clapped her hands together in glee as a child might do.

"Very well." He bid her to follow.

"Ah, so now I might rise from my place at last?"

"The danger is past. The cauldron will settle now, ready for use, but no danger to . . ." He gestured toward her hair, which hung wild about her face and down her back.

"Is the furnace fire yet ablaze? Have you not work—?" As she approached, Gaelan showed her a foot pedal at the base of the platform. "A small device to calm the blaze. Maintain the heat, but not douse it. But come. See."

He led Caitrin to his workbench. "Observe! But do not close your eyes, not even a blink. No matter how you may wish to do so. You must witness every moment."

Gaelan took up a sledgehammer from his desk, lifting it above the glass drop.

Cate held up her hands. "No! Do not . . . You shall destroy . . . Please!"

"Do not trouble yourself! I only mean to demonstrate my point. That something so apparently fragile may not be quite as we perceive. Now observe. I promise," he added with a smile, "if it breaks, I shall make for you ten more—in all the colors of the rainbow. Now step back and do not close your eyes. Shield them if you think I might blind you with the scattered shards, but . . . do watch!"

Caitrin inhaled a deep breath under Gaelan's attentive gaze. He meant to dazzle her, uncertain why it had become so important—and so suddenly. He'd been immune to the charms of women far more beautiful than she—for decade upon decade, yet . . .

Gaelan hoisted the hammer high above his head and struck a blow, hitting the drop straight on, startling himself with the ferocity of the strike and its thunderous blow.

"You see, my lady? It did not break. It did quite dent my metal tray, but the glass drop is intact. Not even a chip!"

Gaelan handed it to her, removing a transparent glass beaker from a shelf. He held up a finger. "Now my lady, if you will clip the drop like so . . ." Gaelan slipped a small implement into her hand, holding the teardrop above the beaker.

"One, two, three, and . . . now," he encouraged Caitrin. "Cut it . . . right . . . there."

She snipped the fine thread of glass that extended from the glass bauble and it exploded into the beaker—a shower of color and fine sparkling powder like fine blue snow.

Her reaction was as he'd hoped. Delight as if she'd not a care in the world. It would do for now, until the reality of her situation renewed itself in her thoughts. "I've no time now, but perhaps later I might fashion for you a jar in which you might keep the tiny shards!"

"But how? How is it possible to work this sorcery?"

"It is naught but physics. I do not understand it. Not completely. Yet, I know it is true. Parlor trick though it is, the science of it is compelling, is it not? Something so hard, so durable that it might not be fractured by a hammer's blow would disintegrate to powder by a single snip at the neck?"

"Very like the human body, I daresay. Tough and sturdy, yet so very fragile that a single knife-blow to the neck might destroy it."

Strong, fragile. The hardness of bone, enough to support the body, yet brittle enough to break with a direct blow. Yet the organs, fragile for the filigree of vessels running through and between: liver to spleen to heart to lung, soft and placid but a powerful engine. The lungs. That was the key to taming this dragon.

"My lady Caitrin, yes! Thank you! Of course! It is brilliant!" An idea, unrelated on its face, but inspired. Brilliant. He must set to work. Immediately.

CHICAGO, PRESENT DAY

CHAPTER 25

Anne readied the small examining room for her new patient—her only patient. Two days later, she was still shaken by her experience at the glass museum; the tips of her fingers still tingled, peculiar and electric. As if they'd connected in some way, she and Gaelan, through glass. She swore she'd seen him, heard his voice, the most fleeting moment. Intellectually, it was her grief and nothing more. Gaelan was dead. *Just bloody get on with it!*

The girl—Erin—and her father were due any minute. The large examination room, provided by Alcott's money and contacts, was a physician's—a geneticist's—dream. But she could not afford to be lulled by magically arranged office suites and high-tech medical toys.

Erin Alcott was the innocent here, the victim of a horrific disease. Whatever the father's ambitions, the girl could not be blamed. And if Anne could save her life, the lives of others stricken with GPC? So be it.

She turned down Alcott's offer of a hotel suite at the Four Seasons as a bit too chummy, even if more convenient than commuting to and from Simon's house some thirty miles up the coast. If the consult went on too long, Anne would well afford a room at her own expense. If she found herself too drawn in, all she need do is imagine his friends at the Galahad Society and their vampiric methods to remain forever young.

As for the fresh approach to the case Anne promised, it was at best a fantasy. GPC was neither curable nor treatable no matter how many pharmaceutical companies Alcott acquired, or how many genetic disease specialists he'd enticed into questing for this particular grail. She understood the allure of it. A cure for GPC? That would be a lifetime's enduring achievement for anyone in her field. A breakthrough to trigger other, bigger, innovations in treating short telomere diseases. A Nobel wasn't an impossibility either. Not for puzzling out this one.

Her office windows offered a glorious view of Navy Pier. The Ferris wheel with its garish spokes and neon lights dominated the scene. But it was the glass museum beneath she could not stop thinking about. It hadn't occurred to her that Gaelan had a life—a full life—more than a century ago. An artist? A master glassmaker? Had he known Tiffany personally? Worked alongside him? How she would love to ask him about life . . . real life . . . in other ages. But he was gone.

Erin Alcott was dropped off by a young woman precisely at ten o'clock. The girl was a bit of a shock. Inquisitive and clever beyond her eight years, but why not? Her father was a certified genius. The Edison of our time—at least that's what his website touted. Had Gaelan met Thomas Edison in 1893 at the World's Fair?

Erin was decidedly unsentimental for such a young kid. She was well versed in every bit of what Anne could only assume was the standard physical examination she'd undergone dozens of times, from dozens of doctors.

"My dad doesn't want me to die, but he doesn't want anyone to die. Ever."

"Ever? We *all* die at some time. Okay, sweetheart, make a good fist for me."

Erin pumped her hand. "I'm gonna die sooner than most. Like Mom. But Dad says it's not gonna happen. I'll never die. Ever. He promises. But I don't believe him."

And well you shouldn't! What sort of bollocks was he feeding the girl? She ignored the comment. "No need to pump. I've got your vein. Hold the fist, though. Well, we'll see about that. I can't make any promises, but—"

"They all say that. You know, you're not the first doctor my dad's taken me to."

"I'm aware. And you know more about GPC than some of my colleagues. Bit of a pinch here. Sorry." Anne inserted the butterfly catheter into Erin's arm, observing the burgundy blood fill the Vacutainer. "One more tube and we're . . . done."

She handed the girl gauze to hold over the insertion point and covered it with a Band-Aid.

"No superhero bandages?"

"I can order some, if you'd like."

"Nah. That's okay. The docs are always trying to make me like them. Superhero bandages seem to be the favorite way. As if it'll rub off on me. Pretty stupid, huh?"

"I've got lollies. Fun flavors, perfect for summer."

Erin smiled. "Blueberry?"

Anne produced a box of lollipops from her messenger bag. "Take your choice. Two if you'd like."

The girl had some of the symptoms, but not severe to an untrained eye. She'd been diagnosed at seven years, so it had been a year. She had patches of a lacy rash on her upper torso, and perhaps some hair loss, along with the signature deteriorated fingernails.

The door opened. "Is she ready to go?"

"Mr. Alcott. Yes. I'm glad you've fetched her. I have one or two questions for you, if you don't mind."

"Sure. Shoot."

"Erin, would you mind having a seat in the waiting room?"

"I'd rather hear."

Anne glanced at Alcott, who shrugged.

Anne looked from father to daughter, deciding not to make an issue of it. "Okay. Your wife. You say she'd been diagnosed with GPC?"

"Yeah. Symptoms started in her early forties."

"How did she die?"

"The GPC." His eyes narrowed. "I don't know where you're going with this."

"Bear with me. People who acquire GPC have variable symptoms, and they often grow more severe in subsequent generations. Your wife didn't show signs until early middle age. Your daughter at seven. Cause of death might be any number of things resulting from the mutation that causes the disease but doesn't cause death on its own. What was the official cause of death?"

"Leukemia."

Anne nodded tightly, briefly glancing at Erin, who flicked her eyes toward Anne before biting off a corner of her lollypop.

Anne returned her attention toward Alcott, clearing her throat. "Your mother-in-law, was she ill? I doubt she would have been diagnosed, but do you know anything about . . . was she . . ."

"She died while my wife was in grad school. Before we met. It's in the history. Didn't you read it among the buried hundreds of pages in her file?"

"Of course I have. I wanted to hear it from you. It does all fit."

"So now what?"

"*Now* I do my tests, study her genetic makeup." She glanced at Erin, uncomfortable to go on with the caveat that she was unlikely to come up with anything that the several doctors had not already thought of. "She definitely shows symptoms of GPC, but you already knew that. I will run the diagnostic tests, run her blood through the gene sequencer, and we shall see."

"And a treatment?"

Anne shook her head, uneasy to say it in front of the girl, who was now observing the exchange with the intensity of a tennis umpire. "Let's see what the tests say, and take it from there, shall we?"

"What if I tell you I may be able to acquire something that will make your job easier—and more?"

"You've granted me a veritable molecular biologist's Christmas wish list. I don't see what else—"

"You will." A self-satisfied smile crossed his face. "Hey, we're going to take a trip up to the zoo. Care to join us?"

Not a chance in hell. "Nope. Got work to do. Besides which, I am terribly far behind in closing out the affairs of a recently departed relative, so I will have to take a pass. Might I speak with you alone? For just a moment. Erin, would you mind going into the waiting room? Your dad will be out in just a minute."

Anne watched the girl leave, closing the door behind her.

"Mr. Alcott, you do your daughter no good to tell her she will live, not to mention 'forever.' It's irresponsible—"

"She's a kid."

"I thought you weren't involved with the Galahad—"

"I'm not. Did she say something about . . . ? I'm not. And that's quite a leap. What exactly did she say to you?" Alcott walked to the window, looking down onto the street. "Nice view. I mean . . . who's to say? Someday. You know I'm right. Your work . . . your colleagues . . . are proving it more each day. That's all those guys in Galahad are looking for. And I'm not involved with them. Not really. A donation. Sizable, yeah, but . . . And who could blame me given . . . Hey, if they can help unlock the cure to Erin's . . . disease . . . save a lot of kids, why not? There's no price tag on the sort of anguish . . ." He gestured toward the door. "Given the circumstances, I do have an interest in *anything* they discover along the way, and why not? My kid's going to die, just like her mother. Unless—"

Anne had no response. She was torn. Erin's test results would be back in two days, she would write up her findings and turn her over to an American doctor—and be done with Preston Alcott. Desperate father or not, he made her bloody uncomfortable. "I will ring you as soon as I have her test results."

Alcott nodded and, and without another word, left her alone in the exam room. Anne blew out a breath as she heard the elevator ding. With the entire afternoon to herself, and all of Chicago's Magnificent Mile to explore, there was only one place she had any interest in visiting.

It was a longer walk to the glass museum than she'd remembered from the other day. Half a mile to the pier and another mile down to its end and the museum, past kiosk vendors, tall ships and excursion boat tours, inviting restaurants, and The Chicago Shakespeare Company and its futuristic glass-windowed complex. Finally, down the stairs and beneath the Great Hall, she arrived. The museum was a contrast to the touristy scene above; besides the bored-looking attendant, Anne was alone.

"Excuse me. Have you a guide brochure for the museum?"

"Not yet. Being produced. Museum's only been open a few months, you know."

"I did not. Do you mind if I ask *you* a question or two?"

"Nope. You'd probably be better off to do what most folks do. Look it up on the website. Quicker—and better information than I have. Probably why the guide book isn't a big priority."

Anne still could not wrap her mind around believing those panels had been created by Gaelan. If he hadn't, the inscriptions, the designs, would have been an incredible coincidence, emphasis on *incredible*. What was it that Einstein had said? Coincidence was God's way of remaining anonymous. If God existed. *Big if.*

"Fair enough. I have a question about the large panels suspended from the ceiling. Did Tiffany create them all?"

"Nope. He had people working for him, far as I know, back in New York, I think. Can't imagine one man making all of these alone, could you?"

"I suppose not. What do you know about that one in particular?" She pointed to the labyrinth panel.

"No clue. Does have a sort of different look than some of the others, more iridescence to it? A sort of symmetry, I guess you'd say. Same with that one over there." She pointed to the Diana's Tree panel, also signed "G.E."

"Thank you. You've been very helpful. Oh. Do you know the name of the artist who designed those two unique pieces?"

"G.E., whoever that was. I don't know. Tiffany had a lot of people in his glass factory from what I understand, which isn't much. For all I know G.E. made the glass and someone else, maybe Tiffany himself, created the panel. I really have no idea. Like I said. Google it, and maybe you'll find out more."

Anne dragged a stool to the Diana's Tree panel and sat. Looking over her shoulder, to see the guard otherwise occupied, and ignoring the "Do not touch!" signs, Anne placed her palm on the glass, waiting for . . . something. But nothing. Cool, smooth glass and no more than that. Half an hour, pausing only when the guard looked her way in the otherwise empty museum. Nothing. And what the hell did she expect? The prickling in her fingers to return? To see a fleeting image of him? Hear his voice as a ghostlike echo haunting her like a phantom?

Disappointed and feeling quite foolish, she left, wondering if she might find something more at Gaelan's—evidence to confirm, if only to herself, that he was the artist "G.E."

The flat had been freed of its abandoned opium den aroma. Still, it could do with a bit more airing out. She opened the windows again and began searching for whatever the bloody hell she was searching for. He lived his life in and among books—why not start there?

A large art-print catalog, *The Works of Louis Comfort Tiffany*, was shelved in the bottom corner of a floor-to-ceiling bookcase. It had been well read; sticky notes of varying colors poked out between the pages of the heavy volume. As she thumbed through it on Gaelan's desk, Anne recognized several of the museum panels, each marked with an asterisk.

Receipts and letters attesting to authenticity, matched to photographs of several of the works she'd seen in the museum display, were scattered among the disaster of folders and papers piled everywhere. So, he'd been in the market for Tiffany's work, searching for it.

She tried to imagine any scenario in which it was possible that Gaelan had been the anonymous museum benefactor. The wildest of thoughts. But was it really? Preserving the works created for the 1893 exhibition, especially if he . . . ? Where the hell would he have obtained the funds to . . . ?

The books. Of course. That collection must be worth a not-insignificant fortune. Sell a few, trade another few . . . maybe a crowdfunding campaign to boot . . . He might easily have done it, and anonymously, too. Simon had thought Gaelan was destitute, but clearly, he was not. By far.

Call it curiosity, but Anne was keen to uncover everything she could find. No, this was more than curiosity—she was obsessing over this Tiffany glass thing. She knew why. The distraction kept her from thinking of Alcott, of her future . . . of what the bloody hell Gaelan was doing in his lab . . .

Perhaps she might find something more in Simon's papers . . . his diary, some note he'd made about what Gaelan had been up to in the latter part of the nineteenth century. Already, she'd discovered they'd remained in contact despite years they did not see each other at all. There must be some reference. Somewhere.

By the time she opened the door to Simon's house, Anne was exhausted. Mrs. O'Malley had left her a delicious casserole in the oven. Perfect; she was also famished.

Three hours later, searching through dusty, yellowed diaries, she located a relevant entry.

11 September 1891

Finally, I heard today from Erceldoune after five years' silence. He's had no luck, even nearly fifty years hence, in locating that damnable book of his, and has, he insists, given it up. Gone, he said, for good. Time to move on. I can never accept that. For to do so would mean to give up all hope of ending this earthly existence so I might be reunited with my beloved Sophia.

Erceldoune has apparently taken up residence in New York City, where he says he will stay for now. He does not believe enough time has yet passed to return to Britain, absurd as it may be. I think it is rather more he cannot face Eleanor, long since married to a cousin of the queen's, and with children and grandchildren, his own descendants amongst them.

He has apparently found employment in glassmaking of all things. Yes, I recall his abilities in this realm. That odd inoculation device of his own design he'd given me during that horrid illness of '26. I'd never seen anything of its like before then. It was then he'd told me he also crafted his own glassware. Indeed, I employed him many a time afterwards to create glass vessels for my own laboratory as well.

I am happy for him, that he has found a trade that utilizes his unique and substantial gifts. He tells me he has made the acquaintance of a Mr. Louis Comfort Tiffany, a pastor of all things, introduced through a fellow Englishman—a Mr. Arthur Nash of the Tiffany Glass and Decorating Company.

Another entry, and she was certain.

2 January 1894

Erceldoune has sent to me and by extension, Eleanor and my niece Ariadne, greetings from New York, where he is still in residence and working at his art. No luck in locating that book. And yes, I know he has all but given up the chase. He was more excited than I have ever known him to be and chatted on and on about the World's Fair—the Columbian Exposition in Chicago last year. He aims one day to relocate there; he likes it better, he says, than New York. He went on and on about meeting a Nicola Tesla, a physicist and engineer, whom he insists will be one of the brightest lights of the coming century. He shall ignite the world in ways we cannot yet understand, he believes.

He was quite pleased to have three glass panels exhibited at the exposition, including one he dedicated to my sister and their

*daughter, Ariadne. But he went on and on about this Tesla chap,
who, he insists, understands the power of glass and of chemistry,
that the two together fused and lit afire are a force that cannot
be beaten. He spoke of Mr. Tesla's tubes filled with elemental
gases, which created colored lights, the likes of which he'd never
seen. More than ever, he says, he believes there is a transcendent
harmony in the excitation of the chemical atoms, music that goes
beyond our hearing and creates an indefinable power that he
does not understand, yet is certain exists, connecting all things,
seen and merely perceived.*

Anne understood exactly what Gaelan meant, even if Simon did
not—or could not. With absolute certainty. That was the energy experienced down to her fingers in that exhibit when she touched that
panel made by Gaelan's own hand. A connection, a tangible spark of
electricity—indefinable, but undeniably real, connecting them in an
indefinable way.

SCOTTISH BORDERS, PRESENT DAY

CHAPTER 26

"Reality" ceased to be relevant for Gaelan Erceldoune. He supposed for him, now, reality was a relative. *Real* compared to *what*? Through which lens? What perspective?

Mad or not, at the gates of hell or not, real or not. This was "it," whether for the next hour, a year, a millennium, for eternity: trapped in a mirrored labyrinth with no escape. It occurred to him that he might simply leave the catacombs, get on a plane, and return to Chicago. What then? London? Do what? What would it prove if it were all in his mind anyway? Would it break the delusion, if, in fact, he'd broken with reality?

And to say he wasn't intrigued by the catacombs would be a lie, and for the moment he had no better options than to accept and adapt as he had so many times in his past after each cataclysm of his life: his father's execution, leaving the sanctuary of Dernwode, the realization that he was immortal, Caitrin's death, and grappling with Iain's supposed death; Eleanor and Simon. The Great War and beyond.

He concentrated on the prisms, their hum a not-unpleasant white noise now. What if their arrangement had been by design? And the glass piece not the imagined avatar of a life he'd left behind but a missing piece, intended for him, and only him, to discover. And Dernwode House—not a convenient refuge of the mind but a place to which he'd managed to drag himself all the way from the coast, the

intuitive impulse of muscle memory? The magnetic pull of some indefinable . . . something . . .

The opalescent teardrop sat beside him on the floor. The way the
light within glowed and sparked, reached out to him, drew him. Yet,
he feared taking hold of it again. Would it return him to that LaSalle
bloke and his interrogation, or some other place—or nowhere at all?
He wasn't ready. Not yet.

Gingerly and with trembling fingers, Gaelan placed the object in
his pocket, ignoring the prisms, which had reverted now to a clattering
chaos of discordant noise. He hurried from the room, relieved to find
himself in the dark corridor—familiar territory.

The network of chambers twisted back on itself, and Gaelan
noticed what he thought might be another chamber in the distance.
Evidently the terminus of catacombs was not the seòmar-criostalan.
Drawn toward the far chamber, he was in the dark. No sconces lined
the walls as they had done through other passages. Had it not been for
a diffuse, distant glow ahead, Gaelan would have believed this section
of the network of little interest, likely never used.

A lit candle in his hand, he drew nearer. But the light he thought
he'd seen did not originate from within a chamber; there was, in fact,
no chamber at all. Only a rock face, gray-black mirror-polished basalt;
its face shimmered, rippling from the center outward in concentric
circles.

Gaelan touched his hand to the smooth surface, surprised when
the wall gently gave beneath his hand, emitting an odd sensation,
which pulsed through his fingers, neither hot nor cold, the waves
infinitesimal and constant. As Gaelan withdrew his hand from it, the
wall retracted, or seemed to. An optical illusion caused by the candlelight, or . . . ?

Curious, Gaelan removed the teardrop from his pocket, holding
it to the peculiar surface, observing as the glass reacted, absorbing
and then reflecting the light. Another illusion? He extinguished the
candle, setting it on the ground, appreciating the honeyed aroma of
melted beeswax.

The absence of flame did not affect the glass piece or its light as it continued to react with the wall. He placed both hands flat against the undulating surface this time. Would the current would move around them or between, disrupting the concentric pattern? Or gravitate toward the glass piece, like iron filings to a magnet?

A subtle vibration, stronger, yet still pleasurable, pulsed through Gaelan's hands and up through his arms, drawing him in until his face met the smooth, glossy surface, which now seemed almost, but not quite, liquid, like glass before it is entirely cooled. Closer and closer, almost as if the wall had enveloped him completely, enfolding him, pressing him forward, eyes closed against a gentle pressure that . . .

Gaelan now stood at the end of a wavering dock, no longer in the catacombs. He knew without glancing over his shoulder that the wall would no longer be there. Water sloshed over a pitted asphalt surface, which overlaid exposed rotting wood. The sky was deep lavender-indigo as the merest glint of red-orange sun bled over the horizon, igniting the water.

He knew this spot. Imprinted, indelible. Crowded afternoons, lonely mornings when the place he now stood was enshrouded in fog. Long after midnight, when the light pollution from office towers and malls, party boats, and sightseeing ships had extinguished, leaving the sky pockmarked with the stars. His favorite time to speed down an empty Lake Shore Drive on his motorbike. Dawn, especially one like this—clear and brilliant—ran a close second. But how was he here?

He closed his eyes, listening for the familiar sounds of morning: the screech of red-tailed hawks on the prowl, the great blue herons shrieking high above as they circled for prey, squawking gulls ornamenting every wood piling and buoy, scanning the water's surface for fresh catch. The gentler clucking of mourning doves and pigeons picking through the leavings from the previous evening.

There was no sound but for the gentle lapping of gray-green waves. Not a bird to be seen. The very air was different too, devoid of the familiar sour pungency of alewives and algae.

Gaelan turned, expecting to be at least somewhat comforted by the sight of the giant Ferris wheel, which dominated the west end of Navy Pier, keeping watch over the pier, the promenade, and the park. Instead, before him lay a city in ruins. As if he'd been transported into a virtual reality disaster movie. He would have screamed if his voice hadn't been tangled up in his throat.

He jammed his fists into his eye sockets, trying to will away the image, knowing somehow it would do no good. Mouth parched, heart throbbing in his chest, he slowly slid his hands from his eyes, steeling himself to be shocked anew, never mind the question of how he found himself incongruously in some surreal version of Chicago, when a moment before he'd been in Scotland. No fucking way this was un-augmented reality. His thoughts shifted back to the poison, trying to parse its possible hallucinogenic effects. What the fuck had he done to himself?

A fucking 3-D disaster movie in every direction but east—the lake itself. He pivoted, turning back toward the open water. At once light-headed, he lost his footing, staggering too close to the edge. He was grateful for the decaying wood bench that caught his fall. He sat, head in his hands, shaking in disbelief. *Let me out of here! Out of this madness! Out of this nightmare!*

The teardrop.

Of course. His escape route. All he needed to do was let it go, and he would return to the catacombs, their blessed, lonely darkness.

From which horrors in Gaelan's past had his mind culled and sub-verted *this* terrifying vision? Better to confront it, understand what it represented. Accept it and move on.

First, focus. He concentrated on the single blaze of sunlight that split the mirror calm of the water in two. He counted, first primes, then the Fibonacci numbers and their primes, then again in base two, and then base three. Well, at least the mathematical side of his brain seemed operational. The logical, rational part. *Well, maybe not so much.* His breathing settled, even as his mind struggled to make sense of the disaster just over his shoulder.

Breathing deeply—once, twice, three times—he stood shakily, too look again, ready to come to terms with what he'd seen. Was it only weeks ago he'd been here, this very bench, a quiet late winter day, snow falling in enormous flakes as he sucked in the pleasures of the most excellent weed for which he'd ever paid?

Opening his eyes, still trembling, Gaelan turned back toward the west, prepared best he could be. He knew the skyline from this vantage so well. The way the morning sun glinted off the glass and steel of Lake Point Tower, hundreds of feet above the shoreline, now deteriorated into a gargantuan birdcage of rusting beams and broken window glass, blinds flapping, silent wings in the whipping wind.

In the far distance, the crumbling, burned-out buildings of downtown Chicago stooped like enormous broken chess pieces. Disintegrating sand castles that had once been the neo-Gothic Tribune Tower and the Wrigley Buildings set against the broken black basalt angles of the John Hancock Tower. Wilson Tower leaned precariously like the Titanic just before it sank.

The pier wobbled and bobbed below Gaelan's feet. No doubt the supporting pylons would be in terrible disrepair: he needed to get off it, get inside. But what would be the state of the mile-long indoor promenade? Was that, too, a ruin? Its glass domes seemed oddly intact and out of sync with everything else around him.

Gaelan noticed now, for the first time, the Ferris wheel, now a mass of bent and twisted metal, its fuchsia and chartreuse spokes wobbling at treacherous angles as if it would at any moment give way. That was it. That's what had seemed familiar, distracted him during LaSalle's interrogation. The Ferris wheel spokes, but out of context. And here, again. Why? Why were they important?

Gaelan made his way along the asphalt, minding the deep ruts every few feet; the ground seemed steadier as he progressed away from the edge and toward the ruined wheel. Sand and soot swirled about his feet, denser as he moved further from the far edge of the pier, gathering into small dunes and drifts as he crossed into the park. Beyond that, what had once been lavish residences and opulent hotels of the Gold Coast was now an avenue of broken, rusted-out cars, charred buildings, trees emptied of their leaves, stripped of their bark.

The sand pooled about his ankles, glittering ashen white in the morning sun. He scooped up a handful. The same material he'd seen in that first vision, recognizing it now as a mélange of beach sand, ground window glass, grains of alabaster, quartz, and marble. The distant hills of that first vision, then obscured by a dust storm, he now realized were Michigan Avenue skyscrapers, long neglected.

No dogs, no birds. As far as Gaelan could determine, he was utterly alone in this eerily familiar wasteland. Nothing at all but a line of kiosks, empty, closed. The placards seemed new, at least, compared to everything else. "Dr. Death's Super Elixir—a bottle away from heaven's gate!" "Club Guillotine—go out in style. Quick and painless. Better—and cheaper—than a bullet to the brain. Reservations only!"

What the fuck?

He turned back toward the long building, ignoring the unnerving advertising signs, unsure he was ready to face whatever awaited inside.

"Hey, you!"

Gaelan whirled toward the sound. A youngish man shuffled through the sand, stopping a couple of feet away. He was joined by several others who emerged from nowhere to surround Gaelan, all dressed in the same uniform: gray hooded tee shirts and sweatpants.

"He looks like one of 'em," another said, edging closer, a broken whisky bottle in one hand and a long, jagged shard of glass in the other. As the man drew near, Gaelan saw the mass of white-gray blistery lesions of differing sizes everywhere his skin was exposed. The first man, who had now backed away to join his friends in the circle, had them, too.

"Do you notice? He's all pure and clean. No tumors," called out a third. "Doc Morely'll pay a lot for one of 'em if can bring him proof."

Proof of what? One of . . . what? He scanned the group, each covered with the lesions. Gaelan barely noticed as one of the men nodded toward another—the one with the broken glass. Too late. Searing pain sliced into Gaelan's right arm, knocking him off his feet.

The teardrop slipped from his grip.

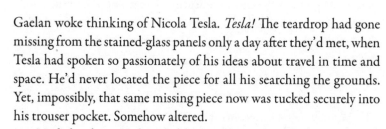

Gaelan welcomed the dark of the catacombs; he was sprawled face-down on the cool floor of the prism room. His arm throbbed, pulsing to the rhythm of his too-fast heartbeat. A familiar cold clamminess began its descent, starting at his forehead and working its way down. He struggled not to lose consciousness before he managed to . . .

Instinct took over, and biting his lower lip hard, Gaelan extracted a long, jagged shard of glass from his upper arm, ignoring as best he could the ripping of tendons, the slicing of muscle and vein. Panting, cold sweat pouring off his head, he removed his shirt, wrapping his arm as best he could.

Disbelief merged into the knowledge of what had just happened. Comprehension would have to bloody wait in line.

Gaelan managed to stand, just barely, and he groped his way along the corridor until he returned to the chamber with the cot. Shivering, he fell into his bed beneath his jacket, giving in to the darkness.

Gaelan woke thinking of Nicola Tesla. *Tesla!* The teardrop had gone missing from the stained-glass panels only a day after they'd met, when Tesla had spoken so passionately of his ideas about travel in time and space. He'd never located the piece for all his searching the grounds. Yet, impossibly, that same missing piece now was tucked securely into his trouser pocket. Somehow altered.

Had that been Tesla? Had he somehow succeeded in mastering

travel between worlds, between times, as he'd aspired? Wouldn't a discovery of that magnitude have been a scientific earthquake with reverberations worldwide? Famous and acclaimed?

Had Tesla died never knowing he'd done it? Gaelan had the proof. Of course, the possibility—a strong possibility—still existed all this was a surreal fabrication of a broken psyche.

Travel through time—and space. An epochal discovery. Like immortality.

Maybe Tesla *had* known of his success, and, considering the consequences, took a breathtaking secret to his grave. Is that not what Gaelan had intended to do with his own monumental secret?

The enormity of the discovery Gaelan could barely comprehend. Travel to another world, another time. Another time, different circumstances, Gaelan would have rejoiced in the brilliance of it. But he was only weary. Of life, of the world, of hiding. He was ready to let go. To die. Little appetite to go round for another ride. And certainly not in the ruined, desolate world to which he'd apparently traversed.

He was frustrated he was not dead. There had to be a way to rectify that. If not the poison, something else, and he would not stop searching until he'd managed it. Did he have the nerve to slice that jagged glass shard through his carotid? His hand might slip; the edge was sharp enough but would not cleanly cut through. Death, if it came at all, would take many painful hours. Too much time; his bloody genetics would foil the effort.

A bullet to the brain? That, too, carried risks. Besides, he did not want his dead body picked over and probed—and exploited. That was the bloody point of the entire enterprise. Something would turn up.

Minding his injured arm, Gaelan rose from the cot, surprised to discover blood continuing to trickle from the wound. By now, the gash should have begun to close, but it had not. Perhaps it was more serious than he'd imagined. He rewrapped it and, grabbing his old shirt and the glass piece, ventured back into the corridor, lantern in hand.

Club Guillotine, now there's an idea!

LONDON, 1826

CHAPTER 27

*E*ureka!

Gaelan's thoughts rushed headlong one into the other as he stood at his laboratory workbench. *Of course, of course.*

"Are you all right, Mr. Erceldoune?"

Caitrin stood beside him, appearing baffled.

"Forgive me. Something you said sparked a rather splendid idea." Whether it had been her or just the random pieces fitting into place of their own accord did not, just at the moment, much matter.

And if it was the sweating sickness that took poor Mr. Barlow's family and afflicted Bell's patient, Gaelan would be prepared for it with shield and dragon-ready lance.

Dragon into dragonfly. Fire and metal. The fragile airiness of a dragonfly's prismatic wings. The water, cool and transformative, strong enough to douse a dragon's fiery breath. Elements all present in the image, that page in the ouroboros book, its careful, incomprehensible design—the alchemist's tools: earth, fire, air, water. He didn't understand it, not the way of it, but he trusted it would work.

But for propriety's sake, Gaelan would have danced her about the laboratory, elated at the discovery.

"My lady . . . Caitrin . . . you must excuse me. I've work to do . . . a direction for . . . I would ask for you to return to the flat. There should yet be sufficient bread and wine, meats as well in the larder."

She startled. "I do not understand. What have I done to—?"

"I've no time to explain, but you, my dear . . . my lady . . . you have shown me the key, and without knowing it, I daresay. But you must let me work!"

Caitrin worried the fabric of her sleeve, visibly distraught. "Allow me to be of assistance. I beg of you. I am quite able, and chemistry, its magic, has always held for me much fascination."

He considered the proposal a brief moment. There was much to do with gathering ingredients, preparing the apparatus, cleaning the glassware; the instructions had to be assembled . . . and all with no apprentice.

Even a fool would be better than nothing, and Lady Caitrin was no fool. The very worst of ideas. Simply not done. *Damnation!* "Indeed, I've work aplenty, and more befitting a scullery maid than a lady, much less the daughter of an earl. Yet, if you insist—"

"I do. I promise I can demonstrate my value. I am no dainty flower, and I am not without skill and education. Indeed, I shall prove myself clever as any apprentice you might take on—"

"Very well," he said with resignation. "And at the end of it, you may craft your own Rupert's drop as payment. I would admonish you, should you feel at any time fatigued, or wont to swoon, you must tell me without hesitation. You are barely recovered, and it will do me little good if you were to once again fall ill."

Her smile lit the room.

"Here. Watch what I do." He spooned a small amount of an orange powder onto a small tin and covered it with an etched clear globe. A soft circle of light spilled onto the workbench around it.

"How did you do that? There is no candle. No—"

Gaelan smiled as he set another globe on the workbench. He could tell her it was magic, and she would surely believe it. "It is but a chemical reaction. A small invention of mine. It casts less light than a candle might, but is safer up here, where fire is an ever-present danger, given all the paper and chemicals about. Besides which, the light casts fewer shadows, and makes for easier work."

He lit two more as he explained the process. Her gaze followed his every move. "Here, you try it." Gaelan handed to her the orange powder and a second jar filled with a white, waxy semiliquid. "One spoon of the orange, one of the white."

She did as instructed and placed the globe. She shook her head as her eyes sparkled. "Incredible!"

"Good. Now, tend to the remainder. This bench and the next only. After you've done, we must prepare the apparatus. Every flask, beaker, crucible, all of it, must be washed and dried—and very carefully. No breakage. And they must be absolutely free of any remaining residues. I've set a tub of soapy water by the window, and a tub of clear water beside it for rinsing. And rags. One rag for cleaning, another for drying. Let me know if the rinse tub becomes too soapy."

He watched as she moved toward the basins. "Wait." Gaelan unboxed a small crate, withdrawing a stiff apron. "Place this over your clothing." She set down the crate of glassware and metal implements at the far end of the laboratory, and satisfied she was busy at work, he went back to his own.

Gaelan settled at his writing table and prepared two phosphorescent globes, which bathed the space in a bright blue-white light, perfect for the detailed work ahead of him. For just a moment, he lingered on the ever-changing leather cover of the ouroboros book, the tree at its center a living thing in the glow of the light globes. He ran his hand along the deeply engraved helices framing the tree; those, too, seemed so alive, undulating, entwined snakes joined like supports of a ladder, twisting in iridescent pewter and bronze.

From within the tree, its scarlet heart of flame, yet another ouroboros, this one of fire, beckoned him. Bade him open its pages and bask in the radiance of its images.

Opening to the dragonfly image, Gaelan matched it to the relevant page in Grandpapa's journal, a copy of a letter to John Caius dated June 1553, after Caius had published his treatise on the sweating sickness.

Removing a rectangle of blank parchment paper from a small inlaid wooden box, he retrieved the ornate metal pen he'd crafted, based upon the instructions of Mr. Frederick Bartholomew Folsch himself.

> *My dear Caius, the dragonfly floats upon the winds of change, the harbinger of renewal—and of the enlightenment for which we and so many of our colleague yearn in these times, and has not yet been seen in our eyes, but which is coming. I feel it in my bones. Already it infuses our art, our music and literature, and only just beginning to inhabit science, if not the healing arts.*
>
> *The dragon is of the old world, steeped in the oldest tales of danger and war: the inscrutable mysteries of plague and disease. But it can be slain through the elemental world of the dragonfly as it takes up wisdom from the tiniest spirits of the plant world, its herbs and flowers, from the spirits of water—the essence of life, of healing. Forgive me, my dear colleague, if I wax once again poetical of the healer Airmid, for my own experience is entwined with her history, as I have before told you. Her legacy mine. Hers is the spirit world of nature, and its taming by means unknowable to the most of us, my poor self amongst them. Some might call it magic; I do not. It be only incomprehensible in the face of our own meager abilities.*
>
> *Yet, I know she is right. Simply put, as you and I both are keenly aware, that means little when it comes to scientific endeavour. You may think me mad, or dabbling in the sorcerer's art, but I do think I have at hand the means for slaying this dragon fever we call the sweating sickness, and that you have so eloquently chronicled in your publication, and which during the great pestilence of it in 1528 I was able to keep from the Scottish border by the means I describe herein. I share this with you colleague to colleague by way of this correspondence, should the dragon Sweate again appear in our midst.*

Another entry suggested that Caius never replied, leaving his grandfather disappointed, for he'd risked much in disclosing the nature of the cure to his colleague. "Whatever John Caius doth think of me, I know what I know," he'd inked in scarlet.

The writings made no further mention of John Caius, which was of no consequence to Gaelan, for in his grandfather's meticulous hand lay the cure to a disease that had been gone from these shores nearly three hundred years. Whether John Caius had believed it or not, Gaelan did.

Symphytum, but only a small bit of the leaf, for too much renders the entire potion poisonous. Must be ground carefully fine, and according to the book of healing exactly, distilled then into a large crucible by fresh water to properly draw forth the curative humors and dried—before mixing to a syrup with dilute elder-berry wine, made from a very strong batch, aged for a year at the least. Into the crucible place a faenugraecum seed, ground well with . . .

Here, there were several symbols unfamiliar to Gaelan, referenced to the ouroboros book. And instructions for a second distillation extract, this one of pansies, violets, and narcissus, and several ingredients noted by the unusual symbols alone, all in proportions as prescribed in the ouroboros book. The two were to be blended in purified alcohol and dried to yellow needle-sharp crystals. Suspended in pure olive, oil, the preparation would be inserted beneath the skin by means of a simple incision into the buttock, thigh, or other fatty place on the body.

Together, these herbs will mitigate the difficult breathing and drain the chest of fluid, which will calm the breathing and ease the heart and kidneys. Thus says the book of healing. The instructions called for ample water, clear, clean water, preferably from a mineral spring. The recipe for a preventive medication followed, utilizing many of the same ingredients, but with the addition of a small amount of blood from a living, but afflicted, soul.

The symbols would match bottles and pouches locked in his

father's ancient apothecary box, which he'd kept close at hand for more than two centuries. Gaelan copied each symbol into a list with the amounts and order of combination.

The leather pouches and small vials in the apothecary box were meticulously organized. Despite the age of the box, its deteriorating condition, the contents seemed fresh enough; even the herbs, though dried, were yet green. What if he needed to treat the whole of Smithfield? Each dose required only a small measure, but would he have enough? Yes, if he took care, but there was little room for error.

The preparation would require hours. Gaelan glanced at the clock. Already near four and he'd yet to open the shop. It had been quiet all the day, no clamor at the door, no pounding on the glass. Perhaps all this was for naught—an academic exercise to file away, hoping never to have need for it.

He stood, stretching, as he listened for the satisfying, gentle snap of sinew as it loosened.

"Mr. Erceldoune. You've finished?"

Caitrin. He'd forgotten her completely. Gaelan's breath caught in his throat. "My lady, still you are here? I had . . . It has been many hours and I would have thought you'd returned—"

"I finished the task quite some time ago, but you'd not dismissed me, and I did not wish to disturb you at your work. I busied myself. For a while at least."

And so she had. The benches were polished clean, the glass sitting neatly on the shelving, ready for him; she'd uncrated several boxes of book and other materials, setting them in good order. He was impressed by her enterprise, but she should not have so exerted herself.

He had nothing to say that might make him look less a fool, less a brute to have neglected her for endless hours. He approached her, mortified. "You've done well, and I am ashamed for not having the simple courtesy to—"

"You were hard at work with your work. My father would have thrashed me had I—"

"That, I assure you, I should never do—to anyone. Not a servant,

not an apprentice, and certainly not one under my care and protection.
I—"

"I have never seen anyone so . . . so deeply . . . You seemed rather
more scholar than what I imagine an apothecary . . . At least what I
know of apothecaries, which is, admittedly, truly little." She shrugged.

The fading light added to her air of melancholy. What glimmer of
joy might reside there—had resided there—once? Before . . . he'd seen
a glimpse of it with the Rupert's drop. Perhaps he would see it again.
Perhaps . . .

Gaelan's eyes were gritty with the sands of sleep, urging his lids
to give in to the rest eluding him for three days now. But Gaelan was
unready to give up the fight just yet. Not now, when he was so very
close.

CHAPTER 28

Long-necked flasks and tubes twisting and turning in spirals awaited Gaelan's skilled hands as he fixed ground glass to ground glass joint, flask to tubing to beaker to retort—a crystal castle. A genuine work of art had it not such practical use as it bubbled and brewed, capturing the impurities, diverting them to a waste vessel, collecting the pure extract in another.

Gaelan enjoyed the challenge of a truly perplexing disease, and this one had puzzled medicine for hundreds of years. Yet, would it not be better this one be not what he thought at all, a simple, fleeting fever instead? Not the epidemic he feared?

And if it were the sweating sickness, from where had it arisen? And how? The riddle was hardly solved, then, was it?

Gaelan collected the distillate into cobalt blue cylinders, protecting the liquid from direct light, before adding the remaining compounds, sealing each with paraffin, melted and secured. The final instruction, to craft a device to inject the substance just beneath the skin, where it would take hold and course through the blood to transform the dragon into a harmless dragonfly.

The good people of Smithfield would likely resist the idea as absurd. Who would believe that a small amount of liquid, inserted beneath the skin, would cure much of anything? Gaelan himself was not fully certain the medicine would work. What if Grandpapa was wrong within the limitations of sixteenth-century scientific knowledge? Even years after being proved and proved again, Jenner's smallpox vaccination was looked upon with suspicion by many men of medicine.

Gaelan crafted an instrument of glass and fused hollow metal, an improvement over Jenner's original device, and vastly more sophisticated than the primitive tool used by Grandpapa. Silver was too soft, but combined with nickel it would do quite well, and be more precise and a bit less terrifying and painful than the method employed by Jenner for his variolae vaccinae smallpox medicine.

For now, it was enough. The preventative medication could wait until the need arose—if ever it did. Gaelan sighed, relieved to at last be finished, as the sunrise sky of pink and indigo filtered through the early morning steam and mist, painting Smithfield in unearthly hues. The view from the laboratory was what Gaelan appreciated most about his new location. The tall mullion windows surrounded the turret shape of the room, offering him the gift of the sky in three directions: east, north, and south.

Once he located his telescope, and this crisis—should it materialize—passed, he would take advantage of the view to observe the asterisms and constellations, galaxies and planets, ever changing, ever constant. He ventured the lady Caitrin might find it amusing as well. He would explain to her the lenses and mirrors—the way glass reflected and refracted within the tube, drawing the heavens closer and more spectacular than imaginable . . .

Stop! Whatever was he thinking? He must be more exhausted than he thought. The girl would be leaving, and soon. She had to go. Somewhere. Anywhere.

Perhaps if he might only sit a moment, close his eyes . . . come back to his senses. A minute or two would suffice . . .

"Mr. Erceldoune! Mr. Erceldoune!" a woman wailed from below. The shouts were loud enough to be heard from the third story. Had she not thought to use the doorbell?

"Yes, yes. I'm coming!" he muttered, carefully placing the medicine vials and the injector device into a large, soft leather pouch before flying down the two flights of steep stairs.

He'd reached the second landing when he heard it. A long, keening wail from the street below through the open windows of his flat. A loud commotion, equal parts terror and confusion. Then pounding on the window glass of the shop.

Taking the stairs two at a time, he managed to tuck his shirt tails into his trousers and fasten his waistcoat. A sweep of hair from his brow—a useless endeavor on any day—and he thought himself modestly presentable.

A crowd had gathered in front of the shop. An elderly woman, breathless and red-faced, stopped slamming her open hand against the door. At the front of the crowd was Simon Bell, staring through the window glass.

Gaelan opened the door a mere crack, anxious that none be trampled coming over the threshold.

Bell came through first, followed by the remaining crowd, as Gaelan pulled the door wider. "I shall be a moment; please be patient." He ushered Bell behind the counter. "What is it? What's happened?"

"Mr. Erceldoune. My patient took quite a turn overnight. He succumbed just an hour past. And *these* . . ." Bell gestured behind him. "Your own neighbors. I have taken the liberty to enquire . . . The symptoms they describe would seem to suggest that . . ."

Gaelan barely listened as he observed the gathered crowd for their symptoms, prioritizing the most urgently in need. Still, how might he attend to so many sick at once?

Only two showed any obvious sign of the illness. The remainder? Perhaps; perhaps not. Yet they would require examination, if only later. Showing the two men into the examining room, where they might be seated, Gaelan turned his attention to those standing about the shop.

"I would ask that if you do not require medical care for yourself, to please return this afternoon."

Several protested, shouting over each other about sisters, mothers, wee ones at home.

"If you would all be so kind to write your addresses and names, I promise I shall call as soon as I am able at your homes. Await me there." He pulled a sheet of paper from a box, placing a quill and ink bottle on the counter.

Some nodded their assent; others stood, glancing about, expressions vaguely confused. *Of course. This was not Hay Hill.*

"If you cannot write . . ." He turned to Bell. "Would you be so kind, Dr. Bell? And then follow me, when you are finished, into the examination room?"

Bell froze. "Mr. Erceldoune, I did not come here to . . . You would dare ask of me to act as clerk? To an apothecary? I have heard—"

Of all the . . . Gaelan had no time for . . . He called on all his will to avoid rolling his eyes and escalate the conflict. Indeed, to Bell, it would seem the insult, never considering the practicality of it while Gaelan attended to *his own* patients. He'd no inclination to argue the subject. Not now.

"Please, *sir.* If you would do me this service, I would be most in your debt." Gaelan punctuated each word with a solicitude he did not feel. "Now if you do not mind, sir, I must attend to my examining room. Please follow as soon as you might. I've prepared something during the past night that might prove effective against this disease!"

Where to start? Each patient exhibited the same symptoms he and Bell had seen earlier, but at differing stages. All suffered lancing headaches and quaked with chills and extreme sweating. One clutched his chest, his breathing laborious and noisy.

Bell came through to the room. "I've done it." Bell handed the paper to Gaelan, smiling.

"Look here, Mr. Erceldoune, I apolo—"

"Have you used one of these?" Gaelan handed Bell a small wooden tube, wider at one end, ignoring the Bell's irrelevant apology. "I can better hear the heart sounds, but also the lungs."

"I have only read of it. Stethoscope? Laennec. In France? It is an odd-looking device."

"The idea, yes, Laennec, but they are yet too hard to acquire. This is of my own design. It works well."

Bell raised an eyebrow. "Indeed."

Gaelan handed him the device. "I have prepared a treatment." He declined to suggest that he also had the means to prevent the disease entirely. Bell would certainly balk at the notion.

"Truly? Well done, you. And this stethoscope, quite the instrument!"

Gaelan retrieved a bottle of clear liquid from a shelf, pouring a small amount in each of several cups. "Hear me out before you dismiss what I say." He handed the cups to Bell. "Would you mind? One for each."

Bell scoffed but did as Gaelan asked. "Is *this* your treatment?"

"It is but the same salt solution I gave to you earlier. No. I have come across something quite old—an ancestor who'd served the Scottish court long ago. As you likely are aware, symptoms such as these appeared during Tudor England—decimated the court of Henry VIII, and several of his family succumbed."

"You are *serious*, sir? Henry VIII? Tudor England. Do you mean to say . . . Surely you do not suggest this is the English sweating sickness? This is beyond comprehension. I've no time to—"

"Yes." Gaelan knew this would be difficult, near impossible, but at least that Bell would hear him out. "Indeed, I am *well aware* that *sudor anglicus*," he continued, using the disease's formal name, "disappeared from these shores by the mid-sixteenth century, yet . . ."

Bell was having none of this—that much was obvious as he impatiently tapped his foot and pinned Gaelan with a cold, disbelieving stare. Gaelan had erred in suggesting it; perhaps a less potentially controversial suggestion might have better served, but it was now too late. He'd assumed Bell's mind was as open to the unconventional as Benjamin's. A particularly vicious influenza would have been far easier for to Bell accept. An error of tactics.

"Perhaps it is the sweat, perhaps not, but it must be something related—the symptoms match up too well. Its progress is far too swift for the influenza. You know this, otherwise you would have not consulted *me*."

"Obviously. There *exists* no effective treatment for the influenza. Useless bleeding, elixirs, potions with ridiculous names that do nothing. In the end, one recovers, or one does not. I did not come here to be told—"

"Do you not see the resemblance in the presentation . . . from your medical education? Surely, it was discussed in lecture . . . in required readings . . ." Of course, he did not see it. He would have read of it, a single paragraph, perhaps a chapter in a medical text on an extinct disease. Why bother with it? History *never* repeats, then, does it? "Allow me, sir, to explain at least the method of treatment. I believe you will find it useful—whatever we wish to call the affliction—"

"And this ancestor of yours? An apothecary as well? An alchemist? Perhaps the court conjurer?"

Gaelan stalked across the room to sit beside the elderly patient, his hands clenched in frustration. He was in no mood to defend . . . "My . . . ancestor . . . served Queen Mary of Scotland as court physician. An accomplished alchemist and apothecary, but were they not all practitioners of medicine of the time? All curious of alchemy? Witness Sir Isaac Newton."

Gaelan had no time to waste upon such debate. "It does not render the diagnosis—or the treatment—any less valid." Gaelan hoped he did not seem overly defensive of a long-ago, supposedly long-forgotten relation. "He was quite famous in his time. A close correspondent of John Caius. It is said that his skill kept the sweat from the Scottish border. That is, at least, the family legend."

Bell threw up his hands. "But, really, the English sweat? Surely—"

"At the least, do me the courtesy to hear me out. I've used his meticulous notes and those of contemporaries. John Caius included. You have read Caius, of course?"

"Anyone may acquire the Caius manuscript. It is famous, discussed in every medical college. The disease, simply put, no longer exists. Has not for a long time now. How can you expect me to accept what you say?"

Gaelan strode through the curtains and back into the shop, fuming, leaving Bell in the examining room. Bell's grandfather had a far more open mind about medicine. Is that not always the way, resting for generations on the laurels of famed forebears? Bell would dismiss him. So be it.

Bell followed, taking up his coat and hat. "Those texts to which you refer were written three centuries past! You cannot be serious about attempting... You, sir, would be no better than the street mountebanks who hawk their salves and potions in the market. I came to you because of your reputation, and you tell me of ancient diseases and magical cure-alls. Perhaps if there was something more definitive. Persuasive. My dear sir, I've no wish to grieve you. Nor to suggest—"

"Well, then, what do *you* propose to do? I have nothing else. No proof, other than . . . I do aim to test my theory. The patients in my examination room would be the first to receive it."

"I have already three dead from whatever this is, and four more ill in a neighboring house. I've no time to listen to any more of such imprudent, irresponsible *theories*."

Three more? Bell had not before mentioned others. "Then pray, Dr. Bell, it does not sweep like a fury from home to home, until it reaches the Thames." But Gaelan was certain, now, it would, spreading death like a black smoke settling upon neighborhood after neighborhood, choking all in its path. "Mine is but one theory—undoubtedly your fellow physicians at the Royal Academy and your club have theirs. And we shall see who fares the better taming this dragon!"

"Mr. Erceldoune, I wish neither to provoke nor to disdain you. For you appear to be an honest man and quite skilled, and I might see us do a good business together over time. Perhaps you are right that I may be better served following convention this time. And so, I bid you a good morning, so you might return to your . . . customers."

"Dr. Bell, one more thing before you take your leave."

"I am listening."

"You must be aware that your own grandfather was a brilliant apothecary-surgeon."

"Of course I am aware; my dear grandfather was the most gifted of all—a true innovator in both surgery and medicine. He died when I was boy, yet his—"

"And might I add, one who did not eschew a medical idea simply for its improbability or its, perhaps, obscure or arcane nature."

"You speak as if you know him yourself."

"I do!" Gaelan paused, shaken by the involuntary admission. "That is to say . . . his works. I have read every one of his treatises; he was, as you say, the most gifted of surgeons. His publications on everything from ulcers to anesthesia to . . ." Gaelan knew he had to stop himself. "Suffice to say I know his work very well, and I would think—"

"I've no time for this *Mr.* Erceldoune. Nor do you. I will bid you a good day, and best of luck in pursuit of a treatment for this unwieldy disease that so threatens London. If you like, I would be honored to share with you any *effective* treatment of which I might learn."

Of course, these men of medicine would never enter Smithfield's alleyways and overcrowded flats to treat the ill themselves. "And I would be willing to hear it. I will, likewise, be most interested to share whatever success I may have. Permit me one more question, sir."

Bell nodded tightly.

"Is it unheard of for an ailment thought long ago disappeared to reappear quite suddenly and without explanation, taking all by surprise?"

"Possible, yes, but you, with your ancient remedies from an ancestor three centuries gone. Do you not realize how you harm your own reputation? Those of your trade?"

Bell had a point. A colossal error of judgment to mention the sweat at all, one that might cost many, many lives. *Damnation!*

"If you should be successful," Bell continued, his tone softer, conciliatory. "If you *should* happen upon a *genuinely* effective treatment, I would be happy to hear of it." Bell paused, his hand on the door, turning back to Gaelan, a satisfying sheepishness in his countenance. "Forgive me, but before I take my leave, I wonder, do you have additional bottles of that salt elixir to spare? I would pay you an excellent price for it."

Touché.

"Of course. Without charge, for had you not come to me with your original patient, I never would have . . ." No, Gaelan had no time to repeat the argument. He removed three large amber bottles from beneath the counter. "This should serve your needs. It is quite concentrated, so you must mix with water two parts to one."

"You are very kind. Then I bid you a good day."

Gaelan bowed and left Bell standing in the shop as he disappeared behind the curtain to his examining room.

CHICAGO'S NORTH SHORE, PRESENT DAY

CHAPTER 29

Hours since returning from the glass museum, Anne's fingers still tingled. Unable to resist just one more visit, if only to prove . . . something . . . to herself, Anne touched the glass panel, and again perceived Gaelan's presence, if only out of the corner of her eye, a sputtering, grainy, colorless light going in and out of focus. A blink, and he vanished. She propped three pillows behind her and sank into the bed. Her imagination, and nothing more. A conspiracy of grief and a grand dollop of her bloody romanticism.

Pressing down on her eyelids did no good diminishing the tension behind her eyes. She sighed, feeling trapped, a tire caught in a muddy rut. At least, she'd be rid of Preston Alcott in a few days' time, a polite apology that no, she was no miracle worker and could do no better than the several other physicians who'd already told him the same thing. She could get back to . . . What, exactly? Obsessing over a glass exhibit? Over Gaelan? For what possible purpose?

A vastly better, healthier choice would be to finish up with Erin Alcott, put Simon's house with an estate agent, clear out Gaelan's shop and flat, and get the bloody hell home to the UK.

To what? To her mother, the rest of her family with their ceaseless barrage of questions about an inheritance that came out of nowhere from a relative of whom none them had ever heard? Back to Paul Gilles—bygones being gone?

Oxford. She could resume teaching, and Oxford would do

quite well as a retreat to reset her life. One thing for certain, her intended midafternoon nap was not going to happen, tired as she was.

Oh God! It had been two days since she'd cleaned out her email inbox. *No time like the present, eh?* Days ago, she'd set her search engine alerts to the Galahad Society and all those cited in the article she'd read.

Cheers! Three emails, all pointing to the same item on a website of which she'd never heard. *Two Minutes to Midnight Newsletter.* What the bloody hell was that?

The Galahad Society Claims to Have Identified the Missing Piece for Human Immortality!

The Galahad Society. The name may be familiar to you only if you're a fan of Arthurian legend. But it is a well-funded organization, dedicated to finding the Holy Grail as did the Arthurian knight for whom the society is named. Immortality is its high-stakes, high-reward game, and it aims to be the first to lay claim to it, to win the patent for it, and to make a fortune off it in the most mercenary ways. As our readers are well aware, whoever holds this key to immortality will wield the most power in the world. Wars have been fought over much less. And they're still going on, underground, and increasingly in the light of day.

The CTO of the Galahad Society, Mr. John Brady, pictured left, owns a chain of blood banks one might better associate with vampires and Gothic fables. The blood banks are an essential arm of the Galahad Society and its long-term agenda, supplying it with ample reserves of fresh blood for its research goals, and, as an anonymous former member revealed to us, providing members an interim fountain of youth through direct transfusion of blood from the youngest, healthiest donors.

Very recently, the Galahad Society has stepped up its activities. Brady claims they have found "the final puzzle piece" just as they had begun to give up the quest—in a pint of blood donated by a walk-in client, he claims, at one of his Chicago, Illinois, blood banks. They are, he said, doing more extensive testing, including what they hope will be a promising in vivo experiment. Stay tuned for more news to come.

The missing link to the puzzle of immortality. How many times had she read that one? Heard it even at professional conferences. And this piece had all the signatures of a conspiracy theorist at his trade. And the name? *Two Minutes to Midnight?* Read: Two Minutes to the Apocalypse!

What was it Alcott had promised the day before? Something special to help along her treatment for Erin? Was it coincidence a Chicago blood bank was the source of the blood? It fit. What if Alcott or one of his cronies at the Galahad Society had stolen the samples? Or paid someone to do it. Hospital workers here in the U.S. were poorly compensated. What about the waste disposal company? And even sensationalist, conspiracy-mongering rags got it right from time to time, didn't they?

She read the article one more time and the truth of it sucker punched her in the gut. The missing tissue samples. Had to be. She'd earlier dismissed the two phone calls as bad record-keeping or sloppiness in the lab.

She scarcely made it to the guest bathroom before losing the entire contents of her stomach. She sat on the bathroom floor, surrounded by the mess and stink of her own vomit, until she could stand without falling.

Her clothes were a ruin.

"Dr. Shawe, are you all right?" Mrs. O'Malley was running up the stairs, her feet thudding even on the carpeting. Did she have bat ears, that she heard the vomiting from all the way downstairs? Anne would have to remember that.

"I'm fine, Mrs. O'Malley. No need to—"

Too late.

"Dr. Shawe! Let me—"

Fuck. Anne slowly rose from the floor, catching a glance of herself in the mirror. *What a fucking mess!*

An hour later, Anne was cleansed by the freshening breeze wafting up from the lake, surrounding her in the sweet perfume of Simon's garden. She sipped at the spice tea Mrs. O'Malley prepared. "Extra ginger," she'd noted. "For your tummy, dear."

Closing her eyes, she tried to shove all thought from her mind, but that fucking article, Samuelson's phone call, and Alcott's "surprise" lingered like a fucking colony of mosquitoes buzzing about her ears on summer's evening.

She wanted not to believe. *Two Minutes to Midnight Newsletter—really?* But the evidence, circumstantial as it was, had piled too high to dismiss entirely. Erin Alcott's GPC was real enough, and even if Alcott were the ringleader of the entire enterprise—for which there was absolutely *no* evidence—Anne was a physician, and she owed it to the girl. To do otherwise would violate every oath she'd taken as a doctor.

Twilight had rendered the eastern sky in dusky red, transforming the water into sculpted clay in the onshore breeze. It had been a long day, and she was more tired than she'd been since arriving in Chicago. By now, Erin Alcott's genomic scans would be back from the lab. One quick look, and then off to bed, take two.

Thankfully, Mrs. O'Malley was nowhere to be seen.

Anne sighed as she sank into the down coverlet and feather pillows, which surrendered and swathed her in the softest of cocoons. Erin Alcott's genome scans could wait until morning, couldn't they?

As if her curiosity would allow her to sleep. And the gnawing anxiety from that article would eat away at the edges of sleep until she was full up and dawn had broken. She did not need a sleepless night. Fine. A quick look, and then to bed. Straightaway!

Wrapping herself in the down comforter, Anne retrieved her tablet, opening the relevant email. "Scans attached. Useable, however, unidentified artifacts present on all images. Should not affect visual inspection and analysis."

Fucking brilliant. As if she weren't already in a black mood. *Arti-*

facts? How the bloody hell had that happened?

Tomorrow. First thing, she'd examine them, artifacts or not, and be done. She didn't want to redraw Erin's blood; she wanted to rid herself of Preston Alcott—*stat*.

Right? Now . . . to bed!

With the bedroom windows full open, Anne hoped the rhythmic sloshing of the waves back and forth, back and forth, cascading over the rocks below and drawing back would lull her to dreamless, deep sleep.

Yeah, right! As soon as she closed off all thought of the scans, her suspicions about Alcott rose up to harass her. Finally, to the music of Vivaldi, Anne managed to force Alcott and his daughter from her thoughts. The music faded as she floated between sleep and wakefulness, thinking of the exquisite glass panel Gaelan had created so long ago, in another lifetime.

The images danced in the far reaches of her retinas and reflected on her eyelids as they closed, drawing her in until she found herself somehow inside Ariadne's labyrinth—circles within circles, hedgerows within concentric hedgerows, like those at her cousin's large country home, but in a palette of impossible color, shimmering like the lake at sunrise.

The Minotaur grunted and sputtered in the distance, spoiling for combat. With whom? Her? Who was she, Ariadne or Theseus—or a mere spectator, sitting among the throngs on the sidelines waiting, watching?

A wind chime pinged and tinged, gentle, but somehow discordant at the edges of sleep, an anchor beyond the labyrinth as she drifted beyond wakefulness. The melody familiar yet completely foreign, a single note played on the harmonics of her old, beat-up guitar. The twelfth fret vibrating beneath her index finger, clear and high as fine crystal, piercing, yet barely audible. The lone note resonated, diffusing into undulating waves, encroaching upon her field of vision until the labyrinth exploded into a fractional dimension of blazing color.

Then she saw him. Theseus at battle with the Minotaur and being savagely beaten. *No! That is not the way it's supposed to go. That's not the story at all.* The Minotaur split itself into six and surrounded the wounded Theseus. She cried out, willing him on to prevail as he had in the myth, as depicted in the glass panel. Theseus turned toward her, as if he'd heard her pleas. But the face was not that of Theseus; Gaelan's piercing black gaze bore through her from the center of the labyrinth just before he fell, and the Minotaur leapt upon him with a howl, igniting the very air. Gaelan skittered out of reach, and Anne was grateful for the Minotaur's lumbering efforts, slow and clumsy, powerful as it was.

"Gaelan!" she shouted. "Watch out!" But the strange harmonic tones of the wind chimes stifled her voice; nothing emerged that she could discern.

The labyrinth gave way to reveal a new tableau, bathed in the strange luminescence of refracted light, painted on a black canvas of gleaming rock. Here too, Gaelan took center stage, speaking to someone, but none she could see. His lips moved, yet she could not hear his voice. He sat on the floor beneath a spiral maze of glass prisms, differing shapes casting colored patterns that arced against every surface, projecting in bridges of color, wall to wall, a surreal crystal forest, blinding as it was brilliant.

"Gaelan!" She called his name repeatedly, but her voice was swallowed by the constant hum of the prisms vibrating through the room, louder and louder, finally waking her. The scene disintegrated into her pillow, minute fractals of color and sound, the wind chimes gently pinging in the cool late spring breeze drifting through the screened window.

Perspiration had dampened the bedcovers, waking her and leaving her hot and sticky despite her shivering. Her pulse was racing—better than one hundred beats per minute. Anne flung away the covers and ran to the window to breathe in the fresh air wafting through the screen. Slowly, her respiration leveled as she shook free of the nightmare.

The rough-smooth facets of the labyrinth necklace caught the moonlight. It twinkled against her collarbone in harmony with the reflection of the full moon against the lake. In the distance, a chorus of cicadas added rhythm, out of time, but somehow fitting the strangeness of her life these days.

Anne was completely awake, wired and restless. Who was she kidding? She'd never fall back to sleep, not now. *May as well get some work done. Tackle Erin Alcott's genome scans.* And those supposed artifacts. Hopefully, they'd not catastrophically affected the relevant chromosomal regions.

First, a cup of tea.

The dream refused to dissipate, even as Anne found her way down to the kitchen and put up the kettle. Instead, it reprised in disparate afterimages randomly stimulating her retinas—spectral figments, like she'd stared too long at a camera's flash.

She sighed, inhaling the fragrant citrus spice of the tea as it steeped, adding a splash of cream and one sugar cube. Finally, sinking into the deep cushions of the library sofa, she opened her laptop and clicked on the first pdf image of Erin Alcott's genome.

What the fuck is that? Anne drew the computer closer, refusing to believe what her own eyes told her. She opened another. The same thing. And then the third. Each scan, right across the middle, had imprinted identical patterns of small dots. They almost seemed to be pinholes of light. Whatever they were, they obscured the central image, but Anne was more concerned with the telomere region, which was clear as it needed to be for interpretation. *Thank God for small favors, at least.*

Still, they needed to be redone. Anne had no deep desire to delay things by even an hour, much less the time it would take to rerun the sample through the electron microscope.

What the bloody hell was that bizarre pattern, and how the devil had it . . . ? A defect in the microscope? Impurities in the substrate? Or the preparation of the sample, or a million other things that might have gone awry before the image had been made. Yes, she'd used an experimental microscope, hybrid open-air scanning electron and light, but there was no way for another object to project, even with the unconventional protocol she'd used.

She opened the image in a different computer application and clicked on "enhance image," so she could gain a closer, more detailed view of the offending object. She printed out the three images and held them beneath a light.

There were minor differences. Not in the genome—that was stable in each. The telomeres were clear, at least, if damning in their confirmation of Erin's GPC. But what was it with the artifact—or whatever it was? In each image, their relative position had changed, as if they'd moved—somehow.

The small points radiated into a spiral from a fuzzy, indistinct nucleus, like cytochrome-C protein structures during cell death. Something tied to Erin's GPC? It would make no sense; she'd never heard of a connection, and the structures did not appear to be part of the image itself, but imposed from an altogether different source.

She glanced down, noticing the glint of her necklace, shimmering in the bright incandescence of the table lamp. The light reflected off the gemstones' facets, projecting a spray of tiny dots onto the sofa, and the nearest wall. The same configuration, more or less. Slightly different coloration, but also a spiral pattern. Coincidence? Random chance?

Highly likely. But how could the necklace be the culprit? The electron microscope would have so magnified the stones they would have obscured the entire image—and then some. The scale in no way matched reality. Anne unlatched the delicate gold chain, and the necklace fell into her cupped hand.

The ouroboros book had been returned to the fae, or so Gaelan had told her, and in its place had been left this lovely, but not-so-unusual, necklace. Not anything unique about it; she'd seen pendants of its like in Harrods, in online jewelry shops—semiprecious gems set into a circular labyrinth. She recognized peridot, garnet, aquamarine, others as well. For all she knew, they were colorful zircons. Or glass.

And . . . there was *nothing* in the stones to suggest even remotely what she'd seen projected onto the scan. She looked closer, shining her phone's flashlight directly on the pattern.

Drawing the desk lamp near, she studied the variation of the randomly placed stones as they framed the circular labyrinth. Thirty-six stones formed the spokes of the maze. Delicate gold filigree, fine as silk thread, formed spokes that joined the spiral together at varying distances. In the center sparkled a single clear crystal, its seemingly infinite facets rendering it far from colorless. The LED light caught the depth and edges of each plane, crossing and diffracting into pink, orange, yellow, and deep sapphire blue, but changing, second by second, and with the angle of the light.

The labyrinth grew out from the center in both spokes and a continuous spiral outward. One deep blue stone followed, seeming nearly black from afar and in juxtaposition to the clarity and brilliance of the central stone. Then a solitary ruby—or garnet—that seemed to draw color as well from the blue stone, rendering it a garish electric purple.

The gems danced, alive and constantly changing in the light, more brilliant than the mere showy sparkle of a diamond in a jewelry shop showcase. Two tiny opals blazed beside the ruby, their inner fire astonishing for their tiny size, followed by a series of three peridots, which lent their pastel green to the opals to at once cool the fire.

The next in the series was light blue quartz. Aquamarine? Five stones. Anne's eyes began to sting from her close scrutiny of the necklace. There were two remaining sets, one of eight yellow-hued stones and thirteen of amethyst. All very well. All quite beautiful. Yet the central question remained. How could a projection from the labyrinth, radiating facets or not, have created a spray of microscopic dots on the micrograph? It was a giant leap to think it an even remote possibility.

What would the stones look like under an electron microscope? An expensive experiment for a mega-giant "what if?" Of course, she'd have to arrange for the time—and charge it to the project. And then explain it to Alcott. *Fuck*. No; it was none of his damn business. Maybe Dana Spangler had access to an EM she might use away from Alcott's enquiring eyes.

She would ring her up first thing.

CHAPTER 30

"There. Do you see it?" Anne directed Dana's gaze to the computer screen in Dana's lab.

"What? What are we looking at? This is obviously not your patient's chromosome. Not a chromosome at all. Even I, a lowly postdoc, know that."

"Obviously. And there it is again."

"What?" Dana repeated, more insistently. "I don't—"

"Movement."

"What? What is it?"

"A gem. An amethyst to be exact."

"Okay. Can you tell me why the hell we are looking at an amethyst in my $2.7 million machine?"

"Curiosity?"

"Anne—"

"Okay, so it's more than curiosity. I can't tell you, not yet anyway, because I'm not sure myself."

Dana scrunched closer to the video screen, pointing to a tentacle-like structure. "It looks like a phage. Maybe."

"That's not possible. It's a stone. You know, an *inanimate* object, meaning *not* bloody alive? You think something's caught in it, like a mosquito in amber?"

"Yeah, but a mosquito in amber doesn't move. Oh!" The phage jumped and Dana leapt back from the video screen.

"Yeah. That."

"I see what you mean."

Anne pushed back from the video screen. "Well . . . ?"

"Where exactly did you get this stone of yours? I'm guessing *not* rock collecting at Oak Street beach."

Anne removed her necklace, placing it in Dana's hand.

"That's from your *necklace*? I don't—"

"Neither do I. My patient's genetic scans came back from the lab with really weird artifacts—a pattern. Dots of light."

"Yeah, but—"

"Hang on. That's what I thought, too. Then I noticed the diffraction pattern given off by my necklace under an LED light—and there it was. The same patterning." Anne pointed to one of the amethysts in her necklace. "What we just saw? A vid capture of that stone. Courtesy of your brilliant EM."

"So you're saying that the artifact . . . but the scale doesn't make any sense."

"Yeah. There is that. Well, I guess I'm not going to wear it to work from now on." Anne wanted to change the subject. "We're having lunch later, right? That new little fish shack near Navy Pier?" Nice try.

"Sure. But aren't you curious? Where did you get it? You never noticed it before?"

Of course, she was curious. "It's new. Only had it a couple weeks. A gift."

Anne watched Dana do the math.

"From Gaelan."

Anne nodded. "I mean, yeah, he's a bit of a strange . . ." She could not go there. "I'm not sure where *he* got it . . . I mean he deals . . . dealt in all sorts of odd . . . antiquities, was it?"

"Yeah." Dana opened her phone. "Shit. I've gotta get back to it, Anne. I'm presenting at group tomorrow afternoon and—"

"Oh, how I not-so-fondly remember those days. See you in an hour, eh?"

Curious as Anne was, it would have to wait. Preston Alcott's text message said he'd sent over a "present," which was awaiting her in the laboratory refrigerator. From a scientist friend of his, he said, working on novel gene therapies.

"I don't know if it will help you, but the guy is Erin's godfather—a good friend of my wife's from college," he explained in a follow-up email. "He's a basic researcher. Not a doctor. Figured it was worth a look. He mentioned something he called super-enhanced hepatic TERT—SEP TERT? He said you'd understand. I sure as hell don't. A cell line he's developing, he says."

What the fuck was "super" enhanced TERT? Liver. Telomerase reverse transcriptase. Yes, it was worth a look. TERT was organ-specific. Erin's condition wasn't organ-specific—it was . . . *everywhere.*

She'd never seen research on treating GPC with TERT, human or otherwise. And nothing about a "super" enhanced anything of the sort. Yes, it was the activating ingredient in immortalizing a telomere, but . . .

She emailed Alcott for the name of the researcher in case she had any questions. She knew most of the researchers in the field, and would know him by name, if nothing else.

Back in her own lab, Anne prepped the "gift"—a sample of hepatic tissue—to examine the telomeres at the subcellular level and placed it in the scope. She poured a coffee and sat down at the video screen, dropping her cup when she looked up at the display. *What the fuck . . . ?*

"Improbable." "Unlikely." "Coincidence." None of these sufficed for what her mind tried its best to reject as completely impossible. But there it was. Again, on the video image, not an artifact on a scan, not the image of whatever was encased in her necklace's gemstones, but now in the tissue sample Alcott had provided her courtesy of his researcher friend. It wasn't similar; it was the exact phenomenon she'd observed, yet on a completely different scale.

Small specks of light scattered all along the telomere loop. Not ordered, like in her necklace, but exhibiting the same radiance, this time in scale with the rest of the scan. The dots were bound up in the genome, but only at the telomere segment. *What the fuck is this?*

Professional skepticism had always been one of Anne's most useful skills—trained into her as an Oxford first-year, and throughout her schooling. The best fallback position whenever anything seemed too coincidental. If it's too good to be true, it is.

Coincidences are *not*, and if they *seem* to be, it's because you haven't done your homework. Or forgot to drop your bias at the lab door. "Coincidences are God's way of remaining anonymous," Einstein said. Anne didn't know if she believed in God, whatever that meant, but if he—or she—wanted to play anonymously amongst the human folk, it was a bloody good way.

The miracle of a breakthrough when least expecting it. Stage four cancer that goes into remission with no explanation. Those were the coincidences—the miracles. Where this one fell, she wasn't sure. It wasn't a "miracle," but it was a bloody big coincidence. And Anne didn't believe it was . . . a coincidence—not for one fucking second.

She'd never seen the phenomenon before, not in fifteen years of telomere research. Never read of it, not so much as a tiny research note of a speculation in an obscure genetics journal no one read.

What would be the function? And why the bloody hell hadn't the researcher shouted it from the rooftops, published in *Nature* and every journal in the field? It made no sense. At all.

"You ready for greasy deep fried?"

Had she really been staring at the screen for an hour?

"Not quite. I want to show you something. Come here." Anne held up two scans.

"Okay. So the first one, you showed me before? The gem. I'd love a copy of it. The crystals are really cool . . . and that phage thing. I still can't figure that puzzle out. Love to try, though."

"Phage thing*s*," Anne corrected, smiling. "Lots of them. And I owe you that at least. It was your multimillion-dollar machine, after all."

"So, what's the other one?"

"Look closer."

"Okay . . . chromosome pair. Male. Good telomere presentation. What kind of dye did you use?"

"Closer. Do you see them?"

"The little dots? What are they?"

Anne ignored the question. "So, the researcher who provided the tissue sample said the telomeres were boosted with hTERT . . . hepatic hTERT."

"Why? Your patient has a liver issue?"

"Some novel gene therapy—for GPC."

"GPC? Wow, that would be great if it worked, but others have tried boosting the telomeres. It hasn't. What's different? So, the dots are—?"

"My client said it's the specific cell line. He did something to it. Enhanced it with superhero reverse transcriptase . . . or something. I need to take a closer look. It's nothing I've ever seen. It must be something completely new. If it was a thing, I'd know about it, and I'm completely baffled."

"Your client. The kid's father? You didn't talk to the primary investigator?"

"He 'prefers to remain anonymous,' so says Daddy. But now I'm going to push the issue. My first call after lunch." A knot had formed in the pit of Anne's stomach from the first moment she'd glanced at the new image, and it had only tightened, nudging her toward a theory she'd rather ignore despite the rather loud klaxon horns blaring away in her head. "Let's get out of here. I'm famished."

A gorgeous day. The sort of cloudless afternoon when it was hard to tell where the sky ended and the water began. The walk down to the shore helped a bit with Anne's mood. She couldn't get the weird coincidence from her mind. "Mind if we visit the glass museum as long as we're here? I could use a good clearing of the cobwebs, and that museum . . ." It was only a short walk down the pier.

"Sure. Gotta be back for a team meeting at two-thirty, though."

"Oh, we don't have to go, if you've got to prep. Been there, and all that."

"All set. So. How well did you know our Gaelan?"

"Well enough, but not very well at all, I suppose. We were close—for a very, very short time. Until—"

"We're here." They went through the swinging door of a weathered wooden shack that looked like it would topple with the next big wind gust. "I'll order." Dana turned to talk to the counter man. "My usual. Two, please."

"How much do I owe—"

"My treat today." A tray with two small paper bags was passed over the high counter and they sat at a small umbrella table just above a small beach. "So, Gaelan . . . he never mentioned you. I mean, knowing I was a molecular biologist, I would have thought—"

"We only just met . . . after his accident." Anne had told Dana nothing about her involvement with Transdiff or how she and Gaelan had connected. Some information was better left unshared. "Hey. These little fish are delicious. What are they called?"

"Smelts. And for about a month, you can get them. And then no more for a year. At least not local smelts. These little shacks make the best. Deep fried and greasy as hell. Trigger a coronary in the healthiest of hearts. And right on top of the equally dripping French fries. Guess you'd call it Chicago-style fish 'n' chips. Minus the newspaper wrapper."

"Think they've got malt vinegar?"

Dana pointed her toward a small card table leaned up against the shack.

The tissue sample continued to nibble at the edges of Anne's mind. "Dana, you're going to think me quite mad, but I have this niggling notion about those little points in the scan."

"And . . ."

"And I wonder if those dots are the same as those in my necklace."

"That's quite a leap, don't you think?"

"Yeah. Crazy, huh?"

"Yeah. I mean think about it. You see a strange artifact on a scan; yeah, it's weird, and the thingies in your necklace are *all sorts* of weird. Actually, weird doesn't begin to describe it. Anyway. Now you see it in this completely different image. An interesting coincidence? Yes. Worthy of further study? Perhaps. You can always do the same sort of scan you did with the pendant. See them up close."

"That was to be my next step. You know, I think I'm going to take a pass at the museum. Maybe I'll stop by after work, if they're open, but something just occurred to me. You do know that leaps like that are what make for the best discoveries ever? What if I've stumbled onto something?"

"From your necklace? Really? Something you're not telling me? Care to share with the class?"

"Just a hunch. I'd rather not say, for now, anyway. You go ahead. I have to get back home—"

Dana nodded. "You sure you're all right? You seem distracted."

Anne shrugged. "Yeah, maybe. See you later. Meet for a beer?"

"Sorry. Date with my wife. Tomorrow?"

Anne hoped she was wrong, and knew she wasn't. The coincidence was too striking to be anything but what she'd already guessed. There was really only one way to tell, and it was easy. The vial of blood Gaelan had given her still sat packed in dry ice at the back of Simon's refrigerator. Two days—if she was lucky—to culture Gaelan's blood sample into a useable cell strain. Then she would know whether the mystery cell line—Alcott's "present"—and Gaelan's were one and the same. And if she were right? What then?

What if the superhero cell line originated with Gaelan—and represented a genuine breakthrough? Could it lead to a treatment, if not a cure, for all those telomere-deficient diseases? So many questions. But they would wait until she knew what—and who—she was dealing with.

The wind picked up, and it had suddenly become freezing cold at the end of the mile-long pier, especially in a sleeveless top. Perhaps she would duck into the glass museum after all, at least to warm up for a bit, have a think about how to proceed with Alcott's cell line, with Erin, with what she knew in her heart was the answer to the question she'd only just begun to ask herself.

The museum was deserted but for the guard. The track lighting painted the walls in refracted color, projections of the stained-glass artwork, fuzzy images, indistinct of their fine workmanship and the intricate stories each piece told.

But she was only interested in two pieces. Planting herself in front of the panels, she stared into them until the colors blurred, as if by so doing she might better understand Gaelan Erceldoune. She glanced around, assuring herself she was still alone, and the guard at the door was still occupied with her smart phone. Drawing near the Minotaur panel, she placed her palms in the center of the panel, peering through its translucence to the refracted image it projected on the wall. Nothing. What the fuck had she been thinking? *You want to believe, Dr. Anne Shawe—and that's bloody dangerous!*

SCOTLAND, PRESENT DAY

CHAPTER 31

Events had transpired too quickly for Gaelan to absorb even a fraction of the impact. He could do little more than react. He'd taken no time to consider the magnitude of what had just happened, much less come to terms with the faint but growing possibility it was all, in fact, *real*.

How could he accept, much less comprehend, what he now knew might well be true? The injury to his arm and the jagged shard of glass—if nothing else, they were empirical evidence, a piece of the "other" world transported through time and space. A starting point.

Evidence, but not proof, that beneath what had once been Dernwode House, there existed a portal between present and future, Scotland and Chicago, linked by a single moment. A chance meeting with Nicola Tesla. The off-handed answer to a question he'd never really thought about since that day. A glass teardrop gone missing shortly after their conversation, fusing past to present to future. He'd never made the connection; there had been none to make. Gaelan allowed the improbability of it to settle to mere unlikelihood.

Theories about such gateways between alternative universes had floated about for centuries, had they not? Never proved, but never entirely dismissed.

Gaelan leafed through Conan Doyle's journal again, finding a particular passage.

If only we understand the means, expand our horizons, and believe it is possible, not with wishes and old wives' tales, nor the conjuring of magic, but with good science. It is there for us to reach out and take hold of the merely imagined. It has been my enduring frustration that as yet I've not the ability to interact with them, the fairy folk, but only to see them. To hear, but not touch. Perhaps I've not the ability at all, but to perceive without grasping entirely. Perhaps you who find this by happenstance, or design, if you will, may possess what I lack.

The separation between our worlds is thin as an invisible membrane, the vibration in the spectra of color as from a prism, a whisper barely audible, but ever-present, if only one might learn to see with particular eyes, enlightened to the vastness of the universe, its many realms. I have been to their world. So shall you. My good friend Wells postulated such a . . . shall we say . . . portal. I implore you to read his "Crystal Egg." Fiction though it may be, the story rings true to my own experience in its way, I quite believe.

Our ideas must be as broad as nature to truly comprehend it, Conan Doyle had said. He'd observed what Gaelan had, understood it, if only through his Victorian prism. And perhaps that was the problem.

Conan Doyle witnessed illusion through a broken mirror and beheld a wondrous, amazing universe. He wanted so much to believe in an alternate world where fairies dwelled in castles and filigreed forests, that he could not see it clearly for what it was: an island sitting in the middle of a destroyed world that spread far beyond the oasis to a nearly deserted wasteland. Had he never seen what Gaelan had—the total annihilation of a city? Or in the century since Conan Doyle had ventured through the portal, had so much changed in that world? Would he even recognize it now?

Gaelan owed it to Conan Doyle's memory, to Tesla, to himself, to return, discover what it really was lay beyond the portal. How the world, at least Chicago, had come to be destroyed.

Club Guillotine. A frightening image flashed through Gaelan's mind. Why had the guillotine made a comeback, and in Chicago? He pushed aside a fleeting thought as he traversed the corridor toward the prism chamber.

Should he pass it by and return through the amorphous wall to the dock? His arm still throbbed; he could barely move it. He didn't much want to run into that gang again. And he dreaded facing the inestimable horror of what lay beyond the Chicago skyline. Better to face the interrogator LaSalle. Two bad options, yet . . .

Clutching the teardrop in his fist, Gaelan stepped through to the prism room and waited, closing his eyes, listening for the cacophony of glass to settle into a sublime harmony, and be transported.

Gaelan stood once again just outside the structure; the air was calm. No sign of that LaSalle fellow. The sand at his feet, recognizable now as the detritus of a long-ago massive destruction of a postmodern White City, pulverized into a powder, soft as it was abrasive.

The deep blue sky contrasted with the few luminous clouds that dotted it. No dust, no mist. A perfect Chicago day.

The skyline from this angle seemed more distant than it had from the Ferris wheel park—the hills that first day obscured then in the whirlwind of a dust storm.

More birdcage high-rises, missing windows, the shine of their polished granite facades, pitted and dull. In the other direction, the water's edge, which had crept above the bike path he'd walked so many times in summer. Joe's Fish Shack still stood just above on a small knoll, boarded up, its signage weathered and decayed. What the hell had happened? And how far into the future was this? How many centuries had it taken to reach this point of deterioration?

Gaelan shoved against the wall and it opened into the tiny alcove where he'd first been. An eternity ago, it seemed. Another push and he was again surrounded by forest. He tried to see it as Conan Doyle had, through his nineteenth-century prism. How easy to misinterpret twenty-first-century invention as otherworldly and magical.

LaSalle had snuck up as quiet as a spider, whispering close to his ear, and Gaelan jumped, his heart caught in his throat.

"So, Mr. Erceldoune, you grace us with your presence once again. Your journey was easier this time round? No windstorms? No gangs? Just straight on into our little paradise. Fantastic."

Gaelan followed LaSalle through the now familiar maze of trees and bridges, which twisted and wound beneath and over the river, finally arriving at LaSalle's tentacled interrogation chair. Not this time; Gaelan chose a straight-backed wooden card chair. No arms to conceal restraints. He brushed his hand across and beneath the seat, searching for any other appendage that might be used to shackle him.

LaSalle shrugged. "One seat's as good as another, and I don't think I have to tie you to your chair—not this time. We've piqued your curiosity, haven't we? Please, sit. By the way, how is that arm?" LaSalle's solicitousness was in deep contrast to his earlier demeanor, chilling in its niceness.

"You knew?"

"We saw. Bravo for dropping the glass piece. Handy escape, dude!"

Gaelan drew back tense and coiled, hands balled into fists, ready to flee to the catacombs. But not before he learned what had happened and how long ago. "That gang. Who are they anyway?"

"Right." LaSalle indicated Gaelan's arm. "They want us. Need us. Can't get to us in here, so they wait. We have pretty good defenses. There aren't a lot of us in here, but we know what we're doing. The last of a dying breed, so to speak. But we must go outside sometime. Gather what supplies we can't produce in-house."

"The last time I was here, you fed my belief that this was hell. And that I was dead. I'm not, am I?"

"Did I? I confirmed nothing at all. I listened . . . You *thought* you were in hell, and perhaps you are. Perhaps we all are. Something's changed . . . You've begun to accept . . ." LaSalle gestured broadly left and right. ". . . all this, haven't you?" He looked too pleased with himself.

"What are you talking about?"

"Before. You were still uncertain—"

"I took a poison. I meant to commit suicide, but—"

"Ah, and so we come to the point. You should be dead but are not. The question is, 'why?'"

"Well, yes. That *is* the question. The only question that matters—to me. That, and how to put it to rights. I'm not supposed to be alive, you see."

"You must have more questions than that one, pretty damn narcissistic question, I might add, and I will give all the answers you want. But I sense you're not one hundred percent ready to abandon your disbelief."

"How would you know that? And why do you care? Who am I to you? How do you know me at all?"

"Legends are like that. Known, but somehow elusive."

"*Legends?*"

"Yup. You will be happy to know you are quite the mythic character in our world. Not quite so famous as your ancestor Thomas, but still . . . No one really cares anymore, except us. In here."

As if Gaelan could not be more confused. Frustrated. "Is that how I came to be here?"

"No. That was all you. We'd hoped that someday . . . No one really believed it, except for one incredibly determined person. First things first. How you got here, on this . . . side—"

Finally. This, Gaelan *was* curious to hear. He sat up straighter. "I'm listening."

"There are . . . doors . . . some call them portals, others, wormholes, gates, whatever you want to call them—they're all synonymous with each other in our well-developed scientific understanding. We know they exist. Have proven it. You're proof of it. But we don't know *how* they work, not exactly. There's no . . . consistent pattern. One day a portal opens, the next it's closed. Some can enter, some can only look, like a department store window display.

"They exist all over the world; for example, the Borders of Scotland. Quite a few, actually, all through the UK. Ireland as well, where the divide is as thin as a sheet of graphene. Chicago, too—full of 'em. Peepholes into other worlds. This is ours. All myths have a grain of truth or they wouldn't survive."

"This is some sort of alternate universe, then? A different time, clearly, but a place familiar to me. How?"

"Some portals are natural, but this one was human-generated, created near the turn of the twentieth century, far as we can tell. And we *know* how this one operates."

"How would that be even possible? Back then, I mean." Gaelan already knew the answer. LaSalle could confirm it.

"You, Mr. E. It was you who presented the coordinates, give or take a meter or two, to the creator of the portal in the first place. And, double bonus, the divide here happens to be quite thin between worlds, so . . . part luck, part not. Or maybe the portal's creator knew more than we give him credit for."

So, it *had* been Tesla. He'd actually done it. But Gaelan wasn't ready to admit it—not to LaSalle, at any rate. "How could you possibly know it was me? What sort of instrumentation would specify that one Gaelan Erceldoune at an inexactly measured time did present some proto–time traveler exact coordinates for some unknowable portal in—"

"Scotland. Not far from Earlston, I think. Anyway, we guessed. An educated guess, but still a lucky guess. That piece of glass you're holding onto as if it's the only thing anchoring you in time and space? It's yours, isn't it? Missing from an art piece *you* made. A long, long time ago."

"Yes. In 1893—" An admission Gaelan hadn't wanted to make.

"Well, there you have it."

"Yes." It was all Gaelan could think to say.

"Would you care for tea? You liked the spice tea, but we've also got fresh mint. With honey. Bees are quite a rarity, as you can imagine, and we've got an apiary, though it's small. We're trying to bring the species back, and it's a tough road."

"Where are all the people?"

"I'm sorry. I don't get—"

"The people. Chicago is . . . was—"

"Most have left the city; those that choose to remain—or have no choice—live in little enclaves like this one. There are more renewables outside the city, but it's far from abandoned—"

"But earlier, when I was out . . ." Gaelan realized it had been just after sunrise. Few would be about, even on a normal day. "Tell me what happened?" He whispered the question, almost involuntarily.

A woman's laugh, bitter and abrasive, came out of the trees behind LaSalle. She appeared as if by magic, floating to his side from between two willows. Small blades at her feet retracted as she settled next to him, taking a seat in the tentacle chair. Gaelan stared at her feet. She noticed.

LaSalle rose from his seat, extending his hand toward Gaelan. Gaelan declined it.

"Well, in any event," he said affably, retracting the proffered hand, "my job here is done." He nodded to the woman. She returned it. A silent conversation through furtive glances Gaelan did not understand.

"Mini drones," she said once LaSalle was gone. "We developed them to ease transport outside as well as in here. It's quick and the Burkies don't have the tech. So. You want to know what happened."

Burkies. Again. He'd find out sooner or later, he guessed. Gaelan nodded. The woman was beautiful, at once angelic and hard, her long, flowing hair hanging loose about a white iridescent cloak. Metallic thread twined through the strands of her hair and her cloak, lending her an ethereal quality. Otherworldly. *Fairy-like.*

"Tea?"

Gaelan shook her off. Did he really want to know? Did he care?

So what? He'd traversed a portal to the future that was something out of a postapocalyptic nightmare. Why should he give a fuck?

This wasn't his world. What the bloody hell had it to do with him? Nothing. Not a fucking thing. He'd thought maybe he'd find a clue about his state of . . . being. Some clarity, and a way to end it, get out of this fucking labyrinth of confusion.

And if it turned out he was alive, all he'd really have to do is drop the glass, return to the catacombs and set the whole bloody thing ablaze. Destroy it, the prisms, the portal, himself. Self-immolation would do just fine. A gallon of kerosene and a match. Done. He was fairly sure by the time it was over, he would be but ash, a small unidentifiable mound among the destruction. Nothing left of him to study or exploit. It was the perfect solution. Why had he not thought of it before?

Yes, the monks would frown, be upset he'd destroyed what they'd worked so hard to preserve, and Gaelan felt truly bad about that. But they were dead and gone. And so would he be, by morning's first light.

An image of his father skittered through his mind. He could feel the heat of the flames as they licked up Papa's legs, melting away his flesh. The sweet stench of fat and blood as it incinerated. He gagged on the memory, still too vivid, half a millennium later. He did not possess the stomach for it—to light the match, dishonor his father, his mother, his family.

Perhaps something rather more explosive would do it. Make it quick. Painless, if possible. He was a skilled chemist, after all, was he not? He could do it, and easily enough. He'd need money; perhaps there was a bit of cash to be had by selling off a few of those prisms. He wouldn't need much. Just enough to blow the whole bloody catacombs to smithereens, and one Gaelan Erceldoune along with it.

He tucked the teardrop in his pocket, and once again, he was in the prism chamber. Exhausted and in agony, the biting, slicing pain in his arm unabated, he slid down the wall until he was sitting, knees drawn up until he could rest his head on them. What a fucking coward he'd become. When did *that* happen? But was the act of courage going through with it, or seeing this scenario to the end, whatever it brought?

LaSalle had said he was infamous. Not infamous. Legendary.

Why? What had he done? He wasn't so sure he really wanted to know. Was that the issue, then? Afraid to face up to whatever "it" was?

What would his father think of him setting himself afire? Blowing himself up? Not very much. What would Gaelan say to him if ever they were to meet in some version of an afterlife—if such a thing existed at all? *Fuck.*

And what of the—shrinking—possibility he was already dead, or dying. Was he so certain this all was not some grand illusion? Elaborate delusion? A poison-induced, psychedelic dream? Even the pain in his arm. Could that, too, be part of the delusion? A test of some sort . . . ?

The phantom pain above the stump of his left hand had never subsided, not nearly two centuries later—not until . . . not until his fingers had been inexplicably restored in his sleep. He'd little difficulty believing that trick, had he not?

Why not play along, then, for just a bit longer? See it through to the final act. He'd figure something out; he always had. Just awhile longer.

Once again, he made his way into the seòmar-criostalan to the music of the prisms.

LONDON, 1826

CHAPTER 32

"Mr. Erceldoune?"

Gaelan turned toward the voice.

"I cannot—" Caitrin entered the examining room through the stairway, reaching for balance; she caught Gaelan's arm before tumbling to the floorboards.

She was feverish again. *Damnation!* Had she, too, fallen victim to the sweating sickness . . . or whatever this was? She had not been in the examining room, not since that night. Aye, but she had been around *him*. Been living in his flat. Breathing in the air he breathed out. How could he know whether he carried the disease within himself and had passed it to her? *Dear God.*

Gaelan glanced at the leather pouch, still clutched in his hand. Dare he try it on her? Take the risk and pray it saved her life? She would not survive the sweat, that much was certain. Yet, she had already been in a weakened condition and too many uncertainties loomed with the new preparation. And was he not about to inject the stricken men, now coughing through every breath as they lay on their cots? What of the risks to them?

No doubt, Caitrin showed the signs: the sweating, the quaking chills; her hands and face were feverish. She would be the one to pay the price for his indecisiveness. Gently, he carried her back to the flat, settling her in his bed, where she now lay still and pale. "Caitrin, can you hear me?"

She nodded weakly, her gaze glassy as polished marble.

"Does your head hurt?"

"It feels . . . it will explode at any moment . . . I fear," she gasped, each word punctuated with a shallow breath.

"I have a medicine that might work to . . . but I must be certain . . . I shall be but a moment."

"No! Do not go! My God! My fingers—they burn and prick. I can scarce feel them."

Gaelan took gentle hold of her hand. It was red and hot as flame. Her breathing had deteriorated. The progress of the illness was so rapid as to defy comprehension.

He needed his notes. He must read through them one last time— to have no doubt he was doing the right thing by her. "I'll return in a moment's time. I promise." With all haste, Gaelan took the stairs up to his laboratory two at a time and fell into his chair while locating the needed entry in Grandpapa's journal.

For many who fall prey to the sweating sickness, it comes on with the fury of a dragon—sudden, unrelenting, breathing fire. He might be in perfect health one moment and deathly in the next. Gone to bed fit and fine, he might awaken suddenly, the sweating so profuse as to soak the bedclothes and bedding. The sweat seems to flow from the body as if all the pores of the skin opened into streams.

There attends the sufferer a sense of dread, terrified of demons only he can see. The heart beats hard and very swift, so much so, I fear it will seize and give out at any moment. I see this over and over as the dragon breathes, stealing its victims' dying gasps to fuel its own fire. There are few instances here thus far, yet I fear with all my being that it shall consume the English border and find its way to Edinburgh. I shall take the risk that needs be taken and inoculate the court, at the very least to stem the tide 'ere it reaches our fair capital. As for the regions to the east and south, nearer the border, I shall rely upon our friends at Dernwode House and prevail upon them to dispense what I carry to them myself, as they are the first outpost on the Scottish frontier of this most deadly battle.

Gaelan read to the end of the page by candlelight as he made his way down to the flat, reviewing one last time the disease's progress and first signs of imminent death. The delirium, the dizziness, the breathing. The blisters. And now the tingling sensations. All appeared in Caitrin in the exact order described.

By the time Gaelan returned to her side, she was drenched, almost as if she'd been immersed in a vat of water. *Damnation.* Why did not have her drink the salt tonic? The bedding was sodden, and her clothing. Small droplets of water had appeared on her bare arms. No, these were not beads of sweat, but small blisters. They were clear, not red, like a rash or the pox. Yes, the blisters. These, too, were part of the pattern as described in Grandpapa's notes.

He poured a tumbler of the salt elixir, but she would not open her parched lips to sip. If this ailment was not *sudor anglicus*, the treatment alone may well kill her. And it would be his fault, his arrogance—as if he'd murdered her himself. He tried to dismiss the idea so he might concentrate on the task at hand.

If he believed in God, Gaelan would have prayed for the wisdom to do what was right, but God had betrayed him more than two centuries before. He had only to rely upon his skill and the knowledge of those who came before him—and the strange recipes of the ouroboros book, which had well served his father, his grandfather, and all before them.

He took hold of Caitrin's hand, his fingers settled on the inside of her wrist. The pulse throbbed against his hand, nearly one beat atop the next.

"Caitrin."

Her eyes remained closed, as if she had not heard, her breaths shallow, rapid puffs. There was no more time to lose; if he was going to do it, he must administer the medicine immediately.

"Caitrin," he repeated, holding up the device. "With this, I believe I can make you better. Do you understand?"

Her eyes fluttered open, a vacant stare, going wide as Gaelan showed her the glass and metal injecting device. "Do you understand?" he repeated. "I cannot guarantee . . . I have never tried . . . But if I do nothing—"

She nodded, her lips pursed into a tight line. "I . . . I . . . trust you," she breathed, each word an effort. Her eyes once again closed; the shivering had recommenced.

If this failed, if Caitrin were to die, Kinston would surely learn of it. And Gaelan would answer for it, not with his life—that was an impossibility—but with a fate much worse. He had no doubt Lord Kinston was the most vengeful of creatures.

Yet, had he any choice here . . . and now?

He drew up a small amount of the liquid into the inoculation device, but where to make the injection? Jenner used the arm to place his smallpox vaccine, but would it be correct for this disease? Or did it not matter where?

Gaelan sought for a spot where there were no blisters and eased in the sharp tip, ignoring the small amount of blood that seeped around the tool's metal. He released the lever and pushed the upper part of the glass through the tube slowly, observing as the liquid rose into a small bubble beneath the skin.

Removing the device, he wiped away the blood and waited. Gaelan listened through the open door of the flat for any sound from down below in the shop, hoping the two men in the examining room might remain asleep for now. *Do not die yet; it is all I ask. Hold on but a while longer.*

Nothing but silence but for the clip-clop of hooves and the dull, uneven roar of wooden wheels upon the cobblestones in the street below the window. Every few moments the rhythm was interrupted by a distant shout for help—a call for the undertakers. Not a good sign at all. He stared at his watch as it ticked off the seconds, each an eternity, so loud in the quiet of the room, he could swear it would echo throughout all London.

Restless, Gaelan paced the room one end to the other, pausing at the window to glance down into the market. Few were out and about.

Minutes passed: five, ten, fifteen. He stared at Caitrin until his eyes burned and she was a blur of color and ragged breaths. She coughed and with it, her entire body shook, followed by long, gasping, noisy breaths.

Thirty-four minutes passed, and Caitrin sat up in the bed.

"What happened? I—Where am I?" Her voice was strong; her breathing seemed less distressed.

Gaelan placed a calming hand on her arm, easing her back against the pillows. "You fell quite ill, nearly took a tumble down the stairs. Do you not recall?"

"No, I don't. I was . . . here. No . . . in the sitting room. Then . . . ? I am . . . don't . . . what happened?"

"You swooned, and I've given you a medicine that should put it to rights, but you must not stand. Not yet." He handed her the tumbler of salt tonic. "Drink this. It will help you regain your strength."

"I do not . . . Is it . . . is it the same . . . the illness . . . as what I had . . . I mean—"

"No, it is not. As I mentioned before, there is a pestilence spreading over London. Just at its start, I believe. I fear it shall become epidemic. You were stricken by it, nearly succumbed to it. The medicine I gave you . . . should work. Already has begun. At least I believe it so."

Her eyes closed again. "I am quite fatigued and should like to sleep, if that is all right."

"Finish the contents in the cup, and then you may rest. Both are important."

He eyed the leather bag. He would try it on the men down in the shop. If it worked with them . . .

Sally Mills awaited him as he came down from the flat; she was agitated, pacing, her hands gripped into tight fists. Her worried gaze darted from the window to the examining room and back to Gaelan.

"What is it, Mrs. Mills? Are there others fallen ill?"

"So many more, so many sick at the Owl. What to do? What to do?"

Gaelan glanced toward the examining room. No sound but the rasping of two patients came through the curtain.

Gaelan placed the leather bag on the countertop. He ushered her over to a chair.

"Sit for a while, then, Mrs. Mills. I've a medicine I believe will help, though I have only tried it on one so far. I've two asleep in the examining room, and after I administer it them, we both shall see. Then I shall fly forthwith to the White Owl and do what I might. That is all I can promise."

She nodded, tears streaming down her round, reddened cheeks. "Have you never seen anything of its like, Mr. Erceldoune?"

"No." It was the simplest answer, if not the most honest. "Forgive me a moment." Gaelan handed her a handkerchief and went through to the examining room.

The men had been quiet the entire time Gaelan had been upstairs, but their rest, it seemed, had been fitful as they thrashed and flailed about. Who knew what visions they wrestled in their dreams? A twitch, a gasp, their hands reaching out from deep within their sleep. One muttered quietly, whispering to one only he could see.

They had endured the symptoms many hours by now—longer than had Caitrin. Yet they seemed no worse than she had after only just a few minutes. Was there a point, then, in the course of the illness when a status quo might be maintained—until it entered a deadlier phase?

Would the injection be effective in all cases or only just at the start? Yes, Caitrin had only just fallen ill, but was already in a weakened condition. Gaelan knew that fevers affected different people differently. There were yet very many questions he could not answer, nor his grandfather's notes had explained, but he could not delay a moment longer. He knew nothing in medicine was ever a certainty. And if what Sally Mills had reported was close to the truth . . . ?

He sucked in a breath and repeated the procedure used on Caitrin, and, minding his pocket watch, waited. The first opened his eyes in twenty-three minutes, confused as to what he was doing in a sodden cot and not in his own bed.

"You've been ill, sir, but you need to rest a while more. I shall see to changing the bedding, and you will be much more comfortable." Gaelan handed him a bottle with the salt solution, admonishing him to drink it all.

The other one was much older, and Gaelan was unsure if anything would help him at this point. He cursed himself for not better understanding the intricacies of the ouroboros book better, and on his own—not relying upon notes written centuries ago by men of limited knowledge by modern standards.

Had he been more skilled, wiser, he might better comprehend the nuances of the dosing. What if it was too much? Too little? Too early? Too late? The answers had to be there, if only he might see them.

And what if the turn for the better was but fleeting and . . . Gaelan heard the gasp, as the elderly man began to cough. Clear, frothy liquid poured from his mouth as he tried to sit up, as if half-drowned. Gaelan leapt to his side, helping him to sit, and held a cloth beneath his chin. The fluid was now tinged with blood as the coughing did not abate.

"Easy, now. Try to take a breath, but not too deeply." Gaelan rubbed the man's back in large circles, hoping it would ease the attack and calm him. His breathing slowed, and the coughing along with it. The fluid turned once again clear. "That's good. Like that. Slow, steady breaths. Just like that, now." Gaelan gathered more blankets to set beneath the heads of the ailing men.

Another half hour and the man seemed much improved, though still quite feverish, whether from the vigor of the coughing attack or the illness Gaelan had no idea.

But he'd done it. The experiment had been a success. And now to face the horror that undoubtedly lay beyond his threshold. He shivered at the thought.

"I must be off for a bit, gentlemen. Mrs. Mills from the White Owl is beyond that curtain. Call out for her should you require anything or you take a turn. She will be in shortly to see to your comfort. He placed a large bottle of the salt tonic beside each cot. "I would admonish you to drink—all of it. Small sips, but finish it."

He did not wait for them to respond.

Sally Mills stood at the window, peering into the street. "I went back there, Mr. Erceldoune. To the Owl. Couldn't help myself." She was white with fear, shaking her head slowly side to side, muttering under her breath. When she again spoke it was as if from within a dream. "Couldn't help myself, y'see. Needed to find . . . Didn't want to believe . . . You were taking god-awful long in there, and I went back. I went back. I—"

Gaelan blew out a sharp breath and ushered her to a chair. He kneeled before her, taking both her hands in his. She was shaking, though not from fever. He addressed her as gently as he would a small child. "Mrs. Mills. You must listen to me—"

She turned her gaze on him, her eyes red-rimmed. "All gone. All of 'em. Dead. How's it possible when last night they's all drinkin' and eatin' . . . ? It's as if the Owl herself's been possessed of an evil that—"

"Not an evil, an illness. A dragon of a pestilence, but one that might be van . . ." He couldn't say it. Not to her. "Are you certain they are dead? All your customers? All? Perhaps they are only ill. Then I might yet—"

"Up in the rooms, they're all blue-faces, eyes like smoke and glass, just starin', damning me for—"

"It is not your fault, Mrs. Mills. This disease, it is like none I've ever seen. Swift and merciless, it is. I will, myself, go to the Owl and see if there is anything to be done."

Did Sally really see what she thought she had? Or was she afflicted, and this was the start of it—the delirium? The panic.

"Mrs. Mills, if you would be so kind to look in on the men convalescing behind that curtain. Insist they drink up the contents of the bottles I've left with them. It is of great importance they do so. Not too quickly, mind, but all of it. And within the hour, by which time I hope to have returned."

Gaelan collected his leather bag, assuring himself the vials, the injector, and other needed items were packed securely. "If any should come here seeking me, tell them I shall be back soon as I can, but do *not*—under any circumstance—come to find me at the Owl. Do you understand? If any require an item from the shop's shelves, you may give them, but do not trouble yourself with collecting monies. I will see to it later. All right?"

She nodded tentatively, still shaking. Galen put a hand on her shoulder. "Do not worry yourself, Mrs. Mills. I shall see to the Owl."

If Sally Mills was even half-right about what she'd seen, he would be far too late.

CHICAGO, PRESENT DAY

CHAPTER 33

"So. How goes the research? Any progress with that new cell line?"

Alcott. She'd barely made it to the lab when her mobile went off.

She struggled to keep her suspicions well under wraps. For now. "No. Not yet. It's only been—"

Anne's first task of the day was to prepare Gaelan's blood sample for closer examination, hoping that what she suspected was merely a giant illogical leap, easily disprovable. Allay her fears—then she could get on with it, use the enhanced cell line provided by Alcott's friend to treat Erin and see if she had in her hands the unlikely Nobel-laureate-worthy miracle of an easy cure to a fatal disease. "Hey. I don't mean to pressure you. Just asking."

Bollocks. She breathed, inhaling slowly, and then again, for all the good it did. Her knuckles had gone completely white as she gripped her mobile. "Sorry. I'm a bit under the gun here . . . Look, actually, I *may* be onto something. With the cell line, I mean. Tell your . . . friend . . . 'good work on that.' What was his name again?"

"I don't think I ever said. Let's just say it prefers to remain anonymous."

"I'd really like to . . ." Why bother? Time enough later. "Might I give you a ring later, when I know something more definitive?"

"Dinner?"

"Perhaps another time." Perhaps never. Not. Ever.

"Look, there are some folks I'd like you to meet. They are very much interested in your research. Its practical application. Venture capitalists. Not really friends, more colleagues, you'd say. Funded my first project—and bought into every one since then. And some tech people in your field. They're anxious to meet you too."

The knot in her stomach tightened another notch. *I'll bet they are.* "Like your friend Mr. Anonymous?"

"Possibly."

"Maybe at the end of all this. If I can find a way to treat Erin—"

"Fair 'nough."

She sighed; this was far from the end. Carefully, she drew the small Styrofoam sample box from her messenger bag, fetching the tubes from within the nest of dry ice packs. She had to sequence the DNA, analyze the telomere region, an expensive proposition—and out of view of Preston Alcott. She hated to ask Dana again, but she didn't see much choice.

As if on cue, Dana appeared at the lab door, bearing two coffees. "Leave it to a Chicago June. One hundred degrees one day, fifty the next. Pretty crazy how the temp dropped yesterday afternoon, though. One café noisette for you. One for me."

"Yeah. Thanks for the coffee. You don't have any sweets possibly …?"

She pulled out a brown paper bag, raising an eyebrow. "Hazelnut croissants."

Anne smiled.

"You said you like hazelnuts."

"Doesn't everybody? You didn't bring that jar of that fab chocolate hazelnut spread over from your lab, did you?"

Dana produced a small jar. "Voila!"

"You sure you don't want to do a postdoc with me if I ever go back to academia?"

"Nope. Just got nabbed by Cornell for next year. Associate professor posting."

"Bravo! Well done, m'dear. We can celebrate. Drinks on me. However, I do need a bit of a favor and quickly."

"Sure. I mean—"

"I need a DNA assay and I can't—"

Dana cocked an eyebrow. "Why do you need me for that? You *have* privileges. And I've already—"

"Two reasons. First, your machine has the magic. You told me yourself. How much that cost, again? And, second, it's not for the project I'm on . . . not exactly. And to be honest, I really don't wish my employer to know."

"It's an experimental machine. The only one in existence. Genetic mojo magic."

"Ha!"

Dana sat. "Sounds nefarious. Is it?"

"No. Not really. Can you do it?"

"I guess. It will cost. Someone's gotta pay for the magic. Sure you don't want to ask your client?"

"Yes, I'm quite certain about that. I can pay how many ever thousands of dollars required. Out of my own pocket. Cost is no object. Let me know, I will write the check. Just tell me to whom."

"Deal. Okay, what is it? Can you tell me that at least?"

"Just a DNA sample. Blood. Legally obtained. With consent."

"It can't be 'just a blood sample.' C'mon. What is it? I'm not interested in getting involved with anything illegal or unethical—"

"Nor am I, and it's neither." Anne considered whether to tell her the truth. *Fine.* "It's Gaelan's blood."

"Gaelan? Why? Where did you get it? I'd heard a rumor about a couple of samples destined for the biohazard disposal that went missing after the accident. They asked everyone about it, from techs to docs and nurses—even the maintenance guys."

"No. This one he gave to me."

"What? Why?"

"It's a longer story than I want to tell right now. Will you do it, then?"

"Sure. Gaelan's blood? Oh, I get it." Dana smiled. "A paternity test?"

Anne closed her eyes. "Like that would require your machine? But I suppose it's as good as any reason, and I'll need those cool super high-res scans."

She trusted Dana, but she barely knew the woman. "Hey, on second thought, do you mind if I run the scans myself? It's a bit delicate, as you might imagine. I want to make certain—"

"Privacy. Sure." Dana shrugged. "Whatever. Really? Gaelan? I thought he was completely celibate . . . sworn off women, men, sex of any kind."

"People change."

"No. They don't!"

"I suppose not, but . . . And thanks. I'd like to get started ASAP."

"I'll check the schedule and let you know."

Three days. An eternity, and finally she had the results. They were as she'd feared, but were now fixed onto paper, proven. Anne reran the tests three times before believing it. The "enhanced" hepatic TERT cell strain and Gaelan's blood were from the same person. No doubt remained.

Gaelan had suffered liver damage in his fall down the bluff in the ravines—that much she knew from his hospital chart. The hepatic TERT had been most definitely rendered from his liver tissue.

Anne aimlessly wandered the main floor of Simon's house, room to room, conscious of it only when her boot heels clacked on the marble tiles in the foyer. Weary of the effort, she threw open the French doors of the refrigerator, scanning the shelves for something palatable to eat. The blueberry pie looked good, and she sat at the table, staring into the tin, for several minutes until she shoved it away. No appetite.

She should text Alcott. She had been delaying it for a day, holed up, hiding from him, from Dana, from everyone. She had no idea of what to do, and no one to talk to about it. That was a lie. She knew exactly what she needed to do. And it would not get easier in an hour or five. Or five months.

Anne's fingers trembled on her phone as she ran her finger over the keyboard. "I've changed my mind about dinner. I would very much like to meet your friends, including the . . ." How should she put it? She backspaced, erasing the sentence she'd begun. "I would like to meet the scientist who . . ."

Who what? Stole a tissue sample? Exploited the DNA of a private human being without consent? Sought to discover the key to human immortality? Well, that was a leap she was unwilling to make, at least not yet.

Perhaps it was all innocent; the tiniest niggle of doubt remained. A scientist with access, coming to the aid of a friend with a dying child, not out of the question . . . She didn't believe it, but until she was absolutely certain . . . Dinner would hopefully land her on one or the other side of the question.

She continued typing. " . . . was kind enough to supply the extraordinary cell line. Never have I . . ." More backspacing. No need to overdo it. "I am hopeful this discovery may lead to a way to approach Erin's illness." She hit "send."

She was in way too far over her head with no idea what would come of it. She pulled the report from her briefcase for the fifth time that day, rereading, highlighting, making more notes, before shoving it back in.

It was almost beside the point, given the simultaneously stunning and terrifying results. The addition of Gaelan's cells to Erin's corrected the telomeres—as if by magic. And with a rapidity that . . . The points of light, what Dana called phages, migrated to the telomere loops and repaired the mutation to the guanine pairs. It was like no genome editing, no manipulation she'd ever seen before, even on paper. Had she not witnessed it herself, had not repeated it, filmed it, and watched and re-watched the process too many times to count over the past three days, she would not believe it possible.

The "phages" were possibly protein complexes, activating enzymes to supercharge the cell, but bonded, somehow, to something more mechanical. Like submicroscopic spiders, they reworked and reconfigured the telomeres at a molecular level.

But how? What was the mechanism? The work to study the process of these tiny objects would require months, perhaps years. How was it possible at all that an extract from Gaelan's immortal tissue—presumably part of his physiology for nearly half a millennium—contained materials so technically advanced to be beyond what she knew to be possible, given the current state of research in her field?

And that material, Gaelan insisted, had itself been rendered from a book centuries older than that. The technology appeared to be so far ahead of its time, scientists were only now just beginning to experiment with that sort of biomechanical complexity. But in the lab, not in vivo. Nanobots. Or something like them embedded into the inks of an ancient manuscript? Who would believe such an absurd thing?

Anne went through to the garden, welcoming the fresh air. Her necklace refracted the midmorning sun, sending sprays of colored dots in an array all about the ground. Taking the dirt path, she made her way down to the beach and sat on a large pitted boulder, listening to the waves rushing up against the gravel, hauling it up the sand and back out into the lake, watching a family of mallard ducks meander along the water's edge in a neat row. Imprinting. Learning bit by bit. How it was supposed to go. In research as well, each step earned with sweat and repetition. Not with magic leaps. That's when the pratfalls happen, and worse.

Gaelan had bequeathed her a sample of his blood so she could carry on her work, heal the world if she desired, after he was gone. His notes on the ouroboros book were to be his legacy, her guide. He didn't want her to ignore the discovery, to toss it away, but to use it. Sensibly, for good.

He couldn't have understood the mechanism of his immortality. Had he known, what would he have done? Would he have given her the key and opened the door, or would he have plunged it all into the fire, burned it, destroy it, rather than risk it being used and weaponized, as it well might be? The prospects were more than terrifying. The consequences of such technology misused could be catastrophic.

Anne's mobile rang. Alcott. She wasn't ready to talk to him. Not yet. She hit "ignore," and with a sigh, climbed the steep path back to the garden, stopping for a moment to breathe in the green-spicy aroma of pine needles and the earthy mustiness of decaying leaves left over from last autumn.

A sharp ping. Voice mail. Alcott. Could he not simply text her back? She sat on an iron bench at the edge of a flower bed. Irises in full bloom. "Dinner would be great. Pick you up at six. I have a much better dinner place than the Frothy Pint. Bad memories for us, right?"

Fuck. No. He was not going to pick her up. She had a car. She could bloody well get there herself. She texted him. "Name of the restaurant? Address? I will meet U."

Did Alcott's friend have the faintest comprehension of what he was dealing with? If he did, there'd been no need to involve her at all. So, no. They must not really have a clue about bots. And Anne was determined to keep it that way. Perhaps the friend suspected something about Gaelan's tissue, and that's where she came in. Enter Erin Alcott—victim.

But what to do about *her*? With conventional treatment, Erin Alcott might live another thirty years. Forty—if the disease didn't accelerate. Until then, she would live a relatively normal life—and with the chance that medicine might yet develop an effective treatment . . . ? Who knew?

Anne saw three possibilities. She could use the enhanced TERT cells on Erin. The girl would be cured, and the path to a cure for short telomere diseases, perhaps all diseases, would be shortened by years. Her advances in the field would be Nobel-worthy at the least, but once out in the wild, there would be no way to take it back.

Or she could do nothing at all; tell Alcott his friend's "special superhero" cell line was worse than useless. That it actually further damaged the chromosome, and using it on Erin would kill her far quicker than GPC. Snake oil. A complete fabrication, but Anne was a terrible liar. Hopeless at poker.

Or she could simply *tell* Alcott she'd treated the girl and leave it at that. Give her a placebo to complete the ruse. Eventually it would be apparent the treatment hadn't worked, but that happened in medicine all the time. No magic cure. No miracle. The "enhanced" cell line was useless and any additional samples, stolen or otherwise, derived from it would likely be headed forthwith to the bio-recyclers. End of tale.

In the meantime, Anne would burn the h-TERT, Gaelan's blood samples. And the labyrinth necklace along with all the scans, the reports. Everything. Let science take its regular course. No shortcuts. No playing God with technology beyond the scope of our wisdom. Is that not what Gaelan would have wanted?

Erin's illness was no lie, and failing to treat her when she had the key in her hand . . . ? Where were the ethics in that?

Scientists had already begun to unlock the puzzle of telomere expression. Where could her discovery lead them? Eradication of cancers? That would be amazing. Could it lead to a genuine fountain of youth and make us all live a little longer, healthier?

It came to her in a flash. Clarity, at last. Anne understood exactly what she needed to do.

New text from Alcott. "Fine. Verna's Crab Shack. In the city, right on the water. GPS it. Great seafood. Palatable steaks. Fantastic mai tais. And the best salad bar in town."

LONDON, 1826

CHAPTER 34

The very air breathed death as Gaelan stepped from his shop into the market. A scant few animals wandered about empty stalls, bewildered at the absence of their owners. Few about but for the undertakers.

A young woman moved drunkenly toward him, weaving amongst the dead. "Lookin' for the apothecary. Seen him?"

"You've found him, Miss." She was sick, and better off treated at the shop than in the streets. Perhaps get this one back and then go to the Owl. "Let me see you to my premises. How long have you been ill?"

"Mr. Tremayne told me about you. I was to come to you when—"

So, she was one of Tremayne's girls.

"Don't want to go to your shop. Need to get back to my . . . business."

"Not today, I'm afraid. You are ill. How long have you been . . . like this?"

Her gaze widened as she took in scene, as if for the first time. "All those . . . sick, like me?"

"Dead. Which you will be as well if we do not—"

She laughed bitterly. "Better off, they are."

"How *long*?" he repeated. "How long have you been sick?"

"Hours now. Last night, I think. Felt strange, dizzy, like. Seeing m'dad standing right in front of me while . . . servicing . . . shall we say. M'dad's transported, two years past. Left me mum to take care of. The sods . . . Died on the ship, but there he was, threatening to kill me if I didn't stop . . . Girl's gotta make a living, right, Dad?" She drew her hands into fists, throwing wild punches in Gaelan's direction. Her entire body seized up, and he caught her just before she fell to the ground.

Cradling her neck in his left arm, he reached into his bag, removing a vial and the inoculation device. Rivulets of dirty sweat dripped down her arms, her face. He hoped to locate a clean spot to insert the needle. Pulling down her bodice slightly, he found a spot slightly less filthy than the rest of her, and pulled the lever, watching the medicine collect beneath her skin.

"Mr. Erceldoune, what are you doing cuddling up to old Betts, and in the middle of the market?"

Tremayne! *Damnation!* When had he slithered into the street?

"Have you no shame, Mr. Apothecary? Most especially with all these dying hereabouts! Think you'd be round making a . . . killing . . . in all this." Laughing raucously, Tremayne waved toward the people lying in the street.

Gaelan hid away the device, quickly as he could. "And you, sir? Are you and your . . . employees . . . unaffected? It appears not." He gestured to the young woman.

"So, I should send them round to you, then? You've got the magic cure?"

"I do what I can—"

The young woman opened her eyes, flinching as she noticed Tremayne standing at Gaelan's side. She sat up, trying to wrest herself from Gaelan and stand. "Do not try to stand just yet. Give it a bit, and then we'll get you to the apothecary."

Tremayne reached for her arm. "I see no need for that. Don't you see, see she's quite recovered. The roses are already back in her cheeks. Go on, Betts, back to work with ye."

The only thing Gaelan noticed on her cheeks besides the pallor was a smudge of scarlet face paint. "She cannot, I am afraid, Mr. Tremayne. She needs to *rest*."

"Maybe she weren't sick at all. Drunk on her feet most like." He bent over the girl. "My money, Betts. Did he give it ya?"

"Mr. Tremayne, he went running from the room, crazy-like, like he were being chased by the devil himself, he was. Didn't leave me a farthing. And I showed him a good time, I did. I promise I did."

"You lying little bitch." He raised a large hand, and Betts cringed, ready for the blow.

Gaelan placed himself between the two of them. He grabbed Tremayne's hand to forestall the blow.

"Hear me now, Mr. Tremayne. This woman is ill. Barely half an hour past, she was good as dead."

Tremayne was breathing heavily, rage in his eyes, but he seemed to be backing down, if only a bit. "Don't trust this one, Erceldoune. None of 'em's trustworthy far as you can . . . She better now?"

"Not today, I'm afraid. She'll need rest. I will take her to the apothecary, and she can recover her strength in my facilities." Gaelan did not want to release her to Tremayne, fearing he'd either beat her or force her back to her work, which would possibly make things worse—for everyone. As if there was anyone hereabouts willing to procure a girl's . . . services . . . in the middle of a maelstrom.

"No. She's mine . . . my responsibility—"

"Not today." He still needed to get into the White Owl. He had no more time to argue with Tremayne. "Mr. Tremayne. I do believe you might do some good. You're strong, clearly, and clever. Perhaps you might make yourself useful as they clear the bodies . . . what to do with them. I'd suggest they be placed in a pit, covered with quicklime, then burned. Perhaps there's empty plot can be dug up . . . somewhere." If anyone knew of one, Tremayne certain did. "Would you be so kind?" The undertakers had likely already thought of it, but it would rid himself of Tremayne, for the moment at least.

When Tremayne finally disappeared around a corner, Gaelan helped the young woman stand. The stench about her was overpowering, but he'd seen and smelled worse. Much. "We must get you to my shop. I've a small infirmary there, and we ought to get you cleaned up a bit. Sally Mills is there, and she can see to it. I must leave soon as you're through the door. Is that all right, then?"

She nodded weakly.

"It's right across the way, Miss—"

"Betts is all right. You're very kind, you know. Any time you want . . ." She winked. "You know . . . taking care of . . . yourself, come 'round. No charge."

Not likely. "Never mind that right now."

She grew stronger by the moment. It had to be the medication. Four cases then, treated successfully. Evidence, if not proof, that it worked.

"Here we go . . . Betts. Home we are."

Mrs. Mills was waiting just outside the door. "What's this, now? Did you find this one at the White Owl? I don't recall—"

"She is alive, but I've got to get back to it. Would you be so—?"

Sally wrinkled her nose. "Good God, girl, what've you got yourself into, rolling about like a pig in shit? Well, no matter."

Gaelan showed them to a room he hoped to make his apprentice's quarters and drew a laver of water from a rain barrel. "There's more if you need it. Rags are . . ." He pointed to a long bar hanging by the window. "Make certain she drinks. Water from the barrel." He'd run short of the salt solution. It would be hours until he'd time to make more. Perhaps, with the medicine, it would be unnecessary. "Now if you'll both excuse me . . ."

As he made his way the short distance to the Owl, Gaelan wondered what met Bell this morn in his part of London. There were plenty of physicians up there. What would they do to treat it? Bell at least had a small amount of the salt solution, perhaps enough for five or six patients. Then what? Laudanum and leeches. And watch them all perish.

Gaelan hesitated at the door of the White Owl, steeling himself for it, knowing he would be in there for hours to come. Might he transform it into a proper sick house, separate those with *sudor anglicus* from those not yet afflicted? It was certainly a large enough establishment.

He gazed up, memorizing the sapphire blue sky, cloudless and perfect, knowing that the hours ahead would be dark. The ceaseless cawing of ravens had grown increasingly loud as he neared the Owl, where they had undoubtedly discovered the rich feeding grounds of Smithfield. He inhaled a deep breath and went inside.

Not even plague had prepared Gaelan for what greeted him in the White Owl. He'd expected death, the beginnings of decay, the stiffened bodies of the fever's victims.

Perhaps it was the place, teeming with disease already. Add to that the crowded quarters, the offal and waste of animal, their carcasses rotting in the market stalls after slaughter. He'd known the place was overrun with vermin of all sorts: rats, cats, feral dogs that roamed at night to clean up the day's leavings.

The White Owl would need to be stripped bare to the walls, scrubbed and painted once this had passed, but for now there was naught to do but leave the rodents, beetles, and birds to their job. Half the corpses themselves had been stripped of their faces, leaving little but skeletal masks in eternal grins as if to mock the yet living.

Reaching for a thick tallow candle, Gaelan nearly toppled into a mass of gore and innards that had, only hours before, been a human being. A man, he thought absently after lighting the candle. Was there a soul yet alive in this . . . mass grave? He had to look.

Behind the bar, a mangy gray dog of no discernable breed sniffed at a possible bit of dinner. Gaelan watched it lick at the face as if to find a bit of life beneath the grime and dried sweat—a reason not to devour it. A small pack of rats approached, and dog backed off to growl at them, unafraid of the razor teeth. The rats, equally unafraid, continued toward their prize. The dog wheeled in an aggressive stance and snarled viciously, sending the rats scattering away toward another victim.

The dog resumed his sniffing and licking at the prone body, and then sat still at its side, unmoving. Waiting, watching in all directions for the rats to return, tense, its tail swiping at the floor behind it.

Suddenly, the dog moved and again licked at the face and neck, the arms, hands, now with obvious purpose. The body moved.

Gaelan approached cautiously, hoping without hope that the frightened dog would refrain from attacking him. He would never get near enough to examine the man, not with the animal standing guard. Saving even one life in this terrible place would be worth the wait.

A groan, and then another as the person tried to speak. "Help!" A harsh whisper croaked in Gaelan's direction. "It's all right. He won't bite you," he continued with difficulty. "I don't think so anyway. Never bit anyone before." The words were slurred and only barely coherent.

Gaelan approached, observing the man's pallor and the sweating, though it was very hot and stuffy in the Owl, and it could be anything. Could be the fever or not.

"Can you walk?"

The man nodded. "Yeah, I think so." Pushing himself up on his arms, the man sat, and then wobbled to his feet hesitantly before looking about him. "What happened here?"

"All dead. More in the street. Yet, you're alive, aren't you?"

"If y'call it that. I feel like . . ." He began to keel over, nearly falling on the dog, who growled at Gaelan as he caught the man before he hit the floor.

"Let's get you out of here. That your dog?"

"Yeah."

"Good dog. Kept the rats from eating you alive." Gaelan looped an arm around the man's back and dragged him from the Owl as the dog watched him warily. "What's your name?"

"James Wiley. Is it plague, sir?"

"I don't think so. Look, I'm the apothecary here. I've a medicine for the illness, but I must inject it into you. A sharp syringe. Has to go right into your body."

"I don't—"

"I won't do a thing yet. I need to know if what you've got is what . . ." Gaelan pointed toward the door with his thumb. "Is what took all them."

Wiley was weak, but not nearly as bad off as some. And he'd survived the night when all those others in there had not. He was still sweating, though it was cool. And shivering. "Give me your hand." It was ablaze. Perhaps it was just at the beginning of its course, but the man seemed to be suffering the ailment. He seemed strong enough to wait the few moments to extricate him from the mass carnage of the White Owl and get him back to the shop.

"Walk back with me to the apothecary. I've a small infirmary, and there I can better care for you. It is certainly cleaner."

"I don't know if I can . . ." Wiley's breathing began to come in shorter bursts, as if he'd run a great distance. His lips had taken on a blue tinge.

"Let me see you fingers." The nail beds were blue. "I shall need to carry you." There appeared to be no one else alive, as Mrs. Mills had said.

Wiley stood shakily, leaning against Gaelan's shoulder. His scream pierced through Gaelan's ear and through his head as Wiley froze before swooning, taking Gaelan with him, tangling them together with several corpses. The contents of his leather pouch lay scattered amongst the stiffened limbs of the dead.

Damnation! He lunged for the vials, collecting them back into the pouch. He retrieved the inoculation device, quickly examining it for damage before placing it carefully back into the pouch.

Gaelan cursed as he saw the other vial, its ground glass bung sitting next to the bottle, the liquid spilled. He collected the nearly empty bottle and stopper, carefully putting them back together and replacing them in the pouch. Three vials would have to do, or he would need to ride five days to Dernwode and retrieve more of the needed herb, found only there, according to his grandfather's writings.

"Mr. Wiley! Are you . . . ?" The man was not conscious; Gaelan dragged him out into the street, his hands slippery from the oily medication. He wiped them on his trousers.

He was too late. Wiley was dead. The lone survivor of the White Owl was gone. The dog sat beside the dead man, licking away, a useless effort to revive his owner. Gaelan coaxed the animal to follow, knew it would be futile. Best to leave him to find out for himself.

He'd been too late. Would it have made a difference had he treated Wiley then and there in the pub? He'd no way of knowing. One survivor—Gaelan couldn't manage even that. How could he face Sally? Still, there were others—too many others in all of Smithfield, and beyond, who might yet be helped.

Sally was awaiting him in the shop. "Ah, there you are, Mr. Erceldoune. I've done as you asked. The . . . lady is resting. I've cleaned her up best I could. Wrapped her up in a sheet. Didn't know what else—"

"The men in the examining room . . . are they—?"

"Oh, they're just fine. As if they'd not been sick at all. Like magic, I suppose you'd say. Ready to go on home. Least that's what they say."

She hadn't asked about the White Owl. She didn't need to. She'd seen it.

"Mr. Erceldoune. Mind if I go back home now?"

"In a few minutes. There is something . . ." Gaelan pulled back the curtain to the exam room, entering with Sally close behind.

The younger of the men was standing, the sweating subsided; his color seemed good. "Let's just have a look at you, eh? Have a seat."

The fever was gone; it was as if he'd not been ill in the first place. He wanted to leave, but where to? Home, where their families likely had perished by now?

"Best if you stay for at least another hour or two, and we'll see." He poured another tumbler of the salt solution, handing it to him. "Drink up. All of it."

Betts was next. Suddenly, the room spun, sending Gaelan reeling. He reached out for something to support him as he fell, and instead slipped to the ground, back up against the counter, head in his hands as the full impact of this epidemic stuck its blow like a barbed club. Who did he think he was that he might manage such a thing? One man. And where to put the sick? Not the Owl. Not now. Perhaps a week, but by then . . . mass graves. They'd need mass graves. And quicklime. He opened his eyes, shutting them immediately, unable to fight through a new wave of dizziness.

"Mr. Erceldoune?"

Sally Mills stood above him, her brows drawn together in concern.

Gaelan sucked in a breath before moving, shooing her away as he stood, as he took a moment to regain his bearings.

"You all right, Mr. Erceldoune?"

"Fine. I . . . we need to speak. Come with me."

Gaelan led her to his office, sitting her down on a settee, crouching low, taking her red, puffy hands in his. "I must talk to you about the Owl. It is a disaster in there, I'm afraid. You can't go back until . . ." Until when? There had been many a contagious pestilence he'd been through: typhus, malaria, smallpox . . . plague. "Do you know your Bible, Mrs. Mills?"

"Indeed, sir, though not as well as I might. My grandfather was a vicar."

"There is a passage in it concerning leprosy—"

"But, sir . . . this is not—"

"No, it is not, but I believe there might be something useful to be found there for our circumstances. The pestilence must be eradicated, even from the very walls where it might lurk unseen, from the floor-boards, the pottery. Everything must be scrubbed clean. Clothing as well, bedding, everything."

"It is a task to behold, then."

"I am afraid so. An arduous one. I've a good cleaner—a strong one that would serve well to eradicate the contagion from the Owl. From everywhere, in fact."

If only people might employ it, and not scoff at it as yet another apothecary's trick. It was an old formula: soap made of quicklime and mercury salts and washed sand for scrubbing. And with some good fortune and the hard work of volunteers, the White Owl might be suitable for a pest house in hours—once the bodies had been cleared away.

"Mrs. Mills, I shall arrange for the dead to be removed forthwith, and if I might impose upon you to set up in your establishment a sick house once the Owl is cleaned. Temporarily, of course, until this disease has . . . moved on, as it surely will."

"I do not know, sir, if—"

"I must have . . . we must have a place to separate the sick from the well to cut off the killer at its knees. I must know who needs the medicine, and who not." He would treat as many as he could, and make up a batch of the preventative medicine, perhaps this night. Offer it free of charge. Until his supplies ran out entirely. It would have to do.

"I believe you, Mr. Erceldoune, but the Owl—"

"You will have few customers whilst this disease haunts Smithfield, I suspect; this will be a town of ghosts and little else until it is eradicated from our midst."

CHAPTER 35

Gaelan had gone through the three vials within two hours. There was nothing to do now but treat the symptoms best he might. The notes suggested that breathing and the sweating itself were the worst of it. If only he might successfully treat those alone, he might save at least a few.

If only there was a way for him to leave the shop. Get to the Borders and Dernwode House. And its herb garden. Until then, best he could do was treat the symptoms, a small measure, and not reliable.

Mrs. Mills entered the shop, startling Gaelan from his thoughts.

"Mr. Erceldoune. The undertakers have removed the corpses from the Owl, and already the goodly folk have begun the cleaning up. It will be ready for you in an hour; perhaps less."

Gaelan could manage only a tight nod, his eyes closed against the raging pain lancing through his head. "Very good, Mrs. Mills. Let me know when it is read—"

"Mr. Erceldoune." A new voice. Bell. Gaelan ran a shaky hand through his hair, endeavoring to comport himself. He was in no mood for an argument.

"Dr. Bell. I was only just this minute wondering about how you were faring on your end of London with this terrible scourge." Gaelan had read the broadsheet reports of deaths in all parts of London, but he was anxious to hear it from a doctor.

"Not at all well. I've lost at least twenty patients this past day alone. And *you* with your ancient treatment for what you believe is an ancient disease?"

Bell's tone seemed almost conciliatory, no sign of provocation.

"There are many dead; it is impossible to keep apace. Yet, I've had some success with my treatment. Twenty-five treated, and in each case, within minutes all signs of the illness are vanished. It is, I admit, quite something to behold. My only regret is that so many died 'ere I'd been able to create the treatment. And that I lack sufficient quantities to . . . treat more than I've done. However, I am preparing a tonic in my laboratory to treat the sweating itself and the breathing difficulties, which seems on its own to hasten death. A slight alteration to the salt tonic you used with some success the other day . . . My hope—"

"Can you not make more of the medicine that—"

"A rare herb is needed, available only in a place too far off to be practical. Once I've finished with the new tonic, I might risk the long ride to the Scottish Borders, where I might obtain—"

"And this you also learned from those ancient texts?" Once again, there was no antagonism in his voice.

"Yes, I—"

"Easy now, Mr. Erceldoune. I came only to apologize. Something I must tell you about our Mr. Barlow, and you will find it remarkably interesting, I am certain, if a bit unnerving."

Barlow. The first to cross Gaelan's threshold, and quickly succumbing to the illness. "What of him?"

"I heard it being said at the club, word of a Mr. Barlow of Smithfield. Worked at the Man O'War. You've heard of the place?"

"Of course—"

"An incident less than a fortnight ago. A simple grave robbing. Barlow and his . . . colleagues . . . thought it a paupers' grave, not far from here. Bodies ripe for their trade. Proximity to the Man O'War, you see. But it was no paupers' grave."

"Then what is it?"

"Come. I shall show you where I was told it may be found."

"But I don't—"

"Just come. Now."

Gaelan did not budge.

"Please, Mr. Erceldoune. I promise you will not be sorry."

A short walk half a mile outside Smithfield. A field overgrown with lavender but for a gaping hole at its center. A mass grave.

"You see, Mr. Erceldoune. The attire. An incredibly old grave."

Indeed, Gaelan recognized the clothing. "Sixteenth century?"

"So it would seem. Apparently, Barlow and his fellow . . . procurers . . . of corpses opened the grave and found not one body, but hundreds. Rather, the remains."

"The sweating sickness."

"It is impossible to say for certain, but could not the sickness have spread from here into the ether and—"

Indeed. "The remains must be burned. Hot fire, then the covered over with quicklime." Only bones and desiccated clothing remained, but if uncovering even that released *sudor anglicus* into the air about Smithfield and carried it throughout London, there was no telling . . .

Now there was no choice—Gaelan had to get to Dernwode forthwith. It would do little to destroy the source—the point of origin, while those already affected continued to spread it. Until the dragon was slayed.

"I apologize, Mr. Erceldoune, for you know your trade, and your guess about the sweating sickness is extraordinary. I confess I am quite curious about this cure of yours. Would not mind trying it myself, if—"

"As I recall, you rebuffed such an offer only days ago. You called my ways ridiculous—alchemy conjured with ill-conceived magic tricks." No, Gaelan would not exact more of a price to see Bell grovel. It was enough to hear him admit he was wrong.

"My dear sir—"

"As for the medicine, as I said, I've no more of it, even for my own patients, until such time as I might ride to the Borders. Three days there and three back—and that is only if the roads are good and the weather holds."

"Three days seems a long journey to gather herbs."

"It is a unique place. Gardens unlike anywhere else. In any event, upon my return, I would be happy to provide you a vial or two, if you are inclined to put it to use, but I must tell you, the medicine must be inserted beneath the skin. Injected with a device for such purpose."

"A device?"

"Forged of glass with a silver-nickel frame to facilitate the insertion of a fine hollow tube, a syringe. Pierced through the skin. I would be . . . honored . . . to create for you such a device."

"Perhaps when the crisis has passed, I should like the opportunity to beat you, sir. A rematch in chess. But that is for another day, assuming we survive this plague. For now, I must get back to the pesthouse outside Hay Hill and my patients."

"Good day, then." Gaelan bowed slightly and ushered Bell from the shop.

"Is he gone?"

Caitrin Kinston whispered from behind the examining room curtain. In all the chaos, he'd much forgotten about her. "Perhaps you'd best wait until he's down the street a bit more. Should he return—"

"Mr. Erceldoune, I hope I've proved my value to you. I would hope . . . after a while you might reconsider and take me on as your apprentice."

Indeed, the girl had proved herself as good an apprentice as he'd employed in many years. Yet, how could he hire—a woman? It was not possible. Even if she was serious, which was unlikely, as she would eventually grow bored and wish to return to the finery of her father's home. And that was the least of the problems ahead should he . . .

An idea. A test of sorts, but a risk. He needed to ride to the Borders, yet how could leave the shop—the only medical care in the district—shuttered for nearly a week? Perhaps if she would disguise herself. "Dress as a boy. Your hair—"

"Shorn. I have thought of it already."

Then there were the consequences to be paid should she be discovered—by Tremayne. By Bell. By anybody at all. If she should be unmasked, it would ruin them both. It was madness to attempt the ruse. But what choice had he? He had to risk it.

She had been a clever, quick, and kind assistant these past days, untroubled by hard labor; tending to the ill—even as she, herself, recovered her health. "My lady, what do you know of nursing?"

"I've a keen interest in the sciences and I would do whatever you asked of me."

"I cannot afford to keep you, and certainly not as you have been accustomed."

"You need pay me nothing but place a roof over my head and provide me food enough to keep me modestly nourished."

Gaelan blanched. Had she any idea of the danger . . . ? "I cannot keep you here indefinitely; this you must know. It would be at best unseemly, and at worst . . . I cannot fathom what your residing under my roof would do to your—"

"My what? My reputation? Again, you enquire of that? Indeed, it is far too late for me to be considering that, of all things."

"Let us not talk of it again today . . ." He paused, considering the ride ahead. "I tell you what. I must away for several days. I would be most grateful should you mind the shop for me."

Caitrin pursed her lips into a tight line, nodding gravely. "I see . . . . Of course . . . I mean . . . My hair. I should chop it off now?"

The breathy glee in her voice suggested she was ignorant of the hazards that lay ahead on the road about to be traveled. "Yes. Immediately, as I must be off, and very soon. Cover it with a lad's cap. Breeches and a blouse. A leather apron will do to . . . mask your rather . . ." Gaelan watched the blush redden her countenance. "I mean to say—"

"No matter. You are quite right. And so I shall . . . disguise myself."

He mulled other options. Gaelan was not an impulsive man, and this was the very definition of impulsivity. He could ask Mrs. Mills, but she'd enough to worry about at the Owl, nursing the sick. He would make certain Mrs. Mills and Caitrin had plenty of the elixirs on hand to distribute amongst the ailing. Enough for a week. Enough at least to forestall death until his return.

Gaelan wrote out instructions, which products were for which conditions, how to tend the elixirs brewing in the laboratory, and whom to contact in the case of an emergency—the apothecary in Regents Park, a good, capable man and a former apprentice of his, who would do, if needed, anything for Gaelan.

"I shall return quick as I might. The roads should be good, given the weather, and I shall hire the swiftest steed in the stables. Not rest a moment until I return. When this is all past, I shall teach you glass-making—if you are, by then, not bored, or weary of an apprentice's life. Do you understand what I am asking of you? For the next week?"

Caitrin nodded tightly. "I do, and I shall do all in my power to serve you ably these days. It is not past my understanding what you are entrusting to me."

The book. "And, my lady . . . or should I say . . . my boy . . . take from my bookshelf any that might amuse you when not at work in the shop—but for that unusual volume you so admired the other day. I have replaced it in a secure location. So please do not search for it."

"Of course not. As you said the other day—" She had about her that hurt look again.

"I do not mean to—"

"It is of no matter. Now fly! And be back safely soon as you might!"

Protected as Dernwode House had been, hidden away in the hills, barely visible to passersby, the monastery now was but a ruin. A broken building here, a piece of stone archway there, remnant statues, frag-ments strewn about a gone-to-seed field good only for pastureland.

Gaelan had little time for wistful remembrance. He had been exhausted even before three days' ride with little respite. Now he was completely spent. He'd changed horses twice, paying the stablemen a tidy sum for their speediest steeds. And now he would return, hoping for clear weather and better horses that would carry him back to London in time. Before too many more lay dead in their homes.

Gaelan well knew how to locate Dernwode's hidden gardens even among the ruins. The stones, embedded deep in the clay, overgrown by tall grasses, formed a spiral, indelible centuries later.

Removing large leather pouches from the horse's saddle, he gathered quantities of each herb, removing entire plants of each variety to cultivate in his laboratory. The ingredient he needed for the *sudor anglicus* treatment was grown indoors, in the damp dark of the cellarium.

Carefully, Gaelan descended the steep stone stairs. He pictured the strange plant, its odd flowers, twisted and pale, as if seeking sunlight that did not exist below ground. He'd never in all his days seen anything of its like.

He plucked the small patch bare, surprised the strange plant had not overtaken the entire stone stairway. He placed everything carefully in his bag and climbed through the mustiness of the stairway, and into the light.

A skin of water and he would be ready to return to London. He wandered the edges of the garden. Despite his haste, Gaelan could not help but to take a moment to take in the place he'd called his home for years so long ago. Even now, hundreds of years hence, he saw them, but only in his mind's eye. His tutors, magicians with glass and chemicals, medicines and the strange alchemy of healing. His family when he'd had none other.

A last look around; he would not return to Dernwode again. Within the silence of this singular place, as much graveyard as garden, Gaelan could hear the hum of the Quhawme Brethren, their constant debate echoing through more than two centuries; the passion of their learning, their teaching, the sparkle in their eyes upon a new discovery within the secrecy of the hidden buildings, now all gone.

He did not notice the tears until he stood again; his hands were wetted with them. A final pang threaded through his chest before he mounted and rode hard back to London.

The hour was late by the time Gaelan arrived in Smithfield. The street was empty as he dismounted and returned the horse to the stables. His stomach clenched as he considered what he might find as he opened the apothecary door.

"Mr. Erceldoune. Welcome home."

Tremayne. Gaelan would know the slick, silky voice even in the dark. The strike of flint and Gaelan's office was flooded with candle light. Lyle Tremayne had made himself comfortable in Gaelan's chair, as if in wait for an unsuspecting prey. *Caitrin!* Was that why he was here? Had he . . . ?

"Mr. Tremayne." Gaelan stilled his hands, trembling both from the fear that ill had befallen Caitrin and from the anger at Tremayne's intrusion into his private domain. "How . . . ? Did my new apprentice let you in, and freely? I'd given no instruction . . . I shall have his head and send him back swiftly to—"

"Now, now . . . Let us not be so hasty. I've barely met . . . him. Carter, is it? No, I quite let myself in, wondering where you'd got off to . . . after your grand success here in Smithfield. The residents hereabouts think you to be some sort of grand savior, sent by God himself to deliver them from the plague whilst the rest of London perishes. Some of them, anyway . . . And I got to wondering how you managed it when the greatest minds in London are baffled still."

There were many more dead than living, and whatever success he might have had was minimal. Perhaps the elixirs worked better than he thought they would. "How did you get in here?"

"Oh, me? No magician, me. No, sir. I owned this building—the entire corner in fact, until I sold it to you." Tremayne produced a key, setting it on Gaelan's desk.

"You?" That was a surprise. He thought he'd purchased the property from the apothecary who'd served Smithfield before him. "And yet you retain the keys? Hardly seems fair, eh?"

Tremayne shrugged. "Never know when a set of keys comes in handy. Who knows if you might fall into trouble? Be locked in with . . . no way to get out."

There was raw threat in Tremayne's tone—and his words. He would hire a locksmith first thing, change every lock, and install bolts. Gaelan did not much fancy the notion of Tremayne poking about in his work.

Tremayne laughed, slapping his hands on his thighs. "You don't think I'd tell you I had the key if I didn't intend to give it back. I'm no fool, and I think you know that. No. It is in thanks for what you've done these past days. For my Betts. A good girl. Like you'd sprinkled some sort of fairy dust. Some would call it magic—if you believe in such things."

A chill snaked its way up Gaelan's spine. "Do *you*?" Gaelan could hear the hesitation in his own voice. What was Tremayne up to?

Tremayne moved to Gaelan's bookshelves, taking the candlestick with him. "Quite an odd assortment. Old books. What good are they to a supposed man of medicine? Alchemy, perchance? Ah, you see? I knew it! Magic—a sorcerer's receipt! Are they for sale?"

"No . . . no. Nothing like that, I assure you. Just the writings of ages past—men of science, not purveyors of magical cures."

"Well, Mr. Erceldoune, I shall be on my way. On behalf of us all—as the civic leader of your new home in London." He placed a key tied to a leather band on the counter and left. "And that Carter fellow—your apprentice—quite a young one. A pretty boy, methinks. The girls'll swoon, and he'll make you rich for all the young ladies he brings to your shop. Pretty indeed. For a *boy*."

Gaelan pondered the ruffian; he fancied himself royalty of Smithfield, able to designate friend and foe with the drop of a word, or a pilfered key. Undoubtedly there were copies of the keys to all the rooms and doors of the apothecary. Yes. The locksmith at first light.

In the street and here, this night, Tremayne seemed nearly gracious—kind, even. But he wore a veil of chaos that foretold nothing but grief and trouble. Gaelan had more secrets locked in the apothecary than he wished to share—with anyone, much less Tremayne. And Tremayne suspected . . . something; Gaelan was certain of it.

There had not been another moment to tarry, and despite the lack of sleep, Gaelan set to work immediately. Caitrin was asleep on the settee in the flat, dressed in breeches and wearing the leather apron, and he debated whether to awaken her and be updated on the disease, how she'd fared running the shop these past days. She looked too peaceful to disturb.

Gaelan kindled the blue-white phosphorus light globes all about the laboratory, dreading the task of cleaning dozens of glass implements and vessels. But the counters were pristine, polished to a deep shine. The glassware was just as he'd left it, but cleaned to a sparkle, as if was the fairy folk had enchanted the place, knowing the night ahead would be a horror. He knew better. The only fairy princess to grace the third floor had been Caitrin.

Clever girl. A sketch of the distillation setup sat upon the counter, a perfect drawing of every tube, every flask and cylinder in its correct place. She would have drawn it before dismantling it to clean. *Brilliant*! He would thank her on the morrow.

Pinching the bridge of his nose, he set to work, and by morning's first light Gaelan had distilled enough of the medicine to treat the entire district if need be. The glass tube of a second injecting device cooled on the counter along with its metal housing and fine syringe. He would be ready—for anything. And once all was settled in Smithfield, he would be well situated to offer his services in other sections of London.

"You've returned. Welcome home, Mr. Erceldoune."

"Caitrin!" She'd taken him by surprise. He had so much to say to her, yet her presence left him suddenly bereft of speech. "I . . . you . . . brilliant . . . ." He could only gesture, but the act fell short, he knew, for the benches had once again given way to entropy, but for the small neatly labeled bottles of medicine.

"I will set to clean it immediately, sir. I trust you found things in proper order upon your return?"

"That I did, and had you not the great good sense to . . . I am indebted to you, my lady." He bowed deeply. "Do not trouble yourself with the laboratory just yet. Please, return to the flat and dress for the day . . . as my *apprentice*. There is time later to see to the cleaning. I will put up the kettle in the shop. Join me when you are ready. I wish to hear of the past six days. But first . . . anything urgent I must attend to?"

"Only that a note from Dr. Bell . . . from Simon . . . was delivered just yesterday by messenger. He will visit this morning. Ten o'clock, the letter said. I feared that I would have to either meet him . . . or decline. I am very glad you are home to greet him yourself. I do not know what I should have done had he—"

"And what of Tremayne. Has he come round? Has he—?"

"I have seen him lurking about outside, at least I assume it was him. For few others would fit the description you gave me. He chills me to the base of my spine."

"He is of little matter. Much pretense, even more bombast. Yes, he might do the both of us both great harm, and we are better for staying clear of him best we can."

Caitrin smiled, crinkling her eyes at the corners.

"What is it so amuses you, especially regards Mr. Lyle Tremayne?"

"It is not that, Mr. Erceldoune, but your use of 'we' that lightens my spirit. Will you accept me, then, as your apprentice?"

It was not intended. Yes, she was good, and yes, she would make an able, smart assistant. Perhaps a partner at some juncture. Yet there were far too many obstacles. Too many . . . considerations. No. It could not be, for all he wished it might.

"Go. Dress. We shall talk after I am assured that all is well in Smithfield. Perhaps this very night."

CHICAGO, THE FUTURE, TIME INDETERMINATE

CHAPTER 36

In the distance, up on a high ridge, the forest swayed. Gaelan listened, the contours of Navy Pier in his head. A familiar rhythm. They were up against the lake. Context.

A woman sat herself opposite him, drinking tea from a dainty, enameled bone cup.

"Who are you?"

"I heard you'd returned to us. Fine. I'll get right to the point. To some, I am known as Airmid, but it was a long time ago, by your timekeeping. Mostly here, I'm called Arie. I find it a bit pretentious to live the legend, don't you think? Let's sit and chat a bit. My office will do."

She set down the cup and ushered Gaelan through a small stand of lacy willow trees, their branches fringed with long velvety leaves. They came to an area behind an arched curtain of glass beads to a silvered table and delicate chairs. "This is my home. And my office. Have a seat."

Airmid. *Airmid*?

A million questions spun through Gaelan's brain, but his voice was caught, knotted in his throat. *Airmid*?

He had begun to accept the reality of his situation, its possibility. But this? Airmid. Creator of his ouroboros book—the source of anguish and wonder for him and all those in his family who'd come before him. Hundreds of years. In fucking Chicago? In the fucking future? The left side of his brain screamed in protest, muffled by the glittering labyrinthine spider's web suffocating all logical thought.

He tried to push through it. Focus. Something mundane. Ordinary. The chairs would do. From a distance, they'd appeared uniquely beautiful. They shimmered in the diffuse greenish light filtered through the dense stand of trees. Ah, but the reality was different, the effect created by the lighting. An illusion of beauty. The chairs, like the table, were chipped and repaired with silver duct tape. The glass beads, tiny shards of fractured bottles: cobalt, amber, red, green, clear. More illusion.

She was not Airmid, not that *Airmid*, of whom Gaelan had dreamed for centuries. Whose song had kept him sane in his darkest hours at Bedlam, her voice a lullaby. A comforting presence when it was the last thing he wanted. An illusion. One he had to break through.

Finally, he spoke. "You are keeping me from my task."

"Your *curiosity* is keeping you from your task, I think. Which is what, Mr. Erceldoune? To complete your suicide pact with Simon Bell?"

She could not know about Simon. About the poison . . . The pendulum swung the other way as logic fought back, fiercely battling his acceptance of this altered reality. The figment of a shattered psyche. "What else do you know about me?"

"More than you might think. You are quite the . . . Quite famous. Your turn. Tell me what you want to know. About . . . here? Out there. Anything."

Delusion or not, he was curious. She was right about that. "What is my role in this absurdist play?"

She sighed. "Interesting. You're not interested in what . . . happened . . . to Chicago? The world?"

He lied, "Not really."

"Never pegged you as a narcissist, but then again . . . This more than about you. You're a bit player with a decidedly considerable impact. Your story is yet to be fully told in this—as you put it—absurdist play. Nor ours. But our fate is tied up with yours, and I will explain, if only you will have patience. We have been waiting—*and patiently*—for quite some time. Decades. Hoping you would come. And I will do more than tell. I will show you."

The lush greenery, the impossibly beautiful streams. The manner in which they moved, lithe, graceful, almost like human butterflies, but with wings on their feet. Conan Doyle's fairies. Folie à deux.

"Go on. Start where you must."

"Power and hubris, always destructive in combination, even when arisen from the best of intentions. And with the sort of dominion over life and death we possessed, there could have been only one possible ending. Catastrophe. Which we aim . . . hope . . . pray . . . to . . . reverse. That is—"

"But . . . Chicago? And in the middle of some sort of postapocalyptic nightmare of the future? How can I believe—"

"You can believe it or not. It's your choice. I can only say what is true."

"Airmid. Bloody goddess of *healing* Airmid?"

"If you like . . . . We have been known in so many times, so many places. So many different names . . . Wherever the fabric between worlds, between times, is weak or particularly thin we may be perceived. Some perceive us as beings from some other universe, timeline, running in parallel. The fairies. Elves. The Tuatha de Danann."

"Portals. Your friend LaSalle mentioned them. But . . . perceived?"

"Or seen. Is this Elfenhame? The Otherworld? Fairyland? Depends on who is doing the seeing. And when, from their temporal origin point. And where they traverse the divide. Am I human? A magical creature? A messenger of heaven? Perspective is everything. Context is everything. Dependent upon your frame of reference."

"Magic is science we do not yet comprehend."

"Yes. Exactly so."

"My ancestor—

"Lord Thomas Learmont de Ercildoune."

Gaelan nodded.

"He was an especially good man. Poet, philosopher, prophet.

Brilliant. All the House of Learmont have been so ever since. From Thomas to . . . you. He could foretell the future, but it was a future we enabled him to see."

"You showed him . . . this?"

"No, of course not. Thomas observed what his mind, his—frame of reference—would allow. And *only* what we could afford to show him. A forward look into history, but only in bits and pieces. He puzzled out some of the rest, but through his decidedly medieval prism. He was the first keeper of the healing book, what we call the Saf Rafah. I gave to it him myself to carry back into his time. A rather practical reason, if shortsighted."

She was convincing, but Gaelan did his best to remain unconvinced. "Practical?"

"My father was a man with a temper. A genius. Powerful, a great, great healer. Yes. A man, not a god, no more than I am a goddess. You know, of course, the story of the warrior Nuada who lost his hand in battle many hundreds of years ago by your own timeline. It was one of the few times we dared to insert ourselves into the past. Into someone else's business—a disastrous war."

Gaelan knew the legend well enough. Airmid one-upped her father, replacing the silver hand her father, the god of medicine Dian Cecht, had set into the stump of Nuada's wrist with one of flesh and bone. Dian was furious and destroyed Airmid's healing cloak, which contained within it the curing herbs for all illness and disease. With the raging breath of a powerful storm he shook her cloak until it was bare; all the cures had been cast to the four winds, never again to be found.

"My father was furious with me, and with good reason. I'd been driven by arrogance. Stupidity, using technology I had no right to . . . Nuada was a great but damaged man who had the vision to change a world engulfed by darkness. I wanted so much for him to succeed. And I believed, stupidly, without two human, perfect hands he would be worse than dismissed . . . I feared for him, for his safety and his ability to withstand . . . All this is beside the point. When my father learned of what I'd done, he threatened to destroy everything. Legend says it was a cloak into which I'd gathered all healing knowledge, but that is not quite correct. A bit more high-tech than that, but again, it is of little matter and a long time ago. I knew my father would carry through with his threat, and I worried that all medicine, all science, would be lost forever. I created a sort of backup copy."

"The ouroboros book."

"Yes. The Saf Rafah."

Airmid's people, the Tuatha de Danann . . . Historians had been ambiguous. Legend or history? A mythological people or a highly advanced civilization settling eventually in Ireland? Advanced in medicine. Advanced in technology. But from the future? No wonder there had been scholarly confusion—if Gaelan were to believe her.

"You see, Mr. Erceldoune, we are quite human. Throughout history, we have been thought of as magical beings. Magic is mostly about perception, is it not? What was magical to Thomas, to Arthur Conan Doyle, to those a century ago or eight, all science, all technology, is magic. We can fly, yes, but it is explainable. Our miniature pedal drones." She kicked out her feet and touched her wrist. The blades whirred. "Something you, a man of the twenty-first century, can comprehend. Wormholes in your time—only just beginning to be understood. Time travel is a fiction. Even now, we don't know how it works—not exactly, only that it is possible."

Yes, Gaelan could see the sense of it, but. He opened his mouth to ask a question, but Airmid held up a hand.

"We are seen only in glimpses and shadows. Out the corner of people's eyes. The space-time continuum frays and repairs itself continually, regenerating only to fragment in another place, another time. There are many portals to many worlds. This is ours. The world of your future."

"Were you not more than that? More than a glimpse here and there?"

"Yes, particularly in Ireland, and only that one time did we dare make that mistake—Nuada, the result. The consequences that followed. The boundary between worlds is very fragile there, and eventually we were revered as deities, venerated. It did much for the ego, but in the end, we were feared. Too clever for our own good. Especially after—"

"You fixed Nuada's hand. I am certain that would have raised some medieval eyebrows."

"Indeed, and so we fled back to our side of the divide. It was the last time we'd venture that far from . . . home. Since then, we have appeared occasionally to certain people—those who possess an ability to perceive us. Some more than others. But mostly in grainy images, barely seen phantoms. Thomas could see us, could interact with us. Conan Doyle could see us, but not interact with us."

"Conan Doyle wrote as much. A journal he kept. I discovered it . . . It was to his great frustration that he could look but not touch."

"We do not understand what gives one the ability to fully cross such portals from one time, one universe, to another, or how the portals work. All of us—in here—were in Chicago when events started reeling out of control. It is where all the horror began. Ground zero. Had we been in New York or London, it is possible we would never have crossed paths. Your friend Tesla created the portal to connect these exact points. Yet destiny always seems to find a way, does it not?"

Destiny. Was this his, then? To be privy to yet another monumental secret. One he could never disclose? Or did fate have something else in mind?

"It began, you see, not long after your accident in Chicago."

Was it only weeks ago? The image flashed before Gaelan, vivid and too fresh. Tumbling down the limestone cliff, his bike exploding as its fuel tank hit the rocks just above his head. He'd implored the gathered good Samaritans, "Let me be. I'll be fine. No need to call nine-one-one . . ." Gaelan shuddered, and the memory disintegrated into grains of sand.

"Are you listening?"

Gaelan nodded. "Sorry—"

"It seems you nodded off. Are you all right?"

"Yes. Sorry. Go on."

"A medical treatment, that's all it was intended to be. A man's pain seeing his wife stricken by a terrible genetic disease, and then their daughter contracting the same fatal illness. A young girl. A tragic story. At first, a noble instinct to save one life, then the possibility to save many, many lives. Is that not always the way? Not everyone involved in the project was in it for altruistic aims. You see, in the treatment, in the cell strain from which it was to be derived, lay the treasure map right to the Holy Grail. The elixir of life."

"Immortality." How long ago must it have been in their timeline? How many years in his future . . . ? And how had *that* come to *this*?

"Patient X, the individual from whom the cell strain was derived, was a man of unique physiology. His tissues possessed the capability to infinitely regenerate, unheard of in humans at the time. Yet there he was."

Gaelan fidgeted nervously with his fingers. He knew where this was headed.

"The mechanics of the regeneration worked at a subcellular level, wrought of technology so far advanced from anything of which he would have been aware, far beyond whatever advances had so far been accomplished in the realm of genomic manipulation. It would have been incomprehensible to him—to anyone of his time."

"Me." A statement of acceptance. But she spoke of him in the past tense.

"Yes. Your accident last month, by your timeline, was the trigger, but in our world, decades ago. The circumstances surrounding an impossible-to-believe rapid recovery from your traumatic injuries had been largely discredited by hospital and medical officials. Dismissed as a sort of mass hysteria amplified by social media, fake news, and tabloid journalism."

"But I thought you said—"

She ignored the interruption. "However. Not all were quick to dismiss the so-called Miracle Man. One of these, a multibillionaire. A man at the very pinnacle of corporate and political power in the United States. The world. Your world. Our world."

Gaelan thought about the pharmaceutical companies that would have been listening, ears pricked, to the story of a Miracle Man not so easily dismissed as the public might believe. Like Transdiff—Anne's employer.

"The dose makes the poison," Gaelan whispered. It was as valid for Paracelsus as it was now and ever would be.

Arie shook her head. "In this case, not so much. The dose can be infinitesimal. Small as the cannula of the finest-gauge hypodermic needle."

"You created the book. I became immortal because of something I did incorrectly with a formulation in that book. Hundreds of years ago. And the book itself, far older than that. Any discoveries, any misuse of them, the consequences . . . all from *this* world. I don't—"

"A classic paradox. A book created in the future, passed backwards, to Thomas in the thirteenth century . . . set in motion by events seven centuries later that led . . . ultimately . . . to . . . this. This world. This nightmare we all must live in. It was never intended . . ."

Destiny.

"All we can do is hope to find a way back. End the loop. Eliminate the pathway that eventually, always, leads us to this fate."

"You've tried . . . before?"

"Yes. Once or twice. Different ways, but as I said, we don't quite know how the portals work. It's as much luck as anything."

"And my being here . . . a stroke of luck?"

"Destiny that you would come to this place, I suppose. Muscle memory—a return to a safe port . . . ? It doesn't matter. We only want to put things to rights. We think . . . we believe . . . some of us, anyway, that it's possible. This is where you fit into that absurdist play. Will it work this time? We don't know. Can't know. We can only keep trying."

"Did you not realize you were playing with fire? Giving a match to scientific toddlers?"

She looked stricken. "Don't you think I've done nothing, all these years, but regret my lack of . . . judgment? It is why I must . . . we must make it right."

"I have to ask . . . The mechanism . . . I've always wondered how it was possible for me to . . . The specificity of the recipes in the book. Unique to each disease, illness described. Brilliant. Yet, the sensitivity to even the slightest error . . . How could I have known that to err, even in the slightest—"

"Infinite tissue regeneration had never been intended as part of the book, you see. But we were betrayed by one of our collaborators. After my father threatened to destroy every last vestige of medical advancement, I realized something had to be done. To preserve the work into the future, no matter the repercussions. I feared a return to the Dark Ages. And my fears were not misplaced, as you might have already figured out. Not exactly the Enlightenment out there, is it?"

"Why? What happened?"

"When it became known it was possible to accomplish genomic manipulation on such a grand scale, the reverberations were earth-shaking, as you might imagine, and not only for curing disease."

A chill snaked down Gaelan's spine. It wasn't just immortality, but immortal—perfect—humans. A quest that had gone on for millennia, finally achieved. The temptation to drink at that grail . . .

"Researchers were already working on genome editing. CRISPR, for example . . . others in various states of progress. Combined with what we . . . what was discovered in your genetic structures . . . The first superhuman was created in only three years. The technology for it—"

"The beginnings of a master race."

"Yes. Stronger, faster, smarter . . . but only for those who might afford the technology."

History doesn't always repeat itself, but it always rhymes, does it not? *Dear God.* The samples of his blood he'd given Anne. For the good of medicine, he'd told her. And gave her the tools to use it. Was he not equally complicit? And Anne?

"The experimentation was prone to corruption from both the potentially lucrative nature of it and the technology itself. No one knew that the tiny machines—the nanobots—were smart. They adapted, changed, and beyond anyone's real control, for we did not understand how or why."

"The lesions?"

"Yes. As the technology became more widely in use, it was cut with other things. Supply was limited, expensive, so . . . Certain mutations were accompanied by terrible, disfiguring adverse effects and it spread like a virus among the general population. You can live forever but be ever disfigured and in eternal pain."

Gaelan needed time to process this. Could he believe it? Did he want to believe it? She still hadn't explained how he'd come to be immortal. "Tell me how the book works. How it made me—"

"So now you believe? The design of the book is an extraordinary achievement. If only . . ." She stopped. For the first time, he noticed that her hands were trembling. "You see, the inks of the Saf Rafah are coated onto special microscopic membranes. Graphenes, microscopic membranes embedded with extracts, complex molecules all bound up with submicroscopic machines—nanobots—specific to each ailment. Some act upon DNA, activating enzymes. Others attach to virus microphages and destroy them. Others do . . . other things. Incredibly advanced. I couldn't let the technology die completely. To do so would have condemned the world to . . . but you see, I *have* condemned it. Never was it intended to be so misused. I never int . . ." She was sobbing, the tears flowing freely down her face.

Gaelan had read about graphene. Twenty-first-century magic. Nanobots, too. Northwestern University was an international center for their study and development. The pieces had all been there, eventually, even without his tissue, his mutated DNA; how long until, given the state of the genomic research . . . ?

"Forgive me my tears. It has been a long time since I've explained it to anyone. The weight is too much to bear . . . all of this . . . our fault." She sniffled into her flowing sleeve. "You see, the instructions to activate the Saf Rafah's treatments were likewise hidden by language, art. To be used only by any enlightened enough to parse through the layers and layers of coding. Adept at science, at language. We thought we'd accomplished a perfect job of it, creating what appears to be medieval medical book—a grimoire, if you will."

"To send it back to the thirteenth century, it could not be a modern, printed anything!"

"Exactly. I know it's not as romantic as the ballads would have it, but it has the benefit of being true. Several of us were involved in creating it. As you might imagine. The art, the languages, the materials. I was—am—a physician, not an engineer. Not a linguist. Nor an artist. What I did not know was that someone on our team tampered with the complex renderings in the book, hidden within them small detours that if followed by design—or error—would eventually lead back to immortality, despite our best efforts. It was the one thing we did not want. The whole point. Yet..."

"But it did." Gaelan could not forestall the chilling image of the tiny machines swarming throughout his anatomy. He shivered at the thought. He needed to sort this out. He understood little about quantum physics, which would have come in handy right about now. "If the ouroboros book—the Saf Rafah, a book created in my future—came to me through my ancestor who'd acquired it in the thirteenth century..."

"Hence, the paradox. You cannot change the past, but there are many futures that might be triggered by a single event. The Saf Rafah ultimately did nothing to change what we'd become, as we'd hoped it would. Had you not fallen down that ravine, you'd never have become the Miracle Man, and none of this would have happened. Had we not been betrayed in creating it... There were many, many variables along the way. The book was more than a simple means to an end."

"Had I not erred in 1625 in treating plague, I'd never have become immortal. Who knows what... Tell me; where are the animals... birds, fish... Outside, they're—"

"The birds have vanished. All wildlife. Overhunting. Where there are too many people, resources are scarce. People had no choice. Chronic starvation is... uncomfortable, if not fatal. Is it possible to defeat? Perhaps with innovation, but our society is frozen. Paralyzed.

Not quite zombies. The wealthy, the powerful have all settled far from the cities. In little utopian enclaves. Perhaps the top half a percent of the top half percent. The rest of the world lives on . . . a walking, breathing sort of death." She smiled humorlessly. "I hear you ran into a gang of Burkies?"

"Who are they? What do they want?"

"Their aim is to kidnap us, hold us captive as part of their supply chain. We, in here, are immune to the worst of the side effects. One of the few urban enclaves, I suppose. There's a good trade in our body parts, for food, trinkets, whatever. Especially because we can regrow them. Usually."

"Body parts . . . ? The tumors?"

"Yes, they grow quite large. More than disfiguring. Graft one of our hands on someone else's unuseable, disfigured limb . . . ? Brand new hand. Worth a lot of money to those who've got it."

So little had changed through the centuries. "Burkies. As in Burke and Hare."

"Yes. They fashion themselves after the resurrection men of the nineteenth century—"

"Burke and Hare were executed."

"No risk of that here."

"Could you not leave like . . . others? Set up a little enclave in more comfort . . . with less risk?"

"We were waiting. Hoping."

Gaelan stood. He couldn't listen to . . . He leaned his forehead against the far wall to her office, retching. The image of . . . He glanced at the teardrop, still in his hand. All he needed to do was drop it, pocket it. Anything . . .

"And that, my dear Mr. Erceldoune, brings us to your role in all this. Why you are essential to us. Are you listening?" He turned back toward Airmid. She handed him a handkerchief drawn from her bosom.

"I'm listening." He could not pull himself away from the story. His head pounded, throbbing in rhythm with his arm. With his other hand he pushed against the injury as if to still the ache. The fabric with which he'd covered it was still moist. He looked at his hand. Blood. Why had it not stopped? Light-headed, Gaelan fell into the chair. "My arm. It—"

"Let me take a look. I'm a doctor after all." She smiled again.

Gaelan lifted his arm. She ripped the sleeve of his shirt to the shoulder. "Glass can be nasty. Could become infected. It needs to be cleaned. Redressed."

"But I can't . . . it will . . ."

She wasn't listening, turning her attention to a large file cabinet. "This will do."

Unwinding a wide roll of gauze, she wrapped his arm, securing it in a knot on the side opposite the injury. "There. That will do until it's healed. Come with me. There is someone I want you to meet. It is time to know your part. What you must do. For us. For the future."

"No. I'm done."

"Excuse me? What do you mean . . . done?" She stood, standing above Gaelan, hands on hips, her gaze hardened and icy. "Done?" she repeated.

"If," he began, still half-believing, half-hoping it all was in his mind. "If any of this is real, I am finished with this life. I've a way to end it. All I need do is drop this teardrop, return to the catacombs on the other side of the portal, and blow up the entire—"

"You don't want to do that." She paled to almost white. Frustration creased the loveliness of her face as she bit her lower lip, inhaling as if to calm herself. "Not yet. Please. Just another few minutes." She was imploring him. "If, after you've seen what . . . Only a few moments more of your time is all I ask."

Gaelan sighed. "Fine. Only that. I promise nothing else."

"Understood."

Gaelan would see what she had to show him; nothing would change his mind. They proceeded down a long hallway, through overgrown, wild gardens: orchids, poppies, forsythia. Orange trees. Vines with fat grapes. "How is this place possible when all around you—"

"As lovely as all this seems to you, it is a prison. We can never leave, but for a moment. And even then, only under cover of darkness or during a storm."

"Why?"

"I already told you. The Burkies."

They started down a long staircase, as bare and stark as where they had been was lush. The conservatory. That was it. The seasonal exhibits of botanic delights. Unlike the buildings around it, the heavy, lead glass was still intact, impervious to the elements, protecting this . . . prison. And they could grow things here. Infinitely regenerative sustenance.

They went through a door and into a small alcove, dark but for a single dim bulb.

"She never leaves. She sits. Waits."

"Who? For what?"

"For you." Airmid led Gaelan through a curtain.

To the glass museum. His glass museum. It was exactly as he'd left it. With one exception.

A panel. One he'd never placed in the museum, for it had long been missing a small teardrop piece. The one he now held in his hand. The panel was the simplest of the three he'd created in Tiffany's workshop. A young woman draped in a white cloak holding a small child surrounded by yellow daffodils, and when the sunlight hit the panel just right, the two figures would be cast in a glowing radiance. It was as Gaelan had remembered them, before disease took Caitrin, and Iain was stolen from him by Caitrin's father. A son he would never know.

A woman sat on the floor before a glass panel, her back to them. She seemed not to notice they'd entered the room, continuing to stare ahead, chanting something. A parched whisper like a mantra. Over and over. He did not hear what it was.

Arie bowed slightly and left the room. Gaelan barely registered her departure as he gazed at the woman. Her hair was longer; the clothes she wore, rags. A tattered sweater—his.

CHAPTER 37

"Anne."

He did not move; he did not wish to startle her.

"You died."

"Anne," he repeated. "What—?" No. Now was not the time to provoke her with questions. She was fragile; he knew that. No need to . . .

She stood, came up to him, and stared. Straight into his eyes, a frightening, chilling glare. Then shuffled back to where she'd been and sat on the floor.

"You lied to me. Told me to trust you, you fucking bastard. Handed me that fucking bottle of poison, when all the while you had another tucked away. I figured *that* out soon enough."

"I'm sorry" seemed inadequate. "I never . . . I meant for you to trust that my death would be better—"

"For who? For you? Certainly not for me. You are no longer immortal, by the way. You died. 'Bout eighty years ago."

"Glomach?"

"No. Not Glomach. You were found by hikers in the Borders. Near Melrose. You'd been badly burned. Hands, feet. You refused to tell them who you were. But you were taken to a trauma center in Edinburgh unconscious. It was in the papers. On the Internet. Someone recognized you. I recognized you. I was furious. I had to travel to Gattonside to scatter Simon's ashes, so I took a flight, detoured to Edinburgh if only to confirm it was you. But you were already gone. Sepsis. From the burns. Ironic, isn't it?"

Gaelan moved for the first time since entering the museum. Sat on the floor beside her. She skittered away.

"Get the fuck away from me."

"None of that happened." Yet, was that not his plan? To destroy the catacombs and himself? "Yes. I took the poison, I admit. Thought you would be—"

"Not yet. Hasn't happened yet." She stared at him, as if making certain he was real. "Apparently." She looked away again, continuing to stare through the panel. Something about her voice was wrong. The flat affect. No passion. No spark. Gaelan swallowed hard, knowing he'd been the cause of it.

"How did you know about the museum? My part in restoring the—"

"Dana Spangler. Your friend. She's here. Somewhere. Everyone is immortal. Except you. More irony. Are you not amused?"

"I'm—?"

"It was the nanobots, by the way. We figured it out. The poison made you mortal, not dead. Why? That's what we couldn't quite figure out. We knew there must have been something that altered your physiology, so it could not work the way intended. But what? We figured out you'd treated yourself for something, somewhere along the way, but had no idea what or when."

"Yes. Nanobots. Airmid . . . Arie . . . told me."

"I knew you'd 'overdosed' the book's embedded compounds, but not which ones. Not which page. You hadn't used them directly from the book, but from the raw materials. You'd told me that much. You didn't know any better. You'd never—"

"Learned how to use it. It was plague. I had Bubonic plague in 1625."

"That was only part of the riddle. Something else happened to your physiology that made the poison you created destroy the nanobots without killing you. The whole thing was reversed. So, that's what we've been waiting for. The final puzzle pieces, so we can put it back to rights. Or rather, you can. The first part, you just gave me. Plague. What's the second?"

Realization hit with a blunt force. "You used my blood."

"There was a girl. Is a girl. Still a girl. My fault. I didn't understand, you see. Not enough."

She looked over to him, her eyes devastated but dry of tears.

"There were people who'd wanted to . . . Stolen tissues from Evanston Lakeshore Hospital."

It all came back to the fucking accident.

"It all got so confused. I tried to destroy the tissue specimens. But it wasn't enough. Or too late. Your DNA, so closely held for so many centuries, was now out in the wild. It had changed. The nanobots mutated."

"The nanobots? How?"

"You can't destroy machines the way you destroy living tissue, and somehow along the way, the bots hybridized with biomaterial and transformed. Like a virus. Keep the host alive and live off it. Forever."

He didn't quite understand. Anne's halting speech, dreamlike. How much was real? How much the product of a misplaced guilt? "Your fault? How? It was my blood. My error in 1625 started the problem."

"You see, it was me that showed them it could be done. Indirectly, but they figured it out when I'd refused to . . . There were more samples of your tissue. I knew that, but if they didn't know how to use it, they couldn't . . . I destroyed everything to do with the project. My records. Scans, computer backups. Everything. And still they . . . it wasn't fucking enough—"

"Anne, stop. Please. You're . . . it's all right. It's not—" She was reciting, rambling. Like a robot. How many times in a century had she gone over it and over it? There was nothing he could say. A century of guilt, of grief held for so long with no respite. He needed to simply let her talk. Get it out. To listen.

"So much good might have come from it. Eradication of the worst diseases. I couldn't . . . I thought I'd destroyed everything. But they'd captured it all. All my notes, my methodology. Everything. I thought . . . No, I believed I'd destroyed . . .

Perhaps if he got her away from here—this musty relic of a

museum. How long had she been there, just sitting? Waiting. "Come, walk with me. Just a stroll. The sun will do you good."

He knew the way, unless it had been boarded up. A small passageway up through what had been an office straightaway to the edge of the dock. She nodded and let him help her up.

They reached the water's edge. A decaying bench lay on its side nearby. He turned it over and sat, urging Anne to sit beside him with a nod of his head. "Here. Sit by me, but first, breathe."

She nodded and sat at the other end of the bench; stared out at the water toward the horizon.

"It's worse than you can imagine, Gaelan. The mutation causes a terrible, cancer-like illness. Undifferentiated tissue taking over the body, the brain, one bit at a time. Unendurable pain, nothing you can do about it. Disfiguring, but keeping the victim alive. So *they* can live. Forever. Cancer, but not fatal. It's affected nearly everyone, but the few of us who seem to be immune, though no one knows why. We live in an enclave of—they're called . . . we're called . . . immunes. Immune—supposedly to the lesions; able to regenerate entire body parts in a single bound. Not just ordinary immortals, us. No, we're super-immortals."

"Descriptive."

"But not entirely accurate. All of us are beginning to show signs of the mutation. Even here. Even me." She lifted her shirt to expose blister-like lesions. "Perhaps we were meant, the scientists here, to see the destruction of everything whilst we lived unscathed. Now it's our turn to enter hell."

"The Malebloge."

"The what?"

"Never mind."

"What is my role . . . in this . . . now?"

"You, *and only you*, can reverse it."

"Before it ever happens—

"Not quite. For the trigger had been pulled by this point in your timeline. You wouldn't be in time to stop it, but you can fix it before any real damage is done."

"You make it sound simple."

"It is not."

"The final piece of the puzzle is to figure out what you did to alter your physiology . . . what changed the nanobots, caused the mutation in the first place—but after you were already immortal. It had to be something in the Saf Rafah."

"But *I* don't have the lesions. I—"

"No. Then again, it was simply part of your internal ecosystem. Who knows what adaptations your physiology made along the way to compensate? But when your blood was used to create a cell line . . . We must know the pathway from your original tissue regeneration to . . . this mess."

It was getting chilly on the dock. The sun had sunk low in the sky behind them. Gaelan turned toward the fading light, which lent an eerie glow to the destroyed skyline.

"We should get back in. Night is falling, and Burkies will be about."

The dock weaved and bobbed below them as they entered through a side door in the structure. Into darkness. They walked down the corridor in the dark. In the distance, the sound of water lapping up against the pier, but nothing else. Gaelan did not know what he could do to change the inevitable, but he owed something to Anne, to Airmid. To the future. He had to at least try.

"Ah . . . the lights have come back on." She looked into Gaelan's eyes. Hers had come alive as they had not been when he'd first come into the glass museum. "And now you are here. Full circle."

So much for Conan Doyle's fairies. Gaelan could not suppress a laugh.

"What?"

"I was thinking of Conan Doyle. His fairies. His expansive view of the universe. He was a time traveler and never knew it. But fairies? Not so much."

"We have been perceived through time as fairies, and perhaps they do exist, but we are not them. There are many portals to many worlds."

"Can you not simply take blood from me? Use it here? Now?"

"We simply do not have the materials or the technology to do it, not the way the world is now situated. It has been so long, and nanobots out there in the ether for so many years, we cannot know if it would even work. Could make things worse—if that's even possible. No. The only answer is to fix it in your timeline."

"How? How am I supposed to remember what I might have inadvert . . ." Gaelan had used the ouroboros book—the Saf Rafah—only four times. In 1625, when he'd become immortal, then in 1826 . . . the English sweat.

"It was 1826. Must've been."

"I don't understand."

"Anne. I think I know when—and what I did that must have altered my physiology. It was in 1826. A terrible epidemic in London. I'd used the . . . ourobo . . . Saf Rafah, but carefully. Until I had an unfortunate incident with a syringe. That had to have been it."

LONDON, 1826

CHAPTER 38

The morning broadsheet proclaimed the death toll "at least seven hundred succumbing to the mystery disease." No one cared that in Smithfield the tide had begun to be pushed back, and no one was ailing.

Mrs. Mills was quick to report that the ill housed in the White Owl were doing as well as might be expected. And supplies of the two elixirs were running low. Nearly all the pallets in the makeshift pesthouse were filled.

"I treated them as your boy said," she explained, showing Gaelan her dwindling supply of medications.

"My . . . boy?" he nearly said, stopping himself, realizing that she'd meant Caitrin. At least that ruse had worked well enough . . . at least well enough to trick Mrs. Mills. "I've a medicine now will cure them, Mrs. Mills. And whilst I treat them, I would ask that you put word out that I've also the means to prevent the illness entirely. Any who come into Smithfield the first time since the illness struck must stop by my shop straightaway. Before they do anything else. Also, anyone not stricken with the illness, likewise. Please be kind enough to act quick as you might about it so the word will spread."

Gaelan injected the medicine beneath the skin of each, coming at last to the final pallet on the floor of the White Owl. A man of middle years. He was restless, thrashing about the straw. "Mrs. Mills, if you assist me."

"Of course, Mr. Erceldoune. Right away, sir."

"Hold his arm for me while I—"

Gaelan readied the injection device. The man reared up, knocking Gaelan to the floor. *Damnation!* The sharp point had pierced deep, painfully into Gaelan's thigh. The glass tube was half what it had been. *Bloody waste of medicine.*

Gingerly, he dislodged the device, refilling it before treating the man, who was by now much calmer. They waited, Gaelan impatiently counting the minutes on his watch. The preparation did its work as it had with his first batch, and within half an hour each had revived, showing no signs of illness whatsoever.

He returned home just as Simon Bell knocked on the apothecary door.

"Good morrow, Mr. Erceldoune."

"Dr. Bell. Do come in. My . . . apprentice told me you would be calling this morning." Bell looked haggard, more exhausted than Gaelan felt. Dark smudges beneath his eyes and the slowness to his gait gave away his state. "I've a kettle on the stove. You look like you might do with some tea."

Bell nodded slowly, his lips drawn into a tight line.

"Then is it yet not faring well? What of the remedy concocted by your fellows at the Royal Academy? No success there?" Genuine concern for the well-being of both Bell and his patients failed to conceal the sarcasm embedded in the question.

"No. They were wrong, clearly. As you . . . and I . . . suspected. So many dead. More than one thousand in London alone, I hear, and I cannot help but wonder had I employed . . . had I used . . ." He nodded to the broadsheet open on the countertop. "You have read as much. And here? You seem yet rather calm for all the chaos about. No further cases, then?" He cast a look about the shop as if to see evidence of disaster recommenced.

"Smithfield was not spared; there is a pest house set up at the White Owl. I have treated all the ailing there, and the treatment seems to work—and with remarkable speed. Had *I* been but swifter, I might have spared more in Smithfield. As it is, at least one hundred forty-two have perished. And now I have had the time, with the immediate crisis past, to formulate a preventive medicine as well."

"A preventative? There is no such a thing for fevers as this."

"Edward Jenner had much success with his cowpox inoculation—"

"That, sir, is a different thing all together."

"We shall see, shall we not?"

"Indeed. And how long, pray tell, sir? To recover once treated?"

"Less than an hour."

Bell sat, his head in his hands.

"You do not believe me, then?"

"I find it so contrary to what I know in my head, yet . . . Such magic does not exist in medicine. I would think you know this, sir. Even as an apothecary. Yet, I cannot argue with your success. Your brilliant diagnosis of the sweating sickness, beyond all comprehension."

"I quite assure you, sir—" It would be of no use to further explain, and Gaelan felt no need to offer more. "It works. And well. I am willing to part with a vial of each for your use. To test it, I have crafted an inoculating device for you, hoping you might return. Knowing that your medical society cures would not be effective. Not against this scourge."

"In every corner there are your brother apothecaries hawking their wares. Promising to cure this . . . thing. This fever. All it does is prevent good people from good medical care. Do you not agree, sir?"

"I heartily do, Dr. Bell. It sore grieves me to know of too many so-called apothecaries who would do nothing but take money and hide in the next town, knowing the damage they've done. It does nothing for either my reputation or those who grace the great Apothecaries Hall, members of the society. All reputable, and all maligned by your brother physicians quite too often, I think. Have you told them of my theory . . . now, as you see, borne out?"

Bell picked up the inoculator and examined it. "Of whom do you speak?"

"Your brother physicians. You see, Dr. Bell, the needle is quite sharp, but hollow. It makes an exceedingly small, quite shallow puncture through the skin and the medicine is installed just beneath the surface until a small bubble is formed—a pouch, as it were—to hold the medicine whilst it becomes absorbed into the blood of the patient."

"It is ingenious. No, I have not. How can I?"

Gaelan bowed. "I did not invent the technique, but the design of this device is of my own hand."

"I should be laughed out of the Royal Society if I . . . What does it matter its name? Whether it is simply a novel fever come to call on us in London—or an old enemy rearing its head. It kills just the same, and I cannot risk . . . Yet this device is pure genius. I thank you for it. The medicines as well."

"You shall save Hay Hill and the credit will be yours."

"I do not understand your meaning."

"I am an apothecary, no physician. The Royal Society would never listen to me; they would laugh me from town. Such notoriety is of no use to me, nor is fame—nor credit. However, when you are successful, I must exact a price—a game of chess. A reprise."

"Thank you, Mr. Erceldoune. I should like that."

"If you need more, return and I will have more for you. I have little to waste if you decide against it. You must follow the instructions, which I have written out and placed in the leather pouch. Exactly." Gaelan handed Bell the pouch for the inoculator. "I wish you luck, Dr. Bell, and look forward to a return chess match."

"Indeed. And to you as well, sir."

Gaelan watched as Bell turned left into the street and mounted the step to a carriage. What would come of it? Would Bell try the medicine, or was he merely being polite and this was the last he would see of Benjamin Bell's grandson? And if it did work all round London? The illness would disappear, hopefully forever . . . or least for another few centuries. Such things have a way of cycling back repeatedly, like history.

Gaelan had done all he might within his ability. There was nothing left to do but wait.

Lady Caitrin Kinston had been for him an able assistant. He could ask nothing more of even the most gifted apothecary's apprentice, and she had given it freely, without compensation—anticipating the needs, fulfilling them without so much as a request. Surely no complaint. Yet, it was a problem. Too much of a problem; Gaelan knew it with every fiber of his being.

Lyle Tremayne was smart as he was tough; it would take him a very short time to puzzle it out and ruin him. And her. If he had not already.

The hour was late, and the shop was closed for the day. Caitrin awaited him in the laboratory, hoping that he might this night teach a bit of the apothecary's craft. But he owed her a gift. The promise to teach her a bit of glassmaking—allow her to make her own Rupert's drop.

"You have done well . . . Carter. I cannot fathom a better assistant these past days, even as you recover from your own illness. And although I am not yet of a mind to offer you employment, as the crisis has now passed, no matter what the future might portend, you have earned a reward at least. The Rupert's drop I promised you. I shall teach you how to fashion your own. And then we shall see your potential as a glassmaker—for that is one skill needed for any apprentice of mine."

Her smile lit the room.

"Tell me, what is your favorite color?"

An entertainment for the lady—a diversion from a difficult landscape for himself. It was far too easy for him, so long in the desert of emotional entanglement, to fall into the complexities of her eyes, especially should he take her on to apprentice.

"The iridescent turquoise of the teardrop you crafted was indeed gloriously beautiful, yet, if you were to ask me my favorite color, it would be indigo—the deepest, richest blue."

Had it been purple, it might have been a simpler proposition. He sighed, and she met his gaze. "Choose whatever color you wish, I only . . . there is a glass ornament in my father's home of that color, and I shall miss it dearly come Christmas—"

"We shall see." Gaelan searched the shelf of half-filled clear glass jars. "Ah, here it is." He pulled out a small bottle.

He touched his boot to the small pedal and the small cauldron heated quickly; steam rose from beneath it as the fire blazed. "It is a large fire for a small vat, but I've nothing smaller. It is for making glassware and not trinkets—usually. But this is for a simple pleasure, and they are far too few, I fear."

"How many times as a girl I marveled at creation of such beautiful glass wares, wondering how it was done—this transformation. Craving the knowledge to make such exquisite magic for myself!"

He could not suppress a small grin. With no desire for her to think him laughing at her, he diverted his gaze downward, into the cauldron, watching the glass melt and darken, and then lighten again to a pale white as he added more chemicals to the vat. "I confess, it is rather magical, this bit of alchemy. There is something quite extraordinary about glass, Lady Caitrin, is there not?"

"Please do not call me that, not while you are instructing me and so amusing me."

"What is proper, then . . . in this case?"

"It *would* be Lady Caitrin, that is correct, but it will not do. Not here, where I wish to forget such connection to a family that so wronged me. Caitrin, I venture, would well please me."

It was an invitation. Such familiarity after so brief a time—and in such close proximity. When she came to her senses and desired a return home after boredom set in . . . He had no desire to inflame her family's ire—nor *her* regret. Nor his own desires, dormant for so many years, which he had thus far managed to restrain.

"*Lady* Caitrin." He emphasized the distance between them rather more forcefully than needed. "I daresay, I've plenty to occupy myself, making notes of the past few days whilst the cauldron heats. In the meantime, do stay clear of it. Perhaps you will find occupation with this." He handed her a Latin text. "You know Latin, I trust?"

"Yes. My governess insisted upon it, and now I've every reason to thank her, and regret making her life quite more miserable than it had already been. I shall leave you for—"

"A quarter hour should be sufficient to melt the materials."

Gaelan watched her, taking a long breath after the door closed behind her, relieved at the short respite, hopefully adequate to come to his senses. She was far too near, far too vulnerable. This was as dangerous an error as ever he had made since leaving Shoreditch in 1625 . . . after the plague. Loneliness had taken its toll and two hundred years without close companionship were too dear a price to pay.

Despair had been his only mate since then, and for far too many years. And now this lovely, fragile woman had crossed his threshold as if sent to him by the gods. Despair had fled, replaced by her presence, despite what he insisted even to himself.

He endeavored to no avail, busying himself writing notes about the illness to add to those of his grandfather's. She returned. So soon? The clock had moved forward the full fifteen minutes he'd requested. He rose, ushering her to the cauldron.

"Now then, shall we get to working on your Rupert's drop? I see the glass is quite ready."

How to accomplish the task without nearness, which she might take to be improper? Which could lead them both toward a precipice he wished not to plunge from. "My lady, I might instruct you, but it would go more swiftly if I guide your hand. May I—?" He gestured, demonstrating.

Caitrin's warmth seeped through the soft linen of his tunic as he stepped behind her. She shivered, causing Gaelan to take a step back, embarrassed, realizing he had never so instructed a woman; he'd thought nothing of it, stupidly so. "I am sorry. I only meant to guide your hand. I thought you understood. My intentions are to amuse you, and if—"

Of course, she would be fearful, wary after what had transpired between her and her brutal cousin. Gaelan needed to be vigilant, mindful of propriety, given . . . Moving off to her side, a fair distance, Gaelan awaited her reassurance.

"Sir, I took no offense at your nearness. Far from it. You have only been kind and quite a bit more the gentleman than any so-called of my acquaintances. Please, I beg of you. Show me!" Her countenance was serious, but the sparkle in her gaze suggested her delighted anticipation of the enterprise.

"Aye." He caught her right hand in his left, placing there the long metal wire. "Now—" Their hands moved together as they dipped the wire into the black-blue of the cauldron. "Take up a bit of it and move it 'round and 'round thus—" The motion was rhythmic and lulling as they dragged the long wire through the heavy, viscous mix.

"Lift the wire now and hold it above the vat of water higher and higher." The molten glass thinned and thinned as it broke away finally, landing with a "plop" in the cold water.

Fetching the drop from the water, Gaelan dried it on his tunic, placing it then in Caitrin's outstretched hand.

Her eyes sparkled in the firelight, catching the reflection of the iridescent bauble. "It is extraordinary. It is white as snow, yet it possesses an inner fire. How—?"

"It is, as I said, magical. But only the magic that is science. And glass, the most magical substance of all."

Gaelan's low bow concealed the blush that had heated his cheeks. Caitrin's smile penetrated the long years of solitude that followed him now for greater than two centuries. It was too dangerous in so many ways. Her nearness, his isolation—self-denial for good reasons that he had never minded.

"You have been, these past days, a greater comfort than I have ever known, Mr. Erceldoune. I wish there was a way for me to repay your kindness, but I fear that I will only cost you grief, as my father will not likely relent. I am his only child, and he will not rest until I am captive once again. And you, sir, by keeping me in your protection, are more at risk than I—"

"Hush now. Let's not trifle with this when we've to celebrate your first glass creation! Will you break the thread?"

Her eyes widened in shock. "Why no, sir! This shall I keep—a most precious gift, more so than had it been a genuine sapphire."

"Then let me bind it in a leather thong for you, that you may wear it about your neck." He fetched a long twine of leather, which he kept in good supply to bind pouched goods, braiding it about the drop until it was secure, before handing it to her.

"Will you not tie it about my neck?"

He obliged, tying a slip knot that would allow her to easily remove the pendant.

This . . . arrangement . . . far too intimate. He had vastly misjudged himself . . . his feelings for . . . No, it would not do for even the shortest time. Either she would need to leave or . . . An idea struck like summer lightning.

"My lady. Caitrin. I think you and I know it is improper for us to reside beneath the same roof—unmarried. Your reputation would—" He had few choices to secure both her safety and his own. "Yet I have given it some thought, and I have a proposition for you." He'd not given it any thought at all. It was as impulsive a notion as he had ever contemplated, but he could think of nothing else. "Shall we retire to the sitting room, where such things might be more appropriately discussed?"

Brushing by her to open the door, Caitrin flinched, barely perceptibly. Realizing he was again too close by her, he opened the door quickly and allowed her passage, saying nothing further until they were downstairs and Caitrin was seated comfortably upon the sofa.

Gaelan paced, taking up a spot at the window, looking down into the market square below, and inhaled a deep breath before facing her. The Rupert's drop sparkled in the candlelight.

"You, my lady, possess a curiosity I daresay I have rarely observed in one of your sex. You are indeed clever; you know philosophy and literature, and I aver an interest in science which rivals even my own. I . . . as you are well aware . . . I have a need of an assistant, an abundant need—as you know, and have rightly pointed out, and as has been made clear the past week, and—"

He had, in the span of five minutes, already become a babbling fool. She said nothing; at least she did not laugh at him. No. Her gaze met his. Tears had gathered in her eyelashes; her face was flushed.

He cleared his throat, regaining his composure. For this to work, he

would need to keep his distance. He did not socialize with his appren-
tices as a rule. They studied and worked for him. He would give them
lessons in Latin and Greek, chemistry, and a bit of alchemy. How to
properly clean and use the glass contraptions that might be as foreign to
them as any language. And they would retire to their quarters to study,
and he to his books until the morning. It could work, at that.

"You cannot, of course, reside here. It would not do for your reputation. And you ought take on an assumed name, and I shall arrange
with Mrs. Sally Mills for you to sleep at her inn, the White Owl. She
is no gossip." He paused, wondering if he should qualify the statement.
"At least not when it really matters."

"But how soon would it be until someone sees me there? Please let
me stay here with you."

She was frightened, yet she was right, and he knew it. Yet he
couldn't keep her locked away, a prisoner in his laboratory or flat,
either. The apprentice's quarters were too exposed to passersby and
visitors. She would soon arouse suspicion in one way or another.

"Mr. Erceldoune, forgive my forwardness . . . but I must confess to
you a story of a friend—a close friend. Her mother dressed her in men's
clothing and sent her off to Cambridge to study medicine. She passed
all the years of her time there, and still she . . . he practices medicine in
Sussex. No one the wiser."

"But why would her mother—"

"She was widowed. I am certain her husband would never have
allowed it, but her mother wished more than anything to have an
impact on the world beyond teas and balls and taking visitors. That
she'd never had for herself, but she had determined that her daughter
should have that opportunity. The daughter was clever, cleverer than
all her sons, than half the suitors come calling for her hand."

"Would she—the girl, her mother—not wish for husband and
children? This charade at which she plays must wear on her—"

"She has a husband—in secret. Also a physician. But my point is,
sir . . . Would it not be possible for me as well to pass as a boy? Your
apprentice, and live under your roof—and your protection?"

Gaelan, too, knew of women with no other recourse, passing as men. There was Andrew MacFee, with whom he'd attended the anatomy theater at Guy's Hospital in Southwark many years earlier. His deft touch and too-delicate hands. Gaelan always been good at spotting someone with a secret—a kindred soul, whose exposure would cause ruination. He'd never enquired and would not have dared suggest despite his curiosity. Yet, somehow, he knew.

Even as he acknowledged the truth of what Caitrin proposed, Gaelan well comprehended the folly of such an enterprise. "We would need to create story for you—from whence you came, your kinfolk. Yet, it *could* work." He scrutinized her. She might pass. For a while, but only that. "I adjure you, my lady, to think, and very, very hard. For this decision should not be taken lightly." Advice he might well take in himself. But his heart refused to give logic its due.

"I have made it already. The prospect of such work excites me, and as far as home and family, I have none I wish to claim. My father has forsaken me, my mother equally so by her silence. There is nothing to which I can fathom returning."

"Then let it be done." Gaelan sighed, knowing that someday, he might well rue the day he'd allowed it.

CHICAGO, PRESENT DAY

CHAPTER 39

Every biowaste disposal room was the same. The burial crypt of infectious tissue, discarded organs, the stuff of horror novels—yellow and red biohazard bags of blood and gore, discarded needles and organs in the basement, hidden away, the mouth of hell, the purifier of all medical evil. Yet it was sterility of the place that chilled Anne at two in the morning, alone in a desolate hospital basement.

Gowned and gloved, masked in the appropriate ritual gear of the act, it was her turn to play God, decide who shall live and who shall die. Who by fire? Who by withholding medical treatment?

What sort of a place was this to make an impossible decision? She held the key to unimaginable progress—a world free of disease. But equally possible was a world destroyed in a mad quest to possess the secret to immortality and the power and riches it would unlock. The discovery of a lifetime, and she was primed to shove it all into the flames. Incinerate it to ash.

She had decided, but did she have that right? Power, politics, the extreme pressure on the already-strained limits of the world's natural resources should immortality become a commodity. The secret would be sold to the highest bidder, held closely in the hands of a few to control the fate of all. Keep the good stuff for themselves, unleash untold horrors upon perceived enemies, whoever they may be at any given time and place. No one deserved that much power.

The autoclave was inadequate to the task of destroying the tiny machines she'd discovered intricately woven into Gaelan's telomeres, as dangerous in their own way as any pathogen. For this, she needed the destructive power of fire. Incinerate the bloody suckers.

She flipped the wall switch and listened as the grinding thump of the ignitor brought it to life. As she waited until the red light turned to yellow, the heat trickled beads of sweat from beneath her mask, even from across the room, where she waited in the dull glow that leaked from the door, which painted the basement dull red-orange. Half expecting security to burst through the basement doors any second, she counted the minutes until it was ready.

But could she really carry it through? Destroy Erin Alcott's life? Ignore world-altering discovery that might change medicine forever? Change the world? Bring people out of poverty? What if those little phages could be used to create viable crops in drought regions? In places flooded out where cholera and Zika reigned like the angel of death? And polio, which had only just begun to rear its deformed head, mutated and immune to vaccination? Did she have the right to deprive the world of this bizarre phenomenon, whatever its source?

She could not afford this indecisiveness, not hours before she was to meet Alcott and company. But the choice was grave, and not so easy as she thought it would be just an hour ago. What would be the more significant violation of her oath? To condemn Erin Alcott to an early death or cure her and take the risk that Gaelan's DNA, and those tiny machines attached to it, might escape into the wild—by error or design? They were not viruses, much as they resembled phages, didn't behave like them either, so what made her believe they would spread like a virus on a rampage? Gaelan had lived for centuries, and he was the only immortal chap she'd ever heard of. Not that it was dispositive.

Anne guessed that the material needed to be injected directly into the bloodstream. Gaelan had been seriously injured nearly two centuries ago, tortured, his fingers severed. His blood, she imagined, was everywhere in that horrible place. Yet, none of those with whom he'd been in contact were immortal like him, were they? Of course not. It would be known, certainly by now, would it not?

Alcott's friend had already experimented with Gaelan's liver tissue—enough to create the superhero cell line. How far a leap would it be to extract the nanobots and customize them into some sort of bio-genetic weapon? Arms dealers would be salivating over such a weapon. Hell, what about DARPA? Or Qinetiq, the UK's very own chamber of biological horrors? How many research posts had she been offered by both over the years to apply her research? She'd even toyed with the notion herself—once.

She had to destroy all the samples. Find out how many more there were. Maybe offer to buy them up—she had the money to do it, after all—a shell startup, perhaps. Better, offer a partnership. Full funding. Anne Shawe—venture capitalist at your service, gentlemen!

The LED light glowed steady green. Go.

She stood at the mouth of the incinerator, letting the heat coming off it scorch her cheeks through the metal door. Asbestos gloves hung nearby, and with shaking hands, she slipped on the left glove. Setting the Styrofoam box on the cart, she removed the top. Wisps of CO_2 vapor wafted up, chilling her face.

Still, she hesitated. Was she being impulsive? Perhaps she should wait, consider. Ask Dana what she thought about it. Call her mother . . . scratch that.

Each test tube had its value, its potential for good; its potential to unleash humankind's worst impulses. Yet, to hold the key to immortality is to rule the world; it was a myth spawned thousands of years ago. The Holy Grail. The philosopher's stone. Vampire legends. Gilgamesh.

She opened the door; the fire singed, the light blinding as it was compelling, the roar of flame consuming anything daring to cross its path. The fire played off the stones in her labyrinth necklace; they hummed with energy. Or was it her imagination as it grew hot against her collarbone?

From the flames, Anne saw him, and it nearly knocked her from her feet: Gaelan Erceldoune rendered in reds and oranges as he had been in the glass panel. Fighting the Minotaur still. The image melted before her, the monster now a pool of light at the base of the image, and Gaelan stood victorious over it, the remnant glass pouring like water through his fingers.

She was confident of her plan. At last.

Bed had never looked so inviting. Drained and exhausted, Anne fell asleep within seconds of crawling beneath the duvet in her room.

A full six hours' sleep. When had been the last time that happened? Anne looked out her bedroom window, opening it to the lovely spring afternoon. She'd done it. Felt right about it. Regret that Erin Alcott, perhaps her father, would suffer for her decision made her feel like shite. That she'd have to lie about all of it made her feel worse.

She showered, trying to wash away the entire month as the hot water pounded needles into her neck and shoulders. Not even that managed to relax the tension.

Anne had no appetite to be wined and dined by Alcott or his friends, but the meeting was essential to the plan. Dana had pointed out the restaurant the first day—an unassuming little café, she'd noted, with "amazing" seafood and fantastic cocktails. Right next to the Ferris wheel.

Her mobile rang just as she was toweling off.

"It's Dana. What did you end up doing with those weird samples? The phages, the nanobots . . . whatever you said they were?"

Anne sucked in a breath. She couldn't tell her the truth. She couldn't tell anyone. "I did more tests, and whatever was in those cell lines, whatever they were, didn't propagate. After . . ." Anne calculated a reasonable number of hours to observe the effect. "After four hours in vitro . . . they basically consumed Erin's cells and died. Little buggers shredded the entire cell, turned it into some . . ." What? She knew she was making it up as she went along. "Gelatinous goo." Overkill? Hopefully not.

"Wow. Too bad for that kid. Would've killed her."

"Yes. And very quickly. I destroyed everything. No choice. Whatever they were, however innocuous in that cell line . . ."

"And your necklace?"

Fuck. "Chalk it up to weird coincidence. Like . . . like the Virgin Mary in a toasted cheese sandwich." She'd heard about that one on the news. "That one fetched a tidy sum, by the way. Like $30,000, if memory serves."

Anne didn't think the story, as she told it to Dana, would work as well with Alcott's friends, who had, after all, worked with the stolen tissues already. Grown cell lines from it, even if they didn't quite know what they had. They suspected they had something extraordinary. For them, she would need to enhance the lie. Make it perfect.

Anne stepped from her rideshare and into the Ferris wheel plaza. Excited children waited with their parents for the opportunity to soar high above the city's lakefront, feel the adrenaline rush, terror, and delight. Everywhere, all along the shimmering promenade, were smiling people, laughter. A somber counterpoint to Anne, her heart a black stone, freezing her from within, despite the balmy late afternoon.

She checked her watch. An hour until dinner. A charade to be played out to its macabre end. Surrounded by Preston Alcott and his host of ghouls. No matter his noble intention—a grieving husband, a father wanting only to save his little girl—Alcott was complicit in it. The only sacrifice in this would be one little girl, his daughter.

The sun was beginning to make its descent behind the skyscrapers along Michigan Avenue. It gleamed against the black of monolithic monuments to commercial achievement and sparkled against the alabaster marble. To the east, a cloud bank from a storm that blew through an hour ago.

She walked out to the far edge of the pier, looking out at the expanse of water, watching the gulls fight each other over the detritus floating atop the oily surface of the harbor. A boatful of partiers waved as a large sightseeing yacht passed her at the edge of the dock, sounded its klaxon horn. Alone, finally, at the edge of the world.

A glimmer of yellow light played against the indigo backdrop of sky and water, and she watched it grow, its lazy arc emerging from the clouds as rain droplets refracted the sun's rays. Yellow, then orange, red, purple, green, blue, and darker, materialized, as if the heavens themselves were giving birth. A double rainbow right at her eye level. She sat on the edge of the dock and gazed into the horizon. A moment of peace before her stomach took to churning again as she went over again and again the tale she would weave to the assembled group. Or the disaster yet to unfold over crab legs and mai tais.

Tomorrow, she would finish what she had to do with Gaelan's belongings and Simon's estate, and turn the whole thing over to her solicitors. Then home to the UK.

She had just enough time for a final visit to the glass museum. There, she would say her goodbye to Gaelan and try to get back to her life, knowing she never could, not knowing what she now knew. What she had passed up.

She'd never before noticed the Pier Glassworks, a small outdoor kiosk tucked away in an obscure corner of the promenade. A glassblower toiled, barely acknowledged by passersby, seeming not to care if he sold anything or not as he crafted fantastical trinkets in all the colors of the rainbow. Unicorns, fairies, castles, pumpkin coaches. The realm of myth and tall tales. She selected a burgundy rose, the edges of its glass petals dipped in gold, and went down the stairs into the museum.

By now the guard at the glass museum must be somewhat amused by her frequent stops over the past few days.

"Back again, huh?"

Anne shrugged sheepishly. "Who could stay away?"

"Yeah. Well, I think I know who might be able to answer all those questions you had back a few days ago."

"Questions—?"

"About those pieces you're always gawking at. Anyway, he's in the back office. I'd knock first. He's a little moody today." The guard indicated a small passageway in the corner of the museum. "It's just below the stairs."

"Thank you. You're very kind."

Pausing a moment at the Minotaur panel, she thought to place the rose there, her own memorial. But no, that wasn't right. The Diana's Tree. A reminder of that first moment he'd shown her how his book worked as she stood in amazement at his shoulder. The magician at his trade. The moment her life irrevocably altered. For better or worse.

She set down the fragile rose, crouching low to the ground, touching the small circle etched with his initials. "I hope you find peace at last, my dear Gaelan." No vibration. No strange sensation through her fingers. It was a silly notion to even think it would happen again. Sniffling back tears, Anne inhaled deeply and walked through the door.

Gaelan Erceldoune sat behind a long desk scattered with a colorful array of cut-glass pieces, which much resembled a giant unassembled jigsaw puzzle. He picked up one piece, then another, setting each loosely in a metal frame behind him as he worked. He had not looked up.

Anne stood at the doorway, observing, waiting. Her anger bubbled and boiled until it threatened to explode full throttle. How dare he sit there, fine as can be? Not a care in the fucking world. Finally, she could wait no longer and came to stand directly in front of the desk. "You bastard! How dare you show up—"

"Anne. I—"

"No word, not a bloody text message, no phone call. Nothing. Leaving me with the task of sorting it all—" Anne knew she wasn't being fair, but she couldn't stop herself. How long had he been in Chicago? The entire time? Hiding? Where? Here? What a fucking... *You sure know how to pick 'em.*

"I couldn't do it, stay with you. Knew it would end badly, eventually. I would watch you grow old, our children, their children. Long before that, you would have resented me . . ."

He was too calm, too bloody reasonable, and she couldn't stand it. "Well, I bloody resent you now. You . . . you are worse than—"

He went on as if he hadn't heard her at all. "It's not that. Nothing

. . . It's the loss, you see. The grief, over and over, of losing everything . . . everyone you love, yet again and again. I told myself you would be better off. But, you see, the joke was on me. It didn't work. And here I am."

"Asking for my forgiveness."

"No. Only your understanding. Anne, we must talk. There is something you need to know. And you will not believe it. I barely believe it myself, yet, no matter how hard I try, I cannot dismiss it. As much as I would like to do so."

She breathed in deeply, really looking at him for the first time. He did not look well. She approached the desk, sitting opposite him. He was pale and looked like he hadn't slept in a week. Dark circles smudged the area beneath his eyes. "What happened to you?"

"I stared into the abyss. I have seen the future, and it has shaken me to the core."

It was all she could do not to roll her eyes. "Am I to believe you're some sort of prophet come back to life?"

"No! No. Please hear me out." He removed a glass object from his pocket, laying it on the desk. "This . . . bauble . . . is a key that unlocks . . . a portal. A door into the future."

What the fuck had happened to him? Had he lost his bloody mind? "What? What kind of nonsense—"

"I used it," he continued, "and I have seen what terrible misery and anguish—ruin—lie ahead. My accident. The one that brought you, your company, to Chicago. Tissue samples were taken from me during surgery. They were stolen. It led then, years later, to—"

"Wait. What did you say? Stolen? How . . . ?"

It wasn't that he was calm; he was suffering shell shock. He could barely look up; his hands were trembling as he spoke. She wasn't ready to relent, but she was prepared to hear him.

"So? What of it?" She looked at her watch; she would be late for her dinner meeting if she stayed much longer. "I have a dinner engagement. Make it quick."

"With whom?"

"It's none of your bloody business, is it? Look, Gaelan. I understood what you did, maybe even why you lied to me, gave me the vial of poison, led me to believe you wouldn't—"

"You must listen to me. Call your friend. Tell whoever it is you'll be late. I must tell you what I came to tell you. Implore you to do what I ask, even if it is beyond your belief. Even if you think I've gone insane, which might very well be true. Then do what you must. I will leave you to your life; never bother you again."

He was pleading with her. His earnestness, the desperation in his gaze . . . He seemed lost, like a child wandering alone, adrift. "Fine." She texted Alcott, telling him to have drinks, and she would be there in not more than forty-five minutes.

"You have half an hour." She set the timer on her phone. "Starting now."

CHAPTER 40

How to make Anne believe when he barely did himself? He had not yet begun to grapple with the notion he was no longer immortal. Half a millennium he had lived with—survived— the curse and the wonder of it. And now . . . ? But that was for later. After they'd done what needed to be done.

Start with the science, something he couldn't have fabricated, dreamed, hallucinated. Something provable to her, here, now. Something he could not have known but by looking into the future. "My cells have . . . had the ability within them to infinitely repair themselves. It's what made it impossible for me to age, to die."

"This is hardly news. And you know I know it. So?"

"But not the 'why.'"

"Your telomeres—"

"My telomeres are bound up with . . . I find it hard to say it, for it sounds ridiculous, considering how long ago it would have happened . . . nearly half a millennium . . ." How to say it and make her believe? "My DNA is bound with submicroscopic machines. Very specific, infinitesimally tiny machines that had been embossed onto graphene membranes saturated with inks. The intense colorations in the ouroboros book illuminations. The inks, by themselves, are benign, inactive until bound with the correct substrates . . . I realize you don't . . . I—"

"Nanobots. They're called nanobots."

She'd made the discovery already. "Yes. You know, then."

"I observed them. But how could *you* know? I saw what you'd been working on in your flat. The karyograms. Over and over, annually, I think, looking for changes, anomalies, anything to help explain your condition. But you never would have been able to see—"

Perhaps this would not be as difficult as he thought. "You saw them? How?"

"Your friend Dana Spangler helped. You see, I was contracted to help a young girl with a terminal genetic disease."

"Yes. That's how it had started." What Arie . . . Airmid told him. "You used my blood to develop a cell strain?"

"No. Yes, but not the way you think."

It began with the treatment of a little girl, he'd been told. An altruistic motive gone wrong when greed got its filthy paw prints all over it. "Samples of my tissues . . . surgical samples set for disposal were stolen, yes?"

"Yes. But how—"

"You told me. The future 'you' at any rate. All of it. You tried to make it right. Destroy the stolen samples. And mine. The one I gave you before—"

"I . . . ? How could you know this? Gaelan, you're freaking me out, more than a little bit."

"As I said . . ." He grasped the glass object he'd discovered in the catacombs at Dernwode House, showing it to her.

"It's lovely but how . . . ?"

"This stained-glass scene, which you see in pieces on my desk, I created—"

"Yes. You were a glassmaker. An artist for Tiffany. The panels in the museum. The Diana's Tree. The Minotaur. I know all that. Found the papers in your flat—"

"There was a third panel. I'd made it to remember . . . my wife Caitrin and my son, Iain. A long time ago. You know of them, yes?"

"Only what little you've . . . what I read in the letter I found in the ouroboros book. From Ariadne."

"This small object came from . . . was stolen . . . went missing from that panel whilst on display at the 1893 Columbian Exposition. I'd taken such care in making it. You see, I'd made for Caitrin an extraordinary piece shortly after we met. It's called a Rupert's drop. I'd never seen such delight in anyone as the day I helped her craft one for herself.

When the glass piece went missing from the panel, I went nearly insane looking for it. I was devastated when I couldn't locate it. But—"

"But it's not lost. You're holding it in your hand. What does any of this matter?"

"I only just found it, in the most . . . the place . . . a place I hadn't been in more than nearly two centuries, but to which I was somehow drawn after I took the poison."

He shouldn't have mentioned the poison. Gaelan watched anger flare again in her eyes.

"And that led you where? To the future? Gaelan, forgive me, but you are making absolutely no sense. Slow down!"

She was right. "Nicola Tesla. I met him back in 1893." Gaelan explained the how, or at least what he believed had happened. That Tesla had stolen the glass piece and used it, somehow, to, impossibly, create a portal in time and space.

"I walked through a portal, created, presumably, by Tesla in the very spot I'd mentioned that day in 1893. He'd asked me to name a place that meant a great deal to me. A place to which I'd return if ever I could. The day I met him, we were standing on a beach, very near the location we are standing now. And through that portal, I stepped—from a cavern in Scotland—onto Navy Pier, but decades into our future. The portal linked that spot in Scotland with this one. The spot where Navy Pier was constructed decades after my chat with Tesla."

"Why should I believe any of this? It's utter madness. Time travel is a theory. No one has been able to—"

"I have. I thought it completely insane. I thought I'd lost my mind. As much as you do now, perhaps more. But something convinced me. You. Not you, as you are sitting here, but you as you were . . . will be, nearly a century from now. Alive. Unaged. Not a day. That I find you *here*—today—lends an awful lot of credence . . ." Her expression hadn't softened a bit. Another approach might be . . .

"It begins with the treatment of a young girl with a terrible fatal disease. A treatment so far advanced it could have only originated in the future. Nanobots extracted from my cells—from my hepatic tissue—to repair the girl's telomeres." A glimmer of recognition in her eyes. "Yes?"

"Yes, exactly but what—"

"But it somehow all careers out of control, years later, unleashing upon the world a horrific plague: immortality, but with catastrophic consequences."

"The nanobots. I first observed them embedded in the stones of the labyrinth necklace you gave me. I didn't know what they were. An artifact, I thought, but then I was given what I now know to be a cell culture created from your stolen surgical tissues, and I observed the same phenomenon. It made zero sense, but it got me wondering about the connection between the bots and you. So, I examined the blood sample you gave to me at Simon's that morning just after you . . . just before . . . you left for the UK."

An eternity ago, yet it had been only weeks. The blink of an eye in the perspective of the half millennium of his life. Time. But yes, she had begun to place the pieces.

"Your DNA was an exact match to the cell line I'd been given to develop a treatment for the girl. What those nanobots did to her degraded telomeres—the root cause of her disease? Remarkable. Impossible, but there it was. I couldn't . . . But I knew I couldn't use . . . I understood the potential for . . . you'd said it yourself. Why you decided your life must come to an end. You must disappear . . . whatever. The risk—"

"But you destroyed what you had in your possession. I know that, but there are, of course, more samples of my tissues. Surgery would have produced . . . And the cell culture you were given. It could not have been all of it."

"No. Of course not. I'm not an idiot, Gaelan."

"No, my dear, you are quite the opposite."

"Hang on a moment. You said your telomeres *were* bound up with the nanobots. What did you mean by that?"

"They're gone. Destroyed . . . or at least disabled, harmless now.

The poison I made . . ." The impact of that discovery had yet to land even a glancing blow, except perhaps in the throbbing agony of his arm where the glass had pierced through to bone. "My telomeres—"

She looked away, then stood, shoving her chair hard before stalking around the small office, from wall to bookshelf to desk to door. She said nothing as she returned to stand in front of him, the desk between them. She picked up a dark blue piece of glass, turning it in her hand, tapping it on the desk. A ticking clock, a timebomb about to explode, he knew.

"Anne. I know this is . . . difficult."

"Difficult? You cannot begin to bloody imagine—"

"Yes. I lied to you. Left you at the edge of Glomach and intended never to see you again." He looked away, unable to look into her accusing eyes. He had to make this right, but didn't know how. How could he after . . . ? But he had no choice. "I'm truly sorry about leaving you like that. Yes. I took the poison. I intended to . . . end it. I won't go over the reasons again. And I won't justify myself to you. I haven't come here—back to Chicago—because I am happy to be alive. Or to beg your forgiveness, which I have no right to expect—"

"I'm leaving."

"No. Wait. I'm sorry. Please just hear me out until the end, and then it's up to you. We go our separate ways."

She nodded, but the tension was still there, the fury still blazing in her eyes.

"Anne. I'm no longer immortal. My cells live and die . . . I live and die like any other person. If I'm struck by a car . . ." He could die in the middle of the street, no longer invincible. The notion struck as if he'd just realized it for the first time.

"Bully for you. Have a blast; remind me not to call for an ambulance."

"Anne—"

She looked at her phone. "Fine. Fifteen minutes, and I'm gone."

He held up a hand, gripping the edge of the table as a wave of dizziness washed over him, causing the room to spin. He sat unsteadily in his chair as he waited for it to pass before he continued. "The poison should have killed me; it did not. Instead, it killed . . . destroyed . . . the nanobots and my immortality along with it."

"Why?"

Good. Anne was curious—about that at least. "In 1826 I treated a disease long believed extinct even then. In the end, I'd used materials from the ouroboros book. I'd never wanted to do—"

"Tick tock, Gaelan. What has this—"

"I was already immortal, yes?"

She nodded. He held up a hand. "Bear with me. The syringe I used to inoculate those affected . . . I inadvertently jabbed myself. Half a syringe-full—quite a lot. Much more than a dose. Than ten. I remember it as if it was yesterday. I'd had little enough to spare, and I'd wasted . . ." Never mind that. "The nanobots, you see, already swarming in my bloodstream, my tissues, with those little . . ." He still had trouble saying it, much less thinking it. "The tiny machines . . . were now joined by others. It somehow . . . some way must've changed my physiology—"

"How?"

She was still irritated, he could see that, but the pieces were clicking into place.

She held up a hand. "Wait. I think . . . You once told me the poison was specific. It's why you had to create two separate compounds—one for you and one for Simon."

"Yes."

"You're telling me, then, the poison couldn't work the way the instructions told you it would. Because your physiology was no longer tied to that specific page in the ouroboros book. The nanobots tied to your telomeres were different, so the poison—"

"Worked differently. It didn't kill me; it killed the nanobots, instead. They . . . your friends in the future, that is . . . believe if I am able to recreate the poison, taint the cell lines, perhaps all will be put right and what *they* call the immortality virus will be stopped before it begins to do damage. The poison is the key to destroying the

ALCHEMY OF GLASS

immortality nanobots. It is a way out of this . . . bleak destiny of the future. The missing piece had been to answer the question 'why.'"

"No, it's not the only missing piece. Why . . . if any of this is true . . . encode a healing book with something that could cause immortality?"

"It was not intentional. There was a betrayal. They wanted . . . to stop the immortality . . . virus, they called it . . . before it ever started. But they failed."

"The Galahad Society."

"What?"

"The Galahad Society. The Holy Grail. Sir Galahad. Immortality."

Gaelan knew the legend.

"It's a think tank with one aim. To get their hands on the Grail. Immortality."

Was that who'd betrayed Airmid and her colleagues?

Again, she walked away. But she no longer appeared quite so angry.

"*If* I believe you, and that is quite a big if, what exactly am I supposed to do about it? How can I possibly . . . ?" She wheeled on Gaelan. A mix of emotions flared in her eyes. She wanted to not to believe him, but he saw the conflict at play.

"The labyrinth necklace—the one I gave you—has all that's needed, but I've not the skill . . . I only know what I know. What you . . . the future you . . . told me, convinced me of."

"What about the necklace?"

"It is the entire contents of the ouroboros book. They call it the Saf Rafah. It is condensed into the stones, which form a particular pattern, which changes, rotates . . . something I do not pretend to understand. The pages themselves, the instructions, the nanobots. All of it. But with a difference. The images—the graphene—are no longer encoded with anything that might lead to immortality." He observed the muscles in her shoulders and her arms slowly unclench. This was a good sign.

"Yes. It makes sense. The jewels. I saw into them. But I only saw the nanobots, no pages from a book."

Arie had told him he needed the glass object, now altered slightly, to see them. That, and an excellent electron microscope.

"Anne, I can show you the place where the portal exists. Prove all this to you. But it's in Scotland, and there isn't any time."

"Do you know anything of a Preston Alcott, the girl's father?"

"No. I think, in that future world I visited, he has something to do with the community's security. Holography, I think."

"Yes, it makes sense that he—"

She believed him, or was beginning to. He closed his eyes, feeling the adrenaline bleed away like a leaky balloon. The adrenaline that had fueled his way back to Chicago: acquiring funds, airline tickets, hours and hours of travel. He had to make it through this conversation before he collapsed. He focused his gaze on Anne as the rest of the room came in and out of focus.

"I destroyed all of it. All the samples, including the blood sample you gave me that morning."

"You know there must be others. Have to be others."

"Yes. I intend to lie through my teeth. Tell them it didn't work, knowing eventually they would realize I was lying, but hopefully not before I'd acquired all the rest. All of it. I was about to have dinner with Alcott and some of his friends, offer to go into a partnership using Simon's legacy. Get hold of all the cell lines, samples, DNA. Everything and destroy it all."

"Do you really believe they'll give it all to you? Not keep a bit back for themselves? Whatever you do, well intentioned, successful, perfectly executed or not, it won't be enough." It wasn't enough. "No. The only way is to taint the cell lines with the same poison I took. It inactivates . . . or destroys the nanobots." She'd again taken her seat. Her head in her hands, she ground the heels of her palms into her eyes. She was thinking, considering new options. Gaelan wanted to draw her near, to hold her, tell her they could do it—together. Be together now that he was no longer immortal. She wasn't ready, perhaps never would be . . .

"Wait. I have an idea. If you're sure . . . Maybe I can tell them it needs a special enzyme to work. *Et voila*, enter your poison! Of course, I won't call it that . . . But what if they can learn . . . have already discovered . . . what I now know about the bots? I'm not the only expert, you know!"

"They came to you. They trust you. You are the expert in this. And now you can treat the little girl for her disease with no—"

"I told you. I destroyed . . . The necklace. There is a cure for her disease in it?"

"Yes. And done proper, and without my blood for a substrate, it will save her life, fix her telomeres and make for a bloody good cover." The necklace. She wasn't wearing it. "Where is it? Did you destroy—"

"No. Believe me, I wanted to. You don't know how much I did. But I couldn't do it. It was all I had left of you. I spent weeks hating you. Hating you for abandoning me at Glomach, for leaving me your things to go through. But I came to understand why you felt it necessary. You're really no longer immortal?"

"I am not. I didn't believe it myself until I got quite a large gash in my arm. It didn't heal. Got infected, I think. Mind if you take a look? I could use a doctor who won't ask too many of the wrong questions—" Gaelan removed his shirt, allowing Anne to unwrap the bandage Arie had wound around his arm.

"This looks terrible. You're right. It's infected. You need antibiotics. I thought it wasn't possible for you to—"

"Exactly. It's what convinced me in the end that everything I was experiencing was real—"

"What everything?"

"A story for another time. You have a dinner to attend, and I've used up my half hour. And I am about to . . ." He tried to shake off the dizziness that threatened to . . . "I—" He needed to get her on her way before he passed out. She would not leave his side then, and she had to make that meeting. It was their only chance . . .

"The antibiotics. You'll need an IV. I should—"

"Go! I promise not to die whilst you're wining, dining, and spinning your tale."

"Will you still be here later? Or are you going home? Say in an hour or two?"

He swallowed hard, managing a weak smile. "I have nothing more important on my schedule but await your return, my lady."

Gaelan watched her leave, half-believing she would never return. Half-believing he would be dead by the time she did, he collapsed to the floor.

LONDON, 1826

CHAPTER 41

A month had passed, and the mysterious disease that had swept through London disappeared. Whatever small part Gaelan had in taming the dragon of a disease would never be known. And he was quite fine with that. More than quite fine.

The door bells jangled as Simon Bell came into the shop. Exactly on time.

"Ah, Dr. Bell, it is good to see you again. I've got the board set and ready."

Life had calmed; the shop was set up, and the trade was brisk. He had an able apprentice at his service, and thus far, that, too, had worked out well.

"I've meant to thank you, Mr. Erceldoune, for preparing the additional medicine for my use. It was kind, and I do mean to repay you for it."

"I will hear nothing of the sort. How goes it then with the Royal Society?"

"I broached the subject only last week at our regular meeting. As you must have known, the very idea was met with derision, and the threat to boot me from such esteemed company. It was only my relationship with my ever-politically astute cousin Dr. James Bell and the legacy of Benjamin Bell that keep my place amongst the esteemed company."

"I see. I suppose it was to be predicted. I cannot say I expected more from them."

"Please. My dear sir!" The tone was stern, but the smile sincere and warm. "Oh, by the by, how is your new apprentice working out? You've said little enough about him, and I've caught nary a glimpse of him in the shop. You do not work him enough. For he should always be about, fetching your supplies, seeing to your customers, so that you might experiment more." Bell took Gaelan's queen. He'd missed a move he should have seen three before. "You, Mr. Erceldoune, are off your game tonight. I may perchance best you—and for the first time."

"It does appear that way." Gaelan considered the board before moving. Without his queen . . . But Bell never could see ahead quite as far as Gaelan might by taking in the whole, perceiving the end of the game in sight. He might yet prevail. But perhaps not. The distraction was too much. He made a novice move as his next, and Bell had checkmate in three more moves. Done.

"Well, Dr. Bell." Gaelan lifted his glass. "Cheers to you, then." He set down his king in surrender.

Bell lifted his glass in response. "And to you, for many games before this one. I daresay you are not up to your usual self tonight."

"Indeed. I do have something quite weighing on my mind. I mean to address it . . . put it to rights this night. And you, sir, wisely took advantage of my distraction. It shall not happen again, so savor your victory whilst you might. And now, I must bid you a good night. I've some . . . reading before I retire."

"Oh. You were going make me up—"

Where is my mind this night? "Of course. I shall return in a trice."

Caitrin greeted Gaelan as he entered his third-story laboratory. "Has he gone?" Caitrin daren't show her visage while Simon Bell was about. Even with cropped hair and breeches, Simon knew her well enough to recognize her.

"No. He is yet about." They had been careful, with Caitrin secreted away in the laboratory or her rooms behind the shop whenever anyone came in the shop, lest Tremayne or one of her father's lackeys were yet on the prowl for her. But Simon spent more time in the shop than any other of Gaelan's patrons. Long evenings in conversation laced with tea drunk down until the kettle was empty, or decanters of brandy-wine and whisky. The present arrangement could not endure.

"You're miles away, Mr. Erceldoune."

"Aye. Sorry, I . . . Would you hand to me that tall bottle?"

"The mercury."

"Yes. He took it from her, their fingers touching, but barely, igniting a frisson that fled through his fingers down through his torso. He placed ten drops in another bottle—a solution he'd prepared earlier. He laughed, shaking his head, his hair long, unbound hair flying into his eyes. "Dr. Bell shall think I've forgotten him entirely."

Gaelan fled down the stairs and into the shop, swirling the vial, which contained an herbal solution bound up with ten drops of pure quicksilver, sending Bell on his way. He turned to find Caitrin standing close behind him.

She blushed, as if only just aware of how close she had approached to her friend and mentor. "I have been now a month in your service, Mr. Erceldoune. But it shall be only a matter of time before someone realizes that I am not a boy, but a woman in man's attire, especially," she said, her cheeks aflame, "at the time I bleed." She turned from him. "I fear discovery—that most inevitable of days, more than I can say, for if it is Mr. Tremayne or even Simon, how long would it be before word reaches my father's ears? How long before someone realizes that I am the daughter of Lord Kinston and reveals my whereabouts? It is not for myself that I fret, but what shall be done to you. You shall be ruined, if not worse, and I . . ."

"Hush now," Gaelan began, recovered. He knew more than he could admit of her fear. Discovery was just as profoundly his own enemy, what forced him to uproot himself every few years. It was a shadow that followed close behind wherever he settled, whatever affections he might share or ties he might form.

"I shall be sent back to my father, only to be shunned and shut up in my room until a suitable husband might be found to take me in—and with a handsome dowry, no doubt. For my father will be quite certain it is the only way to keep the honor of his oh so noble house!"

She was sobbing, near hysterical, and Gaelan ushered her back to the sofa, a gentle hand at her back.

"What has brought this about, Cate, after a month?" His voice was bare above a whisper, and without half realizing it, he was holding her to his chest, patting her cropped hair. One who would walk in on them now might think something entirely other than it was—that it was a man he was comforting and not a lady in distress.

She shook her head. "I do not know what has come over me, sir, that has me bawling like a babe on your shoulder." She moved, regarding Gaelan with somber eyes.

But he did know. It was too much for any lady, especially one highborn and unaccustomed to life in Smithfield, much less life as an apprentice—a boy apprentice—to bear. And she had borne it upon her narrow shoulders so very, very well. And for all she had gone through besides.

Gaelan met her gaze with equal gravity. "Gretna Green," he whispered, barely above a hush.

"Gretna Green? What of it? What is it—or who?"

"A solution to our dilemma, my lady. Please, before you answer, hear me out." He paused, placing her against the cushions, and padded to the fireplace, staring into the glowing embers. Was that the heat that now set afire to his face? How to explain it?

"Wait. I do know this place . . . have heard of it. Do you mean for us to marry? For that is . . ."

"Aye. It is a marrying place, beyond the eyes of parental interference, and I countenance our . . . current . . . arrangement, perhaps even less than you—"

"But Mr. Erceldoune, I . . ."

He turned, realizing how he might be misconstrued. He sighed, combing his fingers through his hair. "I do not mean to say . . ." He paced to the window frame, glancing briefly at the darkening marketplace below, before returning to the mantel, resting his elbow upon it, unable to meet her gaze. "I understand, Lady Caitrin, that our marriage, such as it shall be, would be for convenience's sake alone. I do not expect that . . . I mean to say . . . You shall maintain your rooms as you see fit and come and go as you desire and . . ."

Her breath prickled at the back of his neck, cool, and the lilac scent of the bath oil he had made for her intoxicated him. He dared not turn, for there she was just behind him. A delicate hand touched his arm, a gentle tugging at the soft linen of his sleeve.

"Mr. Erceldoune, I beg, please face me, that I might see your eyes and understand precisely what you are saying to me—with your heart. Not your head."

Gaelan hoped Caitrin could not perceive the way she so disquieted him by her nearness—and the consequences that lay ahead should she accept him. But quite suddenly they were face to face. Whether he had turned of his own accord, or she, unwilling to wait another instant, forced him to face her, he was not certain, but there they were, embracing.

Sometime, he would need to tell her, to reveal the truth of his life. For the moment, Gaelan allowed himself to be lost in Caitrin's eyes. What color were they? He could not pin it down, likening them to the refracted light of prisms, ever changing, bending in exquisite hues. Somewhere deep within, a voice, insistent as it was hushed, warned that it could come to no good for either of them, and for the first time in many decades, Gaelan paid it no heed.

GATTONSIDE, UK, PRESENT DAY

CHAPTER 42

Gaelan stood at the gates of an ancient cemetery, Anne by his side. Two weeks of antibiotics and he was enough recovered to travel. Recovering from immortality would be a much longer enterprise. Ah, but the benefits of being a mere mortal . . .

"Do you know where to find the gravesite?"

Anne removed her smart phone, tapping in coordinates. "Simon's solicitor told me these coordinates. We should find it in a . . ." She pointed slightly to the right. "About half a mile that way."

They made their way through headstones, modern and ancient, well kept and abandoned. In a clearing, beneath a willow tree, they found it. The headstone of Sophie Bell, wife of Dr. Simon Bell, daughter of Lord and Lady Thomas Wallingford of Gattonside and London. Died, November 1837. Gaelan shivered, remembering. So long ago, yet so vivid still.

Gaelan handed Anne the urn. "He's your ancestor, Anne. You should do it."

"We should do it together. You were his friend. You loved his sister."

They took hold of the urn and scattered Simon Bell's ashes over Sophie's grave. Gaelan closed his eyes. "Be at peace, my old friend," he said aloud. "May you at last be reunited with your Sophie."

"Are you at peace, Gaelan? Now? Finally?"

He sighed, unsure of what to say. That he was no longer immortal was both frightening and filled with remarkable possibilities, starting with Dr. Anne Shawe. He could at last have a life with a woman after so many years. A real life: grow old with her, perhaps children, grand-children he would not be terrified to meet.

Yet, the demons still lurked in the shadows of memory. Those had not vanished. Could he burden Anne with living life with a man tor-mented by hallucinations? Given to periods of bleakness? Night terrors? How could he ask it of her? Yet, she knew him, had traveled with him through some black days after the accident, and still she was at his side. Perhaps there was a chance, not impossible. Improbable? Maybe, but who knew? For now, take it a day at a time and see what happened.

Anne was watching him. He hadn't answered her question. "I won't lie to you. I'm not sure. Not at all, but I'm at more at peace than I have been in a very long time. Terrified by the horror of a future I witnessed, but hopeful we've done our bit to change it." He took her hand in his. "At more peace than I've a right to be."

Anne intertwined her fingers into his and a frisson of pleasure fled up his arm. It would be all right. Gaelan raised her hand to his lips and placed a gentle kiss on her fingers.

They'd done it: recreated the poison from the stones in the neck-lace and the treatment for Erin Alcott's disease. Whether it took was anyone's guess. Time would tell . . . on several counts.

Gaelan witnessed it with his own eyes, staring into the video screen of Dana Spangler's ridiculously expensive microscope. The tiny machines enmeshed in his telomeres destroyed.

Alcott's friends accepted Anne's story, that whatever the plan for the experimental liver tissue would not work without the addition of an activating enzyme.

A simple poison. A simple lie. But had it worked? Had the world been put back to rights? There was but one way to really find out.

Gattonside was only a short drive from the ruins of Dernwode House. They exited the hired car in the middle of a barren field. "There!" Gaelan said finally, spotting the bench he'd cobbled together that morning when first he read Conan Doyle's diary.

They sat. "This is where I heard you call out to me. I would have sworn it was you, so close to my ear I could feel your breath on my cheek."

"I did call out to you. The glass panel of the Minotaur . . . I . . ."

"What?"

"I could sense you. Silly, eh?"

He shrugged. "Perhaps not." The bond formed between them was more secure, more visceral than he might have ever imagined. Not silly at all. "Come. I need to show you."

"No. You don't. I believe everything. There's no need."

"I must see for myself. Please come with me."

She nodded, as he led her down the broken stairs to the catacombs. "Here's where I found the Conan Doyle—" The inscription . . . "There was an inscription . . . right . . ." The retaining wall itself was cleaned of grime and moss, just as he had done, but the engraving was gone. How was that possible?

"A bit spooky down here. Is it haunted?"

"Oh, yes. Very. But the place I need to show you is this way down the corridor." Gaelan pushed a button on a large flashlight.

"It's not necessary, and I'm not certain I want to know—"

They arrived at the prism room. Gaelan shined the torch into the room and daylight flooded the chamber, as the prisms painted the black walls in spiral arrays of every color.

"Fibonacci," she said finally.

"Yes."

"They're beautiful, but how—?"

"A long time ago, a sect of monks, friends and allies to my family, created this. Somehow, after Glomach, I was drawn here. I've no memory of coming here. No idea how I got here. Maybe the poison messed with my mind. Left me with amnesia. Something. But it doesn't matter how I got here, but that I did. This place—the last place I'd felt safe. Protected. Destiny, I suppose. Muscle memory, if that makes more sense—"

"So, what now?"

"So, I took hold of the teardrop and I found myself in the future, like magic—but not, of course. In Chicago. At Navy Pier—but a century or so into the future. If what we did with the poison worked, the future beyond that portal will be different, not the horror movie of the future I experienced first-hand. But something, hopefully, better."

Anne stayed his hand as he reached into his jacket. "Don't."

"You don't want to know?"

"No. You are here. You are no longer immortal. What if what's on the other side is much worse than what you saw? You have no way of knowing. And I'm not sure I want to. No, strike that. I am very sure I don't want to know. Besides, you might not come back. You might—"

"Be killed?"

"Yes. And I'm going to let that happen. Not after all . . . not with the future . . . our future . . . ahead of us. As you said, the fact you're only an ordinary—very mortal—bookseller opens up many possibilities."

He smiled. She might be right. Yes, he did want to know, but the portal pulled him, drew him like a powerful electromagnet. But so did she. In the end, perhaps best to let it be. The prisms were quiet. No cacophony, no sweet melody either. Perhaps the world beyond the portal was different. Better. They were, perhaps, better off not knowing.

"That glass bauble belongs back in that extraordinary piece you created. It belongs in Caitrin's hand. Do you still know how to make them?"

"Which? Stained glass?"

"No. A Rupert's drop?"

"Of course!"

"Then let's go back to Chicago and you can show me that, instead."

The End

ACKNOWLEDGMENTS

In many ways, writing a sequel is more difficult than writing the original. Which threads to pluck? Which unanswered questions to answer? Without the encouragement and support of friends, colleagues, family, and fans, this second Gaelan Erceldoune novel may never have seen the light of day.

I would first like to thank my literary agent, Katharine Sands of Sarah Jane Freymann Literary Agency in New York. Katharine has been my biggest booster and most excellent critic, never "telling" me what's needed to make the story "sing," but guiding me to my own "eureka!" moments and to puzzle it out for myself. So incredibly helpful with a novel as complex as this one.

Thank you to Rene Sears, editorial director at Pyr Books, for shepherding *The Alchemy of Glass* through the publication process, for her thoughtful suggestions and her very kind words about the book. Thank you to my copy editor Marianna Vertullo and the entire team at Pyr Books and Start Media.

Thank you as well to Kaye Publicity for getting the word(s) out there to the critics and readers new and old. I have wanted to work with Dana and her team for a while, and I'm thrilled to have had that opportunity with this novel.

Thank you to my son, Adam, daughter, Shoshanna, and son-in-law, Mike, for their encouragement as I wrote *Alchemy of Glass*. And, of course, to my beloved (and patient) husband, Phillip, who read draft after draft, ever encouraging me to dig deeper and take greater risks with my writing. Whenever I got stuck, whether it was trying to come up with a nineteenth-century medical puzzler adding new dimensions to the plot and characters, Phil was there to brainstorm ideas, offer constructive criticism . . . or simply listen.

The Alchemy of Glass was much inspired by Sir Arthur Conan Doyle's fascination with the fairy folk and all things supernatural. I have long wondered about how the man who created the most rational, logical character in all of fiction (and who was both a physician and a journalist!) could also believe in fairies, and his presence in the novel is (in part) my attempt to explore this apparent paradox.

Last (but not least), I thank you, dear reader, for your continued interest in Gaelan Erceldoune and his universe. Your kind words about *The Apothecary's Curse* encouraged and inspired me to continue the story of my tortured, tormented immortal apothecary.

I hope you enjoyed it!

ABOUT THE AUTHOR

Author photo
© *Cilento Photography*

Barbara Barnett is the author of three books, including *The Apothecary's Curse*, finalist for the prestigious Bram Stoker Award for debut novel. She is publisher and executive editor of Blogcritics (blogcritics.org), an Internet magazine of pop culture, politics, and more, for which she has also contributed nearly 1,000 essays, reviews, and interviews over the past decade. Always a pop-culture and sci-fi geek, Barbara was raised on a steady diet of TV (and TV dinners), but she always found her way to fiction's tragic anti-heroes and misunderstood champions, whether on TV, in the movies, or in literature. (In other words, Spock, not Kirk; Han Solo, not Luke Skywalker!) Her first book, *Chasing Zebras: The Unofficial Guide to House, M.D.* (ECW Press), reflects her passion for these Byronic heroes, and it was inevitable that she would have to someday create one of her own in Gaelan Erceldoune, hero of both *The Apothecary's Curse* and *The Alchemy of Glass*.

She is an accomplished speaker, an annual favorite at MENSA's HalloweeM convention, where she has spoken to standing-room crowds on subjects as diverse as "The Byronic Hero in Pop Culture," "The Many Faces of Sherlock Holmes," "The Hidden History of Science Fiction," "Our Passion for Disaster (Movies)," and "The Conan Doyle Conundrum."

A lifelong resident of the Chicago area, she lives in a Victorian coach house with her husband, Phil, and their border collie–Aussie, Semra, on a bluff along the Lake Michigan shore, an area that serves as the modern-day setting for both Apothecary novels. She is the proud mother of Shoshanna (Mike) and Adam, and the loving *savta* of Ari and Meital.